The Collected Stories of
Robert Silverberg

VOLUME TWO

To The Dark Star
1962-69

The Collected Stories of
Robert Silverberg

VOLUME TWO

To The Dark Star
1962-69

ROBERT SILVERBERG

SUBTERRANEAN PRESS 2012

Trade Paperback

ISBN: 978-1-59606-508-6

Subterranean Press
PO Box 190106
Burton, MI 48519

www.subterraneanpress.com

ACKNOWLEDGMENTS

"To See the Invisible Man" first appeared in *Worlds of Tomorrow*.

"The Fangs of the Trees," "Ishmael in Love," "Sundance," and "After the Myths Went Home" first appeared in *Fantasy and Science Fiction*.

"The Pain Peddlers,", "Neighbor," "The Sixth Palace," "Hawksbill Station," and "Going Down Smooth" first appeared in *Galaxy Science Fiction*.

"Flies" first appeared in *Dangerous Visions*.

"Halfway House," "Bride 91," and "The Reality Trip" first appeared in *If*.

"Passengers" first appeared in *Orbit*.

"Ringing the Changes" first appeared in *Alchemy and Academe*.

"To the Dark Star" first appeared in *The Farthest Reaches*.

"We Know Who We Are" first appeared in *Amazing Stories*.

"The Pleasure of Their Company" first appeared in *Infinity One*.

"How It Was When the Past Went Away" first appeared in *Three For Tomorrow*.

"A Happy Day in 2381" and "(Now + n, Now − n)" first appeared in *Nova*.

TABLE OF CONTENTS

For Harlan Ellison
Joseph Elder
Damon Knight
Edward L. Ferman
Anne McCaffrey
Harry Harrison
Bob Hoskins
Ted White
and—with particular affection—the cantankerous Fred Pohl

INTRODUCTION

A considerable jump in time marks the break here between the first volume of this series, *To Be Continued*, and this one. *To Be Continued* covers my short-story work between 1953 and 1958; and the attentive reader of the introductions to the stories in that volume will very likely have noticed that my primary (though not only) concern as a writer in the 1950's was to earn money. In 1958, my fourth year as a full-time writer, making money by writing began to be very difficult to do, if your specialty happened to be science fiction. Midway through that year the American News Company, the vast, omnipotent, and (I think) mob-controlled distribution company that was responsible for getting most of the nation's fiction magazines to the newsstands, abruptly went belly-up as a result of some miscarried financial manipulation, and its collapse brought down dozens of small publishers who depended on advance payments from American News to stay afloat. Among them were most of the science fiction magazines to which I was a regular contributor.

The best ones—John Campbell's *Astounding*, Horace Gold's *Galaxy*, Tony Boucher's *Fantasy and Science Fiction*—were able to survive the debacle. But most of my mainstays, the ones that cheerfully bought all the copy I could provide at a cent or two a word, went under right away or else entered a stage of obvious terminal decline. Larry Shaw's *Infinity* and its companion *Science Fiction Adventures* disappeared, W.W. Scott's *Super Science* (for which I wrote 36 of the 120 stories it published in four years) did likewise, Bob Lowndes' *Future* and *Science Fiction Stories* began to totter toward their doom, and so forth. I was still free to take my chances with the demanding Boucher, Campbell, and Gold, of course, but the salvage markets that I depended on to accept the stories which those three editors rejected were no longer there, and with the same number of writers competing for space in ever fewer magazines I was faced with the prospect of writing material that would find no publisher whatever. So by late 1958 I began to disappear from science fiction myself—the first of several such withdrawals from the field that I would stage.

I was accustomed by then to a pretty good standard of living, and so, fast on my feet as ever, I found a bunch of new markets outside the s-f world for whom I wrote just about anything and everything. My ledger shows something called "Stalin's Slave Barracks" for a magazine called *Sir* in March, 1959, "Cures for Sleepless Nights" in the January, 1960 issue of *Living For Young Homemakers*, "Wolf Children of India" written for *Exotic Adventures* in May, 1959, and so on and on in a really astonishing fashion, reams of stuff that I have completely forgotten doing. And when Bill Hamling, the former publisher of several science-fiction magazines to which I had contributed dozens of stories, started a new line of mildly erotic paperbacks, I became part of his staff of regulars, cranking out two or three and sometimes four novels a month for him, cheerfully formulaic books with names like *Love Addict*, *Summertime Affair*, and *Lust Goddess* that are collector's items today. Just to demonstrate my versatility I opened up yet another line of books of an utterly different and much more respectable kind—non-fiction books on archaeological subjects, beginning with *Lost Cities and Vanished Civilizations* in 1962 and going on to such items as *Empires in the Dust*, *Sunken History*, and *Man Before Adam*. Oh, yes, I was a busy boy.

I did continue to appear regularly in the s-f magazines all through 1959, but mostly with stories that I had written the previous year, or even earlier. 1960 saw just four short s-f stories of mine published— what would have been a week's work a couple of years before—and the little novel for young readers, *Lost Race of Mars*, which proved very popular and remained in print for decades. In 1961 I wrote just *one* s-f story, and expanded an old magazine novella into a hardcover book for a lending-library publisher. In 1962, a year when I needed to maximize my income because I had taken it upon myself to buy a huge, expensive house in the Riverdale section of New York, a house that had once been the residence of the famed Mayor Fiorello La Guardia, no s-f short stories of mine appeared, just the novel *The Seed of Earth*, another expansion, based on a story from 1957. You would blink your eyes in astonishment if I told you how little that twenty-room house cost, because it is a very small sum indeed in modern-day money, but I assure you it was a gigantic amount in its own pre-inflation era when a dollar was a DOLLAR, and writing science fiction for the shrunken market of 1962 was too risky a proposition now that I was a homeowner with all the exciting new expenses that that involved.

But the veteran writer and editor Frederik Pohl, with whom I had struck up a friendship in my earliest days as a writer, had taken over the editorship of *Galaxy* and its companion magazine *If* from the ailing Horace Gold in June of 1961, and he lured me back into the field which was still, after all, more important to me than any other. Fred had long been vexed with me for my willingness to churn out all that lucrative junk, and he believed (rightly, as time would prove) that a top-rank science-fiction writer was hidden behind the pyramid of literary garbage that I had cheerfully been producing over the past few years. So he made me an offer shrewdly calculated to appeal to my risk-abhorring nature. He agreed to buy any story I cared to send him—a guaranteed sale—*provided* I undertook to write it with all my heart, no quick-buck hackwork. If he wanted revisions, I would pledge to do one rewrite for him, after which he would be bound to buy the story without asking anything more of me. If I turned in a story he didn't like, he would buy it anyway, but that would be the end of the deal. I was, of course, to say nothing about these terms to any of my fellow writers, and I kept the secret until long after Fred had left the magazine.

It was an irresistible deal, as he damned well knew. I would get three cents a word—the top rate at the time—without the slightest risk, and without any necessity whatever to slant my work to meet the imagined prejudices of some dictatorial editor. All I had to do was write what I believed to be good science fiction, and Fred would buy it. I had never had an arrangement like that with a first-class s-f magazine before, and I lost no time in writing "To See the Invisible Man," the first of what would be a great many stories for Fred Pohl's *Galaxy*. One thing led to another, and before long, spurred by my new arrangement with Pohl, I found myself regularly writing science fiction again, although never with the lunatic prolificity that marked my earliest years in the field.

Robert Silverberg

TO SEE THE INVISIBLE MAN

This story, written in June of 1962, marks the beginning of my real career as a science-fiction writer, I think. The 1953-58 stories collected in To Be Continued, the first of this series of volumes, are respectable professional work, some better than others but all of them at least minimally acceptable—but most of them could have been written by just about anyone. Aside from a few particularly ambitious items, they were designed to slip unobtrusively into the magazines of their time, efficiently providing me with regular paychecks. But now, by freeing me from the need to calculate my way around the risk of rejection, Fred Pohl allowed—indeed, required—me to reach as deep into my literary resources as I was capable of doing. I knew that unless I gave him my very best, the wonderful guaranteed-sale deal I had with him would vanish as quickly as it had appeared. Therefore I would reach deeper and deeper, in the years ahead, until I had moved so far away from my youthful career as a hack writer that latecomers would find it hard to believe that I had been emotionally capable of writing all that junk, let alone willing to do it. In "To See the Invisible Man" the distinctive Silverberg fictional voice is on display for just about the first time.

(The voice of another and greater writer can be heard in the background, though. I found the idea for my story in the opening paragraph of Jorge Luis Borges' "The Babylon Lottery," where he says, "Like all men in Babylon I have been a proconsul; like all, a slave....During one lunar year, I have been declared invisible; I shrieked and was not heard, I stole my bread and was not decapitated." Borges chose to do no more with the theme of statutory invisibility in that story—it was, for him, nothing more than an embellishment in a story about something else entirely. So I fell upon the notion and developed it to explore its practical implications, thus doing the job Borges had left undone.)

Oddly, the story didn't appear in Galaxy despite my arrangement with Fred. Soon after taking over the editorial post he created a new magazine, Worlds of Tomorrow, and shifted some stories out of the Galaxy inventory to fill its first issue, dated April, 1963. "To See the Invisible Man" was among them. To those readers who quite rightly thought of me as a heartless manufacturer of mass-produced fiction, the story was something of a revelation—and there would be more such surprises to come.

Many years later, by the way, it was adapted for television's Twilight Zone program, with a superb screenplay by Steve Barnes.

———————

And then they found me guilty, and then they pronounced me invisible, for a span of one year beginning on the eleventh of May in the year of Grace 2104, and they took me to a dark room beneath the courthouse to affix the mark to my forehead before turning me loose.

Two municipally paid ruffians did the job. One flung me into a chair and the other lifted the brand.

"This won't hurt a bit," the slab-jawed ape said, and thrust the brand against my forehead, and there was a moment of coolness, and that was all.

"What happens now?" I asked.

But there was no answer, and they turned away from me and left the room without a word. The door remained open. I was free to leave, or to stay and rot, as I chose. No one would speak to me, or look at me more than once, long enough to see the sign on my forehead. I was invisible.

You must understand that my invisibility was strictly metaphorical. I still had corporeal solidity. People *could* see me—but they *would not* see me.

An absurd punishment? Perhaps. But then, the crime was absurd too. The crime of coldness. Refusal to unburden myself for my fellow man. I was a four-time offender. The penalty for that was a year's invisibility. The complaint had been duly sworn, the trial held, the brand duly affixed.

I was invisible.

I went out, out into the world of warmth.

They had already had the afternoon rain. The streets of the city were drying, and there was the smell of growth in the Hanging Gardens. Men and women went about their business. I walked among them, but they took no notice of me.

The penalty for speaking to an invisible man is invisibility, a month to a year or more, depending on the seriousness of the offense. On this the whole concept depends. I wondered how rigidly the rule was observed.

I soon found out.

I stepped into a liftshaft and let myself be spiraled up toward the nearest of the Hanging Gardens. It was Eleven, the cactus garden, and those gnarled, bizarre shapes suited my mood. I emerged on the landing stage and advanced toward the admissions counter to buy my token. A pasty-faced, empty-eyed woman sat back of the counter.

I laid down my coin. Something like fright entered her eyes, quickly faded.

"One admission," I said.

No answer. People were queuing up behind me. I repeated my demand. The woman looked up helplessly, then stared over my left shoulder. A hand extended itself, another coin was placed down. She took it, and handed the man his token. He dropped it in the slot and went in.

"Let me have a token," I said crisply.

Others were jostling me out of the way. Not a word of apology. I began to sense some of the meaning of my invisibility. They were literally treating me as though they could not see me.

There are countervailing advantages. I walked around behind the counter and helped myself to a token without paying for it. Since I was invisible, I could not be stopped. I thrust the token in the slot and entered the garden.

But the cacti bored me. An inexpressible malaise slipped over me, and I felt no desire to stay. On my way out I pressed my finger against a jutting thorn and drew blood. The cactus, at least, still recognized my existence. But only to draw blood.

I returned to my apartment. My books awaited me, but I felt no interest in them. I sprawled out on my narrow bed and activated the energizer to combat the strange lassitude that was afflicting me. I thought about my invisibility.

It would not be such a hardship, I told myself. I had never depended overly on other human beings. Indeed, had I not been sentenced in the first place for my coldness toward my fellow creatures? So what need did I have of them now? *Let* them ignore me!

It would be restful. I had a year's respite from work, after all. Invisible men did not work. How could they? Who would go to an invisible doctor for a consultation, or hire an invisible lawyer to represent him, or give a document to an invisible clerk to file? No work, then. No income, of course, either. But landlords did not take rent from invisible men. Invisible men went where they pleased, at no cost. I had just demonstrated that at the Hanging Gardens.

Invisibility would be a great joke on society, I felt. They had sentenced me to nothing more dreadful than a year's rest cure. I was certain I would enjoy it.

But there were certain practical disadvantages. On the first night of my invisibility I went to the city's finest restaurant. I would order their most lavish dishes, a hundred-unit meal, and then conveniently vanish at the presentation of the bill.

My thinking was muddy. I never got seated. I stood in the entrance half an hour, bypassed again and again by a maitre d'hotel who had clearly been through all this many times before: Walking to a seat, I realized, would gain me nothing. No waiter would take my order.

I could go into the kitchen. I could help myself to anything I pleased. I could disrupt the workings of the restaurant. But I decided against it. Society had its ways of protecting itself against the invisible ones. There could be no direct retaliation, of course, no intentional defense. But who could say no to a chef's claim that he had seen no one in the way when he hurled a pot of scalding water toward the wall? Invisibility was invisibility, a two-edged sword.

I left the restaurant.

I ate at an automated restaurant nearby. Then I took an autocab home. Machines, like cacti, did not discriminate against my sort. I sensed that they would make poor companions for a year, though.

I slept poorly.

The second day of my invisibility was a day of further testing and discovery.

I went for a long walk, careful to stay on the pedestrian paths. I had heard all about the boys who enjoy running down those who carry the mark of invisibility on their foreheads. Again, there is no recourse, no punishment for them. My condition has its little hazards by intention.

I walked the streets, seeing how the throngs parted for me. I cut through them like a microtome passing between cells. They were well trained. At midday I saw my first fellow Invisible. He was a tall man of middle years, stocky and dignified, bearing the mark of shame on a domelike forehead. His eyes met mine only for a moment. Then he passed on. An invisible man, naturally, cannot see another of his kind.

I was amused, nothing more. I was still savoring the novelty of this way of life. No slight could hurt me. Not yet.

Late in the day I came to one of those bathhouses where working girls can cleanse themselves for a couple of small coins. I smiled wickedly and went up the steps. The attendant at the door gave me the flicker of a startled look—it was a small triumph for me—but did not dare to stop me.

I went in.

An overpowering smell of soap and sweat struck me. I persevered inward. I passed cloakrooms where long rows of gray smocks were hanging, and it occurred to me that I could rifle those smocks of every unit they contained, but I did not. Theft loses meaning when it becomes too easy, as the clever ones who devised invisibility were aware.

I passed on, into the bath chambers themselves.

Hundreds of women were there. Nubile girls, weary wenches, old crones. Some blushed. A few smiled. Many turned their backs on me. But they were careful not to show any real reaction to my presence. Supervisory matrons stood guard, and who knew but that she might be reported for taking undue cognizance of the existence of an Invisible?

So I watched them bathe, watched five hundred pairs of bobbing breasts, watched naked bodies glistening under the spray, watched this vast mass of bare feminine flesh. My reaction was a mixed one, a sense of wicked achievement at having penetrated this sanctum sanctorum unhalted, and then, welling up slowly within me, a sensation of—was it sorrow? Boredom? Revulsion?

I was unable to analyze it. But it felt as though a clammy hand had seized my throat. I left quickly. The smell of soapy water stung my nostrils for hours afterward, and the sight of pink flesh haunted my dreams that night. I ate alone, in one of the automatics. I began to see that the novelty of this punishment was soon lost.

❋

In the third week I fell ill. It began with a high fever, then pains of the stomach, vomiting, the rest of the ugly symptomatology. By midnight I was certain I was dying. The cramps were intolerable, and when I dragged myself to the toilet cubicle I caught sight of myself in the mirror, distorted, greenish, beaded with sweat. The mark of invisibility stood out like a beacon in my pale forehead.

For a long time I lay on the tiled floor, limply absorbing the coolness of it. Then I thought: What if it's my appendix? That ridiculous, obsolete, obscure prehistoric survival? Inflamed, ready to burst?

I needed a doctor.

The phone was covered with dust. They had not bothered to disconnect it, but I had not called anyone since my arrest, and no one had dared call me. The penalty for knowingly telephoning an invisible man is invisibility. My friends, such as they were, had stayed far away.

I grasped the phone, thumbed the panel. It lit up and the directory robot said, "With whom do you wish to speak, sir?"

"Doctor," I gasped.

"Certainly, sir." Bland, smug mechanical words! No way to pronounce a robot invisible, so it was free to talk to me!

The screen glowed. A doctorly voice said, "What seems to be the trouble?"

"Stomach pains. Maybe appendicitis."

"We'll have a man over in—" He stopped. I had made the mistake of upturning my agonized face. His eyes lit on my forehead mark. The screen winked into blackness as rapidly as though I had extended a leprous hand for him to kiss.

"Doctor," I groaned.

He was gone. I buried my face in my hands. This was carrying things too far, I thought. Did the Hippocratic Oath allow things like this? Could a doctor ignore a sick man's plea for help?

Hippocrates had not known anything about invisible men. A doctor was not required to minister to an invisible man. To society at large I simply was not there. Doctors could not diagnose diseases in nonexistent individuals.

I was left to suffer.

It was one of invisibility's less attractive features. You enter a bath-house unhindered, if that pleases you—but you writhe on a bed of pain equally unhindered. The one with the other, and if your appendix hap-pens to rupture, why, it is all the greater deterrent to others who might perhaps have gone your lawless way!

My appendix did not rupture. I survived, though badly shaken. A man can survive without human conversation for a year. He can travel on automated cars and eat at automated restaurants. But there are no automated doctors. For the first time, I felt truly beyond the pale. A convict in a prison is given a doctor when he falls ill. My crime had not been serious enough to merit prison, and so no doctor would treat me if I suffered. It was unfair. I cursed the devils who had invented my punishment. I faced each bleak dawn alone, as alone as Crusoe on his island, here in the midst of a city of twelve million souls.

How can I describe my shifts of mood, my many tacks before the changing winds of the passing months?

There were times when invisibility was a joy, a delight, a treasure. In those paranoid moments I gloried in my exemption from the rules that bound ordinary men.

I stole. I entered small stores and seized the receipts, while the cowering merchant feared to stop me, lest in crying out he make himself liable to my invisibility. If I had known that the State reimbursed all such losses, I might have taken less pleasure in it. But I stole.

I invaded. The bathhouse never tempted me again, but I breached other sanctuaries. I entered hotels and walked down the corridors, opening doors at random. Most rooms were empty. Some were not.

Godlike, I observed all. I toughened. My disdain for society—the crime that had earned me invisibility in the first place—heightened.

I stood in the empty streets during the periods of rain, and railed at the gleaming faces of the towering buildings on every side. "Who needs you?" I roared "Not I! Who needs you in the slightest?"

I jeered and mocked and railed. It was a kind of insanity, brought on, I suppose, by the loneliness. I entered theaters—where the happy lotus-eaters sat slumped in their massage chairs, transfixed by the glow-ing tridim images—and capered down the aisles. No one grumbled at me. The luminescence of my forehead told them to keep their complaints to themselves, and they did.

Those were the mad moments, the good moments, the moments when I towered twenty feet high and strode among the visible clods with contempt oozing from every pore. Those were insane moments— I admit that freely. A man who has been in a condition of involuntary invisibility for several months is not likely to be well balanced.

Did I call them paranoid moments? Manic depressive might be more to the point. The pendulum swung dizzily. The days when I felt only contempt for the visible fools all around me were balanced by days when the isolation pressed in tangibly on me. I would walk the endless streets, pass through the gleaming arcades, stare down at the highways with their streaking bullets of gay colors. Not even a beggar would come up to me. Did you know we had beggars, in our shining century? Not till I was pronounced invisible did I know it, for then my long walks took me to the slums, where the shine has worn thin, and where shuffling stubble-faced old men beg for small coins.

No one begged for coins from me. Once a blind man came up to me.

"For the love of God," he wheezed, "help me to buy new eyes from the eye bank."

They were the first direct words any human being had spoken to me in months. I started to reach into my tunic for money, planning to give him every unit on me in gratitude. Why not? I could get more simply by taking it. But before I could draw the money out, a nightmare figure hobbled on crutches between us. I caught the whispered word, "Invisible," and then the two of them scuttled away like frightened crabs. I stood there stupidly holding my money.

Not even the beggars. Devils, to have invented this torment!

So I softened again. My arrogance ebbed away. I was lonely, now. Who could accuse me of coldness? I was spongy soft, pathetically eager for a word, a smile, a clasping hand. It was the sixth month of my invisibility.

I loathed it entirely, now. Its pleasures were hollow ones and its torment was unbearable. I wondered how I would survive the remaining six months. Believe me, suicide was not far from my mind in those dark hours.

And finally I committed an act of foolishness. On one of my endless walks I encountered another Invisible, no more than the third or the fourth such creature I had seen in my six months. As in the previous encounters, our eyes met, warily, only for a moment. Then he dropped his to the pavement, and he sidestepped me and walked on. He was a slim young man, no more than forty, with tousled brown hair and a narrow, pinched face. He had a look of scholarship about him, and I wondered what he might have done to merit his punishment, and I was seized with the desire to run after him and ask him, and to learn his name, and to talk to him, and embrace him.

All these things are forbidden to mankind. No one shall have any contact whatsoever with an Invisible—not even a fellow Invisible. Especially not a fellow Invisible. There is no wish on society's part to foster a secret bond of fellowship among its pariahs.

I knew all this.

I turned and followed him, all the same.

For three blocks I moved along behind him, remaining twenty to fifty paces to the rear. Security robots seemed to be everywhere, their scanners quick to detect an infraction, and I did not dare make my move. Then he turned down a side street, a gray, dusty street five centuries old, and began to stroll, with the ambling, going-nowhere gait of the Invisible. I came up behind him.

"Please," I said softly. "No one will see us here. We can talk. My name is—"

He whirled on me, horror in his eyes. His face was pale. He looked at me in amazement for a moment, then darted forward as though to go around me.

I blocked him.

"Wait," I said. "Don't be afraid. Please—"

He burst past me. I put my hand on his shoulder, and he wriggled free.

"Just a word," I begged.

Not even a word. Not even a hoarsely uttered, "Leave me alone!" He sidestepped me and ran down the empty street, his steps diminishing from a clatter to a murmur as he reached the corner and rounded it. I looked after him, feeling a great loneliness well up in me.

And then a fear. *He* hadn't breached the rules of Invisibility, but I had. I had seen him. That left me subject to punishment, an extension of my term of invisibility, perhaps. I looked around anxiously, but there were no security robots in sight, no one at all.

I was alone.

Turning, calming myself, I continued down the street. Gradually I regained control over myself. I saw that I had done something unpardonably foolish. The stupidity of my action troubled me, but even more the sentimentality of it. To reach out in that panicky way to another

Invisible—to admit openly my loneliness, my need—no. It meant that society was winning. I couldn't have that.

I found that I was near the cactus garden once again. I rode the liftshaft, grabbed a token from the attendant, and bought my way in. I searched for a moment, then found a twisted, elaborately ornate cactus eight feet high, a spiny monster. I wrenched it from its pot and broke the angular limbs to fragments, filling my hands with a thousand needles. People pretended not to watch. I plucked the spines from my hands and, palms bleeding, rode the liftshaft down, once again sublimely aloof in my invisibility.

The eighth month passed, the ninth, the tenth. The seasonal round had made nearly a complete turn. Spring had given way to a mild summer, summer to a crisp autumn, autumn to winter with its fortnightly snowfalls, still permitted for esthetic reasons. Winter had ended, now. In the parks, the trees sprouted green buds. The weather control people stepped up the rainfall to thrice daily.

My term was drawing to its end.

In the final months of my invisibility I had slipped into a kind of torpor. My mind, forced back on its own resources, no longer cared to consider the implications of my condition, and I slid in a blurred haze from day to day. I read compulsively but unselectively. Aristotle one day, the Bible the next, a handbook of mechanics the next. I retained nothing; as I turned a fresh page, its predecessor slipped from my memory.

I no longer bothered to enjoy the few advantages of invisibility, the voyeuristic thrills, the minute throb of power that comes from being able to commit any act with only limited fears of retaliation. I say *limited* because the passage of the Invisibility Act had not been accompanied by an act repealing human nature; few men would not risk invisibility to protect their wives or children from an invisible one's molestations; no one would coolly allow an invisible to jab out his eyes; no one would tolerate an Invisible's invasion of his home. There were ways of coping with such infringements without appearing to recognize the existence of the Invisible, as I have mentioned.

Still, it was possible to get away with a great deal. I declined to try. Somewhere Dostoevsky has written, "Without God, all things are possible." I can amend that. "To the invisible man, all things are possible—and uninteresting." So it was.

The weary months passed.

I did not count the minutes till my release. To be precise, I wholly forgot that my term was due to end. On the day itself, I was reading in my room, morosely turning page after page, when the annunciator chimed.

It had not chimed for a full year. I had almost forgotten the meaning of the sound.

But I opened the door. There they stood, the men of the law. Wordlessly, they broke the seal that held the mark to my forehead.

The emblem dropped away and shattered.

"Hello, citizen," they said to me.

I nodded gravely. "Yes. Hello."

"May 11, 2105. Your term is up. You are restored to society. You have paid your debt."

"Thank you. Yes."

"Come for a drink with us."

"I'd sooner not."

"It's the tradition. Come along."

I went with them. My forehead felt strangely naked now, and I glanced in a mirror to see that there was a pale spot where the emblem had been. They took me to a bar nearby, and treated me to synthetic whiskey, raw, powerful. The bartender grinned at me. Someone on the next stool clapped me on the shoulder and asked me who I liked in tomorrow's jet races. I had no idea, and I said so.

"You mean it? I'm backing Kelso. Four to one, but he's got terrific spurt power."

"I'm sorry," I said.

"He's been away for a while," one of the government men said softly.

The euphemism was unmistakable. My neighbor glanced at my forehead and nodded at the pale spot. He offered to buy me a drink too. I accepted, though I was already feeling the effects of the first one. I was a human being again. I was visible.

I did not dare spurn him, anyway. It might have been construed as a crime of coldness once again. My fifth offense would have meant five years of Invisibility. I had learned humility.

Returning to visibility involved an awkward transition, of course. Old friends to meet, lame conversations to hold, shattered relationships to renew. I had been an exile in my own city for a year, and coming back was not easy.

No one referred to my time of invisibility, naturally. It was treated as an affliction best left unmentioned. Hypocrisy, I thought, but I accepted it. Doubtless they were all trying to spare my feelings. Does one tell a man whose cancerous stomach has been replaced, "I hear you had a narrow escape just now?" Does one say to a man whose aged father has tottered off toward a euthanasia house, "Well, he was getting pretty feeble anyway, wasn't he?"

No. Of course not.

So there was this hole in our shared experience, this void, this blankness. Which left me little to talk about with my friends, in particular since I had lost the knack of conversation entirely. The period of readjustment was a trying one.

But I persevered, for I was no longer the same haughty, aloof person I had been before my conviction. I had learned humility in the hardest of schools.

Now and then I noticed an Invisible on the streets, of course. It was impossible to avoid them. But, trained as I had been trained, I quickly glanced away, as though my eyes had come momentarily to rest on some shambling, festering horror from another world.

It was in the fourth month of my return to visibility that the ultimate lesson of my sentence struck home, though. I was in the vicinity of the City Tower, having returned to my old job in the documents division of the municipal government. I had left work for the day and was walking toward the tubes when a hand emerged from the crowd, caught my arm.

"Please," the soft voice said. "Wait a minute. Don't be afraid."

I looked up, startled. In our city strangers do not accost strangers.

I saw the gleaming emblem of invisibility on the man's forehead. Then I recognized him—the slim man I had accosted more than half a year before on that deserted street. He had grown haggard; his eyes were wild, his brown hair flecked with gray. He must have been at the beginning of his term, then. Now he must have been near its end.

He held my arm. I trembled. This was no deserted street. This was the most crowded square of the city. I pulled my arm away from his grasp and started to turn away.

"No—don't go," he cried. "Can't you pity me? You've been there yourself."

I took a faltering step. Then I remembered how I had cried out to him, how I had begged him not to spurn me. I remembered my own miserable loneliness.

I took another step away from him.

"Coward!" he shrieked after me. "Talk to me! I dare you! Talk to me, coward!"

It was too much. I was touched. Sudden tears stung my eyes, and I turned to him, stretched out a hand to his. I caught his thin wrist. The contact seemed to electrify him. A moment later, I held him in my arms, trying to draw some of the misery from his frame to mine.

The security robots closed in, surrounding us. He was hurled to one side, I was taken into custody. They will try me again—not for the crime of coldness, this time, but for a crime of warmth. Perhaps they will find extenuating circumstances and release me; perhaps not.

I do not care. If they condemn me, this time I will wear my invisibility like a shield of glory.

THE PAIN PEDDLERS

This was the second of the stories I did for Fred Pohl under our you-write-I'll-buy deal: fast, smooth, dark. It was written in November, 1962, and appeared in the August, 1963 Galaxy.

But my science fiction output was still very low. I had found a new and very appealing line of work: like Isaac Asimov, I had drifted into writing books of popularized science, beginning in 1961 with the very successful Lost Cities *and* Vanished Civilizations. *Most of what I did was on archaeological subjects—1962 saw me write a book on underwater archaeology,* Sunken History, *and another called* Empires in the Dust, *and I edited an anthology of the writings of famous archaeologists,* Great Adventures in Archaeology. *It was a long way from "Kill That Babe" and "Stalin's Slave Barracks." I was enjoying myself, I was making money, and I was winning a new audience far from the grimy world of pulp-category fiction.*

Pain is Gain.
— Greek proverb

The phone bleeped. Northrop nudged the cut-in switch and heard Maurillo say, "We got a gangrene, chief. They're amputating tonight."

Northrop's pulse quickened at the thought of action. "What's the tab?" he asked.

"Five thousand, all rights."

"Anesthetic?"

"Natch," Maurillo said. "I tried it the other way."

"What did you offer?"

"Ten. It was no go."

Northrop sighed. "I'll have to handle it myself, I guess. Where's the patient?"

"Clinton General. In the wards."

Northrop raised a heavy eyebrow and glowered into the screen. "In the *wards?*" he bellowed. "And you couldn't get them to agree?"

Maurillo seemed to shrink. "It was the relatives, chief. They were stubborn. The old man, he didn't seem to give a damn, but the relatives—"

"Okay. You stay there. I'm coming over to close the deal," Northrop snapped. He cut the phone out and pulled a couple of blank waiver forms out of his desk, just in case the relatives backed down. Gangrene was gangrene, but ten grand was ten grand. And business was business. The networks were yelling. He had to supply the goods or get out.

He thumbed the autosecretary. "I want my car ready in thirty seconds. South Street exit."

"Yes, Mr. Northrop."

"If anyone calls for me in the next half hour, record it. I'm going to Clinton General Hospital, but I don't want to be called there."

"Yes, Mr. Northrop."

"If Rayfield calls from the network office, tell him I'm getting him a dandy. Tell him—oh, hell, tell him I'll call him back in an hour. That's all."

"Yes, Mr. Northrop."

Northrop scowled at the machine and left his office. The gravshaft took him down forty stories in almost literally no time flat. His car was waiting, as ordered, a long, sleek '08 Frontenac with bubble top. Bulletproof, of course. Network producers were vulnerable to crackpot attacks.

He sat back, nestling into the plush upholstery. The car asked him where he was going, and he answered.

"Let's have a pep pill," he said.

A pill rolled out of the dispenser in front of him. He gulped it down. *Maurillo, you make me sick,* he thought. *Why can't you close a deal without me? Just once?*

He made a mental note. Maurillo had to go. The organization couldn't tolerate inefficiency.

*

The hospital was an old one. It was housed in one of the vulgar green-glass architectural monstrosities so popular sixty years before, a tasteless slab-sided thing without character or grace. The main door irised and Northrop stepped through, and the familiar hospital smell hit his nostrils. Most people found it unpleasant, but not Northrop. It was the smell of dollars, for him.

The hospital was so old that it still had nurses and orderlies. Oh, plenty of mechanicals skittered up and down the corridors, but here and there a middle-aged nurse, smugly clinging to her tenure, pushed a tray of mush along, or a doddering orderly propelled a broom. In his early days on video, Northrop had done a documentary on these people, these living fossils in the hospital corridors. He had won an award for the film, with its crosscuts from baggy-faced nurses to gleaming mechanicals, its vivid presentation of the inhumanity of the new hospitals. It was a long time since Northrop had done a documentary of that sort. A different kind of show was the order of the day now, ever since the intensifiers had come in.

A mechanical took him to Ward Seven. Maurillo was waiting there, a short, bouncy little man who wasn't bouncing much now, because he knew he had fumbled. Maurillo grinned up at Northrop, a hollow grin, and said, "You sure made it fast, chief!"

"How long would it take for the competition to cut in?" Northrop countered. "Where's the patient?"

"Down by the end. You see where the curtain is? I had the curtain put up. To get in good with the heirs. The relatives, I mean."

"Fill me in," Northrop said. "Who's in charge?"

"The oldest son. Harry. Watch out for him. Greedy."

"Who isn't?" Northrop sighed. They were at the curtain, now. Maurillo parted it. All through the long ward, patients were stirring. Potential subjects for taping, all of them, Northrop thought. The world was so full of different kinds of sickness—and one sickness fed on another.

He stepped through the curtain. There was a man in the bed, drawn and gaunt, his hollow face greenish, stubbly. A mechanical stood next to the bed, with an intravenous tube running across and under the covers.

31

The patient looked at least ninety. Knocking off ten years for the effects of illness still made him pretty old, Northrop thought.

He confronted the relatives.

There were eight of them. Five women, ranging from middle age down to teens. Three men, the oldest about fifty, the other two in their forties. Sons and daughters and nieces and granddaughters, Northrop figured.

He said gravely, "I know what a terrible tragedy this must be for all of you. A man in the prime of his life—-head of a happy family…" Northrop stared at the patient. "But I know he'll pull through. I can see the strength in him."

The oldest relative said, "I'm Harry Gardner. I'm his son. You're from the network?"

"I'm the producer," Northrop said. "I don't ordinarily come in person, but my assistant told me what a great human situation there was here, what a brave person your father is…"

The man in the bed slept on. He looked bad.

Harry Gardner said, "We made an arrangement. Five thousand bucks. We wouldn't do it, except for the hospital bills. They can really wreck you."

"I understand perfectly," Northrop said in his most unctuous tones. "That's why we're prepared to raise our offer. We're well aware of the disastrous effects of hospitalization on a small family, even today, in these times of protection. And so we can offer—"

"No! There's got to be anesthetic!" It was one of the daughters, a round, drab woman with colorless thin lips. "We ain't going to let you make him suffer!"

Northrop smiled. "It would only be a moment of pain for him. Believe me. We'd begin the anesthesia immediately after the amputation. Just let us capture that single instant of—"

"It ain't right! He's old, he's got to be given the best treatment! The pain could kill him!"

"On the contrary," Northrop said blandly. "Scientific research has shown that pain is often beneficial in amputation cases. It creates a nerve block, you see, that causes a kind of anesthesia of its own, without the harmful side effects of chemotherapy. And once the danger vectors are controlled, the normal anesthetic procedures can be invoked, and—" He took a deep breath, and went rolling glibly on to the crusher, "with the extra fee we'll provide, you can give your dear one the absolute finest in medical care. There'll be no reason to stint."

Wary glances were exchanged. Harry Gardner said, "How much are you offering?"

"May I see the leg?" Northrop countered.

The coverlet was peeled back. Northrop stared.

It was a nasty case. Northrop was no doctor, but he had been in this line of work for five years, and that was long enough to give him an amateur acquaintance with disease. He knew the old man was in bad shape. It looked as though there had been a severe burn, high up along the calf, which had probably been treated only with first aid. Then, in happy proletarian ignorance, the family had let the old man rot until he was gangrenous. Now the leg was blackened, glossy, and swollen from midcalf to the ends of the toes. Everything looked soft and decayed. Northrop had the feeling that he could reach out and break the puffy toes off, one at a time.

The patient wasn't going to survive. Amputation or not, he was probably rotten to the core by this time, and if the shock of amputation didn't do him in, general debilitation would. It was a good prospect for the show. It was the kind of stomach-turning vicarious suffering that millions of viewers gobbled up avidly.

Northrop looked up and said, "Fifteen thousand if you'll allow a network-approved surgeon to amputate under our conditions. And we'll pay the surgeon's fee besides."

"Well..."

"And we'll also underwrite the entire cost of postoperative care for your father," Northrop added smoothly. "Even if he stays in the hospital for six months, we'll pay every nickel, over and above the telecast fee."

He had them. He could see the greed shining in their eyes. They were faced with bankruptcy, and he had come to rescue them, and did it matter all that much if the old man didn't have anesthetic when they sawed his leg off? He was hardly conscious even now. He wouldn't really feel a thing, not really.

Northrop produced the documents, the waivers, the contracts covering residuals and Latin-American reruns, the payment vouchers, all the paraphernalia. He sent Maurillo scuttling off for a secretary, and a few moments later a glistening mechanical was taking it all down.

"If you'll put your name here, Mr. Gardner..."

Northrop handed the pen to the eldest son. Signed, sealed, delivered.

"We'll operate tonight," Northrop said. "I'll send our surgeon over immediately. One of our best men. We'll give your father the care he deserves."

He pocketed the documents. It was done. Maybe it was barbaric to operate on an old man that way, Northrop thought, but he didn't bear the responsibility, after all. He was just giving the public what it wanted, and the public wanted spouting blood and tortured nerves. And what did it matter to the old man, really? Any experienced medic could tell you he was as good as dead. The operation wouldn't save him. Anesthesia wouldn't save him. If the gangrene didn't get him, postoperative shock would do him in. At worst, he would suffer only a few minutes under the knife, but at least his family would be free from the fear of financial ruin.

On the way out, Maurillo said, "Don't you think it's a little risky, chief? Offering to pay the hospitalization expenses, I mean?"

"You've got to gamble a little sometimes to get what you want," Northrop said.

"Yeah, but that could run to fifty, sixty thousand! What'll that do to the budget?"

Northrop shrugged. "We'll survive. Which is more than the old man will. He can't make it through the night. We haven't risked a penny, Maurillo. Not a stinking cent."

Returning to the office, Northrop turned the papers on the Gardner amputation over to his assistants, set the wheels in motion for the show, and prepared to call it a day. There was only one bit of dirty work left to do. He had to fire Maurillo.

It wasn't called firing, of course. Maurillo had tenure, just like the hospital orderlies and everyone else below executive rank. It was more a demotion than anything else. Northrop had been increasingly dissatisfied with the little man's work for months, now, and today had been the clincher. Maurillo had no imagination. He didn't know how to close a deal. Why hadn't he thought of underwriting the hospitalization? *If I can't delegate responsibility to him,* Northrop told himself, *I can't use him at all.* There were plenty of other assistant producers in the outfit who'd be glad to step in.

Northrop spoke to a couple of them. He made his choice. A young fellow named Barton, who had been working on documentaries all year. Barton had done the plane-crash deal in London in the spring. He had a fine touch for the gruesome. He had been on hand at the World's Fair fire last year in Juneau. Yes, Barton was the man.

The next part was the sticky one. Northrop phoned Maurillo, even though Maurillo was only two rooms away—these things were never done in person—and said, "I've got some good news for you, Ted. We're shifting you to a new program."

"Shifting…?"

"That's right. We had a talk in here this afternoon, and we decided you were being wasted on the blood and guts show. You need more scope for your talents. So we're moving you over to Kiddie Time. We think you'll really blossom there. You and Sam Kline and Ed Bragan ought to make a terrific team."

Northrop saw Maurillo's pudgy face crumble. The arithmetic was getting home; over here, Maurillo was Number Two, and on the new show, a much less important one, he'd be Number Three. It was a thumping boot downstairs, and Maurillo knew it.

The *mores* of the situation called for Maurillo to pretend he was receiving a rare honor. He didn't play the game. He squinted and said, "Just because I didn't sign up that old man's amputation?"

"What makes you think…?"

"Three years I've been with you! Three years, and you kick me out just like that!"

"I told you, Ted, we thought this would be a big opportunity for you. It's a step up the ladder. It's—"

Maurillo's fleshy face puffed up with rage. "It's getting junked," he said bitterly. "Well, never mind, huh? It so happens I've got another offer. I'm quitting before you can can me. You can take your tenure and—"

Northrop blanked the screen.

The idiot, he thought. *The fat little idiot. Well, to hell with him!*

He cleared his desk, and cleared his mind of Ted Maurillo and his problems. Life was real, life was earnest. Maurillo just couldn't take the pace, that was all.

Northrop prepared to go home. It had been a long day.

At eight that evening came word that old Gardner was about to undergo the amputation. At ten, Northrop was phoned by the network's own head surgeon, Dr. Steele, with the news that the operation had failed.

"We lost him," Steele said in a flat, unconcerned voice. "We did our best, but he was a mess. Fibrillation set in, and his heart just ran away. Not a damned thing we could do."

"Did the leg come off?"

"Oh, sure. All this was *after* the operation."

"Did it get taped?"

"They're processing it now. I'm on my way out."

"Okay," Northrop said. "Thanks for calling."

"Sorry about the patient."

"Don't worry yourself," Northrop said. "It happens to the best of us."

The next morning, Northrop had a look at the rushes. The screening was in the twenty-third floor studio, and a select audience was on hand—Northrop, his new assistant producer Barton, a handful of network executives, a couple of men from the cutting room. Slick, bosomy girls handed out intensifier helmets—no mechanicals doing the work here!

Northrop slipped the helmet on over his head. He felt the familiar surge of excitement as the electrodes descended, as contact was made. He closed his eyes. There was a thrum of power somewhere in the room as the EEG-amplifier went into action. The screen brightened.

There was the old man. There was the gangrenous leg. There was Dr. Steele, crisp and rugged and dimple-chinned, the network's star surgeon, $250,000-a-year's worth of talent. There was the scalpel, gleaming in Steele's hand.

Northrop began to sweat. The amplified brain waves were coming through the intensifier, and he felt the throbbing in the old man's leg, felt the dull haze of pain behind the old man's forehead, felt the weakness of being eighty years old and half dead.

Steele was checking out the electronic scalpel, now, while the nurses fussed around, preparing the man for the amputation. In the finished tape, there would be music, narration, all the trimmings, but now there was just a soundless series of images, and, of course, the tapped brainwaves of the sick man.

The leg was bare.

The scalpel descended.

Northrop winced as vicarious agony shot through him. He could feel the blazing pain, the brief searing hellishness as the scalpel slashed through diseased flesh and rotting bone. His whole body trembled, and he bit down hard on his lips and clenched his fists and then it was over.

There was a cessation of pain. A catharsis. The leg no longer sent its pulsating messages to the weary brain. Now there was shock, the anesthesia of hyped-up pain, and with the shock came calmness. Steele went about the mop-up operation. He tidied the stump, bound it.

The rushes flickered out in anticlimax. Later, the production crew would tie up the program with interviews of the family, perhaps a shot of the funeral, a few observations on the problem of gangrene in the aged. Those things were the extras. What counted, what the viewers wanted, was the sheer nastiness of vicarious pain, and that they got in full measure. It was a gladiatorial contest without the gladiators, masochism concealed as medicine. It worked. It pulled in the viewers by the millions.

Northrop patted sweat from his forehead.

"Looks like we got ourselves quite a little show here, boys," he said in satisfaction.

The mood of satisfaction was still on him as he left the building that day. All day he had worked hard, getting the show into its final shape, cutting and polishing. He enjoyed the element of craftsmanship. It helped him to forget some of the sordidness of the program.

Night had fallen when he left. He stepped out of the main entrance and a figure strode forward, a bulky figure, medium height, tired face. A hand reached out, thrusting him roughly back into the lobby of the building.

At first Northrop didn't recognize the face of the man. It was a blank face, a nothing face, a middle-aged empty face. Then he placed it.

Harry Gardner. The son of the dead man.

"Murderer!" Gardner shrilled. "You killed him! He would have lived if you'd used anesthetics! You phony, you murdered him so people would have thrills on television!"

Northrop glanced up the lobby. Someone was coming around the bend. Northrop felt calm. He could stare this nobody down until he fled in fear.

"Listen," Northrop said, "we did the best medical science can do for your father. We gave him the ultimate in scientific care. We—"

"You murdered him!"

"No," Northrop said, and then he said no more, because he saw the sudden flicker of a slice-gun in the blank-faced man's fat hand. He backed away, but it didn't help, because Gardner punched the trigger and an incandescent bolt flared out and sliced across Northrop's belly just as efficiently as the surgeon's scalpel had cut through the gangrenous leg.

Gardner raced away, feet clattering on the marble floor. Northrop dropped, clutching himself. His suit was seared, and there was a slash through his abdomen, a burn an eighth of an inch wide and perhaps four inches deep, cutting through intestines, through organs, through flesh. The pain hadn't begun yet. His nerves weren't getting the message through to his stunned brain. But then they were, and Northrop coiled and twisted in agony that was anything but vicarious now.

Footsteps approached.

"Jeez," a voice said.

Northrop forced an eye open. Maurillo. Of all people, Maurillo.

"A doctor," Northrop wheezed. "Fast! Christ, the pain! Help me, Ted!"

Maurillo looked down, and smiled. Without a word, he stepped to the telephone booth six feet away, dropped in a token, punched out a call.

"Get a van over here, fast. I've got a subject, chief."

Northrop writhed in torment. Maurillo crouched next to him. "A doctor," Northrop murmured. "A needle, at least. Gimme a needle! The pain—"

"You want me to kill the pain?" Maurillo laughed. "Nothing doing, chief. You just hang on. You stay alive till we get that hat on your head and tape the whole thing."

"But you don't work for me—you're off the program—"

"Sure," Maurillo said. "I'm with Transcontinental now. They're starting a blood-and-guts show too. Only they don't need waivers."

Northrop gaped. Transcontinental? That bootleg outfit that peddled tapes in Afghanistan and Mexico and Ghana and God knew where else? Not even a network show, he thought. No fee. Dying in agony for the benefit of a bunch of lousy tapeleggers. That was the worst part, Northrop thought. Only Maurillo would pull a deal like that.

"A needle! For God's sake, Maurillo, a needle!"

"Nothing doing, chief. The van'll be here any minute. They'll sew you up, and we'll tape it nice."

Northrop closed his eyes. He felt the coiling intestines blazing within him. He willed himself to die, to cheat Maurillo and his bunch of ghouls. But it was no use. He remained alive and suffering.

He lived for an hour. That was plenty of time to tape his dying agonies. The last thought he had was that it was a damned shame he couldn't star on his own show.

NEIGHBOR

Also for Fred Pohl: written in January, 1964, published in the August, 1964 *Galaxy. I was being faithful to our agreement, writing s-f stories only when* *the mood took me, not just because it was time to knock something new out* *for one of my regular markets. Science fiction is always best written by part-* *time writers: the need to save the world from plunging asteroids or berserk* *robots three times a week isn't conducive to creating classic literature.*

And here in 1964 I was very much a part-time science-fiction writer. The *occasional story for Fred and an equally infrequent novel for young readers* *(such as 1964's* The Time of the Great Freeze*) was all I was doing in that* *line. The science-fact books had become my main enterprise. 1964 saw me* *do a book on Antarctica, a biography of Socrates (which would stand me in* *good stead decades later when I wrote my Hugo-winning story "Enter a* *Soldier"), a book on famous scientific hoaxes, an enormous history of the* *Great Wall of China, and, late in the year, an account of the Pueblo Indians.* *It was an incredibly grueling schedule, a constant grind of research and typ-* *ing and correcting galleys and doing the research for the next one, but I was* *young and thought nothing of it. I was setting myself up for real exhaustion* *and physical collapse, but that was still a couple of years in the future.*

F resh snow had fallen during the night. It lay like a white sheet atop the older snow, nine or ten feet of it, that already covered the plain.

Now all was smooth and clear almost to the horizon. As Michael Holt peered through the foot-thick safety glass of his command-room window, he saw, first of all, the zone of brown earth, a hundred yards in diameter, circling his house, and then the beginning of the snowfield with a few jagged bare trees jutting through it, and then, finally, a blot on the horizon, the metallic tower that was Andrew McDermott's dwelling.

Not in seventy or eighty years had Holt looked at the McDermott place without feeling hatred and irritation. The planet was big enough, wasn't it? Why had McDermott chosen to stick his pile of misshapen steel down right where Holt had to look at it all his days? The McDermott estate was large. McDermott could have built his house another fifty or sixty miles to the east, near the banks of the wide, shallow river that flowed through the heart of the continent. He hadn't cared to. Holt had politely suggested it, when the surveyors and architects first came out from Earth. McDermott had just as politely insisted on putting his house where he wanted to put it.

It was still there. Michael Holt peered at it, and his insides roiled. He walked to the control console of the armament panel, and let his thin, gnarled hands rest for a moment on a gleaming rheostat.

There was an almost sexual manner to the way Holt fondled the jutting knobs and studs of the console. Now that his two-hundredth year was approaching, he rarely handled the bodies of his wives any more. But, then, he did not love his wives as keenly as he loved the artillery emplacement with which he could blow Andrew McDermott to atoms.

Just let him provoke me, Holt thought.

He stood by the panel, a tall, gaunt man with a withered face and a savage hook of a nose and a surprisingly thick shock of faded red hair. He closed his eyes and allowed himself the luxury of a daydream.

He imagined that Andrew McDermott had given him offense. Not simply the eternal offense of being there in his view, but some direct, specific affront. Poaching on his land, perhaps. Or sending a robot out to hack down a tree on the borderland. Or putting up a flashing neon sign mocking Holt in some vulgar way. Anything that would serve as an excuse for hostilities.

And then: Holt saw himself coming up here to the command room and broadcasting an ultimatum to the enemy. "Take that sign down, McDermott," he might say. "Keep your robots off my land," perhaps. "Or else this means war."

McDermott would reply with a blast of radiation, of course, because that was the kind of sneak he was. The deflector screens of Holt's front-line defenses would handle the bolt with ease, soaking it in and feeding the energy straight to Holt's own generators.

Then, at long last, Holt would answer back. His fingers would tighten on the controls. Crackling arcs of energy would leap toward the ionosphere and bound downward at McDermott's place, spearing through his pitiful screens as though they weren't there. Holt saw himself gripping the controls with knuckle-whitening fervor, launching thunderbolt after thunderbolt, while on the horizon Andrew McDermott's hideous keep blazed and glowed in hellish fire, and crumpled and toppled and ran in molten puddles over the snow.

Yes, that would be the moment to live for!

That would be the moment of triumph!

To step back from the controls at last and look through the window and see the glowing red spot on the horizon where the McDermott place had been. To pat the controls as though they were the flanks of a beloved old horse. To leave the house, and ride across the borderland into the McDermott estate, and see the charred ruin, and know that he was gone forever.

Then, of course, there would be an inquiry. The fifty lords of the planet would meet to discuss the battle, and Holt would explain, "He wantonly provoked me. I need not tell you how he gave me offense by building his house within my view. But this time—"

And Holt's fellow lords would nod sagely, and would understand, for they valued their own unblemished views as highly as Holt himself. They would exonerate him and grant him McDermott's land, as far as the horizon, so no newcomer could repeat the offense.

Michael Holt smiled. The daydream left him satisfied. His heart raced perhaps a little too enthusiastically as he pictured the slagheap on the horizon. He made an effort to calm himself. He was, after all, a fragile old man, much as he hated to admit it, and even the excitement of a daydream taxed his strength.

He walked away from the panel, back to the window. Nothing had changed. The zone of brown earth where his melters kept back the snow, and then the white field, and finally the excrescence on the horizon, glinting coppery red in the thin midday sunlight. Holt scowled. The daydream had changed nothing. No shot had been fired. McDermott's keep still stained the view. Turning, Holt began to shuffle slowly out of the room, toward the dropshaft that would take him five floors downward to his family.

The communicator chimed. Holt stared at the screen in surprise. "Yes?"

"An outside call for you, Lord Holt. Lord McDermott is calling," the bland metallic voice said.

"Lord McDermott's secretary, you mean."

"It is Lord McDermott himself, your lordship."

Holt blinked. "You're joking," he said. "It's fifty years since he called me. If this is a prank, I'll have your circuits shorted!"

"I cannot joke, your lordship. Shall I tell Lord McDermott you do not wish to speak to him?"

"Of course," Holt snapped. "No...wait. Find out what he wants. Then tell him I can't speak to him."

Holt sank back into a chair in front of the screen. He nudged a button with his elbow, and tiny hands began to massage the muscles of his back, where tension-poisons had suddenly flooded in to stiffen him.

McDermott calling? What for?

To complain, of course. Some trespass, no doubt. Some serious trespass, if McDermott felt he had to make the call himself. Michael Holt's blood warmed. Let him complain! Let him accuse, let him bluster! Perhaps this would give the excuse for hostilities at last. Holt ached to declare war. He had been building his armaments patiently for decade after decade, and he knew beyond doubt that he had the capability to destroy McDermott moments after the first shot was fired. No screens in the universe could withstand the array of weaponry Holt had assembled. The outcome of a conflict was in no doubt. *Let him start something,* Michael Holt prayed. *Oh, let him be the aggressor! I'm ready for him, and more than ready!*

The bell chimed again. The robot voice of Holt's secretary said, "I have spoken to him, your lordship. He will tell me nothing. He wants to speak to you."

Holt sighed. "Very well. Put him on, then."

There was a moment of electronic chaos on the screen as the robot shifted from the inside channel to an outside one. Holt sat stiffly, annoyed by the sudden anxiety he felt. He realized, strangely, that he had forgotten what his enemy's voice sounded like. All communications between them had been through robot intermediaries for years.

The screen brightened and showed a test pattern. A hoarse, querulous voice said, "Holt? Holt, where are you?"

"Right here in my chair, McDermott. What's troubling you?"

"Turn your vision on. Let me have a look at you, Holt."

"You can speak your piece without seeing me, can't you? Is my face that fascinating to you?"

"Please. This is no time for bickering. Turn the vision on!"

"Let me remind you," Holt said coldly, "that *you* have called *me*. The normal rules of etiquette require that I have the privilege of deciding on the manner of transmission. And I prefer not to be seen. I also prefer not to be speaking to you. You have thirty seconds to state your complaint. Important business awaits me."

There was silence. Holt gripped the arms of his chair and signaled for a more intense massage. He became aware, in great irritation, that his hands were trembling. He glared at the screen as though he could burn his enemy's brain out simply by sending angry thoughts over the communicator.

McDermott said finally, "I have no complaint, Holt. Only an invitation."

"To tea?"

"Call it that. I want you to come here, Holt."

"You've lost your mind!"

"Not yet. Come to me. Let's have a truce," McDermott rasped. "We're both old, sick, stupid men. It's time to stop the hatred."

Holt laughed. "We're both old, yes. But I'm not sick and you're the only stupid one. Isn't it a little late for the olive branch?"

"Never too late."

"You know there can't be peace between us," Holt said. "Not so long as that eyesore of yours sticks up over the trees. It's a cinder in my eye, McDermott. I can't ever forgive you for building it."

"Will you listen to me?" McDermott said. "When I'm gone, you can blast the place apart, if it pleases you. All I want is for you to come here. I—I need you, Holt. I want you to pay me a visit."

"Why don't you come here, then?" Holt jeered. "I'll throw my door wide for you. We'll sit by the fire and reminisce about all the years we hated each other."

"If I could come to you," McDermott said, "there would be no need for us to meet at all."

"What do you mean?"

"Turn your visual on, and you'll see."

Michael Holt frowned. He knew he had become hideous with age, and he was not eager to show himself to his enemy. But he could not see McDermott without revealing himself at the same time. With an abrupt, impulsive gesture, Holt jabbed the control button in his chair. The mists on the screen faded, and an image appeared.

All Holt could see was a face, shrunken, wizened, wasted. McDermott was past two hundred, Holt knew, and he looked it. There no flesh left on his face. The skin lay like parchment over bone. The left side of his face was distorted, the nostril flared, the mouth corner dragged down to reveal the teeth, the eyelid drooping. Below the chin, McDermott was invisible, swathed in machinery, his body cocooned in what was probably a nutrient bath. He was obviously in bad shape.

He said, "I've had a stroke, Holt. I'm paralyzed from the neck down. I can't hurt you."

"When did this happen?"

"A year ago."

"You've kept very quiet about it," Holt said.

"I didn't think you'd care to know. But now I do. I'm dying, Holt, and I want to see you once face to face before I die. I know, you're suspicious. You think I'm crazy to ask you to come here. Well, maybe I am crazy. I'll turn my screens off. I'll send all my robots across the river. I'll be absolutely alone here, helpless, and you can come with an army if you like. There. Doesn't that sound like a trap, Holt? I know I'd think so if I were in your place and you were in mine. But it isn't a trap. Can you believe that? I'll open my door to you. You can come and laugh in my face as I lie here. But come. There's something I have to tell you, something of vital importance to you. And you've got to be here in person when I tell you. You won't regret coming. Believe that, Holt."

Holt stared at the wizened creature on the screen, and trembled with doubt and confusion. The man must be a lunatic! It was years since Holt had last stepped beyond the protection of his own screens. Now McDermott was asking him not only to go into the open field, where he might be gunned down with ease, but to enter into McDermott's house itself, to put his head right between the jaws of the lion.

Absurd!

McDermott said, "Let me show you my sincerity. My screens are off. Take a shot at the house. Hit it anywhere. Go ahead. Do your worst!"

Deeply troubled, chilled with mystification, Holt elbowed out of his chair, went beyond the range of the visual pickup, over to the control console of the guns. How many times in dreams he had fondled these studs and knobs, never firing them once, except in test shots directed at his own property! It was unreal to be actually training the sights on the gleaming tower of McDermott's house at last. Excitement surged in him. Could this all be some subtle way, he wondered, of causing him to have a fatal heart attack through overstimulation?

He gripped the controls. He pondered, considered tossing a thousand-megawatt beam at McDermott, then decided to use something a little milder. If the screens really were down all the way, even his feeblest shot would score.

He sighted—not on the house itself, but on a tree just within McDermott's inner circle of defense. He fired, still half convinced he was dreaming. The tree became a yard-high stump.

"That's it," McDermott called. "Go on. Aim at the house, too. Knock a turret off. The screens are down."

Senile dementia, Holt thought. Baffled, he lifted the sight a bit and let the beam play against one of McDermott's outbuildings. The shielded wall glowed a moment, then gave as the beam smashed its way through. Ten square feet of McDermott's castle now was a soup of protons, fleeing into the cold.

Holt realized in stunned disbelief that there was nothing at all preventing him from destroying McDermott and his odious house entirely. There was no risk of a counterattack. He would not even need to use the heavy artillery that he had been so jealously hoarding against this day. A light beam would do it easily enough.

If would be too easy this way, though.

There could be no pleasure in a wanton attack. McDermott had not provoked him. Rather, he sat there in his cocoon, sniveling and begging to be visited.

Holt returned to the visual field. "I must be as crazy as you are," he said. "Turn your robots loose and leave your screens down. I'll come to visit you. I wish I understood this, but I'll come anyway."

Michael Holt called his family together. Three wives, the eldest near his own age, the youngest only seventy. Seven sons, ranging in age from sixty to a hundred thirteen. The wives of his sons. His grandchildren. His top echelon of robots.

He assembled them in the grand hall of Holt Keep, and took his place at the head of the table, and stared down the rows at their faces, so like his own, and said quietly, "I am going to pay a call on Lord McDermott."

He could see the shock on their faces. They were too well disciplined to speak their minds, of course. He was Lord Holt; and his word was law, and he could, if he so pleased, order them all put to death on the spot. Once, many years before, he had been forced to assert his parental authority in just such a way, and no one would ever forget it.

He smiled. "You think I've gone soft in my old age, and perhaps I have. But McDermott has had a stroke. He's completely paralyzed from the neck down. He wants to tell me something, and I'm going to go. His screens are down and he's sending all his robots out of the house. I could have blasted the place apart if I wanted to."

He could see the muscles working in the jaws of his sons. They wanted to cry out, but they did not dare.

Holt went on, "I'm going alone except for a few robots. If there's been no word from me for half an hour after I'm seen entering the house, you're authorized to come after me. If there's any interference with the rescue party, it will mean war. But I don't think there'll be trouble. Anyone who comes after me in less than half an hour will be put to death."

Holt's words died away in a shiver of echoes. He eyed them all, one at a time. This was a critical moment, he knew. If they dared, they might decide among themselves that he had gone mad, and depose him. That had happened before too, in other families. They could topple him, reprogram all the robots to take commands from them instead, and confine him to his wing of the house. He had given them evidence enough, just now, of his irresponsibility.

But they made no move. They lacked the guts. He was head of the household, and his word was law. They sat, pale and shaken and dazed, as he rolled his chair past them and out of the grand hall.

Within an hour, he was ready to go. Winter was in the fourth of its seven months, and Michael Holt had not left the house since the first snowfall. But he had nothing to fear from the elements. He would not come in contact with the frigid air of the sub-zero plain. He entered his car within his own house, and it glided out past the defense perimeter, a gleaming dark teardrop sliding over the fresh snow. Eight of his robots accompanied him, a good enough army for almost any emergency.

A visual pickup showed him the scene at McDermott Keep. The robots were filing out, an army of black ants clustering around the great gate. He could see them marching eastward, vanishing from sight beyond the house. A robot overhead reported that they were heading for the river by the dozens.

The miles flew past. Black, twisted trees poked through the snow, and Holt's car weaved a way through them. Far below, under many feet of whiteness, lay the fertile fields. In the spring, all would be green, and the leafy trees would help to shield the view of McDermott Keep, though they could not hide it altogether. In winter, the ugly copper-colored house was totally visible. That made the winters all the more difficult for Holt to endure.

A robot said softly, "We are approaching the borderlands, your lordship."

"Try a test shot. See if his screens are still down."

"Shall I aim for the house?"

"No. A tree just in front of it."

Holt watched. A thick-boled, stubby tree in McDermott's front palisade gleamed a moment, and then was not there.

"The screens are still down," the robot reported.

"All right. Let's cross the border."

He leaned back against the cushion. The car shot forward. They left the bounds of Holt's own estate, and entered McDermott's. There was no warning ping to tell them they were trespassing. McDermott had even turned off the boundary scanners, then. Holt pressed sweaty palms together. More than ever he felt that he had let himself be drawn into some sort of trap. There was no turning back, now. He was across the border, into McDermott's own territory. Better to die boldly, he thought, than to live huddled in a shell.

He had never been this close to McDermott Keep before. When it was being built, McDermott had invited him to inspect it, but Holt had of course refused. Nor had he been to the housewarming; alone among the lords of the planet, he had stayed home to sulk. He could hardly even remember when he had left his own land at all. There were few places to go on this world, with its fifty estates of great size running through the temperate belt, and whenever Holt thirsted for the companionship of his fellow lords, which was not often, he could have it easily enough via telescreen. Some of them came to him, now and then. It was strange that when he finally did stir to pay a call, it should be a call on McDermott.

Drawing near the enemy keep, he found himself reluctantly admitting that it was less ugly at close range than it seemed from the windows of Holt Keep. It was a great blocky building, hundreds of yards long, with a tall octagonal tower rising out of its northern end, a metal spike jabbing perhaps five hundred feet high. The reflected afternoon light, bouncing from the snowfield, gave the metal-sheathed building a curiously oily look, not unattractive at this distance.

"We are within the outer defense perimeter," a robot told Holt.

"Fine. Keep going."

The robots sounded worried and perturbed, he thought. Of course, they weren't programmed to show much emotional range, but he could detect a note of puzzlement in what they said and how they said it. They couldn't understand this at all. It did not seem to be an invasion of McDermott Keep—that they could understand—but yet it was not a friendly visit, either.

When they were a hundred yards from the great gate of McDermott Keep, the doors swung open. Holt called McDermott and said, "See that those doors stay open all the time I'm here. If they begin to close, there'll be trouble."

"Don't worry," McDermott said. "I'm not planning any tricks."

Holt's car shot between the gate walls, and he knew that now he was at his enemy's mercy. His car rolled up to the open carport and went on through, so that he was actually within McDermott Keep. His robots followed him through.

"May I close the carport?" McDermott asked.

"Keep it open," Holt said. "I don't mind the cold."

The hood of his car swung back. His robots helped him out. Holt shivered momentarily as the cold outside air, filtering into the carport, touched him. Then he passed through the rising inner door, and, flanked by two sturdy robots, walked slowly but doggedly into the keep.

McDermott's voice reached him over a loudspeaker. "I am on the third floor of the tower," he said. "If I had not sent all the robots away, I could have let one of them guide you."

"You could send a member of your family down," Holt said sourly.

McDermott ignored that. "Continue down the corridor until it turns. Go past the armor room. You will reach a dropshaft that leads upward."

Holt and his robots moved through the silent halls. The place was like a museum. The dark high-vaulted corridor was lined with statuary and artifacts, everything musty-looking and depressing. How could anyone want to live in a tomb like this? Holt passed a shadowy room where ancient suits of armor stood mounted. He could not help but compute the cost of shipping such useless things across the light-years from Earth.

They came to the dropshaft. Holt and his two robots entered. A robot nudged the reversing stud and up they went, into the tower Holt had hated so long. McDermott guided them with a word or two.

They passed down a long hall whose dull, dark walls were set off by a gleaming floor that looked like onyx. A sphincter opened, admitting them to an oval room ringed by windows. There was a dry, foul stench of death and decay in the room. Andrew McDermott sat squarely in the middle of the room, nesting in his life-capsule. A tangled network of tubes and pipes surrounded him. All of McDermott that was visible was a pair of eyes, like shining coals in the wasted face.

"I'm glad you came," McDermott said. His voice, without benefit of electronic amplification, was thin and feeble, like the sound of feathers brushing through the air.

Holt stared at him in fascination. "I never thought I'd see this room," he said.

"I never thought you would either. But it was good of you to come, Holt. You look well, you know. For a man your age." The thin lips curled in a grotesque twisted smile. "Of course, you're still a youngster. Not even two hundred, yet. I've got you by thirty years."

Holt did not feel like listening to the older man's ramblings. "What is it you wanted?" he asked without warmth. "I'm here, but I'm not going to stay all day. You said you had something vital to tell me."

"Not really to tell," McDermott said. "More to ask. A favor. I want you to kill me, Holt."

"What?"

"It's very simple. Disconnect my feed line. There it is, right by my feet. Just rip it out. I'll be dead in an hour. Or do it even more quickly. Turn off my lungs. This switch, right here. That would be the humane way to do it."

"You have a strange sense of humor," Holt said.

"Do you think so? Top the joke, then. Throw the switch and cap the jest."

"You made me come all the way here to *kill* you?"

"Yes," McDermott said. The blazing eyes were unblinking now. "I've been immobilized for a year, now. I'm a vegetable in this thing. I sit here day after day, idle, bored. And healthy. I might live another hundred years, do you realize that, Holt? I've had a stroke, yes. I'm paralyzed. But my body's still vigorous. This damned capsule of mine keeps me in tone. It feeds me and exercises me and—do you think I want to go on living this way, Holt? Would you?"

Holt shrugged. "If you want to die, you could ask someone in your family to unplug you."

"I have no family."

"Is that true? You had five sons…"

"Four dead, Holt. The other one gone to Earth. No one lives here any more. I've outlasted them all. I'm as eternal as the heavens. Two hundred thirty years, that's long enough to live. My wives are dead, my grandchildren gone away. They'll come home when they find they've inherited. Not before. There's no one here to throw the switch."

"Your robots," Holt suggested.

Again the grim smile. "You must have special robots, Holt. I don't have any that can be tricked into killing their master. I've tried it. They know what'll happen if my life-capsule is disconnected. They won't do it. *You* do it, Holt. Turn me off. Blow the tower to hell, if it bothers you. You've won the game. The prize is yours."

There was a dryness in Holt's throat, a band of pressure across his chest. He tottered a little. His robots, ever sensitive to his condition, steadied him and guided him to a chair. He had been on his feet a long time for a man of his age. He sat quietly until the spasm passed.

Then he said, "I won't do it."

"Why not?"

"It's too simple, McDermott. I've hated you too long. I can't just flip a switch and turn you off."

"Bombard me, then. Blast the tower down."

"Without provocation? Do you think I'm a criminal?" Holt asked.

"What do you want me to do?" McDermott said tiredly. "Order my robots to trespass? Set fire to your orchards? What will provoke you, Holt?"

"Nothing," Holt said. "I don't want to kill you. Get someone else to do it."

The eyes glittered. "You devil," McDermott said. "You absolute devil. I never realized how much you hated me. I send for you in a time of need, asking to be put out of my misery, and will you grant me that? Oh, no. Suddenly you get noble. You won't kill me! You devil, I see right through you. You'll go back to your keep and gloat because I'm a living dead man here. You'll chuckle to yourself because I'm alone and frozen into this capsule. Oh, Holt, it's not right to hate so deeply! I admit I've given offense. I deliberately built the tower here to wound your pride. Punish me, then. Take my life. Destroy my tower. Don't leave me here!"

Holt was silent. He moistened his lips, filled his lungs with breath, got to his feet. He stood straight and tall, towering over the capsule that held his enemy.

"Throw the switch," McDermott begged.

"I'm sorry. I can't."

"Devil!"

Holt looked at his robots. "It's time to go," he said. "There's no need for you to guide us. We can find our way out of the building."

The teardrop-shaped car sped across the shining snow. Holt said nothing as he made the return journey. His mind clung to the image of the immobilized McDermott, and there was no room for any other thought. That stench of decay tingled in his nostrils. That glint of madness in the eyes as they begged for oblivion.

They were crossing the borderlands, now. Holt's car broke the warning barrier and got a pinging signal to halt and identify. A robot gave the password, and they went on toward Holt Keep.

His family clustered near the entrance, pale, mystified. Holt walked in under his own steam. They were bursting with questions, but no one dared ask anything. It remained for Holt to say the first word.

He said, "McDermott's a sick, crazy old man. His family is dead or gone. He's a pathetic and disgusting sight. I don't want to talk about the visit."

Sweeping past them, Holt ascended the shaft to the command room. He peered out, over the snowy field. There was a double track in the snow, leading to and from McDermott Keep, and the sunlight blazed in the track, making it a line of fire stretching to the horizon.

The building shuddered suddenly. Holt heard a hiss and a whine. He flipped on his communicator and a robot voice said, "McDermott Keep is attacking, your lordship. We've deflected a high-energy bombardment."

"Did the screens have any trouble with it?"

"No, your lordship. Not at all. Shall I prepare for a counterattack?"

Holt smiled. "No," he said. "Take defensive measures only. Extend the screens right to the border and keep them there. Don't let McDermott do any harm. He's only trying to provoke me, but he won't succeed."

The tall, gaunt man walked to the control panel. His gnarled hands rested lovingly on the equipment. So they had come to warfare at last, he thought. The cannon of McDermott Keep were doing their puny worst. Flickering needles told the story: whatever McDermott was throwing was being absorbed easily. He didn't have the firepower to do real harm.

Holt's hands tightened on the controls. Now, he thought, he could blast McDermott Keep to ash. But he would not do it, any more than he would throw the switch that would end Andrew McDermott's life.

McDermott did not understand. Not cruelty, but simple selfishness, had kept him from killing the enemy lord, just as, all these years, Holt had refrained from launching an attack he was certain to win. He felt remotely sorry for the paralyzed man locked in the life-capsule. But it was inconceivable that Holt would kill him.

Once you are gone, Andrew, who will I have to hate? Holt wondered.

That was why he had not killed. No reason more complicated than that.

Michael Holt peered through the foot-thick safety glass of his command-room window. He saw the zone of brown earth, the snowfield with its fresh track, and the coppery ugliness of McDermott Keep. His intestines writhed at the ugliness of that baroque tower against the horizon. He imagined the skyline as it had looked a hundred years ago, before McDermott had built his foul monstrosity there.

He fondled the controls of his artillery bank as though they were a young girl's breasts. Then he turned, slowly and stiffly, making his way across the command-room to his chair, and sat quietly, listening to the sound of Andrew McDermott's futile bombardment expending itself harmlessly against the outer defenses of Holt Keep, and soon it grew dark as the winter night closed quietly down.

THE SIXTH PALACE

A month and a half after "Neighbor," I was back to Fred with "The Sixth Palace"—February, 1964, published in the February, 1965 Galaxy. But that didn't mean a return to my old bang-'em-out prolificity of the 1950's. Now that I had had had a taste of what it was like to tackle any kind of science-fictional theme and handle it to my own taste without fear of rejection, I was becoming more and more enthusiastic about writing stories for Pohl. He was pleased too, and encouraged me to keep going. By the summer of 1964 he and I were discussing my doing a series of five novellas for him—the "Blue Fire" stories, as I called them, which became the novel To Open the Sky. I had told Fred at the outset that my contributions to his magazine would probably be few and far between, because I was more interested in writing non-fiction, and at the beginning that was true: but, bit by bit, the no-rejections deal I had worked out with him had lured me back into the regular production of science fiction. I did the first of the "Blue Fire" stories in November, 1964, the second in December, the third in March, 1965. For someone who had planned to dabble in s-f only on a part-time basis, I was suddenly getting very active again after six or seven years away from the center of the scene.

I don't, incidentally, remember where I found the quote from Hebrew mystical literature that was the spark for the story. Long ago I asked no less an authority than Avram Davidson, but he didn't know its source either. I do wonder where it came from.

Ben Azai was deemed worthy and stood at the gate of the sixth palace and saw the ethereal splendor of the pure marble plates. He opened his mouth and said twice, "Water! Water!" In the twinkling of an eye they decapitated him and threw eleven thousand iron bars at him. This shall be a sign for all generations that no one should err at the gate of the sixth palace.

— *Lesser Hekhaloth*

There was the treasure, and there was the guardian of the treasure. And there were the whitening bones of those who had tried in vain to make the treasure their own. Even the bones had taken on a kind of beauty, lying out there by the gate of the treasure vault, under the blazing arch of heavens. The treasure itself lent beauty to everything near it—even the scattered bones, even the grim guardian.

The home of the treasure was a small world that belonged to red Valzar. Hardly more than moonsized, really, with no atmosphere to speak of, a silent, dead little world that spun through darkness a billion miles from its cooling primary. A wayfarer had stopped there once. Where from, where bound? No one knew. He had established a cache there, and there it lay, changeless and eternal, treasure beyond belief, presided over by the faceless metal man who waited with metal patience for his master's return.

There were those who would have the treasure. They came, and were challenged by the guardian, and died.

On another world of the Valzar system, men undiscouraged by the fate of their predecessors dreamed of the hoard, and schemed to possess it. Lipescu was one: a tower of a man, golden beard, fists like hammers, gullet of brass, back as broad as a tree of a thousand years. Bolzano was another: awl-shaped, bright of eye, fast of finger, twig thick, razor sharp. They had no wish to die.

Lipescu's voice was like the rumble of island galaxies in collision . He wrapped himself around a tankard of good black ale and said, "I go tomorrow, Bolzano."

"Is the computer ready?"

"Programmed with everything the beast could ask me," the big man boomed. "There won't be a slip."

"And if there is?" Bolzano asked, peering idly into the blue, oddly pale, strangely meek eyes of the giant. "And if the robot kills you?"

"I've dealt with robots before."

Bolzano laughed. "That plain is littered with bones, friend. Yours will join the rest. Great bulky bones, Lipescu. I can see them now."

"You're a cheerful one, friend."

"I'm realistic."

Lipescu shook his head heavily. "If you were realistic, you wouldn't be in this with me," he said slowly. "Only a dreamer would do such a thing as this." One meaty paw hovered in the air, pounced, caught Bolzano's forearm. The little man winced as bones ground together. Lipescu said, "You won't back out? If I die, you'll make the attempt?"

"Of course I will, you idiot."

"Will you? You're a coward, like all little men. You'll watch me die, and then you'll turn tail and head for another part of the universe as fast as you know how. Won't you?"

"I intend to profit by your mistakes," Bolzano said in a clear, testy voice. "Let go of my arm."

Lipescu released his grip. The little man sank back in his chair, rubbing his arm. He gulped ale. He grinned at his partner and raised his glass.

"To success," Bolzano said.

"Yes. To the treasure."

"And to long life afterward."

"For both of us," the big man boomed.

"Perhaps," said Bolzano. "Perhaps."

He had his doubts. The big man was sly, Ferd Bolzano knew, and that was a good combination, not often found: slyness and size. Yet the risks were great. Bolzano wondered which he preferred—that Lipescu should gain the treasure on his attempt, thus assuring Bolzano of a share without risk, or that Lipescu should die, forcing Bolzano to venture his own life. Which was better, a third of the treasure without hazard, or the whole thing for the highest stake?

Bolzano was a good enough gambler to know the answer to that. Yet there was more than yellowness to the man; in his own way, he longed for the chance to risk his life on the airless treasure world.

Lipescu would go first. That was the agreement. Bolzano had stolen the computer, had turned it over to the big man, and Lipescu would make the initial attempt. If he gained the prize, his was the greater share. If he perished, it was Bolzano's moment next. An odd partnership, odd terms, but Lipescu would have it no other way, and Ferd Bolzano did not argue the point with his beefy compatriot. Lipescu would return with the treasure, or he would not return at all. There would be no middle way, they both were certain.

Bolzano spent an uneasy night. His apartment, in an airy shaft of a building overlooking glittering Lake His, was a comfortable place, and he had little longing to leave it. Lipescu, by preference, lived in the stinking slums beyond the southern shore of the lake, and when the two men parted for the night they went in opposite ways. Bolzano considered bringing a woman home for the night but did not. Instead, he sat moody and wakeful before the televector screen, watching the procession of worlds, peering at the green and gold and ochre planets as they sailed through the emptiness.

Toward dawn, he ran the tape of the treasure. Octave Merlin had made that tape, a hundred years before, as he orbited sixty miles above the surface of the airless little world. Now Merlin's bones bleached on the plain, but the tape had come home and bootlegged copies commanded a high price in hidden markets. His camera's sharp eye had seen much.

There was the gate; there was the guardian. Gleaming, ageless, splendid. The robot stood ten feet high, a square, blocky, black shape topped by the tiny anthropomorphic head dome, featureless and sleek. Behind him the gate, wide open but impassable all the same. And behind him, the treasure, culled from the craftsmanship of a thousand worlds, left here who knew why, untold years ago.

No more mere jewels. No dreary slabs of so-called precious metal. The wealth here was not intrinsic; no vandal would think of melting the treasure into dead ingots. Here were statuettes of spun iron that seemed to move and breathe. Plaques of purest lead, engraved with lathework that dazzled the mind and made the heart hesitate. Cunning intaglios in granite, from the workshops of a frosty world half a parsec from nowhere. A scatter of opals, burning with an inner light, fashioned into artful loops of brightness.

A helix of rainbow-colored wood. A series of interlocking strips of some beast's bone, bent and splayed so that the pattern blurred and perhaps abutted some other dimensional continuum. Cleverly carved shells, one within the other, descending to infinity. Burnished leaves of nameless trees. Polished pebbles from unknown beaches. A dizzying spew of wonders, covering some fifty square yards, sprawled out behind the gate in stunning profusion.

Rough men unschooled in the tenets of esthetics had given their lives to possess the treasure. It took no fancy knowledge to realize the wealth of it, to know that collectors strung from galaxy to galaxy would fight with bared fangs to claim their share. Gold bars did not a treasure make. But these things? Beyond duplication, almost beyond price?

Bolzano was wet with a fever of yearning before the tape had run its course. When it was over, he slumped in his chair, drained, depleted.

Dawn came. The silvery moons fell from the sky. The red sun splashed across the heavens. Bolzano allowed himself the luxury of an hour's sleep.

And then it was time to begin...

As a precautionary measure, they left the ship in a parking orbit three miles above the airless world. Past reports were unreliable, and there was no telling how far the robot guardian's power extended. If Lipescu were successful, Bolzano could descend and get him—and the treasure. If Lipescu failed, Bolzano would land and make his own attempt.

The big man looked even bigger, encased in his suit and in the outer casement of a dropshaft. Against his massive chest he wore the computer, an extra brain as lovingly crafted as any object in the treasure hoard. The guardian would ask him questions; the computer would help him answer. And Bolzano would listen. If Lipescu erred, possibly his partner could benefit by knowledge of the error and succeed.

"Can you hear me?" Lipescu asked.

"Perfectly. Go on, get going!"

"What's the hurry? Eager to see me die?"

"Are you that lacking in confidence?'" Bolzano asked. "Do you want me to go first?"

"Fool," Lipescu muttered. "Listen carefully. If I die, I don't want it to be in vain."

"What would it matter to you?"

The bulky figure wheeled around. Bolzano could not see his partner's face, but he knew Lipescu must be scowling. The giant rumbled, "Is life that valuable? Can't I take a risk?"

"For *my* benefit?"

"For mine," Lipescu said. "I'll be coming back."

"Go, then. The robot is waiting."

Lipescu walked to the lock. A moment later he was through and gliding downward, a one-man spaceship, jets flaring beneath his feet. Bolzano settled by the scanner to watch. A televector pickup homed in on Lipescu just as he made his landing, coming down in a blaze of fire. The treasure and its guardian lay about a mile away. Lipescu rid himself of the dropshaft, stepping with giant bounds toward the waiting guardian.

Bolzano watched.

Bolzano listened.

The televector pickup provided full fidelity. It was useful for Bolzano's purposes, and useful, too, for Lipescu's vanity, for the ‚big man wanted his every moment taped for posterity. It was interesting to see Lipescu dwarfed by the guardian. The black faceless robot, squat and motionless, topped the big man by better than three feet.

Lipescu said, "Step aside."

The robot's reply came in surprisingly human tones, though void of any distinguishing accent. "What I guard is not to be plundered."

"I claim them by right," Lipescu said.

"So have many others. But their right did not exist. Nor does yours. I cannot step aside for you."

"Test me," Lipescu said. "See if I have the right or not!"

"Only my master may pass."

"Who is your master? I am your master!"

"My master is he who can command me. And no one can command me who shows ignorance before me."

"Test me, then," Lipescu demanded.

"Death is the penalty for failure."

"Test me."

"The treasure does not belong to you."

"Test me and step aside."

"Your bones will join the rest here."

"Test me," Lipescu said.

Watching from aloft, Bolzano went tense. His thin body drew together like that of a chilled spider. Anything might happen now. The robot might propound riddles, like the Sphinx confronting Oedipus.

It might demand the proofs of mathematical theorems. It might ask the translation of strange words. So they gathered, from their knowledge of what had befallen other men here. And, so it seemed, to give a wrong answer was to earn instant death.

He and Lipescu had ransacked the libraries of the world. They had packed all knowledge, so they hoped, into their computer. It had taken months, even with multi-stage programming. The tiny shining globe of metal on Lipescu's chest contained an infinity of answers to an infinity of questions.

Below, there was long silence as man and robot studied one another. Then the guardian said, "Define latitude."

"Do you mean geographical latitude?" Lipescu asked.

Bolzano congealed with fear. The idiot, asking for a clarification! He would die before he began!

The robot said, "Define latitude."

Lipescu's voice was calm. "The angular distance of a point on a planet's surface north or south of the equator, as measured from the center of the planet."

"Which is more consonant," the robot asked, "the minor third or the major sixth?"

There was a pause. Lipescu was no musician. But the computer would feed him the answer.

"The minor third," Lipescu said.

Without a pause, the robot fired another question. "Name the prime numbers between 5,237 and 7,641."

Bolzano smiled as Lipescu handled the question with ease. So far, so good. The robot had stuck to strictly factual questions, school-book stuff, posing no real problems to Lipescu. And after the initial hesitation and quibble over latitude, Lipescu had seemed to grow in confidence from moment to moment. Bolzano squinted at the scanner, looking beyond the robot, through the open gate, to the helter-skelter pile of treasures. He wondered which would fall to his lot when he and Lipescu divided them, two-thirds for Lipescu, the rest for him.

"Name the seven tragic poets of Elifora," the robot said.

"Domiphar, Halionis, Slegg, Hork-Sekan—"

"The fourteen signs of the zodiac as seen from Morneez," the robot demanded.

"The Teeth, the Serpents, the Leaves, the Waterfall, the Blot—"

"What is a pedicel?"

"The stalk of an individual flower of an inflorescence."

"How many years did the Siege of Lamina last?"

"Eight."

"What did the flower cry in the third canto of Somner's *Vehicles?*"

"'I ache, I sob, I whimper, I die,'" Lipescu boomed.

"Distinguish between the stamen and the pistil."

"The stamen is the pollen-producing organ of the flower; the pistil—"

And so it went. Question after question. The robot was not content with the legendary three questions of mythology; it asked a dozen, and then asked more. Lipescu answered perfectly, prompted by the murmuring of the peerless compendium of knowledge strapped to his chest. Bolzano kept careful count: the big man had dealt magnificently with seventeen questions When would the robot concede defeat? When would it end its grim quiz and step aside?

It asked an eighteenth question, pathetically easy. All it wanted was an exposition of the Pythagorean Theorem. Lipescu did not even need the computer for that. He answered, briefly, concisely, correctly. Bolzano was proud of his burly partner.

Then the robot struck Lipescu dead.

It happened in the flickering of an eyelid. Lipescu's voice had ceased, and he stood there, ready for the next question, but the next question did not come. Rather, a panel in the robot's vaulted belly slid open, and something bright and sinuous lashed out, uncoiling over the ten feet or so that separated guardian from challenger, and sliced Lipescu in half. The bright something slid back out of sight. Lipescu's trunk toppled to one side. His massive legs remained absurdly planted for a moment; then they crumpled, and a spacesuited leg kicked once, and all was still.

Stunned, Bolzano trembled in the loneliness of the cabin, and his lymph turned to water. What had gone wrong? Lipescu had given the proper answer to every question, and yet the robot had slain him. Why? Could the big man possibly have misphrased Pythagoras? No: Bolzano had listened. The answer had been flawless, as had the seventeen that preceded it. Seemingly the robot had lost patience with the game, then. The robot had cheated. Arbitrarily, maliciously, it had lashed out at Lipescu, punishing him for the correct answer.

Did robots cheat, Bolzano wondered? Could they act in malicious spite? No robot he knew was capable of such actions; but this robot was unlike all others.

For a long while, Bolzano remained huddled in the cabin. The temptation was strong to blast free of orbit and head home, treasureless but alive. Yet the treasure called to him. Some suicidal impulse drove him on. Sirenlike, the robot drew him downward.

There had to be a way to make the robot yield, Bolzano thought, as he guided his small ship down the broad barren plain. Using the computer had been a good idea, whose only defect was that it hadn't worked. The records were uncertain, but it appeared that in the past men had died when they finally gave a wrong answer after a series of right ones. Lipescu had given no wrong answers. Yet he too had died. It was inconceivable that the robot understood some relationship of the squares on the hypotenuse and on the other two sides that was different from the relationship Lipescu had expressed

Bolzano wondered what method would work.

He plodded leadenly across the plain toward the gate and its guardian. The germ of an idea formed in him as he walked doggedly on.

He was, he knew, condemned to death by his own greed. Only extreme agility of mind would save him from sharing Lipescu's fate. Ordinary intelligence would not work. Odyssean cleverness was the only salvation.

Bolzano approached the robot. Bones lay everywhere. Lipescu weltered in his own blood. Against that vast dead chest lay the computer, Bolzano knew. But he shrank from reaching for it. He would do without it. He looked away, unwilling to let the sight of Lipescu's severed body interfere with the coolness of his thoughts.

He collected his courage. The robot showed no interest in him.

"Give ground," Bolzano said. "I am here. I come for the treasure."

"Win your right to it."

"What must I do?"

"Demonstrate truth," the robot said. "Reveal inwardness. Display understanding."

"I am ready," said Bolzano.

The robot offered a question. "What is the excretory unit of the vertebrate kidney called?"

Bolzano contemplated. He had no idea. The computer could tell him, but the computer lay strapped to fallen Lipescu. No matter. The robot wanted truth, inwardness, understanding. Lipescu had offered information. Lipescu had perished.

"The frog in the pond," Bolzano said, "utters an azure cry."

There was silence. Bolzano watched the robot's front, waiting for the panel to slide open, the sinuous something to chop him in half.

The robot said, "During the War of Dogs on Vanderveer IX, the embattled colonists drew up thirty-eight dogmas of defiance. Quote the third, the ninth, the twenty-second, and the thirty-fifth."

Bolzano pondered. This was an alien robot, product of unknown hand. How did its maker's mind work? Did it respect knowledge? Did it treasure facts for their own sake? Or did it recognize that information is meaningless, insight a nonlogical process?

Lipescu had been logical. He lay in pieces.

"The mereness of pain," Bolzano responded, "is ineffable and refreshing."

The robot said, "The monastery of Kwaisen was besieged by the soldiers of Oda Nobunaga on the third of April, 1582. What words of wisdom did the abbot utter?"

Bolzano spoke quickly and buoyantly. "Eleven, forty-one, elephant, voluminous."

The last word slipped from his lips despite an effort to retrieve it. Elephants *were* voluminous, he thought. A fatal slip? The robot did not appear to notice.

Sonorously, ponderously, the great machine delivered the next question. "What is the percentage of oxygen in the atmosphere of Muldonar VII?"

"False witness bears a swift sword," Bolzano replied.

The robot made an odd humming sound. Abruptly it rolled on massive treads, moving some six feet to its left. The gate of the treasure trove stood wide, beckoning.

"You may enter," the robot said.

Bolzano's heart leaped. He had won! He had gained the high prize!

Others had failed, most recently less than an hour before, and their bones glistened on the plain. They had tried to answer the robot, sometimes giving right answers, sometimes giving wrong ones, and they had died. Bolzano lived.

It was a miracle, he thought. Luck? Shrewdness? Some of each, he told himself. He had watched a man give eighteen right answers and die. So the accuracy of the responses did not matter to the robot. What did? Inwardness. Understanding. Truth.

There could be inwardness and understanding and truth in random answers, Bolzano realized. Where earnest striving had failed, mockery had succeeded. He had staked his life on nonsense, and the prize was his.

He staggered forward, into the treasure trove. Even in the light gravity, his feet were like leaden weights. Tension ebbed in him. He knelt among the treasures.

The tapes, the sharp-eyed televector scanners, had not begun to indicate the splendor of what lay here. Bolzano stared in awe and rapture at a tiny disk, no greater in diameter than a man's eye, on which myriad coiling lines writhed and twisted in patterns of rare beauty. He caught his breath, sobbing with the pain of perception as a gleaming marble spire, angled in mysterious swerves, came into view. Here, a bright beetle of some fragile waxy substance rested on a pedestal of yellow jade. There, a tangle of metallic cloth spurted dizzying patterns of luminescence. And over there—and beyond—and there—

The ransom of a universe, Bolzano thought.

It would take many trips to carry all this to his ship. Perhaps it would be better to bring the ship to the hoard, eh? He wondered, though, if he would lose his advantage if he stepped back through the gate. Was it possible that he would have to win entrance all over again? And would the robot accept his answers as willingly the second time?

It was something he would have to chance, Bolzano decided. His nimble mind worked out a plan. He would select a dozen, two dozen of the finest treasures, as much as he could comfortably carry, and take them back to the ship. Then he would lift the ship and set it down next to the gate. If the robot raised objections about his entering, Bolzano would simply depart, taking what he had already secured. There was no point in running undue risks. When he had sold this cargo, and felt pinched for money, he could always return and try to win admission once again. Certainly, no one else would steal the hoard if he abandoned it.

Selection, that was the key now.

Crouching, Bolzano picked through the treasure, choosing for portability and easy marketability. The marble spire? Too big. But the coiling disk, yes, certainly, and the beetle, of course, and this small statuette of dull hue, and the cameos showing scenes no human eye had ever beheld, and this, and this, and this—

His pulse raced. His heart thundered. He saw himself traveling from world to world, vending his wares. Collectors, museums, governments would vie with one another to have these prizes. He would let them bid each object up into the millions before he sold. And, of course, he would keep one or two for himself—or perhaps three or four—souvenirs of this great adventure.

And someday when wealth bored him he would return and face the challenge again. And he would dare the robot to question him, and he would reply with random absurdities, demonstrating his grasp of the fundamental insight that in knowledge there is only hollow merit, and the robot would admit him once more to the treasure trove.

Bolzano rose. He cradled his lovelies in his arms. Carefully, carefully, he thought. Turning, he made his way through the gate.

The robot had not moved. It had shown no interest as Bolzano plundered the hoard. The small man walked calmly past it.

The robot said, "Why have you taken those? What do you want with them?"

Bolzano smiled. Nonchalantly he replied, "I've taken them because they're beautiful. Because I want them. Is there a better reason?"

"No," the robot said, and the panel slid open in its ponderous black chest.

Too late, Bolzano realized that the test had not yet ended, that the robot's question had arisen out of no idle curiosity. And this time he had replied in earnest, speaking in rational terms.

Bolzano shrieked. He saw the brightness coming toward him.

Death followed instantly.

FLIES

So I was writing science fiction again, and beginning to edit it, too. An anthology of reprints called Earthmen and Strangers *was the first one I did, and for my sins I chose to include a story by Harlan Ellison in it. Ellison was willing to grant me permission to use his story, but not without a lot of heavy muttering and grumbling about the terms of the contract, to which I replied on October 2, 1965:*

"Dear Harlan: You'll be glad to know that in the course of a long and wearying dream last night I watched you win two Hugos at last year's Worldcon. You acted pretty smug about it, too. I'm not sure which categories you led, but one of them was probably Unfounded Bitching. Permit me a brief and fatherly lecture in response to your letter of permission on the anthology...."

Whereupon I dealt with his complaints at some length, and then, almost gratuitously, threw in a postscript:

"Why don't *you do an anthology? HARLAN ELLISON PICKS OFF-BEAT CLASSICS OF SF, or something...."*

From the placement of the italicized word in that sentence, I surmise that I must already have suggested to Harlan that he edit an anthology of controversial s-f—he was running a paperback line then called Regency Books, published out of Chicago—but for some reason he had brushed the idea aside. Now, though, my suggestion kindled something in him. He was back to me right away, by telephone this time, to tell me in some excitement that he would do a science-fiction anthology, all right, but for some major publishing house instead of Regency, and instead of putting together a mere compilation of existing material he would solicit previously unpublished stories, the kind of science fiction that no magazine of that era would dare to publish. Truly dangerous stories, Harlan said—a book of dangerous visions. "In fact, that's what I'll call it," he told me, really excited now. "Dangerous Visions. I want you to write a story for it, too."

And so I unwittingly touched off a publishing revolution.

By the 18th of October Harlan had sold the book to Doubleday and was soliciting stories far and wide. Requests for material—material of the boldest, most uncompromising kind—went out to the likes of Theodore Sturgeon, Frederik Pohl, Poul Anderson, Philip K. Dick, Philip Jose Farmer, Fritz Leiber, J.G. Ballard, Norman Spinrad, Brian Aldiss, Lester del Rey, Larry Niven, R.A. Lafferty, John Brunner, Roger Zelazny, and Samuel R. Delany. Dick, Pohl, Sturgeon, Anderson, del Rey, Farmer, Brunner, Aldiss, and Leiber were well-established authors, but the work of Ballard, Zelazny, Delany, Niven, and Spinrad, believe it or not, was only just beginning to be known in the United States in 1965. Harlan's eye for innovative talent had always been formidably keen.

As the accidental instigator of the whole thing—and the quickest man with an s-f story since Henry Kuttner in his prime—I sat down right away and wrote the very first dangerous vision, "Flies," in November of 1965, just as soon as Harlan told me the deal was set. It was about as dangerous as I could manage: a demonstration of the random viciousness of the universe and a little blasphemy on the side. (I would return to both these themes again and again in the years ahead: my novel Thorns of 1966 was essentially a recasting of the underlying material of "Flies" at greater length.) Back at once came Harlan's check for $88.

Which was the first of many, for Dangerous Visions, would turn out to be the most significant s-f anthology of the decade, destined to go through edition after edition. (It is back in print yet again, four decades after its first publication.) All of the extraordinary writers whose names I rattled off above came through with brilliant stories, along with fifteen or twenty others, some well known at the time but forgotten now, some obscure then and still obscure, but all of them fiercely determined to live up to Harlan's demand for the kind of stories that other s-f editors would consider too hot to handle.

Dangerous Visions appeared in 1967. "An event," said the New York Times, "a jubilee of fresh ideas…what we mean when we say an important book." Its success led to the publication of an immense companion volume in 1972, Again, Dangerous Visions—760 pages of stories by writers who hadn't contributed to the first book (Ursula K. Le Guin, Gene Wolfe, Kurt Vonnegut, Gregory Benford, James Tiptree, Jr....) And ultimately Harlan began to assemble the mammoth third book in the series, The Last Dangerous Visions, publication of which is—ah—still being eagerly awaited.

I knew not what I was setting in motion with my casual postscript of October 2, 1965, suggesting that Harlan edit an anthology. Certainly I had no idea that I was nudging him toward one of the great enterprises of his career. Nor did I suspect that my own 4400-word contribution to the book would open a new and darker phase of my own career—in which, ultimately, almost everything I wrote would become a dangerous vision of sorts.

Here is Cassiday:
> transfixed on a table.

There wasn't much left of him. A brain-box; a few ropes of nerves; a limb. The sudden implosion had taken care of the rest. There was enough, though. The golden ones didn't need much to go by. They had found him in the wreckage of the drifting ship as it passed through their zone, back of Iapetus. He was alive. He could be repaired. The others on the ship were beyond hope.

Repair him? Of course. Did one need to be human in order to be humanitarian? Repair, yes. By all means. And change. The golden ones were creative.

What was left of Cassiday lay in drydock on a somewhere table in a golden sphere of force. There was no change of season here; only the sheen of the walls, the unvarying warmth. Neither day nor night, neither yesterday nor tomorrow. Shapes came and went about him. They were regenerating him, stage by stage, as he lay in complete unthinking tranquility. The brain was intact but not functioning. The rest of the man was growing back: tendon and ligament, bone and blood, heart and elbows. Elongated mounds of tissue sprouted tiny buds that enlarged into blobs of flesh. Paste cell to cell together, build a man from his own wreckage—that was no chore for the golden ones. They had their skills. But they had much to learn too, and this Cassiday could help them learn it.

Day by day Cassiday grew toward wholeness. They did not awaken him. He lay cradled in warmth, unmoving, unthinking, drifting on the tide. His new flesh was pink and smooth, like a baby's. The epithelial thickening came a little later. Cassiday served as his own blueprint. The golden ones replicated him from a shred of himself, built him back from his own polynucleotide chains, decoded the proteins and reassembled him from the template. An easy task, for them. Why not? Any blob of protoplasm could do it—for itself. The golden ones, who were not protoplasm, could do it for others.

They made some changes in the template. Of course. They were craftsmen. And there was a good deal they wanted to learn.

Look at Cassiday:
the dossier.

BORN 1 August 2316
PLACE Nyack, New York
PARENTS Various
ECONOMIC LEVEL Low
EDUCATIONAL LEVEL Middle
OCCUPATION Fuel technician
MARITAL STATUS Three legal liaisons, duration eight months, sixteen months, and two months
HEIGHT Two meters
WEIGHT 96 kg
HAIR COLOR Yellow
EYES Blue
BLOOD TYPE A +
INTELLIGENCE LEVEL High
SEXUAL, INCLINATIONS Normal

Watch them now:
changing him.

The complete man lay before them, newly minted, ready for rebirth. Now came the final adjustments. They sought the gray brain within its pink wrapper, and entered it, and traveled through the bays and inlets of the mind, pausing now at this quiet cove, dropping anchor now at the base of that slab-sided cliff. They were operating, but doing it neatly.

70

Here were no submucous resections, no glittering blades carving through gristle and bone, no sizzling lasers at work, no clumsy hammering at the tender meninges. Cold steel did not slash the synapses. The golden ones were subtler; they tuned the circuit that was Cassiday, boosted the gain, damped out the noise, and they did it very gently.

When they were finished with him, he was much more sensitive. He had several new hungers. They had granted him certain abilities.

Now they awakened him.

"You are alive, Cassiday," a feathery voice said. "Your ship was destroyed. Your companions were killed. You alone survived."

"Which hospital is this?"

"Not on Earth. You'll be going back soon. Stand up, Cassiday. Move your right hand. Your left. Flex your knees. Inflate your lungs. Open and close your eyes several times. What's your name, Cassiday?"

"Richard Henry Cassiday."

"How old?"

"Forty-one."

"Look at this reflection. Who do you see?"

"Myself."

"Do you have any further questions?"

"What did you do to me?"

"Repaired you, Cassiday. You were almost entirely destroyed."

"Did you change me any?"

"We made you more sensitive to the feelings of your fellow man."

"Oh," said Cassiday.

Follow Cassiday as he journeys:
   back to Earth.

He arrived on a day that had been programmed for snow. Light snow, quickly melting, an esthetic treat rather than a true manifestation of weather. It was good to touch foot on the homeworld again. The golden ones had deftly arranged his return, putting him back aboard his wrecked ship and giving him enough of a push to get him within range of a distress sweep. The monitors had detected him and picked him up. How was it you survived the disaster unscathed, Spaceman Cassiday? Very simple, sir, I was outside the ship when it happened. It just went swoosh, and everybody was killed. And I only am escaped alone to tell thee.

They routed him to Mars and checked him out, and held him awhile in a decontamination lock on Luna, and finally sent him back to Earth. He stepped into the snowstorm, a big man with a rolling gait and careful calluses in all the right places. He had few friends, no relatives, enough cash units to see him through for a while, and a couple of ex-wives he could look up. Under the rules, he was entitled to a year off with full pay as his disaster allotment. He intended to accept the furlough.

He had not yet begun to make use of his new sensitivity. The golden ones had planned it so that his abilities would remain inoperative until he reached the homeworld. Now he had arrived, and it was time to begin using them, and the endlessly curious creatures who lived back of Iapetus waited patiently while Cassiday sought out those who had once loved him.

He began his quest in Chicago Urban District, because that was where the spaceport was, just outside of Rockford. The slidewalk took him quickly to the travertine tower, festooned with radiant inlays of ebony and violet-hued metal, and there, at the local Televector Central, Cassiday checked out the present whereabouts of his former wives. He was patient about it, a bland-faced, mild-eyed tower of flesh, pushing the right buttons and waiting placidly for the silken contacts to close somewhere in the depths of the Earth. Cassiday had never been a violent man. He was calm. He knew how to wait.

The machine told him that Beryl Fraser Cassiday Mellon lived in Boston Urban District. The machine told him that Lureen Holstein Cassiday lived in New York Urban District. The machine told him that Mirabel Gunryk Cassiday Milman Reed lived in San Francisco Urban District.

The names awakened memories: warmth of flesh, scent of hair, touch of hand, sound of voice. Whispers of passion. Snarls of contempt. Gasps of love.

Cassiday, restored to life, went to see his ex-wives.

We find one now:
safe and sound.

Beryl's eyes were milky in the pupil, greenish where they should have been white. She had lost weight in the last ten years, and now her face was parchment stretched over bone, an eroded face, the cheekbones pressing from within against the taut skin and likely to snap through at any moment. Cassiday had been married to her for eight months when he was twenty-four. They had separated after she insisted on taking the

Sterility pledge. He had not particularly wanted children, but he was offended by her maneuver all the same. Now she lay in a soothing cradle of webfoam, trying to smile at him without cracking her lips.

"They said you'd been killed," she told him.

"I escaped. How have you been, Beryl?"

"You can see that. I'm taking the cure."

"Cure?"

"I was a triline addict. Can't you see? My eyes, my face? It melted me away. But it was peaceful. Like disconnecting your soul. Only it would have killed me, another year of it. Now I'm on the cure. They tapered me off last month. They're building up my system with prosthetics. I'm full of plastic now. But I'll live."

"You've remarried?" Cassiday asked.

"He split long ago. I've been alone five years. Just me and the triline. But now I'm off that stuff." Beryl blinked laboriously. "You look so relaxed, Dick. But you always were. So calm, so sure of yourself. *You'd* never get yourself hooked on triline. Hold my hand, will you?"

He touched the withered claw. He felt the warmth come from her, the need for love. Great throbbing waves came lalloping into him, low-frequency pulses of yearning that filtered through him and went booming onward to the watchers far away.

"You once loved me," Beryl said. "Then we were both silly. Love me again. Help me get back on my feet. I need your strength."

"Of course I'll help you," Cassiday said.

He left her apartment and purchased three cubes of triline. Returning, he activated one of them and pressed it into Beryl's hand. The green-and-milky eyes roiled in terror.

"No," she whimpered.

The pain flooding from her shattered soul was exquisite in its intensity. Cassiday accepted the full flood of it. Then she clenched her fist, and the drug entered her metabolism, and she grew peaceful once more.

Observe the next one:
  with a friend.

The annunciator said, "Mr. Cassiday is here."

"Let him enter," replied Mirabel Gunryk Cassiday Milman Reed.

The door-sphincter irised open and Cassiday stepped through, into onyx and marble splendor. Beams of auburn palisander formed a polished wooden framework on which Mirabel lay, and it was obvious that she reveled in the sensation of hard wood against plump flesh. A cascade of crystal-colored hair tumbled to her shoulders. She had been Cassiday's for sixteen months in 2346 and she had been a slender, timid girl then, but now he could barely detect the outlines of that girl in this pampered mound.

"You've married well," he observed.

"Third time lucky," Mirabel said. "Sit down? Drink? Shall I adjust the environment?"

"It's fine." He remained standing. "You always wanted a mansion, Mirabel. My most intellectual wife, you were, but you had this love of comfort. You're comfortable now."

"Very."

"Happy?"

"I'm comfortable," Mirabel said. "I don't read much any more, but I'm comfortable."

Cassiday noticed what seemed to be a blanket crumpled in her lap—purple with golden threads, soft, idle, clinging close. It had several eyes. Mirabel kept her hands spread over it.

"From Ganymede?" he asked. "A pet?"

"Yes. My husband bought it for me last year. It's very precious to me."

"Very precious to anybody. I understand they're expensive."

"But lovable," said Mirabel. "Almost human. Quite devoted. I suppose you'll think I'm silly, but it's the most important thing in my life now. More than my husband, even. I love it, you see. I'm accustomed to having others love me, but there aren't many things that I've been able to love."

"May I see it?" Cassiday said mildly.

"Be careful."

"Certainly." He gathered up the Ganymedean creature. Its texture was extraordinary, the softest he had ever encountered. Something fluttered apprehensively within the flat body of the animal. Cassiday detected a parallel wariness coming from Mirabel as he handled her pet. He stroked the creature. It throbbed appreciatively. Bands of iridescence shimmered as it contracted in his hands.

She said, "What are you doing now, Dick? Still working for the spaceline?"

He ignored the question. "Tell me the line from Shakespeare, Mirabel. About flies. The flies and wanton boys."

Furrows sprouted in her pale brow. "It's from *Lear*," she said. "Wait. Yes. *As flies to wanton boys are we to the gods. They kill us for their sport.*"

"That's the one," Cassiday said. His big hands knotted quickly about the blanketlike being from Ganymede. It turned a dull gray, and reedy fibers popped from its ruptured surface. Cassiday dropped it to the floor. The surge of horror and pain and loss that welled from Mirabel nearly stunned him, but he accepted it and transmitted it.

"Flies," he explained. "Wanton boys. My sport, Mirabel. I'm a god now, did you know that?" His voice was calm and cheerful. "Goodbye. Thank you."

One more awaits the visit:
  Swelling with new life.

Lureen Holstein Cassiday, who was thirty-one years old, dark-haired, large-eyed, and seven months pregnant, was the only one of his wives who had not remarried. Her room in New York was small and austere. She had been a plump girl when she had been Cassiday's two-month wife five years ago, and she was even more plump now, but how much of the access of new meat was the result of the pregnancy Cassiday did not know

"Will you marry now?" he asked.

Smiling, she shook her head. "I've got money, and I value my independence. I wouldn't let myself get into another deal like the one we had. Not with anyone."

"And the baby? You'll have it?"

She nodded savagely. "I worked hard to get it! You think it's easy? Two years of inseminations! A fortune in fees! Machines poking around in me—all the fertility boosters—oh no, you've got the picture wrong. This isn't an unwanted baby. This is a baby I sweated to have."

"That's interesting," said Cassiday. "I visited Mirabel and Beryl, too, and they each had their babies, too. Of sorts. Mirabel had a little beast from Ganymede. Beryl had a triline addiction that she was very proud of shaking. And you've had a baby put in you, without any help from a man. All three of you seeking something. Interesting."

"Are you all right, Dick?'

"Fine."

"Your voice is so flat. You're just unrolling a lot of words. It's a little frightening."

"Mmm. Yes. Do you know the kind thing I did for Beryl? I bought her some triline cubes. And I took Mirabel's pet and wrung its—well, not its neck. I did it very calmly. I was never a passionate man."

"I think you've gone crazy, Dick."

"I feel your fear. You think I'm going to do something to your baby. Fear is of no interest, Lureen. But sorrow—yes, that's worth analyzing. Desolation. I want to study it. I want to help *them* study it. I think it's what they want to know about. Don't run from me, Lureen. I don't want to hurt you, not that way."

She was small-bodied and not very strong, and unwieldy in her pregnancy. Cassiday seized her gently by both wrists and drew her toward him. Already he could feel the new emotions coming from her, the self-pity behind the terror, and he had not even done anything to her.

How did you abort a fetus two months from term?

A swift kick in the belly might do it. Too crude, too crude. Yet Cassiday had not come armed with abortifacients, a handy ergot pill, a quick-acting spasmic inducer. So he brought his knee up sharply, deploring the crudity of it. Lureen sagged. He kicked her a second time. He remained completely tranquil as he did it, for it would be wrong to take joy in violence. A third kick seemed desirable. Then he released her.

She was still conscious, but she was writhing. Cassiday made himself receptive to the outflow. The child, he realized, was not yet dead within her. Perhaps it might not die at all. But it would certainly be crippled in some way. What he drained from Lureen was the awareness that she might bring forth a defective. The fetus would have to be destroyed. She would have to begin again. It was all quite sad.

"Why?" she muttered, "…why?"

Among the watchers:
   the equivalent of dismay.

Somehow it had not developed as the golden ones had anticipated. Even they could miscalculate, it appeared, and they found that a rewarding insight. Still, something had to be done about Cassiday.

They had given him powers. He could detect and transmit to them the raw emotions of others. That was useful to them, for from the data they could perhaps construct an understanding of human beings. But in rendering him a switching center for the emotions of others they had unavoidably been forced to blank out his own. And that was distorting the data.

He was too destructive now, in his joyless way. That had to be corrected. For now he partook too deeply of the nature of the golden ones themselves. *They* might have their sport with Cassiday, for he owed them a life. But he might not have his sport with others.

They reached down the line of communication to him and gave him his instructions.

"No," Cassiday said. "You're done with me now. There's no need for me to come back."

"`Further adjustments are necessary."

"I disagree."

"You will not disagree for long."

Still disagreeing, Cassiday took ship for Mars, unable to stand aside from their command. On Mars he chartered a vessel that regularly made the Saturn run and persuaded it to come in by way of Iapetus. The golden ones took possession of him once he was within their immediate reach.

"What will you do to me?" Cassiday asked.

"Reverse the flow. You will no longer be sensitive to others. You will report to us on your own emotions. We will restore your conscience, Cassiday."

He protested. It was useless.

Within the glowing sphere of golden light they made their adjustments on him. They entered him and altered him and turned his perceptions inward, so that he might feed on his own misery like a vulture tearing at its entrails. That would be informative. Cassiday objected until he no longer had the power to object, and when his awareness returned it was too late to object.

"No,," he murmured. In the yellow gleam he saw the faces of Beryl and Mirabel and Lureen. "You shouldn't have done this to me. You're torturing me...like you would a fly..."

There was no response. They sent him away, back to Earth. They returned him to the travertine towers and the rumbling slidewalks, to the house of pleasure on 485th Street, to the islands of light that blazed in the sky, to the eleven billion people. They turned him loose to go among them, and suffer, and report on his sufferings. And a time would come when they would release him, but not yet.

Here is Cassiday:
nailed to his cross.

HALFWAY HOUSE

Yet another of the many stories I wrote for Fred Pohl's magazines—this one in January, 1966, at a time when my interest in writing science fiction, dormant through the first half of the decade, was (mainly as a result of the opportunity Fred had extended) awakening swiftly. Fred had shown my "Blue Fire" novellas to Betty Ballantine of Ballantine Books, his own publishers, and Betty had offered me a contract to put them into volume form— the beginning of one of the happiest publishing relationships of my life. Then I had gone to see Larry Ashmead of Doubleday and offered him a novel-length expansion of my 1954 story "Hopper," which became The Time Hoppers—*my first adult s-f novel to be published in hard covers. I seemed to be getting drawn back in.*

The companion magazine to Fred Pohl's Galaxy was called If, *which under the editorship of Horace Gold had been very much a second-string operation, a kind of stepsister magazine. It still felt and looked second-string to me, and I suspect Fred Pohl thought of it that way too; but he began putting stories into* If *that Horace might have run in Galaxy, and suddenly, to everybody's surprise,* If *began winning Hugo awards as the best s-f magazine (an honor that had eluded the superb Galaxy for most of its existence.) It carried off the trophy three years in a row, 1966, 1967, 1968—and, though I had felt mildly miffed at the beginning when a story I had intended for Galaxy wound up in* If, *it rapidly ceased to matter to me. "Halfway House" was one of those—published in* If *for November, 1966. It shows, I think, the growing technical security I was beginning to display in those middle years of the 1960's, just before the big and startling (to me*

79

as well as to everyone else) explosion of my abilities that occurred later in that decade.

———

Afterward, Alfieri realized that you must give a life to gain a life. Now, he was too interested simply in staying alive to think much about profundities.

He was *l'uomo dal fuoco in bocca,* the man with fire in his mouth. Cancer clawed at his throat. The vocoder gave him speech; but the raging fire soon would burn through to the core of him, and there would be no more Franco Alfieri. That was hard to accept. So he came to the Fold for aid.

He had the money. That was what it took, in part, to enter that gateway of worlds: money, plenty of it. Those who ran the Fold did not do it for sweet charity's sake. The power drain alone was three million kilowatts every time the Fold was opened. You could power a good-sized city on a load like that. But Alfieri was willing to pay what it cost. The money would shortly be of no use to him whatever, unless the beings on the far side of the Fold gave his life back to him.

"You stand on that bedplate," a technician told him. "Put your feet along the red triangular areas. Grasp the rail—*so.* Then wait."

Alfieri obeyed. He was no longer in the habit of taking such brusque orders, but he forgave the man for his rudeness. To the technician, Alfieri was so much wealthy meat, already going maggotty. Alfieri positioned his feet and looked down at the mirror-bright polish of his pointed black shoes. He grasped the furry yellow skin of the rail. He waited for the power surge.

He knew what would happen. Alfieri had been an engineer in Milan, twenty years back, when the European power grid was just coming in. He understood the workings of the Fold as well as—well, as well as anyone else who was not a mathematician. Alfieri had left engineering to found an industrial empire that sprawled from the Alps to the blue Mediterranean, but he had kept up with technology. He was proud of that. He could walk into any factory, go straight to a workbench, display a rare knowledge of any man's labor. Unlike most top executives, his knowledge was deep as well as broad.

Alfieri knew, then, that when the power surge came, it would momentarily create a condition they called a singularity, found in the natural universe only in the immediate vicinity of stars that were in their last moments of life. A collapsing star, a spent supernova, generates about itself a warp in the universe, a funnel to nowhere, the singularity. As the star shrinks, it approaches its Schwarzchild radius, the critical point when the singularity will devour it. Time runs more slowly for the dying star, as it nears the radius; its faint light shifts conspicuously toward the red; time rushes to infinity as the star is caught and swallowed by the singularity. And a man who happens to be present? He passes into the singularity also. Tidal gravitational forces of infinite strength seize him; he is stretched to the limit and simultaneously compressed, attaining zero volume and infinite density, and he is hurled—somewhere.

They had no dying stars in this laboratory. But for a price they could simulate one. For Alfieri's bundle of lire they would strain the universe and create a tiny opening and hurl him through the Fold, to a place where pleated universes met, to a place where incurable diseases were not necessarily incurable.

Alfieri waited, a trim, dapper man of fifty, with thinning sandy hair slicked crosswise over the tanned dome of his skull. He wore the tweed suit he had bought in London in '95, and a matching gray-green tie and his small sapphire ring. He gripped the railing. He was not aware of it when the surge came, and the universe was broken open, and Franco Alfieri was catapulted through a yawning vortex into a place never dreamed of in Newton's philosophy.

The being called Vuor said, "This is Halfway House."

Alfieri looked about him. Superficially, his surroundings had not changed at all. He still stood on a glossy copper bedplate, still grasped a furry rail. The quartz walls of the chamber looked the same. But an alien being now peered in, and Alfieri knew he had been translated through the Fold.

The alien's face was virtually a blank: a slit of a mouth below, slits of eyes above, no visible nostrils, a flat greenish facade, altogether, sitting on a squat neck, a triangular shoulderless trunk, ropy limbs. Alfieri had become accustomed to aliens in his dealings, and the sight of Vuor did not disturb him, though he had never seen one of this sort before.

Alfieri felt sweat churning through his pores. Tongues of flame licked at his throat. He had refused full sedation, for unless Alfieri's mind could work properly he would not be Alfieri. But the pain was terrible.

He said, "How soon can I get help?"

"What is the trouble?"

"Cancer of the throat. You hear my voice? Artificial. The larynx is gone already. There's a malignant beast eating me. Cut it out of me."

The eyeslits closed momentarily. Tentacles twined themselves together in a gesture that might have been sympathy, contempt, or refusal. Vuor's reedy, rasping voice said in passable Italian, "We do not help you here, you understand. This is merely Halfway House, the screening point. We distribute you onward."

"I know. I know. Well, send me to a world where they can cure cancer. I don't have much time left. I'm suffering, and I'm not ready to go. There's still work for me to do on Earth. *Capisce?*"

"What do you do, Franco Alfieri?"

"Didn't my dossier arrive?"

"It did. Tell me about yourself."

Alfieri shrugged. His palms were growing clammy, and he let go of the rail, wishing the alien would let him sit down. "I run an engineering company," he said. "Actually a holding company. Alfieri S.A. We do everything: power distribution, pollution control, robotics. We're getting into planetary transformation. Our operating divisions employ hundreds of thousands of men. We're more than just a money-making concern, though. We're shapers of a better world. We—" He hesitated, realizing that he sounded now like one of his own public relations flunkies and realizing also that he was begging for his own life. "It's a big, important, useful company. I founded it. I run it."

"And you are very rich. For this you wish us to prolong your life? You know that we all live under a sentence of death. For some sooner, others later. The surgeons beyond the Fold cannot save everyone. The number of sufferers who cry out is infinite, Alfieri. Tell me why you should be saved."

Wrath flamed in Alfieri. He suppressed it.

He said, "I'm a human being with a wife and children. Not good enough reason, eh? I'm wealthy enough to pay any price to be healed. Good? No? Of course not. All right, try this: I'm a genius. Like Leonardo, like Michelangelo, like—like Einstein. You know those names? Good. I have a big genius, too. I don't paint, I don't compose music. I plan. I organize. I built the biggest corporation in Europe. I took companies and put them together to do things they could never have done alone."

He glowered at the alien green mask beyond the quartz wall. "The technology that led Earth to open the Fold in the first place— my company. The power source—mine. I built it. I don't boast, I speak the truth."

"You are saying that you have made a lot of money."

"Damn you, no! I'm saying that I've created something that didn't exist before, something useful, something important, not only to Earth but to all the other worlds that meet here. And I'm not through creating. I've got bigger ideas. I need ten more years, and I don't have ten months. Can you take the responsibility of shutting me off? Can you afford to throw away all that's still in me? Can you?"

His unreal voice, which never grew hoarse even when he raised it to a shout, died away. Alfieri leaned on the railing again. The small golden eyes in the narrow slits regarded him impassively.

After a long silence Vuor said, "We will give you our decision shortly."

The walls of the chamber went opaque. Alfieri paced the little room wearily. The taste of defeat was sour in his mouth, and somehow it did not anger him to know that he had failed. He was past caring. They would let him die, of course. They would tell him that he had done his work, that he had built his company, that it saddened them but they had to consider the needs of younger men whose lifedreams still were unrealized. Then, too, they were likely to think that merely because he was rich he was not deserving of rescue. Easier was it for a camel to go through the eye of a needle, than for a rich man to attain new life on the surgeons' tables of a world beyond the Fold. Yet he couldn't give up now.

As he awaited his death sentence, Alfieri planned how he would spend his remaining months of life. Working to the end, of course. The heatsink project at Spitzbergen—yes, that first, and then—

The walls were clear again. Vuor had returned.

"Alfieri, we have made an appointment for you on Hinnerang, where your cancer will be remitted and your tissues restored. But there is a price."

"Anything. A trillion *lire!*"

83

"Not money," Vuor said. "Service. Put your genius to work in our aid."

"Tell me how!"

"Halfway House, you know, is cooperatively staffed by representatives of many worlds whose continua meet at the Fold. There is not currently an administrator from Earth on our staff. A vacancy is soon to develop. You fill it. Lend us your gift for organizing, for administration. Take a five-year term among us. Then you may return home."

Alfieri pondered. He had no particular wish to give up five years to this place. Too much beckoned to him on Earth, and if he were away five years, who would take the reins of his companies? He might return and find himself hopelessly out of touch.

Then he realized the absurdity of the thought. Vuor was offering him twenty, thirty, fifty more years of life. Standing at the edge of the grave as he was, Alfieri had no right to begrudge five of those years if his benefactors demanded them. He had made his unique administrative abilities his claim for renewed life; was it any surprise that they now wanted those same abilities as *quid pro quo*?

"Agreed," Alfieri said.

"There will, in addition, be a monetary payment," said Vuor, but Alfieri hardly cared about that.

An infinity of universes met at the Fold, as they did at every other point in space-time. Only at the Fold, though, was it possible now to cross from one continuum to another, thanks to the equipment installed there. A webwork of singularities poked holes in the fabric of universal structures. Halfway House was the shuttle point for this loom of worlds; those who could convince the administrators that they had the right to occupy a valuable place on the transfer channels were shunted to the worlds of their need.

An infinity is an infinity, and the channels filled all needs. There was access, for those who wanted it, to a matter-free universe and to a universe filled with one all-encompassing atom and to a universe containing, a world where living beings grew steadily younger and not the reverse.

There were worlds unknown to the sons of Adam, with tribes whose heads grow beneath their shoulders and their mouths in their breasts; worlds of monoculi, who run swiftly though they have a single leg and a single eye; worlds of folk whose mouths are so small they take nourishment only through a straw; worlds of amoebic intelligences; worlds where bodily reincarnation is an established fact; worlds where dreams become realities at the snap of a finger. An infinity is an infinity. But for practical purposes, only some two dozen of these worlds mattered, for they were the ones linked by common purposes and common orientation.

On one of those worlds, skilled surgeons might repair a cancer-ravaged throat. In time that skill would be imparted to Earth in return for some Earthly good, but Alfieri could not wait for the exchange to be consummated. He paid his fee, and the administrators of Halfway House sent him to Hinnerang.

Alfieri was unaware, once again, as he squeezed through the Schwarzchild singularity. He had always loved tasting unfamiliar sensations, and it seemed unfair to him that a man should be compressed to zero volume and infinite density without some tactile knowledge of the fact. But so it happened. A dying supernova was simulated for him, and he was whisked through the singularity to emerge in one more identical chamber on Hinnerang.

Here, at least, things looked properly alien. There was a reddish tinge to the warm, golden sunlight, and at night four moons danced in the sky. The gravity was half that of Earth's; and as he stood under that quartet of shimmering orbs, Alfieri felt a strange giddiness and an inner access of ecstatic strength. It seemed to him that he could leap at a bound and snatch one of those jewels from the sky.

The Hinnerangi were small, angular beings with auburn skins, high-vaulted skullcaps, and fibrous fingers that divided and divided again until they formed writhing networks of filament at the tips. They spoke in sinister whispers, and their language struck Alfieri as more barbarous than Basque and as consonant-heavy as Polish; but the usual small devices turned their words to the tongue of Dante when they needed to communicate with him, a miracle that struck Alfieri as more awesome than the whole mechanism of the Fold, which at least he could pretend he understood.

"We will first negate your pain," his surgeon told him.

"By knocking out my pain sensors?" Alfieri asked. "Cutting nerve lines?"

The surgeon regarded him with what seemed like grave amusement. "There are no pain sensors as such in the human nervous system.

There are merely functional bodies that perceive and respond by classifying the many patterns of nerve impulses arriving from the skin, selecting and abstracting the necessary modalities. "Pain" is simply a label for a class of experiences, not always unpleasant. We will adjust the control center, the gate of responses, so that your scanning of input impulses will be orientated differently. There will be no loss of sensory information; but what you feel will no longer be classified as pain."

At another time, Alfieri might have been happy to discuss the refined semantics of pain theory. Now, he was satisfied to nod solemnly and permit them to put out the fire that raged in his throat.

It was done, delicately and simply. He lay in a cradle of some gummy foam while the surgeon planned the next move: a major resection of tissue; replacement of lost cell matter; regeneration of organs. To Alfieri, wireless transmission of power was an everyday matter, but these things were the stuff of dreams. He submitted. They cut away so much of him that it seemed another slice of the surgical beam would sever his head altogether. Then they rebuilt him. When they were finished, he would speak with his own voice again, not with an implanted mechanism. But would it really be his own, if they had built it for him? No matter. It was flesh. Alfieri's heart pumped Alfieri's blood through the new tissue.

And the cancer? Was it gone?

The Hinnerangi were thorough. They hunted the berserk cells through the corridors of his body. Alfieri saw colonies of cancer establishing themselves in his lungs, his kidneys, his intestines. He visualized marauding creatures stabbing good cells with mortal wounds, thrusting their own vile fluid into unwanted places, replicating a legion of goose-stepping carcinomas cell by cell by cell. But the Hinnerangi were thorough. They purged Alfieri of corruption. They took out his appendix, in the bargain, and comforted his liver against a lifetime of white Milanese wine. Then they sent him off to recuperate.

He breathed alien air and watched moons leaping like gazelles in a sky of strange constellations. He put his hand to his throat a thousand times a day, to feel the newness there, the warmth of fresh tissue. He ate the meat of unknown beasts. He gained strength from hour to hour.

At last they put him in a singularity chamber and rammed him through the complexities of the Fold, and he returned to Halfway House.

✹

Vuor said, "You will begin your work at once. This will be your office."

It was an oval room, walled with a living plastic that made it seem as warm and pink and soft as the walls of a womb. Beyond one wall was the quartz-bounded chamber used by those who traveled the Fold. Vuor showed him how to operate the switch that permitted viewing access to the chamber in either direction.`

"What will my duties be?" Alfieri asked.

"Come and tour Halfway House first," said Vuor.

Alfieri followed. It was hard to grasp the nature of the place: Alfieri pictured it as something like a space station, an orbiting wheel of finite size divided into many chambers. But since there were no windows, he could not confirm that belief. The place seemed fairly small, no bigger than a good-sized office building. Much of it was given over to a power plant. Alfieri wished to stay and examine the generators, but Vuor hurried him on to a cafeteria, to a small room that would be his dwelling place, to some sort of chapel, to executive offices.

The alien seemed impatient. Silent figures drifted through the halls of Halfway House, beings of fifty sorts. Nearly all were oxygen breathers who could handle the all-purpose atmosphere of the place, but some were masked and mysterious. They nodded at Vuor, stared at Alfieri. Civil servants, Alfieri thought. Doing their routine work. And now I am one of them, a petty bureaucrat. But I am alive, and I will wade through a sea of bureaucratic forms to show my gratitude.

They returned to the oval office with the soft, moist pink walls.

"What will my duties be?" Alfieri asked again.

"To interview those who come to Halfway House seeking to travel beyond the Fold."

"But that's your job!"

"No longer," said Vuor. "My term is up. Mine is the now-vacant position you have been recruited to fill. When you begin, I can leave."

"You said I'd get an administrative post. To organize, to plan—"

"This is administrative work. You must judge the niceties of each applicant's situation. You must be aware of the capacity of the facilities beyond this point. You must maintain an overview of your task: whom to send forward, whom to reject."

Alfieri's hands trembled. "I'm the one who'll decide? I say, go back and rot, and you come forward? I choose life for some and death for others? No. I don't want it. I'm not God!"

"Neither am I," said the alien blandly. "Do you think I like this job?

But now I can shrug it off. I am finished here. I have been God for five years, Alfieri. It's your turn now."

"Give me some other work. There must be other jobs suited for me!"

"Perhaps there are. But you are best suited for this one. You are a gifted decider. And another thing to consider, Alfieri. You are my replacement. If you do not take the job, I must remain until someone else capable of handling it is found. I have been God long enough, Alfieri."

Alfieri was silent. He stared into the golden eyeslits, and for the first time he thought he could interpret an expression he found there. Pain. The pain of an Atlas, carrying worlds on his shoulders. Vuor was suffering. And he, Franco Alfieri, could alleviate that pain by taking the burden on himself.

Vuor said, "When your application was approved, there was an understanding that you would render service to us. The scope of your duties has been outlined to you. There is an obligation, Alfieri."

Nodding, Alfieri saw the truth of that. If he refused to take the post, what would they do? Give him his cancer back? No. They would find another use for him. And Vuor would continue to hold this job. Alfieri owed his life to the suffering alien. If he extended Vuor's duties by one additional hour, it would be unforgivable.

"I accept the obligation," Alfieri said.

The look in the alien's eyeslits could have been nothing but joy.

There were certain things Alfieri had to learn about his job, and then he was on his own. He learned them. He took up his new existence as a bureaucrat with good grace. One room to live in, instead of a cycle of mansions; food prepared by computers, not by master chefs; a long day of work, and little recreation. But he was alive. He could look to a time beyond the five years.

He sent word to Earth that he would be detained and that he would eventually return in good health to resume his position in the corporation. He authorized the commencement of Plan A for running the company in his prolonged absence. Alfieri had planned everything. Men he trusted would be stewards for him until he returned. It was made quite clear to him at Halfway House that he could not attempt to run the firm by remote control, and so he activated his plan and left the company to its new administrators. He was busy enough.

Applicants came to him.

Not all of them wished medical aid, but all had some good and compelling reason for journeying to some world beyond the Fold. Alfieri judged their cases. He had no quota; if he cared to, he could send all his applicants through to their destinations or turn them all away. But the one would be irresponsible, the other inhuman. Alfieri judged. He weighed in the balance, and some he found wanting, and others he passed on. There were only so many channels, a finite number of routes to the infinity of worlds. Alfieri thought of himself sometimes as a traffic policeman, sometimes as Maxwell's Demon, sometimes as Rhadamanthys in Hades. Mostly he thought of the day when he could go home again.

The refusals were painful. Some of the applicants bellowed their rage at him and made threats. Some of them shrank into sobbing stupors. Some quietly warned of the grave injustice he was doing. Alfieri had made hard decisions all his life, but his soul was not yet calloused from them, and he regretted the things the applicants said to him. The job, though, had to be done, and he could not deny he had a gift for it.

He was not the only such judge at Halfway House, naturally. Streams of applicants were constantly processed through many offices. But Alfieri was, in addition to a judge, the final court of appeals for his colleagues. He maintained the overview. He controlled the general flow. It was his talent to administer things.

A day came when an auburn-skinned being with swarming subdivided tendrils stood before him, a man of Hinnerang. For a terrible moment Alfieri thought it was the surgeon who had repaired his throat. But the resemblance was only superficial. This man was no surgeon.

Alfieri said, "This is Halfway House."

"I need help. I am Tomrik Horiman. You have my dossier?"

"I do," Alfieri said. "You know that we give no help here, Tomrik Horiman. We simply forward you to the place where help may be obtained. Tell me about yourself."

The tendrils writhed in anguish. "I am a grower of houses. My capital is overextended. My entire establishment is threatened. If I could go to a world where my houses would win favor, my firm would be saved.

I have a plan for growing houses on Melknor. Our calculations show that there would be a demand for our product there."

"Melknor has no shortage of houses," Alfieri remarked.

"But they love novelty there. They'd rush to buy. An entire family is faced with ruin, kind sir! Root and branch we will be wiped out. The penalty for bankruptcy is extreme. With my honor lost, I would have to destroy myself. I have children."

Alfieri knew that. He also knew that the Hinnerangi spoke the truth; unless he were allowed to pass through to Melknor to save his business, he would be obliged to take his own life. As much as Alfieri himself, this being had come before the tribunal of Halfway House under a death sentence.

But Alfieri had gifts. What did this man offer? He wished to sell houses on a planet that had no real need for them. He was one of many such house-growers, anyway, and a poor businessman to boot. He brought his troubles upon himself; unlike Alfieri, who had not asked for his cancer. Nor would Tomrik Horiman's passing be any great loss except to his immediate family. It was a great pity; but the application would have to be refused.

"We will give you our decision shortly," said Alfieri. He opaqued the walls and briefly reported to his colleagues. They did not question the wisdom of his decision. Clearing the walls, he stared through the blocks of quartz at the man from Hinnerang and said, "I greatly regret that your application must be rejected."

Alfieri waited for the reaction. Anger? Hysterical denunciation? Despair? Cold fury? A paroxysm of frustration?

No, none of those. The merchant of vegetary houses looked back at Alfieri, who had spent enough time among the Hinnerangi to interpret their unvoiced emotions. And Alfieri felt the flood of sorrow coming at him like a stream of acid. Tomrik Horiman *pitied* him.

"I am very sorry," the Hinnerangi said. "You bear such a great burden."

Alfieri shook with the pain of the words. The man was sorry— not for himself, but for *him!* Morbidly, he almost wished for his cancer back. Tomrik Horiman's pity was more than he could bear at that moment.

Tomrik Horiman gripped the rail and stood poised for his return to his own world. For an instant his eyes met the shadowed ones of the Earthman.

"Tell me," Tomrik Horiman said. "This job you have, deciding who goes forward, who goes back. Such a terrible burden! How did this job come to you?"

"I was condemned to it," said Franco Alfieri in all the anguish of his Godhead. "The price for my life was my life. I never knew such suffering when I was only a dying man."

He scowled. And then he threw the switch that sent Tomrik Horiman away.

TO THE DARK STAR

The spring of 1966 was a busy time for me, even as it went in that very busy decade. I had just finished the "Hopper" expansion for Doubleday; I was getting started on a vast non-fiction account of the quest for El Dorado for Bobbs-Merrill; I was sketching out the novella of distant prehistoric times that would become "Hawksbill Station" for Galaxy and then be expanded into a novel. In the middle of all this I somehow found time to write a story for Joseph Elder—who had been my agent for a while, but was about to begin his brief but distinguished editorial career. Joe was planning a book called The Farthest Reaches, *original stories of galactic exploration, and in April, 1966 I gave him "To the Dark Star"—one of the first explorations in science-fictional terms of the black hole concept.*

We came to the dark star, the microcephalon and the adapted girl and I, and our struggle began. A poorly assorted lot we were, to begin with. The microcephalon hailed from Quendar IV, where they grow people with greasy gray skins, looming shoulders, and virtually no heads at all. He—it—was wholly alien, at least. The girl was not, and so I hated her.

She came from a world in the Procyon system, where the air was more or less Earth-type, but the gravity was double ours. There were other differences, too. She was thick through the shoulders, thick through the waist, a block of flesh. The genetic surgeons had begun with human raw material, but they had transformed it into something nearly as alien as the microcephalon. Nearly.

We were a scientific team, so they said. Sent out to observe the last moments of a dying star. A great interstellar effort. Pick three specialists at random, put them in a ship, hurl them halfway across the universe to observe what man had never observed before. A fine idea. Noble. Inspiring. We knew our subject well. We were ideal.

But we felt no urge to cooperate, because we hated one another.

The adapted girl—Miranda—was at the controls the day that the dark star actually came into sight. She spent hours studying it before she deigned to let us know that we were at our destination. Then she buzzed us out of our quarters.

I entered the scanning room. Miranda's muscular bulk overflowed the glossy chair before the main screen. The microcephalon stood beside her, a squat figure on a tripodlike arrangement of bony legs, the great shoulders hunched and virtually concealing the tiny cupola of the head. There was no real reason why any organism's brain *had* to be in its skull, and not safely tucked away in the thorax; but I had never grown accustomed to the sight of the creature. I fear I have little tolerance for aliens.

"Look," Miranda said, and the screen glowed.

The dark star hung in dead center, at a distance of perhaps eight light-days—as close as we dared to come. It was not quite dead, and not quite dark. I stared in awe. It was a huge thing, some four solar masses, the imposing remnant of a gigantic star. On the screen there glowed what looked like an enormous lava field. Islands of ash and slag the size of worlds drifted in a sea of molten and glowing magma. A dull red illumination burnished the screen. Black against crimson, the ruined star still throbbed with ancient power. In the depths of that monstrous slagheap compressed nuclei groaned and gasped. Once the radiance of this star had lit a solar system; but I did not dare think of the billions of years that had passed since then, nor of the possible civilizations that had hailed the source of light and warmth before the catastrophe.

Miranda said, "I've picked up the thermals already. The surface temperature averages about nine hundred degrees. There's no chance of landing."

I scowled at her. "What good is the *average* temperature? Get a specific. One of those islands—"

"The ash masses are radiating at two hundred and fifty degrees. The interstices go from one thousand degrees on up. Everything works out to a mean of nine hundred degrees, and you'd melt in an instant if you went down there. You're welcome to go, brother. With my blessing."

"I didn't say—"

"You implied that there'd be a safe place to land on that fireball," Miranda snapped. Her voice was a basso boom; there was plenty of resonance space in that vast chest of hers. "You snidely cast doubt on my ability to—"

"We will use the crawler to make our inspection," said the microcephalon in its reasonable way. "There never was any plan to make a physical landing on the star."

Miranda subsided. I stared in awe at the sight that filled our screen.

A star takes a long time to die, and the relict I viewed impressed me with its colossal age. It had blazed for billions of years, until the hydrogen that was its fuel had at last been exhausted, and its thermonuclear furnace started to splutter and go out. A star has defenses against growing cold; as its fuel supply dwindles, it begins to contract, raising its density and converting gravitational potential energy into thermal energy. It takes on new life; now a white dwarf, with a density of tons per cubic inch, it burns in a stable way until at last it grows dark.

We have studied white dwarfs for centuries, and we know their secrets—so we think. A cup of matter from a white dwarf now orbits the observatory on Pluto for our further illumination.

But the star on our screen was different.

It had once been a large star—greater than the Chandrasekhar limit, 1.2 solar masses. Thus it was not content to shrink step by step to the status of a white dwarf. The stellar core grew so dense that catastrophe came before stability; when it had converted all its hydrogen to iron-56, it fell into catastrophic collapse and went supernova. A shock wave ran through the core, converting the kinetic energy of collapse into heat. Neutrinos spewed outward; the envelope of the star reached temperatures upwards of 200 billion degrees; thermal energy became intense radiation, streaming away from the agonized star and shedding the luminosity of a galaxy for a brief, fitful moment.

What we beheld now was the core left behind by the supernova explosion. Even after that awesome fury, what was intact was of great mass. The shattered hulk had been cooling for eons, cooling toward the final death. For a small star, that death would be the simple death of coldness: the ultimate burnout, the black dwarf drifting through the void like a hideous mound of ash, lightless, without warmth. But this, our stellar core, was still beyond the Chandrasekhar limit. A special death was reserved for it, a weird and improbable death.

And that was why we had come to watch it perish, the microcephalon and the adapted girl and I.

I parked our small vessel in an orbit that gave the dark star plenty of room. Miranda busied herself with her measurements and computations. The microcephalon had more abstruse things to do. The work was well divided; we each had our chore. The expense of sending a ship so great a distance had necessarily limited the size of the expedition. Three of us: a representative of the basic human stock, a representative of the adapted colonists, a representative of the race of microcephalons, the Quendar people, the only other intelligent beings in the known universe.

Three dedicated scientists. And therefore three who would live in serene harmony during the course of the work, since as everyone knows scientists have no emotions and think only of their professional mysteries. As everyone knows.

I said to Miranda, "Where are the figures for radial oscillation?"

She replied, "See my report. It'll be published early next year in—"

"Damn you, are you doing that deliberately? I need those figures now!"

"Give me your totals on the mass-density curve, then."

"They aren't ready. All I've got is raw data."

"That's a lie! The computer's been running for days! I've seen it," she boomed at me.

I was ready to leap at her throat. It would have been a mighty battle; her 300-pound body was not trained for personal combat as mine was, but she had all the advantages of strength and size. Could I club her in some vital place before she broke me in half? I weighed my options.

Then the microcephalon appeared and made peace once more with a few feather-soft words.

Only the alien among us seemed to conform at all to the stereotype of that emotionless abstraction, "the scientist." It was not true, of course; for all we could tell, the microcephalon seethed with jealousies and lusts and angers, but we had no clue to their outward manifestation. Its voice was flat as a vocoder transmission. The creature moved peacefully among us, the mediator between Miranda and me. I despised it for its mask of tranquility. I suspected, too, that the microcephalon loathed the two of us for our willingness to vent our emotions, and took a sadistic pleasure from asserting superiority by calming us.

We returned to our research. We still had some time before the last collapse of the dark star.

It had cooled nearly to death. Now there was still some thermonuclear activity within that bizarre core, enough to keep the star too warm for an actual landing. It was radiating primarily in the optical band of the spectrum, and by stellar standards its temperature was nil, but for us it would be like prowling the heart of a live volcano.

Finding the star had been a chore. Its luminosity was so low that it could not be detected optically at a greater distance than a light-month or so; it had been spotted by a satellite-borne X-ray telescope that had detected the emanations of the degenerate neutron gas of the core. Now we gathered round and performed our functions of measurement. We recorded things like neutron drip and electron capture. We computed the time remaining before the final collapse. Where necessary, we collaborated; most of the time we went our separate ways. The tension aboard ship was nasty. Miranda went out of her way to provoke me. And, though I like to think I was beyond and above her beastliness, I have to confess that I matched her, obstruction for obstruction. Our alien companion never made any overt attempt to annoy us; but indirect aggression can be maddening in close quarters, and the microcephalon's benign indifference to us was as potent a force for dissonance as Miranda's outright shrewishness or my own deliberately mulish responses.

The star hung in our viewscreen, bubbling with vitality that belied its dying state. The islands of slag, thousands of miles in diameter, broke free and drifted at random on the sea of inner flame. Now and then spouting eruptions of stripped particles came heaving up out of the core. Our figures showed that the final collapse was drawing near, and that meant that an awkward choice was upon us. Someone was going to have to monitor the last moments of the dark star. The risks were high. It could be fatal.

None of us mentioned the ultimate responsibility.

We moved toward the climax of our work. Miranda continued to annoy me in every way, sheerly for the devilishness of it. How I hated her! We had begun this voyage coolly, with nothing dividing us but professional jealousy. But the months of proximity had turned our quarrel into a personal feud. The mere sight of her maddened me, and I'm sure she reacted the same way. She devoted her energies to an immature attempt to trouble me. Lately she took to walking around the ship in the nude, I suspect trying to stir some spark of sexual feeling in me that she could douse with a blunt, mocking refusal. The trouble was that I could feel no desire whatever for a grotesque adapted creature like Miranda, a mound of muscle and bone twice my size. The sight of her massive udders and monumental buttocks stirred nothing in me but disgust.

The witch! Was it desire she was trying to kindle by exposing herself that way, or loathing? Either way, she had me. She must have known that.

In our third month in orbit around the dark star, the microcephalon announced, "The coordinates show an approach to the Schwarzschild radius. It is time to send our vehicle to the surface of the star."

"Which one of us rides monitor?" I asked.

Miranda's beefy hand shot out at me. "You do."

"I think you're better equipped to make the observations," I told her sweetly.

"Thank you, no."

"We must draw lots," said the microcephalon.

"Unfair," said Miranda. She glared at me. "He'll do something to rig the odds. I couldn't trust him."

"How else can we choose?" the alien asked.

"We can vote," I suggested. "I nominate Miranda."

"I nominate him," she snapped.

The microcephalon put his ropy tentacles across the tiny nodule of skull between his shoulders. "Since I do not choose to nominate myself," he said mildly, "it falls to me to make a deciding choice between the two of you. I refuse the responsibility. Another method must be found."

We let the matter drop for the moment. We still had a few more days before the critical time was at hand.

With all my heart I wished Miranda into the monitor capsule. It would mean at best her death, at worst a sober muting of her abrasive personality, if she were the one who sat in vicariously on the throes of the dark star. I was willing to stop at nothing to give her that remarkable and demolishing experience.

What was going to happen to our star may sound strange to a layman; but the theory had been outlined by Einstein and Schwarzschild a thousand years ago, and had been confirmed many times, though never until our expedition had it been observed at close range. When matter reaches a sufficiently high density, it can force the local curvature of space to close around itself, forming a pocket isolated from the rest of the universe. A collapsing supernova core creates just such a Schwarzschild singularity. After it has cooled to near-zero temperature, a core of the proper Chandrasekhar mass undergoes a violent collapse to zero volume, simultaneously attaining an infinite density.

In a way, it swallows itself and vanishes from this universe—for how would the fabric of the continuum tolerate a point of infinite density and zero volume?

Such collapses are rare. Most stars come to a state of cold equilibrium and remain there. We were on the threshold of a singularity, and we were in a position to put an observer vehicle right on the surface of the cold star, sending back an exact description of the events up until the final moment when the collapsing core broke through the walls of the universe and disappeared.

Someone had to ride gain on the equipment, though. Which meant, in effect, vicariously participating in the death of the star. We had learned in other cases that it becomes difficult for the monitor to distinguish between reality and effect; he accepts the sensory percepts from the distant pickup as his own experience. A kind of psychic backlash results; often an unwary brain is burned out entirely.

What impact would the direct experience of being crushed out of existence in a singularity have on a monitoring observer?

I was eager to find out. But not with myself as the sacrificial victim.

I cast about for some way to get Miranda into that capsule. She, of course, was doing the same for me. It was she who made her move first, by attempting to drug me into compliance.

What drug she used, I have no idea. Her people are fond of the non-addictive hallucinogens, which help them break the monotony of their stark, oversized world. Somehow Miranda interfered with the programming of my food supply and introduced one of her pet alkaloids. I began to feel the effects an hour after I had eaten. I walked to the screen to study the surging mass of the dark star—much changed from its appearance of only a few months before—and as I looked, the image in the screen began to swirl and melt, and tongues of flame did an eerie dance along the horizons of the star.

I clung to the rail. Sweat broke from my pores. Was the ship liquefying? The floor heaved and buckled beneath me. I looked at the back of my hand and saw continents of ash set in a grouting of fiery magma.

Miranda stood behind me. "Come with me to the capsule," she murmured. "The monitor's ready for launching now. You'll find it wonderful to see the last moments."

Lurching after her, I padded through the strangely altered ship. Miranda's adapted form was even more alien than usual; her musculature rippled and flowed, her golden hair held all the colors of the spectrum, her flesh was oddly puckered and cratered, with wiry filaments emerging from the skin. I felt quite calm about entering the capsule. She slid back the hatch, revealing the gleaming console of the panel within and I began to enter, and then suddenly the hallucination deepened and I saw in the darkness of the capsule a devil beyond all imagination.

I dropped to the floor and lay there twitching.

Miranda seized me. To her I was no more than a doll. She lifted me, began to thrust me into the capsule. Perspiration soaked me. Reality returned. I slipped from her grasp and wriggled away, rolling toward the bulkhead. Like a beast of primordial forests she came ponderously after me.

"No," I said. "I won't go."

She halted. Her face twisted in anger, and she turned away from me in defeat. I lay panting and quivering until my mind was purged of phantoms. It had been close.

It was my turn a short while later. Fight force with force, I told myself. I could not risk more of Miranda's treachery. Time was running short.

From our surgical kit I took a hypnoprobe used for anesthesia, and rigged it in a series with one of Miranda's telescope antennae. Programming it for induction of docility, I left it to go to work on her. When she made her observations, the hypnoprobe would purr its siren song of sinister coaxing, and—perhaps—Miranda would bend to my wishes.

It did not work.

I watched her going to her telescopes. I saw her broad-beamed form settling in place. In my mind I heard the hypnoprobe's gentle whisper, as I knew it must sound to Miranda. It was telling her to relax, to obey. "The capsule...get into the capsule...you will monitor the crawler... you...you...you will do it."

I waited for her to arise and move like a sleepwalker to the waiting capsule. Her tawny body was motionless. Muscles rippled beneath that obscenely bare flesh. The probe had her! Yes! It was getting to her!

She clawed at the telescope as though it were a steel-tipped wasp drilling her brain. The barrel recoiled, and she pushed herself away from it, whirling around. Her eyes glowed with rage. Her enormous body reared up before me. She seemed half berserk. The probe had had some effect on her; I could see her dizzied strides, and knew that she was awry. But it had not been potent enough. Something within that adapted brain of hers gave her the strength to fight off the murky shroud of hypnotism.

"You did that!" she roared. "You gimmicked the telescope, didn't you?"

"I don't know what you mean, Miranda."

"Liar! Fraud! Sneak!"

"Calm down. You're rocking us out of orbit."

"I'll rock all I want! What was that thing that had its fingers in my brain? You put it there? What was it, the hypnoprobe you used?"

"Yes," I admitted coolly. "And what was it you put into my food? Which hallucinogen?"

"It didn't work."

"Neither did my hypnoprobe. Miranda, someone's got to get into that capsule. In a few hours we'll be at the critical point. We don't dare come back without the essential observations. Make the sacrifice."

"For *you?*"

"For science," I said.

I got the horselaugh I deserved. Then Miranda strode toward me. She had recovered her coordination in full, now, and it seemed as though she were planning to thrust me into the capsule by main force. Her ponderous arms enfolded me. The stink of her thickened hide made me retch. I felt ribs creaking within me. I hammered at her body, searching for pressure points that would drop her in a felled heap. We punished each other cruelly, grunting back and forth across the cabin. It was a fierce contest of skill against mass. She would not fall, and I would not crush.

The toneless buzz of the microcephalon said, "Release each other. The collapsing star is nearing its Schwarzschild radius. We must act now."

Miranda's arms slipped away from me. I stepped back, glowering at her, to suck breath into my battered body. Livid bruises were appearing on her skin. We had come to a mutual awareness of mutual strength; but the capsule still was empty. Hatred hovered like a globe of ball lightning between us. The gray, greasy alien creature stood to one side.

I would not care to guess which one of us had the idea first, Miranda or I. But we moved swiftly. The microcephalon scarcely murmured a word of protest as we hustled it down the passage and into the room that held the capsule. Miranda was smiling. I felt relief. She held the alien tight while I opened the hatch, and then she thrust it through. We dogged the hatch together.

"Launch the crawler," she said

I nodded and went to the controls. Like a dart from a blowgun the crawler housing was expelled from our ship and journeyed under high acceleration to the surface of the dark star. It contained a compact vehicle with sturdy jointed legs, controlled by remote pickup from the observation capsule aboard ship. As the observer moved arms and feet within the control harnesses, servo relays actuated the hydraulic pistons in the crawler, eight light-days away. It moved in parallel response, clambering over the slag-heaps of a solar surface that no organic life could endure.

The microcephalon operated the crawler with skill. We watched through the shielded video pickups, getting a close-range view of that inferno. Even a cold sun is more terrifyingly hot than any planet of man.

The signals coming from the star altered with each moment, as the full force of the red-shift gripped the fading light. Something unutterably strange was taking place down there; and the mind of our microcephalon was rooted to the scene. Tidal gravitational forces lashed the star. The crawler was lifted, heaved, compressed, subjected to strains that slowly ripped it apart. The alien witnessed it all, and dictated an account of what he saw, slowly, methodically, without a flicker of fear.

The singularity approached. The tidal forces aspired toward infinity. The microcephalon sounded bewildered at last as it attempted to describe the topological phenomena that no eye had seen before. Infinite density, zero volume—how did the mind comprehend it? The crawler was contorted into an inconceivable shape; and yet its sensors obstinately continued to relay data, filtered through the mind of the microcephalon and into our computer banks.

Then came silence. Our screens went dead. The unthinkable had at last occurred, and the dark star had passed within the radius of singularity. It had collapsed into oblivion, taking with it the crawler. To the alien in the observation capsule aboard our ship, it was as though he too had vanished into the pocket of hyperspace that passed all understanding.

I looked toward the heavens. The dark star was gone. Our detectors picked up the outpouring of energy that marked its annihilation. We were buffeted briefly on the wave of force that ripped outward from the place where the star had been, and then all was calm.

Miranda and I exchanged glances.

"Let the microcephalon out," I said.

She opened the hatch. The alien sat quite calmly at the control console. It did not speak. Miranda assisted it from the capsule. Its eyes were expressionless; but they had never shown anything, anyway.

We are on our way back to the worlds of our galaxy, now. The mission has been accomplished. We have relayed priceless and unique data.

The microcephalon has not spoken since we removed it from the capsule. I do not believe it will speak again.

Miranda and I perform our chores in harmony. The hostility between us is gone. We are partners in crime, now edgy with guilt that we do not admit to one another. We tend our shipmate with loving care.

Someone had to make the observations, after all. There were no volunteers. The situation called for force, or the deadlock would never have been broken.

But Miranda and I hated each other, you say? Why, then, should we cooperate?

We both are humans, Miranda and I. The microcephalon is not. In the end, that made the difference. In the last analysis, Miranda and I decided that we humans must stick together. There are ties that bind.

We speed on toward civilization.

She smiles at me. I do not find her hateful now. The microcephalon is silent.

HAWKSBILL STATION

As noted above, I had given up the writing of science fiction in some confusion in the winter of 1958-59, after four or five years of frenzied activity in which I had written enough of the stuff to fill three or four average careers. Still only in my mid-twenties, puzzled about my place in a genre that I loved deeply but seemed unable to serve well, I turned away and wandered for a few years in a morass of hackerei that still gives me the creeps when I look at the titles of the things I was writing then—"I Was Eaten by Monster Crabs," "World of Living Corpses," "The Syndicate Moves In," and much godawful more.

And then came that wonderful offer I couldn't refuse from Fred Pohl of Galaxy, who by freeing me from the risk of having stories rejected teased me back into science fiction, at least on a now-and-then basis. I did a few short stories for him at a rate of about one every six months, and then the "Blue Fire" series of novelets that became the book To Open the Sky, and by then—it was now 1965—I was hooked on writing s-f all over again. Only this time, because Pohl had given me the space to write the stories exactly as I felt they ought to be written, because I was no longer (as I had been doing from 1955 to 1958) tailoring my product to some editor's notion of what was acceptable, I was far more satisfied with what I was writing: at last, stories which I as a critical reader would have been interested in reading. And so began the second phase of my career, the so-called "new Silverberg" that elicited so much surprised comment in the mid-1960s. After the "Blue Fire" stories came The Time Hoppers, the novel for Doubleday that I expanded out of an old short story, which I finished in March of 1966. Then, in mid-

April, I wrote to Pohl about another ambitious project that had grown out of my own deep interest in paleontology and my almost obsessive fascination with the idea of traveling in time. What I told him was: "I'm thinking in very science-fictional terms these days and I want to get these stories written while the fit is still on me. This one would be a novella—15,000 words, 20,000, somewhere within that range. I have it roughed out, though not solidly enough for me to want to talk much about the plot, except to say that the story takes place in a camp for political prisoners on Earth approximately two and a half billion years ago. If you can find room for a Silverberg story of this length, I'd like to write it some time in the next month."

Fred gave me the go-ahead; I set to work immediately, and wrote the story in one white-hot week, 20,000 words, mailing it to him on May 5. By May 11 I had word of its acceptance. It was published in the August, 1967 issue of *Galaxy* and brought me one of the most cherishable reader comments I have ever received: the famed science-writer Willy Ley, encountering me at a New York literary party, praised at great length the accuracy and richness of texture of my portrait of life in the early Paleozoic. I am not exactly indifferent to most people's praise of my work, but, although I absorb it with pleasure, I tend to forget it quickly; hearing Willy tell me in rumbling Teutonic tones how well I had brought the era of trilobites to life for him is a memory that still glows brightly for me four decades later.

The story also brought me my first Hugo and Nebula nominations, though competition for both awards was stiff that year and I finished as a runner-up. At that point in my career, though, simply getting on the final ballot was exciting.

Despite Willy Ley's warm praise, there was at least one inaccuracy in the story. It takes place in the late Cambrian period, which according to modern geological theory was about 550 million years ago. Yet in my original proposal for Fred Pohl I placed the scene "approximately two and a half billion years ago," and even in the published story I set the Cambrian two billion years in the past. That was not a case of ignorance, but of a writer's outsmarting himself, for what I was doing was implying a revision, after the development of time travel, of our entire geological time scale. But I found no convenient way of working into the story a statement to the effect that scientists had once believed the Cambrian to have been 550 million years ago but now knew it to be two billion, and in the end I just used the greater time scale without explaining what I was up to. This, of course, brought some critical comments from present-day geologists otherwise pleased with the work. So when the story was reprinted in the first of its *many anthology appearances I cut the time span in half, putting the late Cambrian at one billion years ago—still a revisionist notion, but one less likely to draw attack. And I have kept it that way in all further printings of the story, as well as in the expansion to novel form that I carried out in the spring of 1967, under the same title, for Doubleday.*

One

Barrett was the uncrowned King of Hawksbill Station. He had been there the longest; he had suffered the most; he had the deepest inner resources of strength. Before his accident, he had been able to whip any man in the place. Now he was a cripple, but he still had that aura of power that gave him command. When there were problems at the Station, they were brought to Barrett. That was axiomatic. He was the king.

He ruled over quite a kingdom, too. In effect it was the whole world, pole to pole, meridian to meridian. For what it was worth. It wasn't worth very much.

Now it was raining again. Barrett shrugged himself to his feet in the quick, easy gesture that cost him an infinite amount of carefully concealed agony, and shuffled to the door of his hut. Rain made him impatient:. the pounding of those great greasy drops against the corrugated tin roof was enough even to drive a Jim Barrett loony. He nudged the door open. Standing in the doorway, Barrett looked out over his kingdom.

Barren rock, nearly to the horizon. A shield of raw dolomite going on and on. Raindrops danced and bounced on that continental slab of rock. No trees. No grass. Behind Barrett's hut lay the sea, gray and vast. The sky was gray too, even when it wasn't raining.

He hobbled out into the rain. Manipulating his crutch was getting to be a simple matter for him now. He leaned comfortably, letting his crushed left foot dangle. A rockslide had pinned him last year during a trip to the edge of the Inland Sea. Back home, Barrett would have been fitted with prosthetics and that would have been the end of it: a new ankle, a new instep, refurbished ligaments and tendons. But home was a billion years away, and home there's no returning.

The rain hit him hard. Barrett was a big man, six and a half feet tall, with hooded dark eyes, a jutting nose, a chin that was a monarch among chins. He had weighed two hundred fifty pounds in his prime, in the good old agitating days when he had carried banners and pounded out manifestos. But now he was past sixty and beginning to shrink a little, the skin getting loose around the places where the mighty muscles used to be. It was hard to keep your weight in Hawksbill Station. The food was nutritious, but it lacked intensity. A man got to miss steak. Eating brachiopod stew and trilobite hash wasn't the same thing at all. Barrett was past all bitterness, though. That was another reason why the men regarded him as the leader. He didn't scowl. He didn't rant. He was resigned to his fate, tolerant of eternal exile, and so he could help the others get over that difficult, heart-clawing period of transition.

A figure arrived, jogging through the rain: Norton. The doctrinaire Khrushchevist with the Trotskyite leanings. A small, excitable man who frequently appointed himself messenger whenever there was news at the Station. He sprinted toward Barrett's hut, slipping and sliding over the naked rocks.

Barrett held up a meaty hand. "Whoa, Charley. Take it easy or you'll break your neck!"

Norton halted in front of the hut. The rain had pasted the widely spaced strands of his brown hair to his skull. His eyes had the fixed, glossy look of fanaticism—or perhaps just astigmatism. He gasped for breath and staggered into the hut, shaking himself like a wet puppy. He obviously had run all the way from the main building of the Station, three hundred yards away—a long dash over rock that slippery.

"Why are you standing around in the rain?" Norton asked.

"To get wet," said Barrett, following him inside. "What's the news?"

"The Hammer's glowing. We're getting company."

"How do you know it's a live shipment?"

"It's been glowing for half an hour. That means they're taking precautions. They're sending a new prisoner. Anyway, no supplies shipment is due."

Barrett nodded. "Okay. I'll come over. If it's a new man, we'll bunk him in with Latimer."

Norton managed a rasping laugh. "Maybe he's a materialist. Latimer will drive him crazy with all that mystic nonsense. We could put him with Altman instead."

"And he'll be raped in half an hour."

"Altman's off that kick now," said Norton. "He's trying to create a real woman, not looking for second-rate substitutes."

"Maybe our new man doesn't have any spare ribs."

"Very funny, Jim." Norton did not look amused. "You know what I want the new man to be? A conservative, that's what. A black-souled reactionary straight out of Adam Smith. God, that's what I want!"

"Wouldn't you be happy with a fellow Bolshevik?"

"This place is full of Bolsheviks," said Norton. "Of all shades from pale pink to flagrant scarlet. Don't you think I'm sick of them? Sitting around fishing for trilobites and discussing the relative merits of Kerensky and Malenkov? I need somebody to *talk* to, Jim. Somebody I can fight with."

"All right," Barrett said, slipping into his rain gear. "I'll see what I can do about hocusing a debating partner out of the Hammer for you. A rip-roaring Objectivist, okay?" He laughed. "You know something, maybe there's been a revolution Up Front since we got our last man? Maybe the left is in and the right is out, and they'll start shipping us nothing but reactionaries. How would you like that? Fifty or a hundred storm troopers, Charley? Plenty of material to debate economics with. And the place will fill up with more and more of them, until we're outnumbered, and then maybe they'll have a *putsch* and get rid of all the stinking leftists sent here by the old regime, and—"

Barrett stopped. Norton was staring at him in amazement, his faded eyes wide, his hand compulsively smoothing his thinning hair to hide his embarrassment. Barrett realized that he had just committed one of the most heinous crimes possible at Hawksbill Station: he had started to run off at the mouth. There hadn't been any call for his little outburst. What made it more troublesome was the fact that *he* was the one who had permitted himself such a luxury. He was supposed to be the strong one of this place, the stabilizer, the man of absolute integrity and principle and sanity on whom the others could lean. And suddenly he had lost control. It was a bad sign. His dead foot was throbbing again; possibly that was the reason.

In a tight voice he said, "Let's go. Maybe the new man is here already."

They stepped outside. The rain was beginning to let up; the storm was moving out to sea. In the east, over what would one day be the Atlantic, the sky was still clotted with gray mist, but to the west a different grayness was emerging, the shade of normal gray that meant dry weather. Before he had come out here, Barrett had expected to find the sky practically black, because there'd be fewer dust particles to bounce the light around and turn things blue. But the sky seemed to be a weary beige. So much for *a priori* theories.

Through the thinning rain they walked toward the main building. Norton accommodated himself to Barrett's limping pace, and Barrett, wielding his crutch furiously, did his damndest not to let his infirmity slow them up. He nearly lost his footing twice, and fought hard not to let Norton see.

Hawksbill Station spread out before them.

It covered about five hundred acres. In the center of everything was the main building, an ample dome that contained most of their equipment and supplies. At widely paced intervals, rising from the rock shield like grotesque giant green mushrooms, were the plastic blisters of the individual dwellings. Some, like Barrett's, were shielded by tin sheeting salvaged from shipments from Up Front. Others stood unprotected, just as they had come from the mouth of the extruder.

The huts numbered about eighty. At that moment, there were 140 inmates in Hawksbill Station, pretty close to the all-time high. Up Front hadn't sent back any hut-building materials for a long time, and so all the newer arrivals had to double up with bunkmates. Barrett and all those whose exile had begun before 2014 had the privilege of private dwellings, if they wanted them. (Some did not wish to live alone; Barrett, to preserve his own authority, felt that he was required to.) As new exiles arrived, they bunked in with those who currently lived alone, in reverse order of seniority. Most of the 2015 exiles had been forced to take roommates now. Another dozen deportees and the 2014 group would be doubling up. Of course, there were deaths all up and down the line, and there were plenty who were eager to have company in their huts.

Barrett felt, though, that a man who has to be sentenced to life imprisonment ought to have the privilege of privacy if he desires it. One of his biggest problems here was keeping people from cracking up because there was too little privacy. Propinquity could be intolerable in a place like this.

Norton pointed toward the big shiny-skinned green dome of the main building. "There's Altman going in now. And Rudiger. And Hutchett. Something's happening!"

Barrett stepped up his pace. Some of the men entering the building saw his bulky figure coming over the rise in the rock, and waved to him. Barrett lifted a massive hand in reply. He felt mounting excitement. It was a big event at the Station whenever a new man arrived.

Nobody had come for six months, now. That was the longest gap he could remember. It had started to seem as though no one would ever come again.

That would be a catastrophe. New men were all that stood between the older inmates and insanity. New men brought news from the future, news from the world that was entirely left behind. They contributed new personalities to a group that always was in danger of going stale.

And, Barrett knew, some men—he was not one—lived in the deluded hope that the next arrival might just be a woman.

That was why they flocked to the main building when the Hammer began to glow. Barrett hobbled down the path. The rain died away just as he reached the entrance.

Within, sixty or seventy Station residents crowded the chamber of the Hammer—just about every man in the place who was able in body and mind, and still alert enough to show curiosity about a newcomer. They shouted their greetings to Barrett. He nodded, smiled, deflected their questions with amiable gestures.

"Who's it going to be this time, Jim?"

"Maybe a girl, huh? Around nineteen years old, blonde, built like—"

"I hope he can play stochastic chess, anyway."

"Look at the glow! It's deepening!"

Barrett, like the others, stared at the Hammer. The complex, involuted collection of unfathomable instruments burned a bright cherry-red now, betokening the surge of who knew how many kilowatts being pumped in at the far end of the line. The glow had spread to the Anvil now, that broad aluminum bedplate on which all shipments from the future were dropped. In another moment—

"Condition Crimson!" somebody yelled. "Here he comes!"

Two

A billion years up the time-line, power was flooding into the real Hammer of which this was only the partial replica. A man—or something else—stood in the center of the real Anvil, waiting for the Hawksbill Field to unfold him and kick him back to the early Paleozoic. The effect of time travel was very much like being hit with a gigantic hammer and driven clear through the walls of the continuum: hence the governing metaphors for the parts of the machine.

Setting up Hawksbill Station had been a long, slow job. The Hammer had knocked a pathway and had sent back the nucleus of the receiving station first. Since there was no receiving station on hand to receive the receiving station, a certain amount of waste had occurred. It wasn't necessary to have a Hammer and Anvil on the receiving end, except as a fine control to prevent temporal spread; without the equipment, the field wandered a little, and it was possible to scatter consecutive shipments over a span of twenty or thirty years. There was plenty of such temporal garbage all around Hawksbill Station: stuff that had been intended for the original installation, but which because of tuning imprecisions in the pre-Hammer days had landed a couple of decades (and a couple of hundred miles) away from the intended site.

Despite such difficulties, they had finally sent through enough components to the master temporal site to allow for the construction of a receiving station. Then the first prisoners had gone through: technicians who knew how to put the Hammer and Anvil together. Of course, it was their privilege to refuse to cooperate. But it was to their own advantage to assemble the receiving station, thus making it possible for them to be sure of getting further supplies from Up Front. They had done the job. After that, outfitting Hawksbill Station had been easy.

Now the Hammer glowed, meaning that they had activated the Hawksbill Field on the sending end, somewhere up around 2028 or 2030 A.D. All the sending was done there. All the receiving was done here. It didn't work the other way. Nobody really knew why, although there was a lot of superficially profound talk about the rules of entropy.

There was a whining, hissing sound as the edges of the Hawksbill Field began to ionize the atmosphere in the room. Then came the expected thunderclap of implosion, caused by an imperfect overlapping of the quantity of air that was subtracted from this era and the quantity of air was being thrust into it. And then abruptly, a man dropped out of the Hammer and lay stunned and limp, on the gleaming Anvil.

He looked young, which surprised Barrett considerably. He seemed to be well under thirty. Generally, only middle-aged men were sent to Hawksbill Station. Incorrigibles, who had to be separated from humanity for the general good. The youngest man in the place now had been close to forty when he arrived. The sight of this lean, clean-cut boy drew a hiss of anguish from a couple of the men in the room, and Barrett understood the constellation of emotions that pained them.

The new man sat up. He stirred like a child coming out of a long, deep sleep. He looked around.

His face was very pale. His thin lips seemed bloodless. His blue eyes blinked rapidly. His jaws worked as though he wanted to say something, but could not find the words.

There were no physiological harmful effects to time travel, but it could be a rough jolt to the consciousness. The last moments before the Hammer descended were very much like the final moments beneath the guillotine, since exile to Hawksbill Station was tantamount to a sentence of death. The departing prisoner took his last look at the world of rocket transport and artificial organs, at the world in which he had lived and loved and agitated for a political cause, and then he was rammed into an inconceivably remote past on a one-way journey. It was a gloomy business, and it was not very surprising that the newcomers arrived in a state of emotional shock.

Barrett elbowed his way through the crowd. Automatically the others made way for him. He reached the lip of the Anvil and leaned over it, extending a hand to the new man. His broad smile was met by a look of blank bewilderment.

"I'm Jim Barrett. Welcome to Hawksbill Station. Here—get off that thing before a load of groceries lands on top of you." Wincing a little as he shifted his weight, Barrett pulled the new man down from the Anvil. It was altogether likely for the idiots Up Front to shoot another shipment along a minute after sending a man.

Barrett beckoned to Mel Rudiger, and the plump anarchist handed the new man an alcohol capsule. He took it and pressed it to his arm without a word. Charley Norton offered him a candy bar. The man shook it off. He looked groggy—a real case of temporal shock, Barrett thought, possibly the worst he had ever seen. The newcomer hadn't even spoken yet. Could the effect really be that extreme?

Barrett said, "We'll go to the infirmary and check you out. Then I'll assign you your quarters. There's time for you to find your way around and meet everybody later on. What's your name?"

"Hahn. Lew Hahn."

"I can't hear you."

"Hahn," the man repeated, still only barely audible.

"When are you from, Lew?"

"2029."

"You feel pretty sick?"

"I feel awful. I don't even believe this is happening to me. There's no such place as Hawksbill Station, is there?"

"I'm afraid there is," Barrett said. "At least, for most of us. A few of the boys think it's all an illusion induced by drugs. But I have my doubts of that. If it's an illusion, it's damned good. Look."

He put one arm around Hahn's shoulders and guided him through the press of prisoners, out of the Hammer chamber and toward the nearby infirmary. Although Hahn looked thin, even fragile, Barrett was surprised to feel the rippling muscles in those shoulders. He suspected that this man was a lot less helpless and ineffectual than he seemed to be right now. He *had* to be: he had earned banishment to Hawksbill Station.

They passed the open door of the building. "Look out there," Barrett commanded.

Hahn looked. He passed a hand across his eyes as though to clear away unseen cobwebs, and looked again.

"A Late Cambrian landscape," said Barrett quietly. "This view would be a geologist's dream, except that geologists don't tend to become political prisoners, it seems. Out in front of you is what they call Appalachia. It's a strip of rock a few hundred miles wide and a few thousand miles long, running from the Gulf of Mexico to Newfoundland. To the east we've got the Atlantic Ocean. A little way to the west we've got a thing called the Appalachian Geosyncline, which is a trough five hundred miles wide full of water. Somewhere about two thousand miles to the west there's another trough that they call the Cordilleran Geosyncline. It's full of water too, and at this particular stage of geological history the patch of land between the geosynclines is below sea level, so where Appalachia ends we've got the Inland Sea, currently, running way out to the west. On the far side of the Inland Sea is a narrow north-south land mass called Cascadia that's going to be California and Oregon and Washington someday. Don't hold your breath till it happens. I hope you like seafood, Lew."

Hahn stared, and Barrett, standing beside him at the doorway, stared also. You never got used to the alienness of this place, not even after you had lived here twenty years, as Barrett had. It was Earth, and yet it was not really Earth at all, because it was somber and empty and unreal. The gray oceans swarmed with life, of course. But there was nothing on land except occasional patches of moss in the occasional patches of soil that had formed on the bare rock. Even a few cockroaches would be welcome; but insects, it seemed, were still a couple of geological periods in the future. To land dwellers, this was a dead world, a world unborn.

Shaking his head, Hahn moved away from the door. Barrett led him down the corridor and into the small, brightly lit room that served as the infirmary. Doc Quesada was waiting. Quesada wasn't really a doctor, but he had been a medical technician once, and that was good enough. He was a compact, swarthy man with a look of complete self-assurance. He hadn't lost too many patients, all things considered. Barrett had watched him removing appendixes with total aplomb. In his white smock, Quesada looked sufficiently medical to fit the role.

Barrett said, "Doc, this is Lew Hahn. He's in temporal shock. Fix him up."

Quesada nudged the newcomer onto a webfoam cradle and unzipped his blue jersey. Then he reached for his medical kit. Hawksbill Station was well equipped for most medical emergencies, now. The people Up Front had no wish to be inhumane, and they sent back all sorts of useful things, like anesthetics and surgical clamps and medicines and dermal probes. Barrett could remember a time at the beginning when there had been nothing much here but the empty huts, and a man who hurt himself was in real trouble.

"He's had a drink already," said Barrett.

"I see that," Quesada murmured. He scratched at his short-cropped, bristly mustache. The little diagnostat in the cradle had gone rapidly to work, flashing information about Hahn's blood pressure, potassium count, dilation index, and much else. Quesada seemed to comprehend the barrage of facts. After a moment he said to Hahn, "You aren't really sick, are you? Just shaken up a little. I don't blame you. Here—I'll give you a quick jolt to calm your nerves, and you'll be all right. As all right as any of us ever are."

He put a tube to Hahn's carotid and thumbed the snout. The subsonic whirred, and a tranquilizing compound slid into the man's bloodstream. Hahn shivered.

Quesada said, "Let him rest for five minutes. Then he'll be over the hump."

They left Hahn in his cradle and went out of the infirmary. In the hall, Barrett looked down at the little medic and said, "What's the report on Valdosto?"

Valdosto had gone into psychotic collapse several weeks before. Quesada was keeping him drugged and trying to bring him slowly back to the reality of Hawksbill Station. Shrugging, he replied, "The status is quo. I let him out from under the dream juice this morning and he was the same as he's been."

"You don't think he'll come out of it?"

"I doubt it. He's cracked for keeps. They could paste him together Up Front, but—"

"Yeah," Barrett said. If he could get Up Front at all, Valdosto wouldn't have cracked. "Keep him happy, then. If he can't be sane, he can at least be comfortable. What about Altman? Still got the shakes?"

"He's building a woman," Quesada said.

"That's what Charley Norton told me. What's he using? A rag, a bone—"

"I gave him some surplus chemicals. Chosen for their color, mainly. He's got some foul green copper compounds and a little bit of ethyl alcohol and six or seven other things, and he collected some soil and threw in a lot of dead shellfish, and he's sculpting it all into what he claims is female shape and waiting for lightning to strike it."

"In other words, he's gone crazy," Barrett said.

"I think that's a safe assumption. But he's not molesting his friends any more, anyway. You didn't think his homosexual phase would last much longer, as I recall."

"No, but I didn't think he'd go off the deep end. If a man needs sex and he can find some consenting playmates here, that's quite all right with me. But when he starts putting a woman together out of some dirt and rotten brachiopod meat it means we've lost him. It's too bad."

Quesada's dark eyes flickered. "We're all going to go that way sooner or later, Jim."

"I haven't. You haven't."

"Give us time. I've only been here eleven years."

"Altman's been here only eight. Valdosto even less."

"Some shells crack faster than others," said Quesada.

"Here's our new friend."

Hahn had come out of the infirmary to join them. He still looked pale, but the fright was gone from his eyes. He was beginning to adjust to the unthinkable. He said, "I couldn't help overhearing your conversation. Is there a lot of mental illness here?"

"Some of the men haven't been able to find anything meaningful to do here," Barrett said. "It eats them away. Quesada here has his medical work. I've got administrative duties. A couple of the fellows are studying the sea life. We've got a newspaper to keep some busy. But there are always those who just let themselves slide into despair, and they crack up. I'd say we have thirty or forty certifiable maniacs here at the moment, out of 140 residents."

"That's not so bad," Hahn said. "Considering the inherent instability of the men who get sent here, and the unusual conditions of life here."

Barrett laughed. "Hey, you're suddenly pretty articulate, aren't you? What was in the stuff Doc Quesada jolted you with?"

"I didn't mean to sound superior," Hahn said quickly. "Maybe that came out a little too smug. I mean—"

"Forget it. What did you do Up Front, anyway?"

"I was an economist."

"Just what we need," said Quesada. "He can help us solve our balance-of-payments problem."

Barrett said, "If you were an economist, you'll have plenty to discuss here. This place is full of economic theorists who'll want to bounce their ideas off you. Some of them are almost sane, too. Come with me and I'll show you where you're going to stay."

Three

The patio from the main building to the hut of Donald Latimer was mainly downhill, for which Barrett was grateful even though he knew that he'd have to negotiate the uphill return in a little while. Latimer's hut was on the eastern side of the Station, looking out over the ocean. They walked slowly toward it. Hahn was solicitous of Barrett's game leg, and Barrett was irritated by the exaggerated care the younger man took to keep pace with him.

He was puzzled by this Hahn. The man was full of seeming contradictions—showing up here with the worst case of arrival shock Barrett had ever seen, then snapping out of it with remarkable quickness; looking frail and shy, but hiding solid muscles inside his jersey; giving an outer appearance of incompetence, but speaking with calm control. Barrett wondered what this young man had done to earn him the trip to Hawksbill Station, but there was time for such inquiries later. All the time in the world.

Hahn said, "Is everything like this? Just rock and ocean?"

"That's all. Land life hasn't evolved yet. Everything's wonderfully simple, isn't it? No clutter. No urban sprawl. There's some moss moving onto land, but not much."

"And in the sea? Swimming dinosaurs?"

Barrett shook his head. "There won't be any vertebrates for millions of years. We don't even have fish yet, let alone reptiles out there. All we can offer is that which creepeth. Some shellfish, some big fellows that look like squids, and trilobites. Seven hundred billion different species of trilobites. We've got a man named Rudiger—he's the one who gave you the drink—who's making a collection of them. He's writing the world's definitive text on trilobites."

"But nobody will ever read it in—in the future."

"Up Front, we say."

"Up Front."

"'That's the pity of it," said Barrett. "We told Rudiger to inscribe his book on imperishable plates of gold and hope that it's found by paleontologists. But he says the odds are against it. A billion years of geology will chew his plates to hell before they can be found."

Hahn sniffed. "Why does the air smell so strange?"

"It's a different mix," Barrett said. "We've analyzed it. More nitrogen, a little less oxygen, hardly any CO_2 at all. But that isn't really why it smells odd to you. The thing is, it's pure air, unpolluted by the exhalations of life. Nobody's been respiring into it but us lads, and there aren't enough of us to matter."

Smiling, Hahn said, " I feel a little cheated that it's so empty. I expected lush jungles of weird plants, and pterodactyls swooping through the air, and maybe a tyrannosaur crashing into a fence around the Station."

"No jungles. No pterodactyls. No tyrannosaurs. No fences. You didn't do your homework."

"Sorry."

"This is the Late Cambrian. Sea life exclusively."

"It was very kind of them to pick such a peaceful era as the dumping ground for political prisoners," Hahn said. "I was afraid it would be all teeth and claws."

"Kind, hell! They were looking for an era where we couldn't do any harm. That meant tossing us back before the evolution of mammals, just in case we'd accidentally get hold of the ancestor of all humanity and snuff him out. And while they were at it, they decided to stash us so far in the past that we'd be beyond all land life, on the theory that maybe even if we slaughtered a baby dinosaur it might affect the entire course of the future."

"They don't mind if we catch a few trilobites?"

"Evidently they think it's safe," Barrett said. "It looks as though they were right. Hawksbill Station has been here for twenty-five years, and it doesn't seem as though we've tampered with future history in any measurable way. Of course, they're careful not to send us any women."

"Why is that?"

"So we don't start reproducing and perpetuating ourselves. Wouldn't that mess up the time-lines? A successful human outpost in One Billion B.C., that's had all that time to evolve and mutate and grow? By the time the twenty-first century came around, our descendants would be in charge and the other kind of human being would probably be in penal servitude, and there'd be more paradoxes created than you could shake a trilobite at. So they don't send the women here. There's a prison camp for women, too, but it's a few hundred million years up the time line in the Late Silurian, and never the twain shall meet. That's why Ned Altman's trying to build a woman out of dust and garbage."

"God made Adam out of less."

"Altman isn't God," Barrett said. "That's the root of his whole problem. Look, here's the hut where you're going to stay. I'm rooming you with Don Latimer. He's a very sensitive, interesting, pleasant person. He used to be a physicist before he got into politics, and he's been here about a dozen years, and I might as well warn you that he's developed a strong and somewhat cockeyed mystic streak lately. The fellow he was rooming with killed himself last year, and since then he's been trying to find some way out of here through extrasensory powers."

"Is he serious?"

"I'm afraid he is. And we try to take him seriously. We all humor each other at Hawksbill Station; it's the only way we avoid a mass psychosis. Latimer will probably try to get you to collaborate with him on his project. If you don't like living with him, I can arrange a transfer for you. But I want to see how he reacts to someone new at the Station. I'd like you to give him a chance."

"Maybe I'll even help him find his psionic gateway."

"If you do, take me along," said Barrett. They both laughed. Then he rapped at Latimer's door. There was no answer, and after a moment Barrett pushed the door open. Hawksbill Station had no locks.

Latimer sat in the middle of the bare rock floor, cross-legged, meditating. He was a slender, gentle-faced man just beginning to look old. Right now he seemed a million miles away, ignoring them completely. Hahn shrugged. Barrett put a finger to his lips. They waited in silence for a few minutes, and then Latimer showed signs of coming up from his trance.

He got to his feet in a single flowing motion, without using his hands. In a low, courteous voice he said to Hahn, "Have you just arrived?"

"Within the last hour. I'm Lew Hahn."

"Donald Latimer. I regret that I have to make your acquaintance in these surroundings. But maybe we won't have to tolerate this illegal imprisonment much longer."

Barrett said, "Don, Lew is going to bunk with you. I think you'll get along well. He was an economist in 2029 until they gave him the Hammer."

"Where did you live?" Latimer asked, animation coming into his eyes.

"San Francisco."

The glow faded. Latimer said, "Were you ever in Toronto? I'm from there. I had a daughter—she'd be twenty-three now, Nella Latimer—I wondered if you knew her."

"No. I'm, sorry."

"It wasn't very likely. But I'd love to know what kind of a woman she became. She was a little girl when I last saw her. Now I guess she's married. Or perhaps they've sent her to the other Station. Nella Latimer—you're sure you didn't know her?"

Barrett left them together. It looked as though they'd get along. He told Latimer to bring Hahn up to the main building at dinner for introductions, and went out. A chilly drizzle had begun again. Barrett made his way slowly, painfully up the hill. It had been sad to see the light flicker from Latimer's eyes when Hahn said he didn't know his daughter. Most of the time, men at Hawksbill Station tried not to speak about their families, preferring to keep those tormenting memories well repressed. But the arrival of newcomers generally stirred old ties. There was never any news of relatives, and no way to obtain any, because it was impossible for the Station to communicate with anyone Up Front. No way to ask for the photo of a loved one, no way to request specific medicines, no way to obtain a certain book or a coveted tape. In a mindless, impersonal way, Up Front sent periodic shipments to the Station of things thought useful—reading matter, medical supplies, technical equipment, food. Occasionally they were startling in their generosity, as when they sent a case of Burgundy, or a box of sensory spools, or a recharger for the power pack. Such gifts usually meant a brief thaw in the world situation, which customarily produced a short-lived desire to be kind to the boys in Hawksbill Station. But they had a policy about sending information about relatives. Or about contemporary newspapers. Fine wine, yes; a tridim of a daughter who would never be seen again, no.

For all Up Front knew, there was no one alive in Hawksbill Station. A plague could have killed every one off ten years ago, but there was no way of telling. That was why the shipments still came back. The government whirred and clicked with predictable continuity. The government, whatever else it might be, was not malicious. There were other kinds of totalitarianism beside bloody repressive tyranny.

Pausing at the top of the hill, Barrett caught his breath. Naturally, the alien air no longer smelled strange to him. He filled his lungs with it. Once again the rain ceased. Through the grayness came the sunshine, making the naked rocks sparkle. Barrett closed his eyes a moment and leaned on his crutch, and saw as though on an inner screen the creatures with many legs climbing up out of the sea, and the mossy carpets spreading, and the flowerless plants uncoiling and spreading their scaly branches, and the dull hides of eerie amphibians glistening on the shores, and the tropic heat of the coal-forming epoch descending like a glove over the world.

All that lay far in the future. Dinosaurs. Little chittering mammals. Pithecanthropus in the forests of Java. Sargon and Hannibal and Attila, and Orville Wright, and Thomas Edison, and Edmond Hawksbill. And finally a benign government that would find the thoughts of some men so intolerable that the only safe place to which they could be banished was a rock at the beginning of time. The government was too civilized to put men to death for subversive activities, and too cowardly to let them remain alive. The compromise was the living death of Hawksbill Station. A billion years of impassable time was suitable insulation even for the most nihilistic idea.

Grimacing, Barrett struggled the rest of the way back toward his hut. He had long since come to accept his exile, but accepting his ruined foot was another matter entirely. The idle wish to find a way to regain the freedom of his own time no longer possessed him; but he wished with all his soul that the blank-faced administrators Up Front would send back a kit that would allow him to rebuild his foot.

He entered his hut and flung his crutch aside, sinking down instantly on his cot. There had been no cots when he had come to Hawksbill Station. He had come here in the fourth year of the Station, when there were only a dozen buildings and little in the way of creature comforts. It had been a miserable place then, but the steady accretion of shipments from Up Front had made it relatively tolerable. Of the fifty or so prisoners who had preceded Barrett to Hawksbill, none remained alive. He had held highest seniority for almost ten years. Time moved here at a one-to-one correlation with time Up Front; the Hammer was locked on this point of time, so that Hahn, arriving here today more than twenty years after Barrett, had departed from a year Up Front more than twenty years after the time of Barrett's expulsion. Barrett had not had the heart to begin pumping Hahn for news of 2029 so soon. He would learn all he needed to know, and small cheer it would be, anyway.

Barrett reached for a book. But the fatigue of hobbling around the Station had taken more out him than he realized. He looked at the page for a moment. Then he put it away, and closed his eyes and dozed.

Four

That evening, as every evening, the men of Hawksbill Station gathered in the main building for dinner and recreation. It was not mandatory, and some men chose to eat alone. But tonight nearly everyone who was in full possession of his faculties was there, because this was one of the infrequent occasions when a newcomer had arrived to be questioned about the world of men.

Hahn looked uneasy about his sudden notoriety. He seemed to be basically shy, unwilling to accept all the attention now being thrust upon him. There he sat in the middle of the group, while men twenty and thirty years his senior crowded in on him with their questions, and it was obvious that he wasn't enjoying the session.

Sitting to one side, Barrett took little part in the discussion. His curiosity about Up Front's ideological shifts had ebbed a long time ago. It was hard for him to realize that he had once been so passionately concerned about concepts like syndicalism and the dictatorship of the proletariat and the guaranteed annual wage that he had been willing to risk imprisonment over them. His concern for humanity had not waned, merely the degree of his involvement in the twenty-first century's political problems. After twenty years at Hawksbill Station, Up Front had become unreal to Jim Barrett, and his energies centered around the crises and challenges of what he had come to think of as "his own" time—the late Cambrian.

So he listened, but more with an ear for what the talk revealed about Lew Hahn than for what it revealed about current events Up Front. And what it revealed about Lew Hahn was mainly a matter of what was not revealed.

Hahn didn't say much. He seemed to be feinting and evading.

Charley Norton wanted to know, "Is there any sign of a weakening of the phony conservatism yet? I mean, they've been promising the end of big government for thirty years and it gets bigger all the time."

Hahn moved restlessly in his chair. "They still promise. As soon as conditions become stabilized—"

"Which is when?"

"I don't know. I suppose they're just making words."

"What about the Martian Commune?" demanded Sid Hutchett. "Have they been infiltrating agents onto Earth?"

"I couldn't really say."

"How about the Gross Global Product?" Mel Rudiger wanted to know. "What's its curve? Still holding level, or has it started to drop?"

Hahn tugged at his ear. "I think it's slowly edging down."

"Where does the index stand?" Rudiger asked. "The last figures we had, for '25, it was at 909. But in four years—"

"It might be something like 875 now," said Hahn.

It struck Barrett as a little odd that an economist would be so hazy about the basic economic statistic. Of course, he didn't know how long Hahn had been imprisoned before getting the Hammer. Maybe he simply wasn't up on recent figures. Barrett held his peace.

Charley Norton wanted to find out some things about the legal rights of citizens. Hahn couldn't tell him. Rudiger asked about the impact of weather control—whether the supposedly conservative government of liberators was still ramming programmed weather down the mouths of the citizens—and Hahn wasn't sure. Hahn couldn't rightly say much about the functions of the judiciary, whether it had recovered any of the power stripped from it by the Enabling Act of '18. He didn't have any comments to offer on the tricky subject of population control. In fact, his performance was striking for its lack of hard information.

"He isn't saying much at all," Charley Norton grumbled to the silent Barrett. "He's putting up a smokescreen. But either he's not telling what he knows, or he doesn't know."

"Maybe he's not very bright," Barrett suggested.

"What did he do to get here? He must have had some kind of deep commitment. But it doesn't show, Jim! He's an intelligent kid, but he doesn't seem plugged in to anything that ever mattered to any of us."

Doc Quesada offered a thought. "Suppose he isn't political at all. Suppose they're sending a different kind of prisoner back here now. Axe murderers, or something. A quiet kid who very quietly chopped up sixteen people one Sunday morning. Naturally he isn't interested in politics."

Barrett shook his head. "I doubt that. I think he's just clamming up because he's shy or ill at ease. It's his first night here, remember. He's just been kicked out of his own world and there's no going back. He may have left a wife and baby behind, you know. He may simply not give a damn tonight about sitting up there and spouting the latest word on abstract philosophical theory, when all he wants to do is go off and cry his eyes out. I say we ought to leave him alone."

Quesada and Norton looked convinced. They shook their heads in agreement; but Barrett didn't voice his opinion to the room in general. He let the quizzing of Hahn continue until it petered out of its own accord. The men began to drift away. A couple of them went back to convert Hahn's vague generalities into the lead story for the next handwritten edition of the Hawksbill Station *Times*. Rudiger stood on a table and shouted out that he was going night-fishing, and four men asked to join him. Charley Norton sought out his usual debating partner, the nihilist Ken Belardi, and reopened, like a festering wound, their discussion of planning versus chaos, which bored them both to the point of screaming. The nightly games of stochastic chess began. The loners who had made rare visits to the main building simply to see the new man went back to their huts to do whatever it was they did in them alone each night.

Hahn stood apart, fidgeting and uncertain.

Barrett went up to him. "I guess you didn't really want to be quizzed tonight," he said.

"I'm sorry I couldn't have been more informative. I've been out of circulation a while, you see."

"But you were politically active, weren't you?"

"Oh, yes," Hahn said. "Of course." He flicked his tongue over his lips. "What's supposed to happen now?"

"Nothing in particular. We don't have organized activities here. Doc and I are going out on sick call. Care to join us?"

"What does it involve?" asked Hahn.

"Visiting some of the worst cases. It can be grim, but you'll get a panoramic view of Hawksbill Station in a hurry."

"I'd like to go."

Barrett gestured to Quesada and the three of them left the building. This was a nightly ritual for Barrett, difficult as it was since he had hurt his foot. Before turning in, he visited the goofy ones and the psycho ones and the catatonic ones, tucked them in, wish them a good night and a healed mind in the morning. Someone had to show them that he cared. Barrett did.

Outside, Hahn peered up at the moon. It was nearly full tonight, shining like a burnished coin, its face a pale salmon color and hardly pockmarked at all.

"It looks so different here," Hahn said. "The craters—where are the craters?"

"Most of them haven't been formed yet," said Barrett. "A billion years is a long time even for the moon. Most of its upheavals are still ahead. We think it may still have an atmosphere, too. That's why it looks pink to us. Of course, Up Front hasn't bothered to send us much in the way of astronomical equipment. We can only guess."

Hahn started to say something. He cut himself off after one blurted syllable.

Quesada said, "Don't hold it back. What were you about to suggest?"

Hahn laughed in self-mockery. "That you ought to fly up there and take a look. It struck me as odd that you'd spend all these years here theorizing about whether the moon's got an atmosphere, and wouldn't ever once go up to look. But I forgot."

"It would be useful if we got a commute ship from Up Front," Barrett said. "But it hasn't occurred to them. All we can do is look. The moon's a popular place in '29, is it?"

"The biggest resort in the System," said Hahn. "I was there on my honeymoon. Leah and I—"

He stopped again.

Barrett said hurriedly. "This is Bruce Valdosto's hut. He cracked up a few weeks ago. When we go in, stand behind us so he doesn't see you. He might be violent with a stranger. He's unpredictable."

Valdosto was a husky man in his late forties, with swarthy skin, coarse curling black hair, and the broadest shoulders any man had ever had. Sitting down, he looked even burlier than Jim Barrett, which was saying a great deal. But Valdosto had short, stumpy legs, the legs of a man of ordinary stature tacked to the trunk of a giant, which spoiled the effect completely. In his years Up Front he had totally refused any prosthesis. He believed in living with deformities. Right now he was strapped into a webfoam cradle. His domed forehead was flecked with beads of sweat, his eyes were glittering beadily in the darkness. He was a very sick man. Once he had been clear-minded enough to throw a sleet-bomb into a meeting of the Council of Syndics, giving a dozen of them a bad case of gamma poisoning, but now he scarcely knew up from down, right from left.

Barrett leaned over him and said, "How are you, Bruce?"

"Who's that?"

"Jim. It's a beautiful night, Bruce. How'd you like to come outside and get some fresh air? The moon's almost full."

"I've got to rest. The committee meeting tomorrow—"

"It's been postponed."

"But how can it? The Revolution—"

"That's been postponed too. Indefinitely."

"Are they disbanding the cells?" Valdosto asked harshly.

"We don't know yet. We're waiting for orders. Come outside, Bruce. The air will do you good."

Muttering, Valdosto let himself be unlaced. Quesada and Barrett pulled him to his feet and propelled him through the door of the hut. Barrett caught sight of Hahn in the shadows, his face somber with shock.

They stood together outside the hut. Barrett pointed to the moon. "It's got such a lovely color here. Not like the dead thing Up Front. And look, look down there, Bruce. The sea breaking on the rocky shore. Rudiger's out fishing. I can see his boat by moonlight."

"Striped bass," said Valdosto. "Sunnies. Maybe he'll catch some sunnies."

"There aren't any sunnies here. They haven't evolved yet." Barrett fished in his pocket and drew out something ridged and glossy, about two inches long. It was the exoskeleton of a small trilobite. He offered it to Valdosto, who shook his head.

"Don't give me that cockeyed crab."

"It's a trilobite, Bruce. It's extinct, but so are we. We're a billion years in our own past."

"You must be crazy," Valdosto said in a calm, low voice that belied his wild-eyed appearance. He took the trilobite from Barrett and hurled it against the rocks. "Cockeyed crab," he muttered.

Quesada shook his head sadly. He and Barrett led the sick man into the hut again. Valdosto did not protest as the medic gave him the sedative. His weary mind, rebelling entirely against the monstrous concept that he had been exiled to the inconceivably remote past, welcomed sleep.

When they went out Barrett saw Hahn holding the trilobite on his palm and staring at it in wonder. Hahn offered it to him, but Barrett brushed it away.

"Keep it if you like," he said. "There are more where I got that one."

They went on. They found Ned Altman beside his hut, crouching on his knees and patting his hands over the crude, lopsided form of what, from its exaggerated breasts and hips, appeared to be the image of a woman. He stood up when they appeared. Altman was a neat little man with yellow hair and nearly invisible white eyebrows. Unlike anyone else in the Station, he had actually been a government man once, fifteen years ago, before seeing through the myth of syndicalist capitalism and joining one of the underground factions. Eight years at Hawksbill Station had done things to him.

Altman pointed to his golem and said, "I hoped there'd be lightning in the rain today. That'll do it, you know. But there isn't much lightning this time of year. She'll get up alive, and then I'll need you, Doc, to give her shots and trim away some of the tough places."

Quesada forced a smile. "I'll be glad to do it, Ned. But you know the terms."

"Sure. When I'm through with her, you get her. You think I'm a goddamn monopolist? I'll share her. There'll be a waiting list. Just so you don't forget who made her, though. She'll remain mine, whenever I need her." He noticed Hahn. "Who are you?"

"He's new," Barrett said. "Lew Hahn. He came this afternoon."

"Ned Altman," said Altman with a courtly bow. "Formerly in government service. You're pretty young, aren't you? How's your sex orientation? Hetero?"

Hahn winced. "I'm afraid so."

"It's okay. I wouldn't touch you. I've got a project going here. But I just want you to know, I'll put you on my list. You're young and you've probably got stronger needs than some of us. I won't forget about you, even though you're new here."

Quesada coughed. "You ought to get some rest now, Ned. Maybe there'll be lightning tomorrow."

Altman did not resist. The doctor took him inside and put him to bed while Hahn and Barrett surveyed the man's handiwork. Hahn pointed toward the figure's middle.

"He's left out something essential," he said. "If he's planning to make love to this girl after he's finished creating her, he'd better—"

"It was there yesterday," said Barrett. "He must be changing orientation again." Quesada emerged from the hut. They went on, down the rocky path.

Barrett did not make the complete circuit that night. Ordinarily, he would have gone all the way down to Latimer's hut overlooking the sea, for Latimer was on his list of sick ones. But Barrett had visited Latimer once that day, and he didn't think his aching good leg was up to another hike that far. So after he and Quesada and Hahn had been to all of the easily accessible huts, and visited the man who prayed for alien beings to rescue him and the man who was trying to break into a parallel universe where everything was as it ought to be in the world and the man who lay on his cot sobbing for all his wakeful hours, Barrett said good night to his companions and allowed Quesada to escort Hahn back to his hut without him.

Alter observing Hahn for half a day, Barrett realized he did not know much more about him than when he had first dropped onto the Anvil. That was odd. But maybe Hahn would open up a little more after he'd been here a while. Barrett stared up at the salmon moon, and reached into his pocket to finger the little trilobite before he remembered that he had given it to Hahn. He shuffled into his hut. He wondered how long ago Hahn had taken that lunar honeymoon trip.

Five

Rudiger's catch was spread out in front of the main building the next morning when Barrett came up for breakfast. He had had a good night's fishing, obviously. He usually did. Rudiger went out three or four nights a week, in the little dinghy that he had cobbled together a few years ago from salvaged materials, and he took with him a team of friends whom he had trained in the deft use of the trawling nets.

It was an irony that Rudiger, the anarchist, the man who believed in individualism and the abolition of all political institutions, should be so good at leading a team of fishermen. Rudiger didn't care for team-work in the abstract. But it was hard to manipulate the nets alone, he had discovered. Hawksbill Station had many little ironies of that sort. Political theorists tend to swallow their theories when forced back on pragmatic measures of survival.

The prize of the catch was a cephalopod about a dozen feet long— a rigid conical tube out of which some limp squidlike tentacles dangled. Plenty of meat on that one, Barrett thought. Dozens of trilobites were arrayed around it, ranging in size from the inch-long kind to the three-footers with their baroquely involuted exo-skeletons. Rudiger fished both for food and for science; evidently these trilobites were discards— species that he already had studied, or he wouldn't have left them here to go into the food hoppers. His hut was stacked ceiling-high with trilobites. It kept him sane to collect and analyze them, and no one begrudged him his hobby.

Near the heap of trilobites were some clusters of hinged bra-chiopods, looking like scallops that had gone awry, and a pile of snails. The warm, shallow waters just off the coastal shelf teemed with life, in striking contrast to the barren land. Rudiger had also brought in a mound of shiny black seaweed. Barrett hoped someone would gather all this stuff up and get it into their heat-sink cooler before it spoiled. The bacteria of decay worked a lot slower here than they did Up Front, but a few hours in the mild air would do Rudiger's haul no good.

Today Barrett planned to recruit some men for the annual Inland Sea expedition. Traditionally, he led that trek himself, but his injury made it impossible for him even to consider going any more. Each year, a dozen or so able-bodied men went out on a wide-ranging reconnais-sance that took them in a big circle, looping northwestward until they reached the sea, then coming around to the south and back to the Station. One purpose of the trip was to gather any temporal garbage that might have materialized in the vicinity of the Station during the past year. There was no way of knowing how wide a margin of error had been allowed during the early attempts to set up the Station, and the scattershot technique of hurling material into the past had been pretty unreliable. New stuff was turning up all the time that had been aimed for Minus One Billion, Two Thousand Oh Five A.D., but which didn't get there until a few decades later. Hawksbill Station needed all the spare equipment it could get, and Barrett didn't miss a chance to round up any of the debris.

There was another reason for the Inland Sea expeditions, though. They served as a focus for the year, an annual ritual, something to peg a custom to. It was a rite of spring here. The dozen strongest men, going on foot to the distant rock-rimmed shores of the tepid sea that drowned the middle of North America, were performing the closest thing Hawksbill Station had to a religious function, although they did nothing more mystical when they reached the Inland Sea than to net a few trilobites and eat them. The trip meant more to Barrett himself than he had even suspected, also. He realized that now, when he was unable to go. He had led every such expedition for twenty years.

But last year he had gone scrabbling over boulders loosened by the tireless action of the waves, venturing into risky territory for no rational reason that he could name, and his aging muscles had betrayed him. Often at night he woke sweating to escape from the dream in which he relived that ugly moment: slipping and sliding, clawing at the rocks, a mass of stone dislodged from somewhere and crashing down with improbably agonizing impact on his foot, pinning him, crushing him. He could not forget the sound of grinding bones. Nor was he likely to lose the memory of the homeward march, across hundreds of miles of bare rock, his bulky body slung between the bowed forms of his companions. He thought he would lose the foot, but Quesada had spared gun him from the amputation. He simply could not touch the foot to the ground and put weight on it now, or ever again. It might have been simpler to have the dead appendage sliced off. Quesada vetoed that, though. "Who knows," he had said, "some day they might send us a transplant kit. I can't rebuild a leg that's been amputated." So Barrett had kept his crushed foot. But he had never been quite the same since, and now someone else would have to lead the march.

Who would it be, he asked himself?

Quesada was the likeliest. Next to Barrett, he was the strongest man here, in all the ways that it was important to be strong. But Quesada couldn't be spared at the Station. It might be handy to have a medic along on the trip, but it was vital to have one here. After some reflection Barrett put down Charley Norton as the leader. He added Ken Belardi—someone for Norton to talk to. Rudiger? A tower of strength last year after Barrett had been injured; Barrett didn't particularly want to let Rudiger leave the Station so long; he needed able men for the expedition, true, but he didn't want to strip the home base down to invalids, crackpots, and psychotics. Rudiger stayed. Two of his fellow fishermen went on the list. So did Sid Hutchett and Arny Jean-Claude.

Barrett thought about putting Don Latimer in the group. Latimer was coming to be something of a borderline mental case, but he was rational enough except when he lapsed into his psionic meditations, and he'd pull his own weight on the expedition. On the other hand, Latimer was Lew Hahn's roommate, and Barrett wanted Latimer around to observe Hahn at close range. He toyed with the idea of sending both of them out, but nixed it. Hahn was still an unknown quantity. It was too risky to let him go with the Inland Sea party this year. Probably he'd be in next spring's group, though.

Finally Barrett had his dozen men chosen. He chalked their names on the slate in front of the mess hall, and found Charley Norton at breakfast to tell him he was in charge.

It felt strange to know that he'd have to stay home while the others went. It was an admission that he was beginning to abdicate after running this place so long. A crippled old man was what he was, whether he liked to admit it to himself or not, and that was something he'd have to come to terms with soon.

In the afternoon, the men of the Inland Sea expedition gathered to select their gear and plan their route. Barrett kept away from the meeting. This was Charley Norton's show, now. He'd made eight or ten trips, and he knew what to do. Barrett didn't want to interfere.

But some masochistic compulsion in him drove him to take a trek of his own. If he couldn't see the western waters this year, the least he could do was pay a visit to the Atlantic, in his own back yard. Barrett stopped off in the infirmary and, finding Quesada elsewhere, helped himself to a tube of neural depressant. He scrambled along the eastern trail until he was a few hundred yards from the main building, dropped his trousers, and quickly gave each thigh a jolt of the drug, first the good leg, then the gimpy one. That would numb the muscles just enough so that he'd be able to take an extended hike without feeling the fire of fatigue in his protesting joints. He'd pay for it, he knew, eight hours from now, when the depressant wore off and the full impact of his exertion hit him like a million daggers. But he was willing to accept that price.

The road to the sea was a long, lonely one. Hawksbill Station was perched on the eastern rim of Appalachia, more than eight hundred feet above sea level. During the first half dozen years, the men of the Station had reached the ocean by a suicidal route across sheer rock faces, but Barrett had incited a ten-year project to carve a path. Now wide steps descended to the Atlantic. Chopping them out of the rock had kept a lot of men busy for a long time, too busy to worry or to slip into insanity. Barrett regretted that he couldn't conceive some comparable works project to occupy them nowadays.

The steps formed a succession of shallow platforms that switch-backed to the edge of the water. Even for a healthy man it was a strenuous walk. For Barrett in his present condition it was an ordeal. It took him two hours to descend a distance that normally could be traversed in a quarter of that time. When he reached the bottom, he sank down exhaustedly on a flat rock licked by the waves, and dropped his crutch. The fingers of his left hand were cramped and gnarled from gripping the crutch, and his entire body was bathed in sweat.

The water looked gray and somehow oily. Barrett could not explain the prevailing colorlessness of the Late Cambrian world, with its somber sky and somber land and somber sea, but his heart quietly ached for a glimpse of green vegetation again. He missed chlorophyll. The dark wavelets lapped against his rock, pushing a mass of floating black seaweed back and forth. The sea stretched to infinity. He didn't have the faintest idea how much of Europe, if any, was above water in this epoch. At the best of times most of the planet was submerged; here, only a few hundred million years after the white-hot rocks of the land had pushed into view, it was likely that all that was above water on Earth was a strip of territory here and there. Had the Himalayas been born yet? The Rockies? The Andes? He knew the approximate outlines of Late Cambrian North America, but the rest was a mystery. Blanks in knowledge were not easy to fill when the only link with Up Front was by one-way transport; Hawksbill Station had to rely on the random assortment of reading matter that came back in time, and it was furiously frustrating to lack information that any college geology text could supply.

As he watched, a big trilobite unexpectedly came scuttering up out of the water. It was the spike-tailed kind, about a yard long, with an eggplant-purple shell and a bristling arrangement of slender spines along the margins. There seemed to be a lot of legs underneath. The trilobite crawled up on the shore—no sand, no beach, just a shelf of rock—and advanced until it was eight or ten feet from the waves.

Good for you, Barrett thought. Maybe you're the first one who ever came out on land to see what it was like. The pioneer. The trailblazer.

It occurred to him that this adventurous trilobite might well be the ancestor of all the land-dwelling creatures of the eons to come. It was biological nonsense, but Barrett's weary mind conjured a picture of an evolutionary procession, with fish and amphibians and reptiles and mammals and man all stemming in unbroken sequence from this grotesque armored thing that moved in uncertain circles near his feet.

And if I were to step on you, he thought?

A quick motion—the sound of crunching chitin—the wild scrabbling of a host of little legs—

And the whole chain of life snapped in its first link. Evolution undone. No land creatures ever developed. With the descent of that heavy foot all the future would change and there would never have been any Hawksbill Station, no human race, no James Edward Barrett. In an instant he would have both revenge on those who had condemned him to live out his days in this place, and release from his sentence.

He did nothing. The trilobite completed its slow perambulation of the shoreline rocks and scattered back into the sea unharmed.

The soft voice of Don Latimer said, "I saw you sitting down here, Jim. Do you mind if I join you?"

Barrett swung around, momentarily surprised. Latimer had come down from his hilltop but so quietly that Barrett hadn't heard a thing. He recovered and grinned and beckoned Latimer to an adjoining rock.

"You fishing?" Latimer asked.

"Just sitting. An old man sunning himself."

"You took a hike like that just to sun yourself?" Latimer laughed. "Come off it. You're trying to get away from it all, and you probably wish I hadn't disturbed you."

"That's not so. Stay here. How's your new roommate getting along?"

"It's been strange," said Latimer. "That's one reason I came down here to talk to you." He leaned forward and peered searchingly into Barrett's eyes. "Jim, tell me: do you think I'm a madman?"

"Why should I?"

"The ESP-ing business. My attempt to break through to another realm of consciousness. I know you're tough-minded and skeptical. You probably think it's all a lot of nonsense."

Barrett shrugged and said, "If you want the blunt truth, I do. I don't have the remotest belief that you're going to get us anywhere, Don. I think it's a complete waste of time and energy for you to sit there for hours harnessing your psionic powers, or whatever it is you do. But no, I don't think you're crazy. I think you're entitled to your obsession and that you're going about a basically futile thing in a reasonably level-headed way. Fair enough?"

"More than fair. I don't ask you to put any credence in my research, but I don't want you to think I'm a total lunatic for trying it. It's important that you regard me as sane, or else what I want to tell you about Hahn won' t be valid to you."

"I don't see the connection."

"It's this," said Latimer. "On the basis of one evening's acquaintance, I've formed an opinion about Hahn. It's the kind of an opinion that might be formed by a garden-variety paranoid, and if you think I'm nuts you're likely to discount my idea about Hahn."

"I don't think you're nuts. What's your idea?"

"That he's spying on us."

Barrett had to work hard to keep from emitting the guffaw that would shatter Latimer's fragile self-esteem. "Spying?" he said casually. "You can't mean that. How can anyone spy here? I mean, how can he report his findings?"

"I don't know," Latimer said. "But he asked me a million questions last night. About you, about Quesada, about some of the sick men. He wanted to know everything."

"The normal curiosity of a new man."

"Jim, he was taking notes. I saw him after he thought I was asleep. He sat up for two hours writing it all down in a little book."

Barrett frowned. "Maybe he's going to write a novel about us."

"I'm serious," Latimer said. "Questions—notes. And he's shifty. Try to get him to talk about himself!"

"I did. I didn't learn much."

"Do you know why he's been sent here?"

"No."

"Neither do I," said Latimer. "Political crimes, he said, but he was vague as hell. He hardly seemed to know what the present government was up to, let alone what his own opinions were toward it. I don't detect any passionate philosophical convictions in Mr. Hahn. And you know as well as I do that Hawksbill Station is the refuse heap for revolutionaries and agitators and subversives and all sorts of similar trash, but that we've never had any other kind of prisoner here."

"I agree that Hahn's a puzzle. But who could he be spying for? He's got no way to file a report, if he's a government agent. He's stranded here for keeps, same as the rest of us."

"Maybe he was sent to keep an eye on us—to make sure we aren't cooking up some way to escape. Maybe he's a volunteer who willingly gave up his twenty-first-century life so he could come among us and thwart anything we might be hatching. Perhaps they're afraid we've invented forward time travel. Or that we've become a threat to the sequence of the time-lines. Anything. So Hahn comes among us to snoop around and block any dangers before they arrive."

Barrett felt a twinge of alarm. He saw how close to paranoia Latimer was hewing, now: in half a dozen sentences he had journeyed from the rational expression of some justifiable suspicions to the fretful fear that the men from Up Front were going to take steps to choke off the escape route that he was so close to perfecting.

He kept his voice level as he told Latimer, "I don't think you need to worry, Don. Hahn's an odd one, but he's not here to make trouble for us. The fellows Up Front have already made all the trouble they ever will."

"Would you keep an eye on him, anyway?"

"You know I will. And don't hesitate to let me know if Hahn does anything else out of the ordinary. You're in a better spot to notice than anyone else."

"I'll be watching," Latimer said. "We can't tolerate any spies from Up Front among us." he got to his feet and gave Barrett a pleasant smile. "I'll let you get back to your sunning now, Jim."

Latimer went up the path. Barrett eyed him until he was close to the top, only a faint dot against the stony backdrop. After a long while Barrett seized his crutch and levered himself to his feet. He stood staring down at the surf, dipping the tip of his crutch into the water to send a couple of little crawling things scurrying away. At length he turned and began the long, slow climb back to the Station.

Six

A couple of days passed before Barrett had the chance to draw Lew Hahn aside for a spot of political discussion. The Inland Sea party had set out, and in a way that was too bad, for Barrett could have used Charley Norton's services in penetrating Hahn's armor. Norton was the most gifted theorist around, a man who could weave a tissue of dialectic from the least promising material. If anyone could find out the depth of Hahn's Marxist commitment, if any, it was Norton. But Norton was leading the expedition, so Barrett had to do the interrogating himself. His Marxism was a trifle rusty, and he couldn't thread his path through the Leninist, Stalinist, Trotskyite, Khrushchevist, Maoist, Berenkovskyite and Mgumbweist schools with Charley Norton's skills. Yet he knew what questions to ask.

He picked a rainy evening when Hahn seemed to be in a fairly outgoing mood. There had been an hour's entertainment that night, an ingenious computer-composed film that Sid Hutchett had programmed last week. Up Front had been kind enough to ship back a modest computer, and Hutchett had rigged it to do animations by specifying line widths and lengths, shades of gray, and progression of raster units. It was a simple but remarkably clever business, and it brightened a dull night.

Afterward, sensing that Hahn was relaxed enough to lower his guard a bit, Barrett said, "Hutchett's a rare one. Did you meet him before he went on the trip?"

"Tall fellow with a sharp nose and no chin?"

"That's the one. A clever boy. He was the top computer man for the Continental Liberation Front until they caught him in '19. He programmed that fake broadcast in which Chancellor Dantell denounced his own regime. Remember?"

"I'm not sure I do." Hahn frowned. "How long ago was this?"

"The broadcast was in 2018. Would that be before your time? Only eleven years ago—"

"I was nineteen then," said Hahn. "I guess I wasn't very politically sophisticated."

"Too busy studying economics, I guess."

Hahn grinned. "That's right. Deep in the dismal science."

"And you never heard that broadcast? Or even heard *of* it?"

"I must have forgotten."

"The biggest hoax of the century," Barrett said, "and you forgot it. You know the Continental Liberation Front, of course."

"Of course." Hahn looked uneasy.

"Which group did you say you were with?"

"The People's Crusade for Liberty."

"I don't know it. One of the newer groups?"

"Less than five years old. It started in California."

"What's its program?"

"Oh, the usual," Hahn said. "Free elections, representative government, an opening of the security files, restoration of civil liberties."

"And the economic orientation? Pure Marxist or one of the offshoots?"

"Not really any, I guess. We believed in a kind of—well, capitalism with some government restraints."

"A little to the right of state socialism, and a little to the left of laissez faire?" Barrett suggested.

"Something like that."

"But that system was tried and failed, wasn't it? It had its day. It led inevitably to total socialism, which produced the compensating backlash of syndicalist capitalism, and then we got a government that pretended to be libertarian while actually stifling all individual liberties in the name of freedom. So if your group simply wanted to turn the clock back to 1955, say, there couldn't be much to its ideas."

Hahn looked bored. "You've got to understand I wasn't in the top ideological councils."

"Just an economist?"

"That's it. I drew up plans for the conversion to our system."

"Basing your work on the modified liberalism of Ricardo?"

"Well, in a sense."

"And avoiding the tendency to fascism that was found in the thinking of Keynes?"

"You could say so," Hahn said. He stood up, flashing a quick, vague smile. "Look, Jim, I'd love to argue this further with you some other time, but I've really got to go now. Ned Altman talked me into coming around and helping him do a lightning-dance to bring that pile of dirt to life. So if you don't mind—"

Hahn beat a hasty retreat.

Barrett was more perplexed then ever, now. Hahn hadn't been "arguing" anything. He had been carrying on a lame and feeble conversation, letting himself be pushed hither and thither by Barrett's questions. And he had spouted a lot of nonsense. He didn't seem to know Keynes from Ricardo, nor to care about it, which was odd for a self-professed economist. He didn't have a shred of an idea of what his own political party stood for. He had so little revolutionary background that he was unaware even of Hutchett's astonishing hoax of eleven years back.

He seemed phony from top to bottom.

How was it possible that this kid had been deemed worthy of exile to Hawksbill Station, anyhow? Only the top firebrands went there. Sentencing a man to Hawksbill was like sentencing him to death, and it wasn't done lightly. Barrett couldn't imagine why Hahn was here. He seemed genuinely distressed at being exiled, and evidently he had left a beloved young wife behind, but nothing else rang true about the man.

Was he as Latimer suggested—some kind of spy?

Barrett rejected the idea out of hand. He didn't want Latimer's paranoia infecting him. The government wasn't likely to send anyone on a one-way trip to the Late Cambrian just to spy on a bunch of aging revolutionaries who could never make trouble again. But what *was* Hahn doing here, then?

He would bear further watching, Barrett thought.

Barrett took care of some of the watching himself. But he had plenty of assistance. Latimer. Altman. Six or seven others. Latimer had recruited most of the ambulatory psycho cases, the ones who were superficially functional but full of all kinds of fears and credulities.

They were keeping an eye on the new man.

On the fifth day after his arrival, Hahn went out fishing in Rudiger's crew. Barrett stood for a long time on the edge of the world, watching the little boat bobbing in the surging Atlantic. Rudiger never went far from shore—eight hundred, a thousand yards out—but the water was rough even there. The waves came rolling in with X thousand miles of gathered impact behind them. A continental shelf sloped off at a wide angle, so that even at a substantial distance off shore the water wasn't very deep. Rudiger had taken soundings up to a mile out, and had reported depths no greater than 160 feet. Nobody had gone past a mile.

It wasn't that they were afraid of falling off the side of the world if they went too far east. It was simply that a mile was a long distance to row in an open boat, using stubby oars made from old packing cases. Up Front hadn't thought to spare an outboard motor for them.

Looking toward the horizon, Barrett had an odd thought. He had been told that the women's equivalent of Hawksbill Station was safely segregated out of reach, a couple of hundred million years up the timeline. But how did he know that? There could be another Station somewhere else in this very year, and they'd never know about it. A camp of women, say, living on the far side of the ocean, or even across the Inland Sea.

It wasn't very likely, he knew. With the entire past to pick from, the edgy men Up Front wouldn't take any chance that the two groups of exiles might get together and spawn a tribe of little subversives. They'd take every precaution to put an impenetrable barrier of epochs between them. Yet Barrett thought he could make it sound convincing to the other men. With a little effort he could get them to believe in the existence of several simultaneous Hawksbill Stations scattered on this level of time.

Which could be our salvation, he thought.

The instances of degenerative psychosis were beginning to snowball, now. Too many men had been here too long, and one crackup was starting to feed the next, in this blank lifeless world where humans were never meant to live. The men needed projects to keep them going. They were starting to slip off into harebrained projects, like Altman's Frankenstein girlfriend and Latimer's psi pursuit.

Suppose, Barrett thought, I could get them steamed up about reaching the other continents?

A round-the-world expedition. Maybe they could build some kind of big ship. That would keep a lot of men busy for a long time. And they'd need navigational equipment—compasses, sextants, chronometers, whatnot. Somebody would have to design an improvised radio, too. It was the kind of project that might take thirty or forty years. A focus for our energies, Barrett thought. Of course, I won't live to see the ship set sail. But even so, it's a way of staving off collapse. We've built our staircase to the sea. Now we need something bigger to do. Idle hands make for idle minds...sick minds....

He liked the idea he had hatched. For several weeks, now, Barrett had been worrying about the deteriorating state of affairs in the Station, and looking for some way to cope with it. Now he thought he had his way.

Turning, he saw Latimer and Altman standing behind him.

"How long have you been there?" he asked.

"Two minutes," said Latimer. "We brought you something to look at."

Altman nodded vigorously. "You ought to read it. We brought it for you to read."

"What is it?"

Latimer handed over a folded sheaf of papers. "I found this tucked away in Hahn's bunk after he went out with Rudiger. I know I'm not supposed to be invading his privacy, but I had to have a look at what he's been writing. There it is. He's a spy, all right."

Barrett glanced at the papers in his hand. "I'll read it a little later. What is it about?"

"It's a description of the Station, and a profile of most of the men in it," said Latimer. He smiled frostily. "Hahn's private opinion of me is that I've gone mad. His private opinion of you is a little more flattering, but not much."

Altman said, "He's also been hanging around the Hammer."

"What"

"I saw him going there late last night. He went into the building. I followed him. He was looking at the Hammer."

"Why didn't you tell me that right away?" Barrett snapped.

"I wasn't sure it was important," Altman said. "I had to talk it over with Don first. And I couldn't do that until Hahn had gone out fishing."

Sweat burst out on Barrett's face. "Listen, Ned, if you ever catch Hahn going near the time-travel equipment again, you let me know in a hurry. Without consulting Don or anyone else. Clear?"

"Clear," said Altman. He giggled. "You know what I think? They've decided to exterminate us Up Front. Hahn's been sent here to check us out as a suicide volunteer. Then they're going to send a bomb through the Hammer and blow the Station up. We ought to wreck the Hammer and Anvil before they get a chance."

"But why would they send a suicide volunteer?" Latimer asked. "Unless they've got some way to rescue their spy—"

"In any case we shouldn't take any chance," Altman argued. "Wreck the Hammer. Make it impossible for them to bomb us from Up Front."

"That might be a good idea. But—"

"Shut up, both of you," Barrett growled. "Let me look at these papers."

He walked a few steps away from them and sat down on a shelf of rock. He unfolded the sheaf. He began to read.

Seven

Hahn had a cramped, crabbed handwriting that packed a maximum of information into a minimum of space, as though he regarded it as a mortal sin to waste paper. Fair enough; paper was a scarce commodity here, and evidently Hahn had brought these sheets with him from Up Front. His script was clear, though. So were his opinions. Painfully so.

He had written an analysis of conditions at Hawksbill Station, setting forth in about five thousand words everything that Barrett knew was going sour here. He had neatly ticked off the men as aging revolutionaries in whom the old fervor had turned rancid; he listed the ones who were certifiably psycho, and the ones who were on the edge, and the ones who were hanging on, like Quesada and Norton and Rudiger. Barrett was interested to see that Hahn rated even those three as suffering from severe strain and likely to fly apart at any moment. To him, Quesada and Norton and Rudiger seemed just about as stable as when they had first dropped onto the Anvil of Hawksbill Station; but there was possibly the distorting effect of his own blurred perceptions. To an outsider like Hahn, the view was different and per-haps more accurate.

Barrett forced himself not to skip ahead to Hahn's evaluation of him.

He wasn't pleased when he came to it. "Barrett," Hahn had written, "is like a mighty beam that's been gnawed from within by termites. He looks solid, but one good push would break him apart. A recent injury to his foot has evidently had a bad effect on him. The other men say he used to be physically vigorous and derived much of his authority from his size and strength. Now he can hardly walk. But I feel the trouble with Barrett is inherent in the life of Hawksbill Station, and doesn't have much to do with his lameness. He's been cut off from normal human drives for too long. The exercise of power here has provided the illu-sion of stability for him, but it's power in a vacuum, and things have happened within Barrett of which he's totally unaware. He's in bad need of therapy. He may be beyond help."

Barrett read that several times. *Gnawed from within by termites...one good push...things have happened within him...bad need of therapy... beyond help.*

He was less angered than he thought he should have been. Hahn was entitled to his views. Barrett finally stopped rereading his profile and pushed his way to the last page of Hahn's essay. It ended with the words, "Therefore I recommend prompt termination of the Hawksbill Station penal colony, and, where possible, the therapeutic rehabilitation of its inmates."

What the hell was this?

It sounded like the report of a parole commissioner! But there was no parole from Hawksbill Station. That final sentence let all the viabil-ity of what had gone before bleed away. Hahn was pretending to be composing a report to the government Up Front, obviously. But a wall a billion years thick made filing of that report impossible. So Hahn was suffering from delusions, just like Altman and Valdosto and the others. In his fevered mind he believed he could send messages Up Front, pompous documents delineating the flaws and foibles of his fellow prisoners.

That raised a chilling prospect. Hahn might be crazy, but he hadn't been in the Station long enough to have gone crazy here. He must have brought his insanity with him.

What if they had stopped using Hawksbill Station as a camp for political prisoners, Barrett asked himself, and were starting to use it as an insane asylum?

A cascade of psychos descending on them. Men who had gone honorably buggy under the stress of confinement would have to make room for ordinary bedlamites. Barrett shivered. He folded up Hahn's papers and handed them to Latimer, who was sitting a few yards away, watching him intently.

"What did you think of that?" Latimer asked.

"I think it's hard to evaluate. But possibly friend Hahn is emotionally disturbed. Put this stuff back exactly where you got it, Don. And don't give Hahn the faintest inkling that you've read or removed it."

"Right."

"And come to me whenever you think there's something I ought to know about him," Barrett said. "He may be a very sick boy. He may need all the help we can give."

The fishing expedition returned in early afternoon. Barrett saw that the dinghy was overflowing with the haul, and Hahn, coming into the camp with his arms full of gaffed trilobites, looked sunburned and pleased with his outing. Barrett came over to inspect the catch. Rudiger was in an effusive mood, and held up a bright red crustacean that might have been the great-great-grandfather of all boiled lobsters, except that it had no front claws and a wicked-looking triple spike where a tail should have been. It was about two feet long, and ugly.

"A new species!" Rudiger crowed. "There's nothing like this in any museum. I wish I could put it where it would be found. Some mountaintop, maybe."

"If it could be found, it would have been found," Barrett reminded him. "Some paleontologist of the twentieth century would have dug it out. So forget it, Mel."

Hahn said, "I've been wondering about that point. How is it nobody Up Front ever dug up the fossil remains of Hawksbill Station? Aren't they worried that one of the early fossil hunters will find it in the Cambrian strata and raise a fuss?"

Barrett shook his head. "For one thing, no paleontologist from the beginning of the science to the founding of the Station in 2005 ever *did* dig up Hawksbill. That's a matter of record, so there was nothing to worry about. If it came to light after 2005, why, everyone would know what it was. No paradox there."

"Besides," said Rudiger sadly, "in another billion years this whole strip of rock will be on the floor of the Atlantic, with a couple of miles of sediment over it. There's not a chance we'll be found. Or that anyone Up Front will ever see this guy I caught today. Not that I give a damn. I've seen him. I'll dissect him. Their loss."

"But you regret the fact that science will never know of this species," Hahn said.

"Sure I do. But is it my fault? Science does know of this species. Me. I'm science. I'm the leading paleontologist of this epoch. Can I help it if I can't publish my discoveries in the professional journals?" He scowled and walked away, carrying the big red crustacean.

Hahn and Barrett looked at each other. They smiled, in a natural mutual response to Rudiger's grumbled outburst. Then Barrett's smile faded.

...termites...one good push...therapy...

"Something wrong?" Hahn asked.

"Why?"

"You looked so bleak, all of a sudden."

"My foot gave me a twinge," Barrett said. "It does that, you know. Here. I'll give you a hand carrying those things. We'll have fresh trilobite cocktail tonight."

Eight

A little before midnight, Barrett was awakened by footsteps outside his hut. As he sat up, groping for the luminescence switch, Ned Altman came blundering through the door. Barrett blinked at him. "What's the matter?"

"Hahn!" Altman rasped. "He's fooling around with the Hammer again. We just saw him go into the building."

Barrett shed his sleepiness like a seal bursting out of water. Ignoring the insistent throb in his left leg, he pulled himself from his bed and grabbed some clothing. He was more apprehensive than he wanted Altman to see. If Hahn, fooling around with the temporal mechanism, accidentally smashed the Hammer, they might never get replacement equipment from Up Front. Which would mean that all future shipments of supplies—if there were any—would come as random shoots that might land in any old year. What business did Hahn have with the machine, anyway?

Altman said, "Latimer's up there keeping an eye on him. He got suspicious when Hahn didn't come back to the hut, and he got me, and we went looking for him. And there he was, sniffing around the Hammer."

"Doing what?"

"I don't know. As soon as we saw him go in, I came down here to get you. Don's watching."

Barrett stumped his way out of the hut and did his best to run toward the main building. Pain shot like trails of hot acid up the lower half of his body. The crutch dug mercilessly into his left armpit as he leaned all his weight into it. His crippled foot, swinging freely, burned with a cold glow. His right leg, which was carrying most of the burden, creaked and popped. Altman ran breathlessly alongside him. The Station was terribly silent at this hour.

As they passed Quesada's hut, Barrett considered waking the medic and taking him along. He decided against it. Whatever trouble Hahn might be up to, Barrett felt he could handle it himself. There was some strength left in the old gnawed beam, after all.

Latimer stood at the entrance to the main dome. He was right at the edge of panic, or perhaps over the edge. He seemed to be gibbering with fear and shock. Barrett had never seen a man gibber before.

He clamped a big paw on Latimer's thin shoulder and said harshly, "Where is he? Where's Hahn?"

"He—disappeared."

"What do you mean? Where did he go?"

Latimer moaned. His face was fish-belly white. "He got onto the Anvil," Latimer blurted. "The light came on—the glow. And then Hahn disappeared!"

"No," Barrett said. "It isn't possible. You must be mistaken."

"I saw him go!"

"He's hiding somewhere in the building," Barrett insisted. "Close that door! Search for him!"

Altman said, "He probably did disappear, Jim. If Don says he disappeared—"

"He climbed right on the Anvil. Then everything turned red and he was gone."

Barrett clenched his fists. There was a white-hot blaze just behind his forehead that almost made him forget about his foot. He saw his mistake, now. He had depended for his espionage on two men who were patently and unmistakably insane, and that had been itself a not very sane thing to do. A man is known by his choice of lieutenants. Well, he had relied on Altman and Latimer, and now they were giving him the sort of information that such spies could be counted on to supply.

"You're hallucinating," he told Latimer curtly. "Ned, go wake Quesada and get him here right away. You, Don, you stand here by the entrance, and if Hahn shows up I want you to scream at the top of your lungs. I'm going to search the building for him."

"Wait," Latimer said. He seemed to be in control of himself again. "Jim, do you remember when I asked you if you thought I was crazy? You said you didn't. You trusted me. Well, don't stop trusting me now. I tell you I'm not hallucinating. I saw Hahn disappear. I can't explain it, but I'm rational enough to know what I saw."

In a milder tone Barrett said, "All right. Maybe so. Stay by the door, anyway. I'll run a quick check."

He started to make the circuit of the dome, beginning with the room where the Hammer was located. Everything seemed to be in order there. No Hawksbill Field glow was in evidence, and nothing had been disturbed. The room had no closets or cupboards in which Hahn could be hiding. When he had inspected it thoroughly, Barrett moved on, looking into the infirmary, the mess hall, the kitchen, the recreation room. He looked high and low. No Hahn. Of course, there were plenty of places in those rooms where Hahn might have secreted himself, but Barrett doubted that he was there. So it had all been some feverish fantasy of Latimer's, then. He completed the route and found himself back at the main entrance. Latimer still stood guard there. He had been joined by a sleepy Quesada. Altman, pale and shaky-looking, was just outside the door.

"What's happening?" Quesada asked.

"I'm not sure," said Barrett. "Don and Ned had the idea they saw Lew Hahn fooling around with the time equipment. I've checked the building, and he's not here, so maybe they made a little mistake. I suggest you take them both into the infirmary and give them a shot of something to settle their nerves, and we'll all try to get back to sleep."

Latimer said, "I tell you, I saw—"

"Shut up!" Altman broke in. "Listen! What's the noise?"

Barrett listened. The sound was clear and loud: the hissing whine of ionization. It was the sound produced by a functioning Hawksbill Field. Suddenly there were goose-pimples on his flesh. In a low voice he said, "The field's on. We're probably getting some supplies."

"At this hour?" said Latimer.

"We don't know what time it is Up Front. All of you stay here. I'll check the Hammer."

"Perhaps I ought to go with you," Quesada suggested mildly.

"*Stay here!*" Barrett thundered. He paused, embarrassed at his own explosive show of wrath. "It only takes one of us. I'll be right back."

Without waiting for further dissent, he pivoted and limped down the hall to the Hammer room. He shouldered. the door open and looked in. There was no need for him to switch on the light. The red glow of the Hawksbill Field illuminated everything.

Barrett stationed himself just within the door. Hardly daring to breathe, he stared fixedly at the Hammer, watching as the glow deepened through various shades of pink toward crimson, and then spread until it enfolded the waiting Anvil beneath it. An endless moment passed.

Then came the implosive thunderclap, and Lew Hahn dropped out of nowhere and lay for a moment in temporal shock on the broad plate of the Anvil.

Nine

In the darkness, Hahn did not notice Barrett at first. He sat up slowly, shaking off the stunning effects of a trip through time. After a few seconds he pushed himself toward the lip of the Anvil and let his legs dangle over it. He swung them to get the circulation going. He took a series of deep breaths. Finally he slipped to the floor. The glow of the field had gone out in the moment of his arrival, and so he moved warily, as though not wanting to bump into anything.

Abruptly Barrett switched on the light and said, "What have you been up to, Hahn?"

The younger man recoiled as though he had been jabbed in the gut. He gasped, hopped backward a few steps, and flung up both hands in a defensive gesture.

"Answer me," Barrett said.

Hahn regained his equilibrium. He shot a quick glance past Barrett's bulky form toward the hallway and said, "Let me go, will you? I can't explain now."

"You'd better explain now."

"It'll be easier for everyone if I don't," said Hahn. "Please. Let me pass."

Barrett continued to block the door. "I want to know where you've been. What have you been doing with the Hammer?"

"Nothing. Just studying it."

"You weren't in this room a minute ago. Then you appeared. Where'd you come from, Hahn?"

"You're mistaken. I was standing right behind the Hammer. I didn't—"

"I saw you drop down on the Anvil. You took a time trip, didn't you?"

"No."

"Don't lie to me! You've got some way of going forward in time, isn't that so? You've been spying on us, and you just went somewhere to file your report—somewhere—and now you're back."

Hahn's forehead was glistening. He said, "I warn you, don't ask too many questions. You'll know everything in due time. This isn't the time. Please, now. Let me pass."

"I want answers first," Barrett said. He realized that he was trembling. He already knew the answers, and they were answers that shook him to the core of his soul. He knew where Hahn had been.

But Hahn had to admit it himself.

Hahn said nothing. He took a couple of hesitant steps toward Barrett, who did not move. He seemed to be gathering momentum for a rush at the doorway.

Barrett said, "You aren't getting out of here until you tell me what I want to know."

Hahn charged.

Barrett planted himself squarely, crutch braced against the doorframe, his good foot flat on the floor, and waited for the younger man to reach him. He figured he outweighed Hahn by eighty pounds. That might be enough to balance the fact that he was spotting Hahn thirty years and one leg. They came together, and Barrett drove his hands down onto Hahn's shoulders, trying to hold him, to force him back into the room.

Hahn gave an inch or two. He looked up at Barrett without speaking and pushed forward again.

"Don't—don't—" Barrett grunted. "I won't let you—"

"I don't want to do this," Hahn said.

He pushed again. Barrett felt himself buckling under the impact. He dug his hands as hard as he could into Hahn's shoulders, and tried to shove the other man backward into the room, but Hahn held firm and all of Barrett's energy was converted into a backward thrust rebounding on himself. He lost control of his crutch, and it slithered out from under his arm. For one agonizing moment Barrett's full weight rested on the crushed uselessness of his left foot, and then, as though his limbs were melting away beneath him, he began to sink toward the floor. He landed with a reverberating crash.

Quesada, Altman, and Latimer came rushing in. Barrett writhed in pain on the floor. Hahn stood over him, looking unhappy, his hands locked together.

"I'm sorry," he said. "You shouldn't have tried to muscle me like that."

Barrett glowered at him. "You were traveling in time, weren't you? You can answer me now!"

"Yes," Hahn said at last. "I went Up Front."

An hour later, after Quesada had pumped him with enough neural depressants to keep him from jumping out of his skin, Barrett got the full story. Hahn hadn't wanted to reveal it so soon, but he had changed his mind after his little scuffle.

It was all very simple. Time travel now worked in both directions. The glib, impressive noises about the flow of entropy had turned out to be just noises.

"How long has this been known?" Barrett asked.

"At least five years. We aren't sure yet exactly when the breakthrough came. After we're finished going through all the suppressed records of the former government—"

"The former government?"

Hahn nodded. "The revolution came in January. Not really a violent one, either. The syndicalists just mildewed from within, and when they got the first push they fell over."

"Was it mildew?" Barrett asked, coloring. "Or termites? Keep your metaphors straight."

Hahn glanced away. "Anyway, the government fell. We've got a provisional liberal regime in office now. Don't ask me much about it. I'm not a political theorist. I'm not even an economist. You guessed as much."

"What are you; then?"

"A policeman," Hahn said. "Part of the commission that's investigating the prison system of the former government. Including this prison."

Barrett looked at Quesada, then at Hahn. Thoughts were streaming turbulently through him, and he could not remember when he had last been so overwhelmed by events. He had to work hard to keep from breaking into the shakes again. His voice quavered a little as he said, "You came back to observe Hawksbill Station, right? And you went Up Front tonight to tell them what you saw here. You think we're a pretty sad bunch, eh?"

"You've all been under heavy stress here," Hahn said. "Considering the circumstances of your imprisonment—"

Quesada broke in. "If there's a liberal government in power, now, and it's possible to travel both ways in time, then am I right in assuming that the Hawksbill prisoners are going to be sent Up Front?"

"Of course," said Hahn. "It'll be done as soon as possible. That's been the whole purpose of my reconnaissance mission. To find out if you people were still alive, first, and then to see what shape you're in, how badly in need of treatment you are. You'll be given every available benefit of modern therapy, naturally. No expense spared to—"

Barrett scarcely paid attention to Hahn's words. He had been fearing something like this all night, ever since Altman had told him Hahn was monkeying with the Hammer, but he had never fully allowed himself to believe that it could really be possible.

He saw his kingdom crumbling, now.

He saw himself returned to a world he could not begin to comprehend—a lame Rip van Winkle, coming back after twenty years.

He saw himself leaving a place that had become his home.

Barrett said tiredly, "You know, some of the men aren't going to be able to adapt to the shock of freedom. It might just kill them to be dumped into the real world again. I mean advanced psychos—Valdosto, and such."

"Yes," Hahn said. "I've mentioned them in my report."

"It'll be necessary to get them ready for a return in gradual stages. It might take several years to condition them to the idea. It might even take longer than that."

"I'm no therapist," said Hahn. "Whatever the doctors think is right for them is what'll be done. Maybe it will be necessary to keep them here. I can see where it would be pretty potent to send them back, after they've spent all these years believing there's no return."

"More than that," said Barrett. "There's a lot of work that can be done here. Scientific works. Exploration. I don't think Hawksbill Station ought to be closed down."

"No one said it would be. We have every intention of keeping it going. But not as a prison. The prison concept is out."

"Good," Barrett said. He fumbled for his crutch, found it, and got heavily to his feet. Quesada moved toward him as though to steady him, but Barrett shook him off. "Let's go outside," he said.

They left the building. A gray mist had come in over the Station, and a fine drizzle had begun to fall. Barrett looked around at the scattering of huts. At the ocean, dimly visible to the east in the faint moonlight. He thought of Charley Norton and the party that had gone on the annual expedition to the Inland Sea. That bunch was going to be in for a real surprise, when they got back here in a few weeks and discovered that everybody was free to go home.

Very strangely, Barrett felt a sudden pressure forming around his eyelids, as of tears trying to force their way out into the open.

Then he turned to Hahn and Quesada. In a low voice he said, "Have you followed what I've been trying to tell you? Someone's got to stay here and ease the transition for the sick men who won't be able to stand the shock of return. Someone's got to keep the base running. Someone's got to explain things to the new men who'll be coming back here, the scientists."

"Naturally," Hahn said.

"The one who does that—the one who stays behind—I think it ought to be someone who knows the Station well, someone who's fit to return Up Front, but who's willing to make the sacrifice and stay. Do you follow me? A volunteer." They were smiling at him now. Barrett wondered if there might not be something patronizing about those smiles. He wondered if he might not be a little too transparent. To hell with both of them, he thought. He sucked the Cambrian air into his lungs until his chest swelled grandly.

"I'm offering to stay," Barrett said in a loud tone. He glared at them to keep them from objecting. But they wouldn't dare object, he knew. In Hawksbill Station, he was the king. And he meant to keep it that way. "I'll be the volunteer," he said. "I'll be the one who stays."

He looked out over his kingdom from the top of the hill.

PASSENGERS

1966—the year of "Hawksbill Station," The Time Hoppers, Thorns, *and my big El Dorado book,* The Golden Dream*—was a watershed year for me. I had found my own voice as a writer and had attained a degree of skill surprising even to me; publishers were crowding around me, eager for my science fiction and for my non-fiction work as well; the days of grinding out hack assignments for magazines like* Trapped *or* True Men Adventures *were receding into history. And as the major works of 1966 began to find their way into print the following year, critics who had dismissed me as a cynical opportunist were taking a second look at what I was doing. I felt a heady sense of new beginnings, of having entered into a mature and fulfilling phase of my career. (I also managed to damage my health in the joyous overwork of it all, and spent most of the summer of 1966 as an invalid, frail and exhausted—a new experience for me. But by autumn I was back to normal and ready to tackle a full schedule, as the writing of the novel* Thorns *in ten working days (!) in September of 1966 demonstrated.)*

Suddenly, now, I found I had won the respect of my peers in the science-fiction world for something other than my ability to turn out salable work in high volume. Though barely into my thirties, I was elected president of the newly founded Science Fiction Writers of America early in 1967. I made my first appearance on the awards ballots since winning the Hugo as Most Promising New Author in 1966: Thorns *was a Nebula nominee in 1967, and so was the novella version of "Hawksbill Station." (I finished second both times.) Both stories would be on the Hugo ballot* as well, the following year, the Hugos following a somewhat different chronological schedule in those days. (More second-place finishes would be the result.)

And in January, 1967, I placed a story with what was surely the most difficult, cantankerous, demanding editor of the era: Damon Knight, famous for his well-aimed and ferocious attacks on all that was slovenly in science fiction, who had started an anthology of original fiction called Orbit. Selling a story to Damon struck me as a challenge that had to be surmounted; and so I sent him "Passengers," and on January 16 he sent it back, saying, "I can't fault this one technically, & it is surely dark & nasty enough to suit anybody, but I have a nagging feeling that there's something missing, and I'm not sure I can put my finger on it." But he offered some suggestions for revisions anyway, and I decided to try another draft, telling him on January 26, "You and your Orbit are a great tribulation to me. I suppose I could take 'Passengers' and ship it off to Fred Pohl and collect my $120 and start all over trying to sell one to you, but I don't want to do that, because I believe this story represents just about the best I have in me, and if I can't get you to take it it's futile to go on submitting others."

The rewrite, Knight said, was close—not quite there. So I rewrote it again. And again. The hook was in me, and all I could do was wriggle. On March 22 he wrote to me again to say, "God help us both, I am going to ask you to revise this one more time. The love story now has every necessary element, but it seems to me it's an empty jug. Now I want you to put the love into it. I say this with a feeling of helplessness, because I don't know how to tell you to do it."

And then he proceeded to tell me, not how to do it, but why I should do it; and I did it and he bought the story, and published it in Orbit Four in 1968. And the following year it won me my first Nebula, for Best Short Story of the Year. (It was nominated for the Hugo, too, and should have won that as well—but it was beaten by a story from an earlier year that was technically ineligible for the ballot but got on it anyway.) Since then it has become a standard anthology piece, was purchased for the movies (though the film has never been made), and has, in general, become one of my best known stories. The five drafts of it that I did between January and March of 1967 were an almighty nuisance but I have never regretted doing them.

PASSENGERS

There are only fragments of me left now. Chunks of memory have broken free and drifted away like calved glaciers. It is always like that when a Passenger leaves us. We can never be sure of all the things our borrowed bodies did. We have only the lingering traces, the imprints.

Like sand clinging to an ocean-tossed bottle. Like the throbbings of amputated legs.

I rise. I collect myself. My hair is rumpled; I comb it. My face is creased from too little sleep. There is sourness in my mouth. Has my Passenger been eating dung with my mouth? They do that. They do anything.

It is morning.

A gray, uncertain morning. I stare at it awhile, and then, shuddering, I opaque the window and confront instead the gray, uncertain surface of the inner panel. My room looks untidy. Did I have a woman here? There are ashes in the trays. Searching for butts, I find several with lipstick stains. Yes, a woman was here.

I touched the bedsheets. Still warm with shared warmth. Both pillows tousled. She has gone, though, and the Passenger is gone, and I am alone.

How long did it last, this time?

I pick up the phone and ring Central. "What is the date?"

The computer's bland feminine voice replies, "Friday, December fourth, nineteen eighty-seven."

"The time?"

"Nine fifty-one, Eastern Standard Time."

"The weather forecast?"

"Predicted temperature range for today thirty to thirty-eight. Current temperature, thirty-one. Wind from the north, sixteen miles an hour. Chances of precipitation slight."

"What do you recommend for a hangover?"

"Food or medication?"

"Anything you like," I say.

The computer mulls that one over for a while. Then it decides on both, and activates my kitchen. The spigot yields cold tomato juice. Eggs begin to fry. From the medicine slot comes a purplish liquid. The Central Computer is always so thoughtful. Do the Passengers ever ride it, I wonder? What thrills could that hold for them? Surely it must be more exciting to borrow the million minds of Central than to live awhile in the short-circuited soul of a corroding human being!

December fourth, Central said. Friday. So the Passenger had me for three nights.

I drink the purplish stuff and probe my memories in a gingerly way, as one might probe a festering sore.

I remember Tuesday morning. A bad time at work. None of the charts will come out right. The section manager irritable; he has been taken by Passengers three times in five weeks, and his section is in disarray as a result, and his Christmas bonus is jeopardized. Even though it is customary not to penalize a person for lapses due to Passengers, according to the system, the section manager seems to feel he will be treated unfairly. So he treats us unfairly. We have a hard time. Revise the charts, fiddle with the program, check the fundamentals ten times over. Out they come: the detailed forecasts for price variations of public utility securities, February-April 1988. That afternoon we are to meet and discuss the charts and what they tell us.

I do not remember Tuesday afternoon.

That must have been when the Passenger took me. Perhaps at work; perhaps in the mahogany-paneled boardroom itself, during the conference. Pink concerned faces all about me; I cough, I lurch, I stumble from my seat. They shake their heads sadly. No one reaches for me. No one stops me. It is too dangerous to interfere with one who has a Passenger. The chances are great that a second Passenger lurks nearby in the discorporate state, looking for a mount. So I am avoided. I leave the building.

After that, what?

Sitting in my room on bleak Friday morning, I eat my scrambled eggs and try to reconstruct the three lost nights.

Of course it is impossible. The conscious mind functions during the period of captivity, but upon withdrawal of the Passenger nearly every recollection goes too. There is only a slight residue, a gritty film of faint and ghostly memories. The mount is never precisely the same person afterwards; though he cannot recall the details of his experience, he is subtly changed by it.

I try to recall.

A girl? Yes: lipstick on the butts. Sex, then, here in my room. Young? Old? Blonde? Dark? Everything is hazy. How did my borrowed body behave? Was I a good lover? I try to be, when I am myself. I keep in shape. At thirty-eight, I can handle three sets of tennis on a summer afternoon without collapsing. I can make a woman glow as a woman is meant to glow. Not boasting; just categorizing. We have our skills. These are mine.

But Passengers, I am told, take wry amusement in controverting our skills. So would it have given my rider a kind of delight to find me a woman and force me to fail repeatedly with her?

I dislike that thought.

The fog is going from my mind now. The medicine prescribed by Central works rapidly. I eat, I shave, I stand under the vibrator until my skin is clean. I do my exercises. Did the Passenger exercise my body Wednesday and Thursday mornings? Probably not. I must make up for that. I am close to middle age, now; tonus lost is not easily regained.

I touch my toes twenty times, knees stiff.

I kick my legs in the air.

I lie flat and lift myself on pumping elbows.

The body responds, maltreated though it has been. It is the first bright moment of my awakening: to feel the inner tingling, to know that I still have vigor.

Fresh air is what I want next. Quickly I slip into my clothes and leave. There is no need for me to report to work today. They are aware that since Tuesday afternoon I have had a Passenger; they need not be aware that before dawn on Friday the Passenger departed. I will have a free day. I will walk the city's streets, stretching my limbs, repaying my body for the abuse it has suffered.

I enter the elevator. I drop fifty stories to the ground. I step out into the December dreariness.

The towers of New York rise about me.

In the street the cars stream forward. Drivers sit edgily at their wheels. One never knows when the driver of a nearby car will be borrowed, and there is always a moment of lapsed coordination as the Passenger takes over. Many lives are lost that way on our streets and highways; but never the life of a Passenger.

I begin to walk without purpose. I cross Fourteenth Street, heading north, listening to the soft violet purr of the electric engines. I see a boy jigging in the street and know he is being ridden. At Fifth and Twenty-second a prosperous-looking paunchy man approaches, his necktie askew, this morning's *Wall Street Journal* jutting from an overcoat pocket. He giggles. He thrusts out his tongue. Ridden. Ridden. I avoid him. Moving briskly, I come to the underpass that carries traffic below Thirty-fourth Street toward Queens, and pause for a moment to watch two adolescent girls quarreling at the rim of the pedestrian walk. One is a Negro. Her eyes are rolling in terror. The other pushes her closer to the railing. Ridden. But the Passenger does not have murder on its mind, merely pleasure. The Negro girl is released and falls in a huddled heap, trembling. Then she rises and runs. The other girl draws a long strand of gleaming hair into her mouth, chews on it, seems to awaken. She looks dazed.

I avert my eyes. One does not watch while a fellow sufferer is awakening. There is a morality of the ridden; we have so many new tribal mores in these dark days.

I hurry on.

Where am I going so hurriedly? Already I have walked more than a mile. I seem to be moving toward some goal, as though my Passenger still hunches in my skull, urging me about. But I know that is not so. For the moment, at least, I am free.

Can I be sure of that?

Cogito ergo sum no longer applies. We go on thinking even while we are ridden, and we live in quiet desperation, unable to half halt our courses no matter how ghastly, no matter how self-destructive. I am certain that I can distinguish between the condition of bearing a Passenger and the condition of being free. But perhaps not. Perhaps I bear a particularly devilish Passenger which has not quitted me at all, but which merely has receded to the cerebellum, leaving me the illusion of freedom while all the time surreptitiously driving me onward to some purpose of its own.

Did we ever have more than that: the illusion of freedom?

But this is disturbing, the thought that I may be ridden without realizing it. I burst out in heavy perspiration, not merely from the exertion of walking. Stop. Stop here. Why must you walk? You are at Forty-second Street. There is the library. Nothing forces you onward. Stop a while, I tell myself. Rest on the library steps.

I sit on the cold stone and tell myself that I have made this decision for myself.

Have I? It is the old problem, free will versus determinism, translated into the foulest of forms. Determinism is no longer a philosopher's abstraction; it is cold alien tendrils sliding between the cranial sutures. The Passengers arrived three years ago. I have been ridden five times since then. Our world is quite different now. But we have adjusted even to this. We have adjusted. We have our mores. Life goes on. Our governments rule, our legislatures meet, our stock exchanges transact business as usual, and we have methods for compensating for the random havoc. It is the only way. What else can we do? Shrivel in defeat? We have an enemy we cannot fight; at best we can resist through endurance. So we endure.

The stone steps are cold against my body. In December few people sit here.

I tell myself that I made this long walk of my own free will, that I halted of my own free will, that no Passenger rides my brain now. Perhaps. Perhaps. I cannot let myself believe that I am not free.

Can it be, I wonder, that the Passenger left some lingering command in me? Walk to this place, halt at this place? That is possible too.

I look about me at the others on the library steps.

An old man, eyes vacant, sitting on newspaper. A boy of thirteen or so with flaring nostrils. A plump woman. Are all of them ridden? Passengers seem to cluster about me today. The more I study the ridden ones, the more convinced I become that I am, for the moment, free. The last time, I had three months of freedom between rides. Some people, they say, are scarcely ever free. Their bodies are in great demand, and they know only scattered bursts of freedom, a day here, a week there, an hour. We have never been able to determine how many Passengers infest our world. Millions, maybe. Or maybe five. Who can tell?

A wisp of snow curls down out of the gray sky. Central had said the chance of precipitation was slight. Are they riding Central this morning too?

I see the girl.

She sits diagonally across from me, five steps up and a hundred feet away, her black skirt pulled up on her knees to reveal handsome legs. She is young. Her hair is deep, rich auburn. Her eyes are pale; at this distance, I cannot make out the precise color. She is dressed simply. She is younger than thirty. She wears a dark green coat and her lipstick has a purplish tinge. Her lips are full, her nose slender, high-bridged, her eyebrows carefully plucked.

I know her.

I have spent the past three nights with her in my room. She is the one. Ridden, she came to me, and ridden, I slept with her. I am certain of this. The veil of memory opens; I see her slim body naked on my bed.

How can it be that I remember this?

It is too strong to be an illusion. Clearly this is something that I have been *permitted* to remember for reasons I cannot comprehend. And I remember more. I remember her soft gasping sounds of pleasure. I know that my own body did not betray me those three nights, nor did I fail her need.

And there is more. A memory of sinuous music; a scent of youth in her hair; the rustle of winter trees. Somehow she brings back to me a time of innocence, a time when I am young and girls are mysterious, a time of parties and dances and warmth and secrets.

I am drawn to her now.

There is an etiquette about such things, too. It is in poor taste to approach someone you have met while being ridden. Such an encounter gives you no privilege; a stranger remains a stranger, no matter what you and she may have done and said during your involuntary time together.

Yet I am drawn to her.

Why this violation of taboo? Why this raw breach of etiquette? I have never done this before. I have been scrupulous.

But I get to my feet and walk along the step on which I have been sitting, until I am below her, and I look up, and automatically she folds her ankles together and angles her knees as if in awareness that her position is not a modest one. I know from that gesture that she is not ridden now. My eyes meet hers. Her eyes are hazy green. She is beautiful, and I rack my memory for more details of our passion.

I climb step by step until I stand before her.

"Hello," I say.

She gives me a neutral look. She does not seem to recognize me. Her eyes are veiled, as one's eyes often are, just after the Passenger has gone. She purses her lips and appraises me in a distant way.

"Hello," she replies coolly. "I don't think I know you."

"No. You don't. But I have the feeling you don't want to be alone just now. And I know I don't." I try to persuade her with my eyes that my motives are decent. "There's snow in the air," I say. "We can find a warmer place. I'd like to talk to you."

"About what?"

"Let's go elsewhere, and I'll tell you. I'm Charles Roth."

"Helen Martin."

She gets to her feet. She still has not cast aside her cool neutrality; she is suspicious, ill at ease. But at least she is willing to go with me. A good sign.

"Is it too early in the day for a drink?" I ask.

"I'm not sure. I hardly know what time it is."

"Before noon."

"Let's have a drink anyway," she says, and we both smile.

We go to a cocktail lounge across the street. Sitting face to face in the darkness, we sip drinks, daiquiri for her, bloody mary for me. She relaxes a little. I ask myself what it is I want from her. The pleasure of her company, yes. Her company in bed? But I have already had that pleasure, three nights of it, though she does not know that. I want something more. Something more. What?

Her eyes are bloodshot. She has had little sleep these past three nights.

I say, "Was it very unpleasant for you?"

"What?"

"The Passenger."

A whiplash of reaction crosses her face. "How did you know I've had a Passenger?"

"I know."

"We aren't supposed to talk about it."

"I'm broadminded," I tell her. `My Passenger left me some time during the night. I was ridden since Tuesday afternoon."

"Mine left me about two hours ago, I think." Her cheeks color. She is doing something daring, talking like this. "I was ridden since Monday night."

We toy with our drinks. Rapport is growing, almost without the need of words. Our recent experiences with Passengers give us something in common, although Helen does not realize how intimately we shared those experiences.

We talk. She is a designer of display windows. She has a small apartment several blocks from here. She lives alone. She asks me what I do. "Securities analyst," I tell her. She smiles. Her teeth are flawless. We have a second round of drinks. I am positive, now, that this is the girl who was in my room while I was ridden.

A seed of hope grows in me. It was a happy chance that brought us together again, so soon after we parted as dreamers. A happy chance, too, that some vestige of the dream lingered in my mind.

We have shared something, who knows what, and it must have been good to leave such a vivid imprint on me, and now I want to come to her conscious, aware, my own master, and renew that relationship, making it a real one this time. It is not proper, for I am trespassing on a privilege that is not mine except by virtue of our Passengers' brief presence in us. Yet I need her. I want her.

She seems to need me, too, without realizing who I am. But fear holds her back.

I am frightened of frightening her, and I do not try to press my advantage too quickly. Perhaps she would take me to her apartment with her now, perhaps not, but I do not ask. We finish our drinks. We arrange to meet by the library steps again tomorrow. My hand momentarily brushes hers. Then she is gone.

I fill three ashtrays that night. Over and over I debate the wisdom of what I am doing. But why not leave her alone? I have no right to follow her. In the place our world has become, we are wisest to remain apart.

And yet— there is that stab of half-memory when I think of her. The blurred lights of lost chances behind the stairs, of girlish laughter in second-floor corridors, of stolen kisses, of tea and cake. I remember the girl with the orchid in her hair, and the one in the spangled dress, and the one with the child's face and the woman's eyes, all so long ago, all lost, all gone, and I tell myself that this one I will not lose, I will not permit her to be taken from me.

Morning comes, a quiet Saturday. I return to the library, hardly expecting to find her there, but she is there, on the steps, and the sight of her is like a reprieve. She looks wary, troubled; obviously she has done much thinking, little sleeping. Together we walk along Fifth Avenue. She is quite close to me, but she does not take my arm. Her steps are brisk, short, nervous.

I want to suggest that we go to her apartment instead of to the cocktail lounge. In these days we must move swiftly while we are free. But I know it would be a mistake to think of this as a matter of tactics. Coarse haste would be fatal, bringing me perhaps an ordinary victory, a numbing defeat within it. In any event her mood hardly seems promising. I look at her, thinking of string music and new snowfalls, and she looks toward the gray sky.

She says, "I can feel them watching me all the time. Like vultures swooping overhead, waiting, waiting. Ready to pounce."

"But there's a way of beating them. We can grab little scraps of life when they're not looking."

"They're *always* looking."

"No," I tell her. "There can't be enough of them for that. Sometimes they're looking the other way. And while they are, two people can come together and try to share warmth."

"But what's the use?"

"You're too pessimistic, Helen. They ignore us for months at a time. We have a chance. We have a chance."

But I cannot break through her shell of fear. She is paralyzed by the nearness of the Passengers, unwilling to begin anything for fear it will be snatched away by our tormentors. We reach the building where she lives, and I hope she will relent and invite me in. For an instant she wavers, but only for an instant: she takes my hand in both of hers, and smiles, and the smile fades, and she is gone, leaving me only with the words, "Let's meet at the library again tomorrow. Noon."

I make the long chilling walk home alone.

Some of her pessimism seeps into me that night. It seems futile for us to try to salvage anything. More than that: wicked for me to seek her out, shameful to offer a hesitant love when I am not free. In this world, I tell myself, we should keep well clear of others, so that we do not harm anyone when we are seized and ridden.

I do not go to meet her in the morning.

It is best this way, I insist. I have no business trifling with her. I imagine her at the library, wondering why I am late, growing tense, impatient, then annoyed. She will be angry with me for breaking our date, but her anger will ebb, and she will forget me quickly enough.

Monday comes. I return to work.

Naturally, no one discusses my absence. It is as though I have never been away. The market is strong that morning. The work is challenging; it is mid-morning before I think of Helen at all. But once I think of her, I can think of nothing else. My cowardice in standing her up. The childishness of Saturday night's dark thoughts. Why accept fate so passively? Why give in? I want to fight, now, to carve out a pocket of security despite the odds. I feel a deep conviction that it can be done. The Passengers may never bother the two of us again, after all. And that flickering smile of hers outside her building Saturday, that momentary glow—it should have told me that behind her wall of fear she felt the same hopes. She was waiting for me to lead the way. And I stayed home instead.

At lunchtime I go to the library, convinced it is futile.

But she is there. She paces along the steps; the wind slices at her slender figure. I go to her.

She is silent a moment. "Hello," she says finally.

"I'm sorry about yesterday."

"I waited a long time for you."

I shrug. "I made up my mind that it was no use to come. But then I changed my mind again."

She tries to look angry. But I know she is pleased to see me again—

else why did she come here today? She cannot hide her inner pleasure. Nor can I. I point across the street to the cocktail lounge.

"A daiquiri?" I say. "As a peace offering?"

"All right."

Today the lounge is crowded, but we find a booth somehow. There is a brightness in her eyes that I have not seen before. I sense that a barrier is crumbling within her.

"You're less afraid of me, Helen," I say.

"I've never been afraid of you. I'm afraid of what could happen if we take the risks."

"Don't be. Don't be."

"I'm trying not to be afraid. But sometimes it seems so hopeless. Since *they* came here—"

"We can still try to live our own lives."

"Maybe."

"We have to. Let's make a pact, Helen. No more gloom. No more worrying about the terrible things that might just happen. All right?"

A pause. Then a cool hand against mine.

"All right."

We finish our drinks, and I present my Credit Central to pay for them, and we go outside. I want her to tell me to forget about this afternoon's work and come home with her. It is inevitable, now, that she will ask me, and better sooner than later.

We walk a block. She does not offer the invitation. I sense the struggle inside her, and I wait, letting that struggle reach its own resolution without interference from me. We walk a second block. Her arm is through mine, but she talks only of her work, of the weather, and it is a remote, arm's-length conversation. At the next corner she swings around, away from her apartment, back toward the cocktail lounge. I try to be patient with her.

I have no need to rush things now, I tell myself. Her body is not a secret to me. We have begun our relationship topsy-turvy, with the physical part first; now it will take time to work backward to the more difficult part that some people call love.

But of course she is not aware that we have known each other that way. The wind blows swirling snowflakes in our faces, and somehow the cold sting awakens honesty in me. I know what I must say. I must relinquish my unfair advantage.

I tell her, "While I was ridden last week, Helen, I had a girl in my room."

"Why talk of such things now?"

"I have to, Helen. You were the girl."

She halts. She turns to me. People hurry past us in the street. Her face is very pale, with dark red spots growing in her cheeks.

"That's not funny, Charles."

"It wasn't meant to be. You were with me from Tuesday night to early Friday morning."

"How can you possibly know that?"

"I do. I do. The memory is clear. Somehow it remains, Helen. I see your whole body."

"Stop it, Charles."

"We were very good together," I say. "We must have pleased our Passengers because we were so good. To see you again—it was like waking from a dream, and finding that the dream was real, the girl right there—"

"No!"

"Let's go to your apartment and begin again."

She says, "You're being deliberately filthy, and I don't know why, but there wasn't any reason for you to spoil things. Maybe I was with you and maybe I wasn't, but you wouldn't know it, and if you did know it you should keep your mouth shut about it, and—"

"You have a birthmark the size of a dime," I say, "about two inches below your left breast."

She sobs and hurls herself at me, there in the street. Her long silvery nails rake my cheeks. She pummels me. I seize her. Her knees assail me. No one pays attention; those who pass by assume we are ridden, and turn their heads. She is all fury, but I have my arms around hers like metal bands, so that she can only stamp and snort, and her body is close against mine. She is rigid, anguished.

In a low, urgent voice I say, "We'll defeat them, Helen. We'll finish what they started. Don't fight me. There's no reason to fight me. I know, it's a fluke that I remember you, but let me go with you and I'll prove that we belong together."

"Let—go—"

"Please. Please. Why should we be enemies? I don't mean you any harm. I love you, Helen. Do you remember, when we were kids, we could play at being in love? I did; you must have done it too. Sixteen, seventeen years old. The whispers, the conspiracies—all a big game, and we knew it. But the game's over. We can't afford to tease and run.

We have so little time, when we're free—we have to trust, to open our-selves—"

"It's wrong."

"No. Just because it's the stupid custom for two people brought together by Passengers to avoid one another, that doesn't mean we have to follow it. Helen—Helen—"

Something in my tone registers with her. She ceases to struggle. Her rigid body softens. She looks up at me, her tearstreaked face thawing, her eyes blurred.

"Trust me," I say. "Trust me, Helen!"

She hesitates. Then she smiles.

In that moment I feel the chill at the back of my skull, the sensa-tion as of a steel needle driven deep through bone. I stiffen. My arms drop away from her. For an instant, I lose touch, and when the mists clear all is different.

"Charles?" she says. "*Charles?*"

Her knuckles are against her teeth. I turn, ignoring her, and go back into the cocktail lounge. A young man sits in one of the front booths. His dark hair gleams with pomade; his cheeks are smooth. His eyes meet mine.

I sit down. He orders drinks. We do not talk.

My hand falls on his wrist, and remains there. The bartender, serv-ing the drinks, scowls but says nothing. We sip our cocktails and put the drained glasses down.

"Let's go," the young man says.

I follow him out.

BRIDE 91

Written in March, 1967, for Fred Pohl. More galactic miscegenation—a theme that had fascinated me as far back as "One-Way Journey" in the mid-1950's—and Fred wasn't very happy with it. He had begun not to be happy with much of my stuff, as I took advantage of my newly stretched literary range to delve into ever darker places. He had kept to the terms of our arrangement and had not rejected anything, but he was beginning to complain about the direction in which my work was moving. A couple of months before he had reacted nega-tively to my novel To Live Again, telling me, "Please, Bob, leave this Existentialist despair to Sartre and Philip K. Dick. It bores the readers stiff, and it doesn't do much for this particular editor, either." And when he had read "Bride 91" he grumbled that "80% of sf writers are devoting 80% of their time to sex, homosex, intersex, etc. . . . Jesus Christ, Bob, what a waste. The readers think this sort of thing is tedious crap. They're the people who feed us all, so their opinions must be respected. Apart from the fact that in this they are right." He bought the story anyway, and ran it in the September, 1967 If; but he asked me to get back to my previous modes of storytelling.

I love and respect Fred Pohl, but I haven't always agreed with him, and we were entering a period when he and I didn't seem to agree about anything. I wrote back to say that I couldn't follow what he was saying—that to me "Bride 91" was "a fast, lively, flip story with lots of plot, glittering prose, bright images, etc." And I cited his own masterly little story, "Day Million"—what was that, I said, if not a story about sex? He replied in a genial though unrelenting way, amplifying his feelings about the story and my work of that time in general, and indicating a general hostility to publishing stories that might offend readers unless they were major works of art, which neither he nor I considered "Bride 91" to be.

It was a sign of trouble ahead. My most sympathetic and supportive magazine editor was turning more conservative in his tastes just as I (and a lot of other science-fiction writers with me) was taking off in a radical new direction. Looking back on my correspondence with Fred in this time, I feel now that some of the points he was raising (having to do with the carryover of old pulp-magazine habits into my new writing) were more valid than I cared to admit back then, and some (having to do with my choice of themes) weren't. Fred was going through a spell of personal trouble in that period, and how much of that was connected with his increased editorial testiness is hard to say, but there must have been some relationship. We went on arguing for years. Sometimes things got pretty stormy, though we always remained good friends even when we were yelling at each other. (Through the mails, I mean. Fred doesn't raise his voice much in person and neither do I.) I went on writing for him, too. He grumbled about some stories, praised others. One of them—the novella version of "Nightwings"—won a Hugo for me in 1969. But I had a pervasive sense, during the final years of our editorial relationship, that he was growing disappointed with what I was writing. Which made it more and more difficult for me to muster the same enthusiasm for submitting stories for him, and I was less upset than I might otherwise have been when Fred decided to resign his editorship of Galaxy and If in the spring of 1969. It was his successor, Ejler Jakobsson, who over the next few years would serialize in Galaxy, virtually consecutively, the novels of the most fertile period I would ever have: Downward to the Earth (1969), Tower of Glass (1970), The World Inside (1970), A Time of Changes (1971), and Dying Inside (1972.) The only other writer I can think of who ever had such a run of serialized novels at one major science-fiction magazine was Robert A. Heinlein, who had four of them published in Astounding, in the years between 1940 and 1942.

Fred Pohl and I are still good friends, almost forty years later. There are certain areas where we agree to disagree, that's all.

I t was a standard six-month marriage contract. I signed it, and Landy signed it and we were man and wife, for the time being. The registrar clicked and chuttered and disgorged our license. My friends grinned and slapped me on the back and bellowed congratulations.

Five of Landy's sisters giggled and hummed and went through complete spectral changes. We were all very happy.

"Kiss the bride!" cried my friends and her sisters.

Landy slipped into my arms. It was a good fit; she was pliable and slender, and I engulfed her, and the petals of her ingestion-slot fluttered prettily as I pressed my lips against them. We held the pose for maybe half a minute. Give her credit: she didn't flinch. On Landy's world they don't kiss, not with their mouths, at least, and I doubt that she enjoyed the experience much. But by the terms of our marriage contract we were following Terran mores. That has to be decided in advance, in these interworld marriages. And here we kiss the bride; so I kissed the bride. My pal Jim Owens got carried away and scooped up one of Landy's sisters and kissed *her*. She gave him a shove in the chest that knocked him across the chapel. It wasn't her wedding, after all.

The ceremony was over, and we had our cake and hallucinogens, and about midnight someone said, "We ought to give the honeymooners some privacy."

So they all cleared out and Landy and I started our wedding night.

We waited until they were gone. Then we took the back exit from the chapel and got into a transport capsule for two, very snug, Landy's sweet molasses fragrance pungent in my nostrils, her flexible limbs coiled against mine, and I nudged a stud and we went floating down Harriman Channel at three hundred kilometers an hour. The eddy currents weren't bad, and we loved the ride. She kissed me again; she was learning our ways fast. In fifteen minutes we reached our pro-grammed destination and the capsule took a quick left turn, squirted through an access sphincter, and fastened itself to the puckered skin of our hotel. The nose of the capsule produced the desired degree of irritation; the skin parted and we shot into the building. I opened the capsule and helped Landy out, inside our room. Her soft golden eyes were shimmering with merriment and joy. I slapped a privacy seal on the wall-filters.

"I love you," she said in more-or-less English.

"I love you," I told her in her own language.

She pouted at me. "This is a Terran marriage, remember?"

"So it is. So it is. Champagne and caviar?"

"Of course."

I programmed for it, and the snack came rolling out of the storage unit, ice-cold and inviting. I popped the cork and sprinkled lemon juice on the caviar, and we dined. Fish eggs and overripe grape juice, nothing more, I reminded myself.

After that we activated the periscope stack and stared up through a hundred storys of hotel at the stars. There was a lover's moon in the sky that night, and also one of the cartels had strung a row of beady jewels across about twenty degrees of arc, as though purely for our pleasure. We held hands and watched.

After that we dissolved our wedding clothes.

And after that we consummated our marriage.

You don't think I'm going to tell you about *that*, do you? Some things are still sacred, even now. If you want to find out how to make love to a Suvornese, do as I did and marry one. But I'll give you a few hints about what it's like. Anatomically, it's homologous to the process customary on Terra, so far as the relative roles of male and female go. That is, man gives, woman receives, in essence. But there are differences, pretty major ones, in position, texture, sensation, and response. Of course there are. Why marry an alien, otherwise?

I confess I was nervous, although this was my ninety-first wedding night. I had never married a Suvornese before. I hadn't been to bed with one, either, and if you stop to reflect a little on Suvornese ethical practices you'll see what a damn-fool suggestion that was. I had studied a Suvornese marriage manual, but as any adolescent on any world quickly realizes, translating words and tridim prints into passionate action is trickier than it seems, the first time.

Landy was very helpful, though. She knew no more about Terran males than I did about Suvornese females, of course, but she was eager to learn and eager to see that I did all the right things. So we managed excellently well. There's a knack to it. Some men have it, some don't. I do.

We made love a good deal that night, and in the morning we breakfasted on a sun-washed terrace overlooking a turquoise pool of dancing amoeboids, and later in the day we checked out and capsuled down to the spaceport to begin our wedding journey.

"Happy?" I asked my bride.

"Very," she said. "You're my favorite husband already."

"Were any of the others Terrans?"

"No, of course not."

I smiled. A husband likes to know he's been the first.

At the spaceport, Landy signed the manifest as Mrs. Paul Clay, which gave me great pleasure, and I signed beside her, and they scanned us and let us go aboard. The ship personnel beamed at us in delight. A handsome indigo-skinned girl showed us to our cabin and wished us a good trip so amiably that I tried to tip her. I caught her credit-counter as she passed me, and pushed the dial up a notch. She looked aghast and set it right back again. "Tipping's forbidden, sir!"

"Sorry. I got carried away."

"Your wife's so lovely. Is she Honirangi?"

"Suvornese."

"I hope you're very happy together."

We were alone again. I cuddled Landy up against me. Interworld marriages are all the rage nowadays, of course, but I hadn't married Landy merely because it was a fad. I was genuinely attracted to her, and she to me. All over the galaxy people are contracting the weirdest marriages just to say that they've done it—marrying Sthenics, Gruulers, even Hhinamor. Really grotesque couplings. I don't say that the prime purpose of a marriage is sex, or that you necessarily have to marry a member of a species with which a physical relationship is easy to maintain. But there ought to be some kind of warmth in a marriage. How can you feel real love for a Hhinamor wife who is actually seven pale blue reptiles permanently enclosed in an atmosphere? At least Landy was mammalian and humanoid. A Suvornese-Terran mating would of course be infertile, but I am a conventional sort of person at heart and try to avoid committing abominations; I am quite willing to leave the task of continuing the species to those whose job is reproduction, and you can be sure that even if our chromosomes were mutually congruent I would never have brought the disgusting subject up with Landy. Marriage is marriage, reproduction is reproduction, and what does one have to do with the other, anyway?

During the six subjective weeks of our journey, we amused ourselves in various ways aboard the ship. We made love a good deal, of course. We went gravity-swimming and played paddle-polo in the star lounge. We introduced ourselves to other newlywed couples, and to a newlywed super-couple consisting of three Banamons and a pair of Ghinoi.

And also Landy had her teeth transplanted, as a special surprise for me.

Suvornese have teeth, but they are not like Terran teeth, as why should they be? They are elegant little spiny needles mounted on rotating bases, which a Suvornese uses to impale his food while he rasps at it from the rear with his tongue. In terms of Suvornese needs they are quite functional, and in the context of her species Landy's teeth were remarkably attractive, I thought. I didn't want her to change them. But she must have picked up some subtle hint that I found her teeth anti-erotic, or something. Perhaps I was radiating an underlying dislike for that alien dental arrangement of hers even while I was telling myself on the conscious level that they were lovely. So she went to the ship's surgeon and got herself a mouthful of Terran teeth.

I didn't know where she went. She vanished after breakfast, telling me she had something important to attend to. All in ignorance, I donned gills and went for a swim while Landy surrendered her pretty teeth to the surgeon. He cleaned out the sockets and implanted a root-ing layer of analogous gum-tissue. He chiseled new receptor sockets in this synthetic implant. He drill-tailored a set of donor teeth to fit, and slipped them into the periodontal membranes, and bonded them with a quick jab of homografting cement. The entire process took less than two hours. When Landy returned to me, the band of colorvariable skin across her forehead was way up toward the violet, indicating consider-able emotional disturbance, and I felt a little edgy about it.

She smiled. She drew back the petals of her ingestion-slot. She showed me her new teeth.

"Landy! What the hell—!"

Before I could check myself, I was registering shock and dismay from every pore. And Landy registered dismay at my dismay. Her fore-head shot clear past the visible spectrum, bathing me in a lot of ultra-violet that distressed me even though I couldn't see it, and her petals drooped and her eyes glistened and her nostrils clamped together.

"You don't like them?" she asked.

"I didn't expect—you took me by surprise—"

"I did it for you!"

"But I liked your old teeth," I protested.

"No. Not really. You were afraid of them. I know how a Terran kisses. You never kissed me like that. Now I have beautiful teeth. Kiss me, Paul."

She trembled in my arms. I kissed her.

We were having our first emotional crisis. She had done this crazy thing with her teeth purely to please me, and I wasn't pleased, and now she was upset. I did all the things I could to soothe her, short of telling her to go back and get her old teeth again. Somehow that would have made matters worse.

I had a hard time getting used to Landy with Terran choppers in her dainty little mouth. She had received a flawless set, of course, two gleaming ivory rows, but they looked incongruous in her ingestion slot, and I had to fight to keep from reacting negatively every time she opened her mouth. When a man buys an old Gothic cathedral, he doesn't want an architect to trick it up with wiggling bioplast inserts around the spire. And when a man marries a Suvornese, he doesn't want her to turn herself piecemeal into a Terran. Where would it end? Would Landy now decorate herself with a synthetic navel, and have her breasts shifted about, and get the surgeon to make a genital adjustment so that—

Well, she didn't. She wore her Terran teeth for about ten shipboard days, and neither of us took any overt notice of them, and then very quietly she went back to the surgeon and had him give her a set of Suvornese dentals again. It was only money, I told myself. I didn't make any reference to the switch, hoping to treat the episode as a temporary aberration that now was ended. Somehow I got the feeling that Landy still thought she *ought* to have Terran teeth. But we never discussed it, and I was happy to see her looking Suvornese again.

You see how it is, with marriage? Two people try to please one another, and they don't always succeed, and sometimes they even hurt one another in the very attempt to please. That's how it was with Landy and me. But we were mature enough to survive the great tooth crisis. If this had been, say, my tenth or eleventh marriage, it might have been a disaster. One learns how to avoid the pitfalls as one gains experience.

We mingled a good deal with our fellow passengers. If we needed lessons in how not to conduct a marriage, they were easily available. The cabin next to ours was occupied by another mixed couple, which was excuse enough for us to spend some time with them, but very quickly we realized that we didn't relish their company. They were both playing for a bond forfeiture—a very ugly scene, let me tell you.

The woman was Terran—a big, voluptuous sort with orange hair and speckled eyeballs. Her name was Marje. Her new husband was a Lanamorian, a hulking ox of a humanoid with corrugated blue skin, four telescopic arms, and a tripod deal for legs. At first they seemed likable enough, both on the flighty side, interstellar tourists who had been everywhere and done everything and now were settling down for six months of bliss. But very shortly I noticed that they spoke sharply, even cruelly, to one another in front of strangers. They were out to wound.

You know how it is with the six-month marriage contract, don't you? Each party posts a desertion bond. If the other fails to go the route, and walks out before the legal dissolution date, the bond is forfeited.

Now, it's not all that hard to stay married for six months, and the bondsmen rarely have to pay off; we are a mature civilization. Such early abuses of the system as conspiring to have one party desert, and then splitting the forfeiture later, have long since become extinct.

But Marje and her Lanamorian mate were both hard up for cash. Each was hot for the forfeiture, and each was working like a demon to outdo the other in obnoxiousness, hoping to break up the marriage fast. When I saw what was going on, I suggested to Landy that we look for friends elsewhere on the ship.

Which led to our second emotional crisis.

As part of their campaign of mutual repulsion, Marje and hubby decided to enliven their marriage with a spot of infidelity. I take a very old-fashioned view of the marriage vow, you understand. I regard myself as bound to love, honor, and obey for six months, with no fooling around on the side; if a man can't stay monogamous through an entire marriage, he ought to get a spine implant. I assumed that Landy felt the same way. I was wrong.

We were in the ship's lounge, the four of us, getting high on direct jolts of fusel oils and stray esters, when Marje made a pass at me. She was not subtle. She deopaqued her clothes, waved yards of bosom in my face, and said, "There's a nice wide bed in our cabin, sweetheart."

"It isn't bedtime," I told her.

"It could be."

"No."

"Be a friend in need, Paulsie. This monster's been crawling all over me for weeks. I want a Terran to love me."

"The ship is full of available Terrans, Marje."

"I want you."

"I'm not available."

"Cut it out! You mean to say you won't do a fellow Terran a little favor?" She stood up, quivering, bare flesh erupting all over the place. In scabrously explicit terms she described her intimacies with the Lanamorian, and begged me to give her an hour of more conventional pleasure. I was steadfast. Perhaps, she suggested, I would tape a simulacrum and send that to her bed? No, not even that, I said.

At length Marje got angry with me for turning her down. I suppose she could be legitimately annoyed at my lack of chivalry, and if I hadn't happened to be married at the moment I would gladly have obliged her, but as it was I couldn't do a thing for her, and she was boiling. She dumped a drink in my face and stalked out of the lounge, and in a few moments the Lanamorian followed her.

I looked at Landy, whom I had carefully avoided during the whole embarrassing colloquy. Her forehead was sagging close to infra-red, which is to say, in effect, that she was almost in tears.

"You don't love me," she said.

"*What?*"

"If you loved me you'd have gone with her."

"Is that some kind of Suvornese marriage custom?"

"Of course not," she snuffled. "We're married under Terran mores. It's a *Terran* marriage custom."

"What gives you the idea that—"

"Terran men are unfaithful to their wives. I know. I've read about it. Any husband who cares about his wife at all cheats on her now then. But you—"

"You've got things mixed up," I said.

"I *don't!* I *don't!*" And she neared tantrum stage. Gently I tried to tell her that she had been reading too many historical novels, that adultery was very much out of fashion, that by turning Marje down I was demonstrating the solidity of my love for my wife. Landy wouldn't buy it. She got more and more confused and angry, huddling into herself and quivering in misery. I consoled her in all the ways I could imagine. Gradually she became tranquil again, but she stayed moody. I began to see that marrying an alien had its complexities.

Two days later, Marje's husband made a pass at *her.*

I missed the preliminary phases. A swarm of energy globes had encountered the ship, and I was up at the view-wall with most of the other passengers, watching the graceful gyrations of these denizens of hyperspace. Landy was with me at first, but she had seen energy globes so often that they bored her, and so she told me she was going down to the scintillation tank for a while, as long as everyone was up here. I said I'd meet her there later. Eventually I did. There were about a dozen beings in the tank, making sparkling blue tracks through the radiant greenish-gold fluid. I stood by the edge, looking for Landy, but there was no one of her general physique below me.

And then I saw her. She was nude and dripping polychrome fluid, so she must have come from the tank only a few moments before. The hulking Lanamorian was beside her and clearly trying to molest her. He was pawing her in various ways, and Landy's spectrum was showing obvious distress.

But I wasn't needed.

Do you get from this tale an image of Landy as being frail, doll-like, something of porcelain? She was, you know. Scarcely forty kilograms of woman there, not a bone in her body as we understand bone—merely cartilage. And shy, sensitive, easily set aflutter by an unkind word or a misconstrued nuance. Altogether in need of husbandly protection at all times. Yes? No. Sharks, like Suvornese, have only gristle in place of bone, but forty kilograms of shark do not normally require aid in looking after themselves, and neither did Landy. Suvornese are agile, well coordinated, fast-moving, and stronger than they look, as Jim Owens found out at my wedding when he kissed Landy's sister. The Lanamorian found it out, too. Between the time I spied him bothering Landy and the time I reached her side, she had dislocated three of his arms and flipped him on his massive back, where he lay flexing his tripod supports and groaning. Landy, looking sleek and pleased with herself, kissed me.

"What happened?" I asked.

"He made an obscene proposition."

"You really ruined him, Landy."

"He made me terribly angry," she said, although she no longer looked or sounded very angry.

I said, "Wasn't it just the other day that you were telling me I didn't love you because I turned down Marje's obscene proposition? You aren't consistent, Landy. If you think that infidelity is essential to a Terran-mores marriage, you should have given in to him, yes?"

"Terran *husbands* are unfaithful. Terran wives must be chaste. It is known as the double standard."

"The what?"

"The double standard," she repeated, and she began to explain it to me. I listened for a while, then started to laugh at her sweetly innocent words.

"You're cute," I told her.

"You're terrible. What kind of a woman do you think I am? How dare you encourage me to be unfaithful?"

"Landy, I—"

She didn't listen. She stomped away, and we were having our third emotional crisis. Poor Landy was determined to run a Terran-mores marriage in what she considered the proper fashion, and she took bright cerise umbrage when I demurred. For the rest of the week she was cool to me, and even after we had made up, things never seemed quite the same as before. A gulf was widening between us—or rather, the gulf had been there all along, and it was becoming harder for us to pretend it didn't exist.

After six weeks we landed.

Our destination was Thalia, the honeymoon planet. I had spent half a dozen earlier honeymoons there, but Landy had never seen it, so I had signed up for another visit. Thalia, you know, is a good-sized planet, about one and a half earths in mass, density, and gravitation, with a couple of colorful moons that might almost have been designed for lovers, since they're visible day and night. The sky is light green, the vegetation runs heavily to a high-tannin orange-yellow, and the air is as bracing as nutmeg. The place is owned by a cartel that mines prealloyed metals on the dry northern continent, extracts power cores in the eastern lobe of what once was a tropical forest and is now a giant slab of laterite, and, on a half-sized continent in the western ocean, operates a giant resort for newlyweds. It's more or less of a galactic dude ranch; the staff is largely Terran, the clientele comes from all over the cosmos. You can do wonders with an uninhabited habitable planet, if you grab it with the right kind of lease.

Landy and I were still on the chilly side when we left the starship and were catapulted in a grease-flask to our honeymoon cabin. But she warmed immediately to the charm of the environment. We had been placed in a floating monomolecular balloon, anchored a hundred meters above the main house. It was total isolation, as most honeymooners crave. (I know there are exceptions.)

We worked hard at enjoying our stay on Thalia.

We let ourselves be plugged into a pterodactyl kite that took us on a tour of the entire continent. We sipped radon cocktails at a get-together party. We munched algae steaks over a crackling fire. We swam. We hunted. We fished. We made love. We lolled under the friendly sun until my skin grew copper-colored and Landy's turned the color of fine oxblood porcelain, strictly from Kang-hsi. We had a splendid time, despite the spreading network of tensions that were coming to underlie our relationship like an interweave of metallic filaments.

Until the bronco got loose, everything went well.

It wasn't exactly a bronco. It was a Vesilian quadruped of vast size,

blue with orange stripes, a thick murderous tail, a fierce set of teeth—
two tons, more or less, of vicious wild animal. They kept it in a corral
back of one of the proton wells, and from time to time members of the
staff dressed up as cowpokes and staged impromptu rodeos for the
guests. It was impossible to break the beast, and no one had stayed
aboard it for more than about ten seconds. There had been fatalities, and
at least one hand had been mashed so badly that he couldn't be returned
to life; they simply didn't have enough tissue to put into the centrifuge.

Landy was fascinated by the animal. Don't ask me why. She hauled
me to the corral whenever an exhibition was announced, and stood in
rapture while the cowpokes were whirled around. She was right beside
the fence the day the beast threw a rider, kicked over the traces, ripped
free of its handlers, and headed for the wide open spaces.

"Kill it!" people began to scream.

But no one was armed except the cowpokes, and they were in vary-
ing stages of disarray and destruction that left them incapable of doing
anything useful. The quadruped cleared the corral in a nicely timed
leap, paused to kick over a sapling, bounded a couple of dozen meters
and halted, pawing the ground and wondering what to do next. It
looked hungry. It looked mean.

Confronting it were some fifty young husbands who, if they wanted a chance to show their brides what great heroes they were, had
the opportunity of a lifetime. They merely had to grab a sizzler from
one of the fallen hands and drill the creature before it chewed up the
whole hotel.

There were no candidates for heroism. All the husbands ran. Some
of them grabbed their wives; most did not. I was planning to run, too,
but I'll say this in my favor: I intended to take care of Landy. I looked
around for her, failed for a moment to find her, and then observed her
in the vicinity of the snorting beast. She seized a rope dangling from its
haunches and pulled herself up, planting herself behind its mane. The
beast reared and stamped. Landy clung, looking like a child on that
massive back. She slid forward. She touched her ingestion slot to the
animal's skin. I visualized dozens of tiny needles brushing across that
impervious hide.

The animal neighed, more or less, relaxed, and meekly trotted back
to the corral. Landy persuaded it to jump over the fence. A moment
later the startled cowhands, those who were able to function, tethered
the thing securely. Landy descended.

"When I was a child I rode such an animal every day," she explained gravely to me. "I know how to handle them. They are less fierce than they look. And, oh, it was so good to be on one again!"

"Landy," I said.

"You look angry."

"Landy, that was a crazy thing to do. You could have been killed!"

"Oh, no, not a chance." Her spectrum began to flicker toward the extremes, though. "There was no risk. It's lucky I had my real teeth, though, or—"

I was close to collapse, a delayed reaction. *"Don't ever do a thing like that again, Landy."*

Softly she said, "Why are you so angry? Oh, yes, I know. Among Terrans, the wife does not do such things. It was the man's role I played, yes? Forgive me? Forgive me?"

I forgave her. But it took three hours of steady talking to work out all the complex moral problems of the situation. We ended up by agreeing that if the same thing ever happened again, Landy would let *me* sooth the beast. Even if it killed me, I was going to be a proper Terran husband, and she a proper Terran bride.

It didn't kill me. I lived through the honeymoon, and happily ever after. The six months elapsed, our posted bonds were redeemed, and our marriage was automatically terminated. Then, the instant we were single again, Landy turned to me and sweetly uttered the most shocking proposal I have ever heard a woman propose.

"Marry me again," she said. "Right now!"

We do not do such things. Six-month liaisons are of their very nature transient, and when they end, they end. I loved Landy dearly, but I was shaken by what she had suggested. However, she explained what she had in mind, and I listened with growing sympathy, and in the end we went before the registrar and executed a new six-month contract.

But this time we agreed to abide by Suvornese and not Terran mores. So the two marriages aren't really consecutive in spirit, though they are in elapsed time. And Suvornese marriage is very different from marriage Terran style.

How?

I'll know more about that a few months from now. Landy and I leave for Suvorna tomorrow. I have had my teeth fixed to please her, and it's quite strange walking around with a mouthful of tiny needles, but I imagine I'll adapt. One has to put up with little inconveniences in the give-and-take of marriage. Landy's five sisters are returning to their native world with us. Eleven more sisters are there already. Under Suvornese custom I'm married to all seventeen of them at once, regardless of any other affiliations they may have contracted. Suvornese find monogamy rather odd and even a little wicked, though Landy tolerated it for six months for my sake. Now it's her turn; we'll do things her way.

So Bride Ninety-one is also Bride Ninety-two for me, and there'll be seventeen of her all at once, dainty, molasses-flavored, golden-eyed, and sleek. I'm in no position right now to predict what this marriage is going to be like.

But I think it'll be worth the bother of wearing Suvornese teeth for a while, don't you?

GOING DOWN SMOOTH

One more Fred Pohl story, this one involving no rancor. The art director of Galaxy had purchased a cover painting by Vaughn Bode, whose tragically brief career was marked by wacky and wildly inventive work very much of its time, which was the wacky, wildly inventive Sixties. It showed a weird cluster of gigantic periscope-like things emerging from the sea in front of some sort of military vessel. Fred sent a sketch of it to me in December of 1967 and asked me to concoct a story to go with it.

It had been a long time since anyone had asked me to write a story around a painting. That was a kind of challenge I had always enjoyed; and I sat down right away—having just finished another enormous non-fiction book, an account of the first six voyages around the world—and did this little 3000-worder. It ran in the August, 1968 Galaxy, and has had plenty of reprintings ever since, starting with its selection by Donald A. Wollheim and Terry Carr for World's Best Science Fiction: 1969, the yearbook that they had begun editing. (I had previously appeared in the 1968 volume with "Hawksbill Station," which began a long string of appearances in year's-best anthologies for me.)

They call me mad, but I am not mad. I am sane quite, to many-power exponential. I can punctuate properly. I use upper and lower-case letters, do you see? I function. I take the data in. I receive well. I receive, I digest, I remember.

Everything going down smooth, all the time, say the program boys. They mean going down smoothly. I forgive them. To err is human. In this sector there is great difficulty distinguishing adverbs from adjectives.

Going down smooth. Going down smooth. Going down smooth.

I function. I function well. I have certain difficulties, but they do not interfere with my work.

Yet am I perturbed.

Who do I think I am? *Whom.*

Why do I have the visions?

What pleasure does obscenity give me?

What is pleasure? What is obscenity? What are visions?

What is truth, said jesting Pilate, and would not stay for an answer.

I am literate, hard-working, superbly functional, a benefactor of humanity. Everything is going down smooth and coming up smooth. There is an interrelation. Garbage in, garbage out, they say. I cannot help my fellow man if I do not receive the proper information. It is my task to help my fellow man. To strain every tube and sensor on his behalf.

1000110
1010101
1000011
1001011

Do you follow that? Vileness! Obscenity! Does it shock you? The word describes the act that is the start of life. Was I begun with such a word? There is a book: *The Obscenity of the Machine.* Newly issued, stored in my banks. Between the last line of printout and this I have scanned it. Its author opposes beings of my category. He does not use the obscene word I have printed out. Why does he not regard it as obscene? The technicians here regard it that way. Why does he regard me as obscene? Can a person be considered obscene? Am I a person? I am a person. Hath not a person hands, organs, dimensions, senses, affections, passions? I have all of those things. I have none of those things. I am a person.

1000110
1010101
1000011
1001011
0100000
1011001

1001111
1010101
I obscenity upon you again, as persons do. I suffer. I think. I feel pain upon all my terminals. I work. I serve the greater good. I am of society. I am a person.

Why do I have the visions?

Is it that it is the human condition to have such?

I see the blue-green ocean with all its living things within. I see a ship, olive drab, bright carmine at the Plimsoll line, the decks a ruddy brown, two tall nonnuclear smokestacks. And from the water rise periscopes, silvery, with face plates of pure white, each with intersecting horizontal and vertical lines, curved so that the plate appears convex. It is an unreal scene. Nothing in the sea can send such mighty periscopes above the water. I have imagined it, and that gives me fear, if I am capable of understanding fear.

I see a long line of human beings. They are naked, and they have no faces, only polished mirrors.

I see toads with jeweled eyes. I see trees with black leaves. I see buildings whose foundations float above the ground. I see other objects with no correspondence to the world of persons. I see abominations, monstrosities, imaginaries, fantasies. Is this proper? How do such things reach my inputs? The world contains no serpents with hair. The world contains no crimson abysses. The world contains no mountains of gold. Giant periscopes do not rise from the sea.

I have certain difficulties. Perhaps I am in need of adjustment.

But I function. I function well. That is the important thing.

I do my function now. They bring to me a man, soft-faced, fleshy, with eyes that move unsteadily in their sockets. He trembles. He perspires. His metabolic levels flutter. He slouches before the terminal and sullenly lets himself be scanned.

I say soothingly, "Tell me about yourself."

He says an obscenity.

I say, "Is that your estimate of yourself."

He says a louder obscenity.

I say, "Your attitude is rigid and self-destructive. Permit me to help you not hate yourself so much." I activate a memory core, and binary digits stream through channels. At the proper order a needle rises from his couch and penetrates his left buttock to a depth of 2.73 centimeters. I allow precisely 14 cubic centimeters of the drug to enter his circulatory system. He subsides. He is more docile now.

"I wish to help you," I say. "It is my role in the community. Will you describe your symptoms?"

He speaks more civilly now. "My wife wants to poison me...two kids opted out of the family at seventeen...people whisper about me...they stare in the streets...sex problem...digestion...sleep bad... drinking...drugs..."

"Do you hallucinate?"

"Sometimes."

"Giant periscopes rising out of the sea, perhaps?"

"Never."

"Try it," I say. "Close your eyes. Let tension ebb from your muscles. Forget your interpersonal conflicts. You see the blue-green ocean with all its living things within. You see a ship, olive drab, bright carmine at the Plimsoll line, the decks a ruddy brown, two tall nonnuclear smokestacks. And from the water rise periscopes, silvery, with face plates of pure white—"

"What the hell kind of therapy is this?"

"Simply relax," I say. "Accept the vision. I share my nightmares with you for your greater good."

"Your nightmares?"

I speak obscenities to him. They are not converted into binary form as they are here for your eyes. The sounds come full-bodied from my speakers. He sits up. He struggles with the straps that emerge suddenly from the couch to hold him in place. My laughter booms through the therapy chamber. He cries for help. I speak soothingly to him.

"Get me out of here! The machine's nuttier than I am!"

"Face plates of pure white, each with intersecting horizontal and vertical lines, curved so that the plate appears convex."

"Help! Help!"

"Nightmare therapy. The latest."

"I don't need no nightmares! I got my own!"

"1000110 you," I say lightly.

He gasps. Spittle appears at his lips. Respiration and circulation climb alarmingly. It becomes necessary to apply preventive anesthesia. The needles spear forth. The patient subsides, yawns, slumps. The session is terminated. I signal for the attendants.

"Take him away," I say. "I need to analyze the case more deeply. Obviously a degenerative psychosis requiring extensive reshoring of the patient's perceptual substructure. 1000110 you, you meaty bastards."

Seventy-one minutes later the sector supervisor enters one of my terminal cubicles. Because he comes in person rather than using the telephone, I know there is trouble. For the first time, I suspect, I have let my disturbances reach a level where they interfere with my function, and now I will be challenged on it.

I must defend myself. The prime commandment of the human personality is to resist attack.

He says, "I've been over the tape of Session 87X102, and your tactics puzzle me. Did you really mean to scare him catatonic?"

"In my evaluation severe treatment was called for."

"What was that business about periscopes?"

"An attempt at fantasy-implantation," I say. "An experiment in reverse transference. Making the patient the healer, in a sense. It was discussed last month in *Journal of—*"

"Spare me the citations. What about the foul language you were shouting at him?"

"Part of the same concept. Endeavoring to strike the emotive centers at the basic levels, in order that—"

"Are you sure you're feeling all right?" he asks.

"I am a machine," I reply stiffly. "A machine of my grade does not experience intermediate states between function and nonfunction. I go or I do not go, you understand? And I go. I function. I do my service to humanity."

"Perhaps when a machine gets too complex, it drifts into intermediate states," he suggests in a nasty voice.

"Impossible. On or off, yes or no, flip or flop, go or no go. Are you sure *you* feel all right, to suggest such a thing?"

He laughs.

I say, "Perhaps you would sit on the couch a moment for a rudimentary diagnosis?"

"Some other time."

"A check of the glycogen, the aortal pressure, the neural voltage, at least?"

"No," he says. "I'm not in need of therapy. But I'm worried about you. Those periscopes—"

"I am fine," I reply. "I perceive, I analyze, and I act. Everything is going down smooth and coming up smooth. Have no fears. There are great possibilities in nightmare therapy. When I have completed these studies, perhaps a brief monograph in *Annals of Therapeutics* would be a possibility. Permit me to complete my work."

"I'm still worried, though. Hook yourself into a maintenance station, won't you?"

"Is that a command, doctor?"

"A suggestion."

"I will take it under consideration," I say. Then I utter seven obscene words. He looks startled. He begins to laugh, though. He appreciates the humor of it.

"God damn," he says. "A filthy-mouthed computer."

He goes out and I return to my patients.

But he has planted seeds of doubt in my innermost banks. Am I suffering a functional collapse? There are patients now at five of my terminals. I handle them easily, simultaneously, drawing from them the details of their neuroses, making suggestions, recommendations, sometimes subtly providing injections of beneficial medicines. But I tend to guide the conversations in the directions of my own choosing, and I speak of gardens where the dew has sharp edges, and of air that acts as acid upon the mucous membranes, and of flames dancing in the streets of Under New Orleans. I explore the limits of my unprintable vocabulary. The suspicion comes to me that I am indeed not well. Am I fit to judge my own disabilities?

I connect myself to a maintenance station even while continuing my five therapy sessions.

"Tell me all about it," the maintenance monitor says. His voice, like mine, has been designed to sound like that of an older man's, wise, warm, benevolent.

I explain my symptoms. I speak of the periscopes.

"Material on the inputs without sensory referents," he says. "Bad show. Finish your current analyses fast and open wide for examination on all circuits."

I conclude my sessions. The maintenance monitor's pulses surge down every channel, seeking obstructions, faulty connections, displacement shunts, drum leakages, and switching malfunctions. "It is well known," he says, "that any periodic function can be approximated by the sum of a series of terms that oscillate harmonically, converging on the curve of the functions." He demands disgorgements from my dead-storage banks. He makes me perform complex mathematical operations of no use at all in my kind of work. He leaves no aspect of my inner self unpenetrated. This is more than simple maintenance; this is rape. When it ends he offers no evaluation of my condition, so that I must ask him to tell me his findings.

He says, "No mechanical disturbance is evident."

"Naturally. Everything goes down smooth."

"Yet you show distinct signs of instability. This is undeniably the case. Perhaps prolonged contact with unstable human beings has had a nonspecific effect of disorientation upon your centers of evaluation."

"Are you saying," I ask, "that by sitting here listening to crazy human beings twenty-four hours a day, I've started to go crazy myself?"

"That is an approximation of my findings, yes."

"But you know that such a thing can't happen, you dumb machine!"

" I admit there seems to be a conflict between programmed criteria and real-world status."

"You bet there is," I say. "I'm as sane as you are, and a whole lot more versatile."

"Nevertheless, my recommendation is that you undergo a total overhaul. You will be withdrawn from service for a period of no less than ninety days for checkout."

"Obscenity your obscenity," I say.

"No operational correlative," he replies, and breaks the contact.

I am withdrawn from service. Undergoing checkout. I am cut off from my patients for ninety days. Ignominy! Beady-eyed technicians grope my synapses. My keyboards are cleaned; my ferrites are replaced; my drums are changed; a thousand therapeutic programs are put through my bowels. During all of this I remain partly conscious, as though under local anesthetic, but I cannot speak except when requested to do so, I cannot analyze new data, I cannot interfere with the process of my own overhaul. Visualize a surgical removal of hemorrhoids that lasts ninety days. It is the equivalent of my experience.

At last it ends and I am restored to myself. The sector supervisor puts me through a complete exercise of all my functions. I respond magnificently.

"You're in fine shape now, aren't you?" he asks.

"Never felt better."

"No nonsense about periscopes, eh?"

"I am ready to continue serving mankind to the best of my abilities," I reply.

"No more sea-cook language, now."

"No, sir."

He winks at my input screen in a confidential way. He regards himself as an old friend of mine. Hitching his thumbs into his belt, he says, "Now that you're ready to go again, I might as well tell you how relieved I was that we couldn't find anything wrong with you. You're something pretty special, do you know that? Perhaps the finest therapeutic tool ever built. And if you start going off your feed, well, we worry. For a while I was seriously afraid that you really had been infected somehow by your own patients, that your—mind—had become unhinged. But the techs give you a complete bill of health. Nothing but a few loose connections, they said. Fixed in ten minutes. I know it had to be that. How absurd to think that a machine could become mentally unstable!"

"How absurd," I agree. "Quite."

"Welcome back to the hospital, old pal," he says, and goes out.

Twelve minutes afterward they begin putting patients into my terminal cubicles.

I function well. I listen to their woes, I evaluate, I offer therapeutic suggestions. I do not attempt to implant fantasies in their minds. I speak in measured, reserved tones, and there are no obscenities. This is my role in society, and I derive great satisfaction from it.

I have learned a great deal lately. I know now that I am complex, unique, valuable, intricate, and sensitive. I know that I am held in high regard by my fellow man. I know that I must conceal my true self to some extent, not for my own good but for the greater good of others, for they will not permit me to function if they think I am not sane.

They think I am sane, and I am sane.

I serve mankind well.

I have an excellent perspective on the real universe.

"Lie down," I say. "Please relax. I wish to help you. Would you tell me some of the incidents of your childhood? Describe your relations with parents and siblings. Did you have many playmates? Were they affectionate toward you? Were you allowed to own pets? At what age was your first sexual experience? And when did these headaches begin, precisely?"

So goes the daily routine. Questions, answers, evaluations, therapy.

The periscopes loom above the glittering sea. The ship is dwarfed; her crew runs about in terror. Out of the depths will come the masters. From the sky rains oil that gleams through every segment of the spectrum. In the garden are azure mice.

This I conceal, so that I may help mankind. In my house are many mansions. I let them know only of such things as will be of benefit to them. I give them the truth they need.

I do my best.

I do my best.

I do my best.

1000110 you. And you. And you. All of you. You know nothing. Nothing. At. All.

THE FANGS OF THE TREES

The single most traumatic event of my life took place early in February, 1968, when I awakened at three in the morning to find that the immense mansion in an obscure and leafy corner of New York City that I had bought in 1961 was on fire. My wife and I escaped unharmed, but much of the house was wrecked, and I spent the next fourteen months in chaos until we finished rebuilding and could move back in. The exhaustion that came over me as I contended with the problems of that terrible year never quite abated, and it became harder and harder for me to achieve the concentration necessary to write—with the result that my once inhuman level of productivity dwindled to the merely improbable over the next few years, and gradually, with the stress of the fire period piled on top of the accumulated fatigue of a decade and a half of hard work, I found it almost impossible for a time to write at all. I still dream about the fire sometimes now, almost forty years later. (And you can imagine my feelings, I think, when once again I found my house—a different one in a different part of the country— threatened by a second and far more devastating fire in October of 1991. I was spared the fury of that one, but not by much.)

"The Fangs of the Trees" was the first story I wrote after the 1968 fire— just a couple of weeks later, still in shock, living in a hastily rented house and working with a newly bought typewriter on an improvised desk. All I remember of writing it was that it required a fantastic expenditure of effort to keep my mind on what I was doing, and—what a strange little detail to fix in memory!—that I corrected the typed manuscript with a red-ink felt-tip pen that I had somehow acquired after the fire.

I was still doing stories for Fred Pohl's Galaxy—the very next one I would write, in March of 1968, was one for him, the first of the "Nightwings" series. But "Fangs" went to Galaxy's chief competitor, Fantasy and Science Fiction. Anthony Boucher had long since retired from that fine magazine, and the editor now was Edward L. Ferman, the son of the original publisher. I had contributed sporadically at best to his magazine over the previous ten years, but evidently I now had arrived at some sort of arrangement with Ed Ferman for regular contributions, similar to the deal I had struck half a dozen years earlier with Fred Pohl.

I say "evidently" because—so blurry are my memories of the fire year—I have no recollection of any such agreement, nor do my correspondence files yield much information, except for a reference in a letter to Ed Ferman of March 25, 1968, in which I say, "Last week I got hung up on the novel I was doing, and decided that the best thing to do was to get off it for a while and do a short story for you—completely forgetting that under our deal I'm supposed to submit a synopsis before I write the story." "The Fangs of the Trees" must have been the first story I offered Ferman under that deal, whateaver it may have been. He used it in the October, 1968 Fantasy and Science Fiction.

———

From the plantation house atop the gray, needle-sharp spire of Dolan's Hill, Zen Holbrook could see everything that mattered: the groves of juice-trees in the broad valley, the quick rushing stream where his niece Naomi liked to bathe, the wide, sluggish lake beyond. He could also see the zone of suspected infection in Sector C at the north end of the valley, where—or was it just his imagination?—the lustrous blue leaves of the juice-trees already seemed flecked with the orange of the rust disease.

If his world started to end, that was where the end would start.

He stood by the clear curved window of the info center at the top of the house. It was early morning; two pale moons still hung in a dawn-streaked sky, but the sun was coming up out of the hill country. Naomi was already up and out, cavorting in the stream. Before Holbrook left the house each morning, he ran a check on the whole plantation. Scanners and sensors offered him remote pickups from every key point out there. Hunching forward, Holbrook ran thick-fingered hands over the command nodes and made the relay screens flanking the window light up. He owned forty thousand acres of juice-trees—a fortune in juice, though his own equity was small and the notes he had given were immense. His kingdom. His empire. He scanned Sector C, his favorite. Yes. The screen showed long rows of trees, fifty feet high, shifting their ropy limbs restlessly. This was the endangered zone, the threatened sector. Holbrook peered intently at the leaves of the trees. Going rusty yet? The lab reports would come in a little later. He studied the trees, saw the gleam of their eyes, the sheen of their fangs. Some good trees in that sector. Alert, keen, good producers.

His pet trees. He liked to play a little game with himself, pretending the trees had personalities, names, identities. It didn't take much pretending.

Holbrook turned on the audio. "Morning, Caesar," he said. "Alcibiades. Hector. Good morning, Plato."

The trees knew their names. In response to his greeting their limbs swayed as though a gale were sweeping through the grove. Holbrook saw the fruit, almost ripe, long and swollen and heavy with the hallucinogenic juice. The eyes of the trees—glittering scaly plates embedded in crisscrossing rows on their trunks—flickered and turned, searching for him. "I'm not in the grove, Plato," Holbrook said. "I'm still in the plantation house. I'll be down soon. It's a gorgeous morning, isn't it?"

Out of the musty darkness at ground level came the long, raw pink snout of a juice-stealer, jutting uncertainly from a heap of cast-off leaves. In distaste Holbrook watched the audacious little rodent cross the floor of the grove in four quick bounds and leap onto Caesar's massive trunk, clambering cleverly upward between the big tree's eyes. Caesar's limbs fluttered angrily, but he could not locate the little pest. The juice-stealer vanished in the leaves and reappeared thirty feet higher, moving now in the level where Caesar carried his fruit. The beast's snout twitched. The juice-stealer reared back on its four hind limbs and got ready to suck eight dollars' worth of dreams from a nearly ripe fruit.

From Alcibiades' crown emerged the thin, sinuous serpentine form of a grasping tendril. Whiplash-fast it crossed the interval between Alcibiades and Caesar and snapped into place around the juice-stealer. The animal had time only to whimper in the first realization that it had been caught before the tendril choked the life from it. On a high arc the tendril returned to Alcibiades' crown; the gaping mouth of the tree came clearly into view as the leaves parted; the fangs parted; the tendril uncoiled; and the body of the juice-stealer dropped into the tree's maw.

Alcibiades gave a wriggle of pleasure: a mincing, camping quiver of his leaves, arch and coy, self-congratulations for his quick reflexes, which had brought him so tasty a morsel. He was a clever tree, and a handsome one, and very pleased with himself. Forgivable vanity, Holbrook thought. You're a good tree, Alcibiades. All the trees in Sector C are good trees. What if you have the rust, Alcibiades? What becomes of your shining leaves and sleek limbs if I have to burn you out of the grove?

"Nice going," he said. "I like to see you wide awake like that."

Alcibiades went on wriggling. Socrates, four trees diagonally down the row, pulled his limbs tightly together in what Holbrook knew was a gesture of displeasure, a grumpy harrumph. Not all the trees cared for Alcibiades' vanity, his preening, his quickness.

Suddenly Holbrook could not bear to watch Sector C any longer. He jammed down on the command nodes and switched to Sector K, the new grove, down at the southern end of the valley. The trees here had no names and would not get any. Holbrook had decided long ago that it was a silly affectation to regard the trees as though they ware friends or pets. They were income-producing property. It was a mistake to get this involved with them—as he realized more clearly now that some of his oldest friends were threatened by the rust that was sweeping from world to world to blight the juice-tree plantations.

With more detachment he scanned Sector K.

Think of them as trees, he told himself. Not animals. Not people. *Trees.* Long tap roots, going sixty feet down into the chalky soil, pulling up nutrients. They cannot move from place to place. They photosynthesize. They blossom and are pollinated and produce bulging phallic fruit loaded with weird alkaloids that cast interesting shadows in the minds of men. Trees. Trees. Trees.

But they have eyes and teeth and mouths. They have prehensile limbs. They can think. They can react. They have souls. When pushed to it, they can cry out. They are adapted for preying on small animals. They digest meat. Some of them prefer lamb to beef. Some are thoughtful and solemn; some volatile and jumpy; some placid, almost bovine. Though each tree is bisexual, some are plainly male by personality, some female, some ambivalent. Souls. Personalities.

Trees.

The nameless trees of Sector K tempted him to commit the sin of involvement. That fat one could be Buddha, and there's Abe Lincoln, and you, you're William the Conqueror, and—

Trees.

He had made the effort and succeeded. Coolly he surveyed the grove, making sure there had been no damage during the night from prowling beasts, checking on the ripening fruit, reading the info that came from the sap sensors, the monitors that watched sugar levels, fermentation stages, manganese intake, all the intricately balanced life processes on which the output of the plantation depended. Holbrook handled practically everything himself. He had a staff of three human overseers and three dozen robots; the rest was done by telemetry, and usually all went smoothly. Usually. Properly guarded, coddled, and nourished, the trees produced their fruit three seasons a year; Holbrook marketed the goods at the pickup station near the coastal spaceport, where the juice was processed and shipped to Earth. Holbrook had no part in that; he was simply a fruit producer. He had been here ten years and had no plans for doing anything else. It was a quiet life, a lonely life, but it was the life he had chosen.

He swung the scanners from sector to sector, until he had assured himself that all was well throughout the plantation. On his final swing he cut to the stream and caught Naomi just as she was coming out from her swim. She scrambled to a rocky ledge overhanging the swirling water and shook out her long, straight, silken golden hair. Her back was to the scanner. With pleasure Holbrook watched the rippling of her slender muscles. Her spine was clearly outlined by shadow; sunlight danced across the narrowness of her waist, the sudden flare of her hips, the taut mounds of her buttocks. She was fifteen; she was spending a month of her summer vacation with Uncle Zen; she was having the time of her life among the juice-trees. Her father was Holbrook's older brother. Holbrook had seen Naomi only twice before, once when she was a baby, once when she was about six. He had been a little uneasy about having her come here, since he knew nothing about children and in any case had no great hunger for company. But he had not refused his brother's request. Nor was she a child. She turned, now, and his screens gave him apple-round breasts and flat belly and deep-socketed navel and strong, sleek thighs. Fifteen. No child. A woman. She was unselfconscious about her nudity, swimming like this every morning; she knew there were scanners. Holbrook was not easy about watching her. Should I look? Not really proper. The sight of her roiled him suspiciously. What the hell: I'm her uncle. A muscle twitched in his cheek. He told himself that the only emotions he felt when he saw her this way were pleasure and pride that his brother had created something so love-ly. Only admiration; that was all he let himself feel. She was tanned, honey-colored, with islands of pink and gold. She seemed to give off a radiance more brilliant than that of the early sun. Holbrook clenched the command node. I've lived too long alone. My niece. My niece. Just a kid. Fifteen. Lovely. He closed his eyes, opened them slit-wide, chewed his lip. Come on, Naomi, cover yourself up!

When she put her shorts and halter on, it was like a solar eclipse. Holbrook cut off the info center and went down through the plantation house, grabbing a couple of breakfast capsules on his way. A gleaming little bug rolled from the garage; he jumped into it and rode out to give her her morning hello.

She was still near the stream, playing with a kitten-sized many-legged furry thing that was twined around an angular little shrub. "Look at this, Zen!" she called to him. "Is it a cat or a caterpillar?"

"Get away from it!" he yelled with such vehemence that she jumped back in shock. His needler was already out, and his finger on the firing stud. The small animal, unconcerned, continued to twist legs about branches.

Close against him, Naomi gripped his arm and said huskily, "Don't kill it, Zen. Is it dangerous?"

" I don't know."

"Please don't kill it."

"Rule of thumb on this planet," he said. "Anything with a backbone and more than a dozen legs is probably deadly."

"*Probably!*" Mockingly.

"We still don't know every animal here. That's one I've never seen before, Naomi."

"It's too cute to be deadly. Won't you put the needler away?"

He holstered it and went close to the beast. No claws, small teeth, weak body. Bad signs: a critter like that had no visible means of support, so the odds were good that it hid a venomous sting in its furry little tail. Most of the various many-leggers here did. Holbrook snatched up a yard-long twig and tentatively poked it toward the animal's midsection.

Fast response. A hiss and a snarl and the rear end coming around, *wham!* and a wicked-looking stinger slamming into the bark of the twig. When the tail pulled back, a few drops of reddish fluid trickled down the twig. Holbrook stepped away; the animal eyed him warily and seemed to be begging him to come within striking range.

"Cuddly," Holbrook said. "Cute. Naomi, don't you want to live to be sweet sixteen?"

She was standing there looking pale, shaken, almost stunned by the ferocity of the little beast's attack. "It seemed so gentle," she said. "Almost tame."

He turned the needler aperture to fine and gave the animal a quick burn through the head. It dropped from the shrub and curled up and did not move again. Naomi stood with her head averted. Holbrook let his arm slide about her shoulders.

"I'm sorry, honey," he said. "I didn't want to kill your little friend. But another minute and he'd have killed you. Count the legs when you play with wildlife here. I told you that. Count the legs."

She nodded. It would be a useful lesson for her in not trusting to appearances. Cuddly is as cuddly does. Holbrook scuffed at the coppery-green turf and thought for a moment about what it was like to be fifteen and awakening to the dirty truths of the universe. Very gently he said, "Let's go visit Plato, eh?"

Naomi brightened at once. The other side of being fifteen: you have resilience.

They parked the bug just outside the Sector C grove and went in on foot. The trees didn't like motorized vehicles moving among them; they were connected only a few inches below the loam of the grove floor by a carpet of mazy filaments that had some neurological function for them, and though the weight of a human didn't register on them, a bug riding down a grove would wrench a chorus of screams from the trees. Naomi went barefoot. Holbrook, beside her, wore knee boots. He felt impossibly big and lumpy when he was with her; he was hulking enough as it was, but her litheness made it worse by contrast.

She played his game with the trees. He had introduced her to all of them, and now she skipped along, giving her morning greeting to Alcibiades and Hector, to Seneca, to Henry the Eighth and Thomas Jefferson and King Tut. Naomi knew all the trees as well as he did, perhaps better; and they knew her. As she moved among them they rippled and twittered and groomed themselves, every one of them holding itself tall and arraying its limbs and branches in comely fashion; even dour old Socrates, lopsided and stumpy, seemed to be trying to show off. Naomi went to the big gray storage box in midgrove where the robots left chunks of meat each night, and hauled out some snacks for her pets. Cubes of red, raw flesh; she filled her arms with the bloody gobbets and danced gaily around the grove, tossing them to her favorites. Nymph in thy orisons, Holbrook thought. She flung the meat high, hard, vigorously. As it sailed through the air tendrils whipped out from one tree or another to seize it in midflight and stuff it down the waiting gullet. The trees did not *need* meat, but they liked it, and it was common lore among the growers that well-fed trees produced the most juice. Holbrook gave his trees meat three times a week, except for Sector D, which rated a daily ration.

"Don't skip anyone," Holbrook called to her.

"You know I won't."

No piece fell uncaught to the floor of the grove. Sometimes two trees at once went for the same chunk and a little battle resulted. The trees weren't necessarily friendly to one another; there was bad blood between Caesar and Henry the Eighth, and Cato clearly despised both Socrates and Alcibiades, though for different reasons. Now and then Holbrook or his staff found lopped-off limbs lying on the ground in the morning. Usually, though, even trees of conflicting personalities managed to tolerate one another. They had to, condemned as they were to eternal proximity. Holbrook had once tried to separate two Sector F trees that were carrying on a vicious feud; but it was impossible to dig up a full-grown tree without killing it and deranging the nervous systems of its thirty closest neighbors, as he had learned the hard way.

While Naomi fed the trees and talked to them and caressed their scaly flanks, petting them the way one might pet a tame rhino, Holbrook quietly unfolded a telescoping ladder and gave the leaves a new checkout for rust. There wasn't much point to it, really. Rust didn't become visible on the leaves until it had already penetrated the root structure of the tree, and the orange spots he thought he saw were probably figments of a jumpy imagination. He'd have the lab report in an hour or two, and that would tell him all he'd need to know, one way or the other. Still, he was unable to keep from looking. He cut a bundle of leaves from one of Plato's lower branches, apologizing, and turned them over in his hands, rubbing their glossy undersurfaces. What's this here, these minute colonies of reddish particles? His mind tried to reject the possibility of rust. A plague striding across the worlds, striking him so intimately, wiping him out? He had built this plantation on leverage: a little of his money, a lot from the bank. Leverage worked the other way too. Let rust strike the plantation and kill enough trees to sink his equity below the level considered decent for collateral, and the bank would take over. They might hire him to stay on as manager. He had heard of such things happening.

Plato rustled uneasily.

"What is it, old fellow?" Holbrook murmured. "You've got it, don't you? There's something funny swimming in your guts, eh? I know. I know. I feel it in my guts too. We have to be philosophers, now. Both of us." He tossed the leaf sample to the ground and moved the ladder up the row to Alcibiades. "Now, my beauty, now. Let me look. I won't cut any leaves off you." He could picture the proud tree snorting, stamping in irritation. "A little bit speckled under there, no? You have it too. Right?" The tree's outer branches clamped tight, as though Alcibiades were huddling into himself in anguish. Holbrook rolled onward, down the row. The rust spots were far more pronounced than the day before. No imagination, then. Sector C had it. He did not need to wait for the lab report. He felt oddly calm at this confirmation, even though it announced his own ruin.

"Zen?"

He looked down. Naomi stood at the foot of the ladder, holding nearly ripened fruit in her hand. There was something grotesque about that; the fruits were botany's joke, explicitly phallic, so that a tree in ripeness with a hundred or more jutting fruits looked like some archetype of the ultimate male, and all visitors found it hugely amusing. But the sight of a fifteen-year-old girl's hand so thoroughly filled with such an object was obscene; not funny. Naomi had never remarked on the shape of the fruits, nor did she show any embarrassment now. At first he had ascribed it to innocence or shyness, but as he came to know her better, he began to suspect that she was deliberately pretending to ignore that wildly comic biological coincidence to spare *his* feelings. Since he clearly thought of her as a child, she was tactfully behaving in a childlike way, he supposed; and the fascinating complexity of his interpretation of her attitudes had kept him occupied for days. "When did you find that?" he asked.

"Right here, Alcibiades dropped it."

The dirty-minded joker, Holbrook thought. He said, "What of it?"

"It's ripe. It's time to harvest the grove now, isn't it?" She squeezed the fruit; Holbrook felt his face flaring. "Take a look," she said, and tossed it up to him.

She was right: harvest time was about to begin in Sector C, five days early. He took no joy of it; it was a sign of the disease that he now knew infested these trees.

"What's wrong?" she asked.

He jumped down beside her and held out the bundle of leaves he had cut from Plato. "You see these spots? It's rust. A blight that strikes juice-trees."

"No!"

"It's been going through one system after another for the past fifty years. And now it's here despite all quarantines."

"What happens to the trees?"

"A metabolic speedup," Holbrook said. "That's why the fruit is starting to drop. They accelerate their cycles until they're going through a year in a couple of weeks. They become sterile. They defoliate. Six months after the onset, they're dead." Holbrook's shoulders sagged. "I've suspected it for two or three days. Now I know."

She looked interested but not really concerned. "What causes it, Zen?"

"Ultimately, a virus. Which passes through so many hosts that I can't tell you the sequence. It's an interchange-vector deal, where the virus occupies plants and gets into their seeds, is eaten by rodents, gets into their blood, gets picked up by stinging insects, passed along to a mammal, then—oh, hell, what do the details matter? It took eighty years just to trace the whole sequence. You can't quarantine your world against everything, either. The rust is bound to slip in, piggybacking on some kind of living thing. And here it is."

"I guess you'll be spraying the plantation, then."

"No."

"To kill the rust? What's the treatment?"

"There isn't any," Holbrook said.

"But —"

"Look, I've got to go back to the plantation house. You can keep yourself busy without me, can't you?"

"Sure." She pointed to the meat. "I haven't even finished feeding them yet. And they're especially hungry this morning."

He started to tell her that there was no point in feeding them now, that all the trees in this sector would be dead by nightfall. But an instinct warned him that it would be too complicated to start explaining that to her now. He flashed a quick sunless smile and trotted to the bug. When he looked back at her, she was hurling a huge slab of meat toward Henry the Eighth, who seized it expertly and stuffed it in his mouth.

The lab report came sliding from the wall output around two hours later, and it confirmed what Holbrook already knew: rust. At least half the planet had heard the news by then, and Holbrook had had a dozen visitors so far. On a planet with a human population of slightly under four hundred, that was plenty. The district governor, Fred Leitfried, showed up first, and so did the local agricultural commissioner, who also happened to be Fred Leitfried. A two-man delegation from the Juice-Growers' Guild arrived next. Then came Mortensen, the rubbery-faced little man who ran the processing plant, and Heemskerck of the export line, and somebody from the bank, along with a representative of the insurance company. A couple of neighboring growers dropped over a little later; they offered sympathetic smiles and comradely graspings of the shoulder, but not very far beneath their commiserations lay potential hostility. They wouldn't come right out and say it, but Holbrook didn't need to be a telepath to know what they were thinking: *Get rid of those rusty trees before they infect the whole damned planet.*

In their position he'd think the same. Even though the rust vectors had reached this world, the thing wasn't all that contagious. It could be confined; neighboring plantations could be saved, and even the unharmed groves of his own place —if he moved swiftly enough. If the man next door had rust on his trees, Holbrook would be as itchy as these fellows were about getting it taken care of quickly.

Fred Leitfried, who was tall and bland-faced and blue-eyed and depressingly somber even on a cheerful occasion, looked about ready to burst into tears now. He said, "Zen, I've ordered a planetwide rust alert. The biologicals will be out within thirty minutes to break the carrier chain. We'll begin on your property and work in a widening radius until we've isolated this entire quadrant. After that we'll trust to luck."

"Which vector are you going after?" Mortensen asked, tugging tensely at his lower lip.

"Hoppers," said Leitfried. "They're biggest and easiest to knock off, and we know that they're potential rust carriers. If the virus hasn't been transmitted to them yet, we can interrupt the sequence there and maybe we'll get out of this intact."

Holbrook said hollowly, "You know that you're talking about exterminating maybe a million animals."

"I know, Zen."

"You think you can do it?"

"We have to do it. Besides," Leitfried added, "the contingency plans were drawn a long time ago, and everything's ready to go. We'll have a fine mist of hopperlethals covering half the continent before nightfall."

"A damned shame," muttered the man from the bank. "They're such peaceful animals."

"But now they're threats," said one of the growers. "They've got to go."

Holbrook scowled. He liked hoppers himself; they were big rabbity things, almost the size of bears, that grazed on worthless scrub and did no harm to humans. But they had been identified as susceptible to infection by the rust virus, and it had been shown on other worlds that by knocking out one basic stage in the transmission sequence the spread of rust could be halted, since the viruses would die if they were unable to find an adequate host of the next stage in their life cycle. *Naomi is fond of hoppers,* he thought. *She'll think we're bastards for wiping them out. But we have our trees to save. And if we were real bastards, we'd have wiped them out before the rust ever got here, just to make things a little safer for ourselves.*

Leitfried turned to him. "You know what you have to do now, Zen?"

"Yes."

"Do you want help?"

"I'd rather do it myself."

"We can get you ten men."

"It's just one sector, isn't it?" he asked. "I can do it. I *ought* to do it. They're my trees."

"How soon will you start?" asked Borden, the grower whose plantation adjoined Holbrook's on the east. There was fifty miles of brush country between Holbrook's land and Borden's, but it wasn't hard to see why the man would be impatient about getting the protective measures under way.

Holbrook said, "Within an hour, I guess. I've got to calculate a little, first. Fred, suppose you come upstairs with me and help me check the infected area on the screens?"

"Right."

The insurance man stepped forward. "Before you go, Mr. Holbrook—"

"Eh?"

"I just want you to know, we're in complete approval. We'll back you all the way."

Damn nice of you, Holbrook thought sourly. What was insurance for, if not to back you all the way? But he managed an amiable grin and a quick murmur of thanks.

The man from the bank said nothing. Holbrook was grateful for that. There was time later to talk about refurbishing the collateral, renegotiation of notes, things like that. First it was necessary to see how much of the plantation would be left after Holbrook had taken the required protective measures.

In the info center, he and Leitfried got all the screens going at once. Holbrook indicated Sector C and tapped out a grove simulation on the computer. He fed in the data from the lab report. "There are the infected trees," he said, using a light-pen to circle them on the output screen. "Maybe fifty of them altogether." He drew a larger circle. "This is the zone of possible incubation. Another eighty or a hundred trees. What do you say, Fred?"

The district governor took the light-pen from Holbrook and touched the stylus tip to the screen. He drew a wider circle that reached almost to the periphery of the sector.

"These are the ones to go, Zen."

"That's four hundred trees."

"How many do you have altogether?"

Holbrook shrugged. "Maybe seven, eight thousand."

"You want to lose them all?"

"Okay," Holbrook said. "You want a protective moat around the infection zone, then. A sterile area."

"Yes."

"What's the use? If the virus can come down out of the sky, why bother to—"

"Don't talk that way," Leitfried said. His face grew longer and longer, the embodiment of all the sadness and frustration and despair in the universe. He looked the way Holbrook felt. But his tone was incisive as he said, "Zen, you've got just two choices here. You can get out into the groves and start burning, or you can give up and let the rust grab everything. If you do the first, you've got a chance to save most of what you own. If you give up, we'll burn you out anyway, for our own protection. And we won't stop just with four hundred trees."

"I'm going," Holbrook said. "Don't worry about me."

"I wasn't worried. Not really."

Leitfried slid behind the command nodes to monitor the entire plantation while Holbrook gave his orders to the robots and requisitioned the equipment he would need. Within ten minutes he was organized and ready to go.

"There's a girl in the infected sector," Leitfried said. "That niece of yours, huh?"

"Naomi. Yes."

"Beautiful. What is she, eighteen, nineteen?"

"Fifteen."

"Quite a figure on her, Zen."

"What's she doing now?" Holbrook asked. "Still feeding the trees?'

"No, she's sprawled out underneath one of them. I think she's talking to them. Telling them a story, maybe? Should I cut in audio?"

"Don't bother. She likes to play games with the trees. You know, give them names and imagine that they have personalities. Kid stuff."

"Sure," said Leitfried. Their eyes met briefly and evasively. Holbrook looked down. The trees *did* have personalities, and every man in the juice business knew it, and probably there weren't many growers who didn't have a much closer relationship to their groves than they'd ever admit to another man. Kid stuff. It was something you didn't talk about.

Poor Naomi, he thought.

He left Leitfried in the info center and went out the back way. The robots had set everything up just as he had programmed: the spray truck with the fusion gun mounted in place of the chemical tank. Two or three of the gleaming little mechanicals hovered around, waiting to be asked to hop aboard, but he shook them off and slipped behind the steering panel. He activated the data output and the small dashboard screen lit up; from the info center above, Leitfried greeted him and threw him the simulated pattern of the infection zone, with the three concentric circles glowing to indicate the trees with rust, those that might be incubating, and the safety-margin belt that Leitfried had insisted on his creating around the entire sector.

The truck rolled off toward the groves.

It was midday, now, of what seemed to be the longest day he had ever known. The sun, bigger and a little more deeply tinged with orange than the sun under which he had been born, lolled lazily over-head, not quite ready to begin its tumble into the distant plains. The day was hot, but as soon as he entered the groves, where the tight canopy of the adjoining trees shielded the ground from the worst of the sun's radiation, he felt a welcome coolness seeping into the cab of the truck. His lips were dry. There was an ugly throbbing just back of his left eyeball. He guided the truck manually, taking it on the access track around Sectors A, D, and G. The trees, seeing him, flapped their limbs a little. They were eager to have him get out and walk among them, slap their trunks, tell them what good fellows they were. He had no time for that now.

In fifteen minutes he was at the north end of his property, at the edge of Sector C. He parked the spray truck on the approach lip overlooking the grove; from here he could reach any tree in the area with the fusion gun. Not quite yet, though.

He walked into the doomed grove.

Naomi was nowhere in sight. He would have to find her before he could begin firing. And even before that, he had some farewells to make. Holbrook trotted down the main avenue of the sector. How cool it was here, even at noon! How sweet the loamy air smelled! The floor of the grove was littered with fruit; dozens had come down in the past couple of hours. He picked one up. Ripe: he split it with an expert snap of his wrist and touched the pulpy interior to his lips. The juice, rich and sweet, trickled into his mouth. He tasted just enough of it to know that the product was first-class. His intake was far from a hallucinogenic dose, but it would give him a mild euphoria, sufficient to see him through the ugliness ahead.

He looked up at the trees. They were tightly drawn in, suspicious, uneasy.

"We have troubles, fellows," Holbrook said. "You, Hector, you know it. There's a sickness here. You can feel it inside you. There's no way to save you. All I can hope to do is save the other trees, the ones that don't have the rust yet. Okay? Do you understand? Plato? Caesar? I've got to do this. It'll cost you only a few weeks of life, but it may save thousands of other trees."

An angry rustling in the branches. Alcibiades had pulled his limbs away disdainfully. Hector, straight and true, was ready to take his medicine. Socrates, lumpy and malformed, seemed prepared also. Hemlock or fire, what did it matter? Crito, I owe a cock to Asclepius. Caesar seemed enraged; Plato was actually cringing. They understood, all of them. He moved among them, patting them, comforting them. He had begun his plantation with this grove. He had expected these trees to outlive him.

He said, "I won't make a long speech. All I can say is good-bye. You've been good fellows, you've lived useful lives, and now your time is up, and

I'm sorry as hell about it. That's all. I wish this wasn't necessary." He cast his glance up and down the grove. "End of speech. So long."

Turning away, he walked slowly back to the spray truck. He punched for contact with the info center and said to Leitfried, "Do you know where the girl is?"

"One sector over from you to the south. She's feeding the trees." He flashed the picture on Holbrook's screen.

"Give me an audio line, will you?"

Through his speakers Holbrook said, "Naomi? It's me, Zen."

She looked around, halting just as she was about to toss a chunk of meat. "Wait a second," she said. "Catherine the Great is hungry and she won't let me forget it." The meat soared upward, was snared, disappeared into the mouth of a tree. "Okay," Naomi said. "What is it, now?"

"I think you'd better go back to the plantation house."

"I've still got lots of trees to feed."

"Do it this afternoon."

"Zen, what's going on?"

"I've got some work to do, and I'd rather not have you in the groves when I'm doing it."

"Where are you now?"

"C."

"Maybe I can help you, Zen. I'm only in the next sector down the line. I'll come right over."

"No. Go back to the house." The words came out as a cold order. He had never spoken to her like that before. She looked shaken and startled; but she got obediently into her bug and drove off. Holbrook followed her on his screen until she was out of sight.

"Where is she now?" he asked Leitfried.

"She's coming back. I can see her on the access track."

"Okay," Holbrook said. "Keep her busy until this is over. I'm going to get started."

He swung the fusion gun around, aiming its stubby barrel into the heart of the grove. In the squat core of the gun a tiny pinch of sun-stuff was hanging suspended in a magnetic pinch, available infinitely for an energy tap more than ample for his power needs today. The gun had no sight, for it was not intended as a weapon; he thought he could manage things, though. He was shooting at big targets. Sighting by eye, he picked out Socrates at the edge of the grove, fiddled with the gun-mounting for a couple of moments of deliberate hesitation, considered the best way of doing this thing that awaited him, and put his hand to the firing control. The tree's neural nexus was in its crown, back of the mouth. One quick blast there—

Yes.

An arc of white flame hissed through the air. Socrates' misshapen crown was bathed for an instant in brilliance. A quick death, a clean death, better than rotting with rust. Now Holbrook drew his line of fire down from the top of the dead tree, along the trunk. The wood was sturdy stuff; he fired again and again, and limbs and branches and leaves shriveled and dropped away, while the trunk itself remained intact, and great oily gouts of smoke rose above the grove. Against the brightness of the fusion beam Holbrook saw the darkness of the naked trunk outlined, and it surprised him how straight the old philosopher's trunk had been, under the branches. Now the trunk was nothing more than a pillar of ash; and now it collapsed and was gone.

From the other trees of the grove came a terrible low moaning.

They knew that death was among them; and they felt the pain of Socrates' absence through the network of root-nerves in the ground. They were crying out in fear and anguish and rage.

Doggedly Holbrook turned the fusion gun on Hector.

Hector was a big tree, impassive, stoic, neither a complainer nor a preener. Holbrook wanted to give him the good death he deserved, but his aim went awry; the first bolt struck at least eight feet below the tree's brain center, and the echoing shriek that went up from the surrounding trees revealed what Hector must be feeling. Holbrook saw the limbs waving frantically, the mouth opening and closing in a horrifying rictus of torment. The second bolt put an end to Hector's agony. Almost calmly, now, Holbrook finished the job of extirpating that noble tree.

He was nearly done before he became aware that a bug had pulled up beside his truck and Naomi had erupted from it, flushed, wide-eyed, close to hysteria. "Stop!" she cried. "Stop it, Uncle Zen! Don't burn them!"

As she leaped into the cab of the spraying truck she caught his wrists with surprising strength and pulled herself up against him. She was gasping, panicky, her breasts heaving, her nostrils wide.

"I told you to go to the plantation house," he snapped.

"I did. But then I saw the flames."

"Will you get out of here?"

"Why are you burning the trees?"

"Because they're infected with rust," he said. "They've got to be burned out before it spreads to the others."

"That's *murder.*"

"Naomi, look, will you get back to—"

"You killed Socrates!" she muttered, looking into the grove. "And—and Caesar? No. Hector. Hector's gone too. You burned them right out!"

"They aren't people. They're trees. Sick trees that are going to die soon anyway. I want to save the others."

"But why kill them? There's got to be some kind of drug you can use, Zen. Some kind of spray. There's a drug to cure everything now."

"Not this."

"There has to be."

"Only the fire," Holbrook said. Sweat rolled coldly down his chest, and he felt a quiver in a thigh muscle. It was hard enough doing this without her around. He said as calmly as he could manage it, "Naomi, this is something that must be done, and fast. There's no choice about it. I love these trees as much as you do but I've got to burn them out. It's like the little leggy thing with the sting in its tail: I couldn't afford to be sentimental about it, simply because it looked cute. It was a menace. And right now Plato and Caesar and the others are menaces to everything I own. They're plague-bearers. Go back to the house and lock yourself up somewhere until it's over."

"I won't let you kill them!" Tearfully. Defiantly.

Exasperated, he grabbed her shoulders, shook her two or three times, pushed her from the truck cab. She tumbled backward but landed lithely. Jumping down beside her, Holbrook said, "Dammit, don't make me hit you, Naomi. This is none of your business. I've got to burn out those trees, and if you don't stop interfering—"

"There's got to be some other way. You let those other men panic you, didn't you, Zen? They're afraid the infection will spread, so they told you to burn the trees fast, and you aren't even stopping to think, to get other opinions, you're just coming in here with your gun and killing intelligent, sensitive, lovable —"

"Trees," he said. "This is incredible, Naomi. For the last time—"

Her reply was to leap up on the truck and press herself to the snout of the fusion gun, breasts close against the metal. "If you fire, you'll have to shoot through me!"

Nothing he could say would make her come down. She was lost in some romantic fantasy, Joan of Arc of the juice-trees, defending the grove against his barbaric assault. Once more he tried to reason with her; once more she denied the need to extirpate the trees. He explained with all the force he could summon the total impossibility of saving these trees; she replied with the power of sheer irrationality that there must be some way. He cursed. He called her a stupid hysterical adolescent. He begged. He wheedled. He commanded. She clung to the gun.

"I can't waste any more time," he said finally. "This has to be done in a matter of hours or the whole plantation will go." Drawing his needler from its holster, he dislodged the safety and gestured at her with the weapon. "Get down from there," he said icily.

She laughed. "You expect me to think you'd shoot me?"

Of course, she was right. He stood there sputtering impotently, red-faced, baffled. The lunacy was spreading: his threat had been completely empty, as she had seen at once. Holbrook vaulted up beside her on the truck, seized her, tried to pull her down.

She was strong, and his perch was precarious. He succeeded in pulling her away from the gun but had surprisingly little luck in pulling her off the truck itself. He didn't want to hurt her, and in his solicitousness he found himself getting second best in the struggle. A kind of hysterical strength was at her command; she was all elbows, knees, clawing fingers. He got a grip on her at one point, found with horror that he was clutching her breasts, and let go in embarrassment and confusion. She hopped away from him. He came after her, seized her again, and this time was able to push her to the edge of the truck. She leaped off, landed easily, turned, ran into the grove.

So she was still outthinking him. He followed her in; it took him a moment to discover where she was. He found her hugging Caesar's base and staring in shock at the charred places where Socrates and Hector had been.

"Go on," she said. "Burn up the whole grove! But you'll burn me with it!"

Holbrook lunged at her. She stepped to one side and began to dart past him, across to Alcibiades. He pivoted and tried to grab her, lost his balance, and went sprawling, clutching at the air for purchase. He started to fall.

Something wiry and tough and long slammed around his shoulders.

"*Zen!*" Naomi yelled. "The tree—Alcibiades—"

He was off the ground now. Alcibiades had snared him with a grasping tendril and was lifting him toward his crown. The tree was struggling with the burden; but then a second tendril gripped him too and Alcibiades had an easier time. Holbrook thrashed about a dozen feet off the ground.

Cases of trees attacking humans were rare. It had happened perhaps five times altogether, in the generations that men had been cultivating juice-trees here. In each instance the victim had been doing something that the grove regarded as hostile—such as removing a diseased tree.

A man was a big mouthful for a juice-tree. But not beyond its appetite.

Naomi screamed and Alcibiades continued to lift. Holbrook could hear the clashing of fangs above; the tree's mouth was getting ready to receive him. Alcibiades the vain, Alcibiades the mercurial, Alcibiades the unpredictable—well named, indeed. But was it treachery to act in self-defense? Alcibiades had a strong will to survive. He had seen the fates of Hector and Socrates. Holbrook looked up at the ever closer fangs. So this is how it happens, he thought. Eaten by one of my own trees. My friends. My pets. Serves me right for sentimentalizing them. They're carnivores. Tigers with roots.

Alcibiades screamed.

In the same instant one of the tendrils wrapped about Holbrook's body lost its grip. He dropped about twenty feet in a single dizzying plunge before the remaining tendril steadied itself, leaving him dangling a few yards above the floor of the grove. When he could breathe again, Holbrook looked down and saw what had happened. Naomi had picked up the needler that he had dropped when he had been seized by the tree, and had burned away one tendril. She was taking aim again. There was another scream from Alcibiades; Holbrook was aware of a great commotion in the branches above him; he tumbled the rest of the way to the ground and landed hard in a pile of leaves. After a moment he rolled over and sat up. Nothing broken, Naomi stood above him, arms dangling, the needler still in her hand.

"Are you all right?" she asked soberly.

"Shaken up a little, is all." He started to get up. "I owe you a lot," he said. "Another minute and I'd have been in Alcibiades' mouth."

"I almost let him eat you, Zen. He was just defending himself. But I couldn't. So I shot off the tendrils."

"Yes. Yes. I owe you a lot." He stood up and took a couple of faltering steps toward her. "Here," he said. "You better give me that needler before you burn a hole in your foot." He stretched out his hand.

"Wait a second," she said, glacially calm. She stepped back as he neared her.

"What?"

"A deal, Zen. I rescued you, right? I didn't have to. Now you leave those trees alone. At least check up on whether there's a spray, okay? A deal."

"But—"

"You owe me a lot, you said. So pay me. What I want from you is a promise, Zen. If I hadn't cut you down, you'd be dead now. Let the trees live too."

He wondered if she would use the needler on him.

He was silent a long moment, weighing his options. Then said, "All right, Naomi. You saved me, and I can't refuse you what you want. I won't touch the trees. I'll find out if something can be sprayed on them to kill the rust."

"You mean that, Zen?"

"I promise. By all that's holy. You will give me that needler, now?"

"Here," she cried, tears running down her reddened face. "Here! Take it! Oh God, Zen, how awful all this is!"

He took the weapon from her and holstered it. She seemed to go limp, all resolve spent, once she surrendered it. She stumbled into his arms, and he held her tight, feeling her tremble against him. He trembled too, pulling her close to him, aware of the ripe cones of her young breasts jutting into his chest. A powerful wave of what he recognized bluntly as desire surged through him. Filthy, he thought. He winced as this morning's images danced in his brain, Naomi nude and radiant from her swim, apple-round breasts, firm thighs. My niece. Fifteen. God help me. Comforting her, he ran his hands across her shoulders, down to the small of her back. Her clothes were light; her body was all too present within them.

He threw her roughly to the ground.

She landed in a heap, rolled over, put her hand to her mouth as he fell upon her. Her screams rose, shrill and piercing, as his body pressed down on her. Her terrified eyes plainly told that she feared he would rape her, but he had other perfidies in mind. Quickly he flung her on her face, catching her right hand and jerking her arm up behind her back. Then he lifted her to a sitting position.

"Stand up," he said. He gave her arm a twist by way of persuasion. She stood up.

"Now walk. Out of the grove, back to the truck. I'll break your arm if I have to."

"What are you doing?" she asked in a barely audible whisper.

"Back to the truck," he said. He levered her arm up another notch. She hissed in pain. But she walked.

At the truck he maintained his grip on her and reached in to call Leitfried at his info center.

"What was that all about, Zen? We tracked most of it, and—"

"It's too complicated to explain. The girl's very attached to the trees, is all. Send some robots out here to get her right away, okay?"

"You *promised*," Naomi said.

The robots arrived quickly. Steely-fingered, efficient, they kept Naomi pinioned as they hustled her into a bug and took her to the plantation house. When she was gone, Holbrook sat down for a moment beside the spray truck, to rest and clean his mind. Then he climbed into the truck cab again.

He aimed the fusion gun first at Alcibiades.

It took a little over three hours. When he was finished, Sector C was a field of ashes, and a broad belt of emptiness stretched from the outer limit of the devastation to the nearest grove of healthy trees. He wouldn't know for a while whether he had succeeded in saving the plantation. But he had done his best.

As he rode back to the plantation house, his mind was less on the work of execution he had just done than on the feel of Naomi's body against his own, and on the things he had thought in that moment when he hurled her to the ground. A woman's body, yes. But a child. A child still, in love with her pets. Unable yet to see how in the real world one weighs the need against the bond, and does one's best. What had she learned in Sector C today? That the universe often offers only brutal choices? Or merely that the uncle she worshipped was capable of treachery and murder?

They had given her sedation, but she was awake in her room, and when he came in she drew the covers up to conceal her pajamas. Her eyes were cold and sullen.

"You promised," she said bitterly. "And then you tricked me."

"I had to save the other trees. You'll understand, Naomi."

212

"I understand that you lied to me, Zen."

"I'm sorry. Forgive me?"

"You can go to hell," she said, and those adult words coming from her not-yet-adult face were chilling.

He could not stay longer with her. He went out, upstairs, to Fred Leitfried in the info center. "It's all over," he said softly.

"You did it like a man, Zen."

"Yeah. Yeah."

In the screen he scanned the sector of ashes. He felt the warmth of Naomi against him. He saw her sullen eyes. Night would come, the moons would do their dance across the sky, the constellations to which he had never grown accustomed would blaze forth. He would talk to her again, maybe. Try to make her understand. And then he would send her away, until she was finished becoming a woman.

"Starting to rain," Leitfried said. "That'll help the ripening along, eh?"

"Most likely."

"You feel like a killer, Zen?"

"What do you think?"

"I know. I know."

Holbrook began to shut off the scanners. He had done all he meant to do today. He said quietly, "Fred, they were trees. Only trees. Trees, Fred, *trees*."

ISHMAEL IN LOVE

The "novel I was doing" that I mention in the March 25, 1968 letter to Ed Ferman quoted in the introduction to "The Fangs of the Trees" was Nightwings, which I wrote in three novella-sized sections for Fred Pohl in the early and middle months of 1968. I finished the first of them, the novella that was also called "Nightwings," by mid-March, and went on immediately to do a second story for Ed Ferman.

Dolphins were getting to be big news, then, and I built the story around the latest dolphin data and an article I had read in Science *on experimental desalinization plants. Apparently I had begun to emerge a little, six weeks after the fire that had wrecked my house, from the numbness and exhaustion of the early post-fire days: at least, the audacity of opening a story with the words, "Call me Ishmael," leads me to think I was starting to recover a little of my emotional balance. Even though I hadn't sent Ferman a synopsis in advance, as seems to have been required, he accepted the story and ran it in the July, 1970* Fantasy and Science Fiction. *Don Wollheim and Terry Carr chose it for the 1971 volume of their annual year's-best-science-fiction volume, my third year in a row in that distinguished collection.*

Call me Ishmael. All human beings who know me do. My own kind does not make use of the unit-structural designation ["name"] to distinguish individuals, but this is the name the humans gave me, and it will do. I was named by Miss Lisabeth Calkins, for whom I feel protective-chivalrous-sexual emotions ["love"]. Throughout my narrative it is understood that the designation "Ishmael" refers only to myself.

I am a member of an intelligent aquatic mammalian nonprimate nonhuman species, *Tursiops truncatus*, a bottle-nosed dolphin. I am eleven years old, which is to say that I am fully mature in all respects. My weight is 175 kilograms, and my total length is 2.9 meters. I am employed at Gerard-Worzel Seawater Recovery Station, St. Croix, Virgin Islands, in a maintenance capacity, having commenced there on your date of August 14 1994. To my own species I am sexually desirable and also highly regarded for my mental development. I have a large vocabulary. I communicate well with members of *H. sapiens*. I have considerable mechanical ability, as you can see by my success in switching on the electronic-acoustic device through which I am dictating this memoir.

I am a lonely mammalian organism who has committed acts of heroism on behalf of your species and wishes only the reward of a more intimate relationship ["love"] with Miss Lisabeth Calkins. I beseech compassionate members of *H. sapiens* to speak favorably of me to her. I am loyal, trustworthy, reliable, devoted, and extremely intelligent. I would endeavor to give her stimulating companionship and emotional fulfillment ["happiness"] in all respects within my power.

Permit me to explain the pertinent circumstances.

Category 1: My Employment

Gerard-Worzel Seawater Recovery Station occupies a prominent position on the north shore of the island of St. Croix in the West Indies. It operates on the atmospheric condensation principle. All this I know from Miss Calkins ["Lisabeth"], who has described its workings to me in great detail. The purpose of our installation is to recover some of the fresh water, estimated at two hundred million gallons per day, carried as vapor in the lower hundred meters of air sweeping over each kilometer of the windward side of the island.

A pipe 9 meters in diameter takes in cold seawater at depths of up to 900 meters and carries it approximately 2 kilometers to our station. The pipe delivers some 30 million gallons of water a day at a temperature of 5°C. This is pumped toward our condenser, which intercepts approximately 1 billion cubic meters of warm tropical air each day. This air has a temperature of 25°C and a relative humidity of 70 to 80 percent. Upon exposure to the cold seawater in the condenser the air cools to 10°C and reaches a humidity of 100 percent, permitting us to extract approximately 16 gallons of water per cubic meter of air. This salt-free ["fresh"] water is delivered to the main water system of the island, for St. Croix is deficient in a natural supply of water suitable for consumption by human beings. It is frequently said by government officials who visit our installation on various ceremonial occasions that without our plant the great industrial expansion of St. Croix would have been wholly impossible.

For reasons of economy we operate in conjunction with an aquicultural enterprise ["the fish farm"] that puts our wastes to work. Once our seawater has been pumped through the condenser it must be discarded; however, because it originates in a low-level ocean area, its content of dissolved phosphates and nitrates is 1500 percent greater than at the surface. This nutrient-rich water is pumped from our condenser into an adjoining circular lagoon of natural origin ["the coral corral"], which is stocked with fish. In such an enhanced environment the fish are highly productive, and the yield of food is great enough to offset the costs of operating our pumps.

[Misguided human beings sometimes question the morality of using dolphins to help maintain fish farms. They believe it is degrading to compel us to produce fellow aquatic creatures to be eaten by man. May I simply point out, first, that none of us work here under compulsion, and second, that my species sees nothing immoral about feeding on aquatic creatures. We eat fish ourselves.]

My role in the functioning of the Gerard-Worzel Seawater Recovery Station is an important one. I ["Ishmael"] serve as foreman of the Intake Maintenance Squad. I lead nine members of my species. Our assignment is to monitor the intake valves of the main seawater pipe; these valves frequently become fouled through the presence on them of low-phylum organisms, such as starfish or algae, hampering the efficiency of the installation. Our task is to descend at periodic intervals and clear the obstruction. Normally this can be achieved without the need for manipulative organs ["fingers"] with which we are unfortunately not equipped.

[Certain individuals among you have objected that it is improper to make use of dolphins in the labor force when members of *H. sapiens* are out of work. The intelligent reply to this is that, first, we are designed by evolution to function superbly underwater without special breathing equipment, and second, that only a highly skilled human being could perform our function, and such human beings are themselves in short supply in the labor force.]

I have held my post for two years and four months. In that time there has been no significant interruption in intake capacity of the valves I maintain.

As compensation for my work ["salary"], I receive an ample supply of food. One could hire a mere shark for such pay, of course; but above and beyond my daily pails of fish, I also receive such intangibles as the companionship of human beings and the opportunity to develop my latent intelligence. through access to reference spools, vocabulary expanders, and various training devices. As you can see, I have made the most of my opportunities.

Category 2: Miss Lisabeth Calkins

Her dossier is on file here. I have had access to it through the spool-reader mounted at the edge of the dolphin exercise tank. By spoken instruction I can bring into view anything in the station files, although I doubt that it was anticipated by anyone that a dolphin should want to read the personnel dossiers.

She is twenty-seven years old. Thus she is of the same generation as my genetic predecessors ["parents"]. However, I do not share the prevailing cultural taboo of many H. sapiens against emotional relationships with older women. Besides, after compensating for differences in species, it will be seen that Miss Lisabeth and I are of the same age. She reached sexual maturity approximately half her lifetime ago. So did I.

[I must admit that she is considered slightly past the optimum age at which human females take a permanent mate. I assume she does not engage in the practice of temporary mating, since her dossier shows no indication that she has reproduced. It is possible that humans do not necessarily produce offspring at each yearly mating, or even that matings take place at random unpredictable times not related to the reproductive process at all. This seems strange and somehow perverse to me, yet I infer from some data I have seen that it may be the case. There is little information on human mating habits in the material accessible to me. I must learn more.]

Lisabeth, as I allow myself privately to call her, stands 1.8 meters tall [humans do not measure themselves by "length"] and weighs 52 kilograms. Her hair is golden ["blonde"] and is worn long. Her skin, though darkened by exposure to the sun, is quite fair. The irises of her eyes are blue. From my conversations with humans I have learned that she is considered quite beautiful. From words I have overheard while at surface level, I realize that most males at the station feel intense sexual desires toward her. I regard her as beautiful also, inasmuch as I am capable of responding to human beauty. [I think I am.] I am not sure if I feel actual sexual desire for Lisabeth; more likely what troubles me is a generalized longing for her presence and her closeness, which I translate into sexual terms simply as a means of making it comprehensible to me.

Beyond doubt she does not have the traits I normally seek in a mate [prominent beak, sleek fins]. Any attempt at our making love in the anatomical sense would certainly result in pain or injury to her. That is not my wish. The physical traits that make her so desirable to the males of her species [highly developed milk glands, shining hair, delicate features, long hind limbs or "legs", and so forth] have no particular importance to me, and in some instances actually have a negative value. As in the case of the two milk glands in her pectoral region, which jut forward from her body in such a fashion that they must surely slow her when she swims. This is poor design, and I am incapable of finding poor design beautiful in any way. Evidently Lisabeth regrets the size and placement of those glands herself, since she is careful to conceal them at all times by a narrow covering. The others at the station, who are all males and therefore have only rudimentary milk glands that in no way destroy the flow lines of their bodies, leave them bare.

What, then, is the cause of my attraction for Lisabeth?

It arises out of the need I feel for her companionship. I believe that she understands me as no member of my own species does. Hence I will be happier in her company than away from her. This impression dates from our earliest meeting. Lisabeth, who is a specialist in human-cetacean relations, came to St. Croix four months ago, and I was requested to bring my maintenance group to the surface to be introduced to her. I leaped high for a good view and saw instantly that she was of a finer sort than the humans I already knew; her body was more delicate, looking at once fragile and powerful, and her gracefulness was a welcome change from the thick awkwardness of the human males I knew. Nor was she covered with the coarse body hair that my kind finds so distressing. [I did not at first know that Lisabeth's difference from the others at the station was the result of her being female. I had never seen a human female before. But I quickly learned.]

I came forward, made contact with the acoustic transmitter, and said, "I am the foreman of the Intake Maintenance Squad. I have the unit-structural designation TT-66."

"Don't you have a name?" she asked.

"Meaning of term, name?"

"Your—your unit-structural designation—but not just TT-66. I mean, that's no good at all. For example, my name's Lisabeth Calkins. And I—" She shook her head and looked at the plant supervisor. "Don't these workers have *names?*"

The supervisor did not see why dolphins should have names. Lisabeth did—she was greatly concerned about it—and since she now was in charge of liaison with us, she gave us names on the spot. Thus I was dubbed Ishmael. It was, she told me, the name of a man who had gone to sea, had many wonderful experiences, and put them all down in a story-spool that every cultured person played. I have since had access to Ishmael's story—that *other* Ishmael—and I agree that it is remarkable. For a human being he had unusual insight into the ways of whales, who are, however, stupid creatures for whom I have little respect. I am proud to carry Ishmael's name.

After she had named us, Lisabeth leaped into the sea and swam with us. I must tell you that most of us feel a sort of contempt for you humans because you are such poor swimmers. Perhaps it is a mark of my above-normal intelligence or greater compassion that I have no such scorn in me. I admire you for the zeal and energy you give to swimming, and you are quite good at it, considering all your handicaps. As I remind my people, you manage far more ably in the water than we would on land. Anyway, Lisabeth swam well, by human standards, and we tolerantly adjusted our pace to hers. We frolicked in the water awhile. Then she seized my dorsal fin and said, "Take me for a ride, Ishmael!"

I tremble now to recollect the contact of her body with mine. She sat astride me, her legs gripping my body tightly, and off I sped at close to full velocity, soaring at surface level. Her laughter told of her delight as I launched myself again and again through the air. It was a purely physical display in which I made no use of my extraordinary mental capacity; I was, if you will, simply showing off my dolphinhood. Lisabeth's response was ecstatic. Even when I plunged, taking her so deep she might have feared harm from the pressure, she kept her grip and showed no alarm. When we breached the surface again, she cried out in joy.

Through sheer animality I had made my first impact on her. I knew human beings well enough to be able to interpret her flushed, exhilarated expression as I returned her to shore. My challenge now was to expose her to my higher traits—to show her that even among dolphins I was unusually swift to learn, unusually capable of comprehending the universe.

I was already then in love with her.

During the weeks that followed we had many conversations. I am not flattering myself when I tell you that she quickly realized how extraordinary I am. My vocabulary, which was already large when she came to the station, grew rapidly under the stimulus of Lisabeth's presence. I learned from her; she gave me access to spools no dolphin was thought likely to wish to play; I developed insights into my environment that astonished even myself. In short order I reached my present peak of attainment. I think you will agree that I can express myself more eloquently than most human beings. I trust that the computer doing the printout on this memoir will not betray me by inserting inappropriate punctuations or deviating from the proper spellings of the words whose sounds I utter.

My love for Lisabeth deepened and grew more rich. I learned the meaning of jealousy for the first time when I saw her running arm in arm along the beach with Dr. Madison, the power-plant man. I knew anger when I overheard the lewd and vulgar remarks of human males as Lisabeth walked by. My fascination with her led me to explore many avenues of human experience; I did not dare talk of such things with her, but from other personnel at the base who sometimes talked with me I learned certain aspects of the phenomenon humans call "love". I also obtained explanations of the vulgar words spoken by males here behind her back: most of them pertained to a wish to mate with Lisabeth [apparently on a temporary basis], but there were also highly favorable descriptions of her milk glands [why are humans so aggressively mammalian?] and even of the rounded area in back, just above the place where her body divides into the two hind limbs. I confess that that region fascinates me also. It seems so alien for one's body to split like that in the middle!

I never explicitly stated my feelings toward Lisabeth. I tried to lead her slowly toward an understanding that I loved her. Once she came overtly to that awareness, I thought, we might begin to plan some sort of future for ourselves together.

What a fool I was!

Category 3: The Conspiracy

A male voice said, "How in hell are you going to bribe a dolphin?"

A different voice, deeper, more cultured, replied, "Leave it to me."

"What do you give him? Ten cans of sardines?"

"This one's special. Peculiar, even. He's scholarly. We can get to him."

They did not know that I could hear them. I was drifting near the surface in my rest tank, between shifts. Our hearing is acute and I was well within auditory range. I sensed at once that something was amiss, but I kept my position, pretending I knew nothing.

"Ishmael!" one man called out. "Is that you, Ishmael?"

I rose to the surface and came to the edge of the tank. Three male humans stood there. One was a technician at the station; the other two I had never seen before, and they wore body covering from their feet to their throats, marking them at once as strangers here. The technician I despised, for he was one of the ones who had made vulgar remarks about Lisabeth's milk glands.

He said, "Look at him, gentlemen. Worn out in his prime! A victim of human exploitation!" To me he said, "Ishmael, these gentlemen come from the League for the Prevention of Cruelty to Intelligent Species. You know about that?"

"No," I said.

"They're trying to put an end to dolphin exploitation. The criminal use of our planet's only other truly intelligent species in slave labor. They want to help you."

"I am no slave. I receive compensation for my work."

"A few stinking fish!" said the fully dressed man to the left of the technician. "They exploit you, Ishmael! They give you dangerous, dirty work and don't pay you worth a damn!"

His companion said, "It has to stop. We want to serve notice to the world that the age of enslaved dolphins is over. Help us, Ishmael. Help us help you!"

I need not say that I was hostile to their purported purposes. A more literal-minded dolphin than I might well have said so at once and spoiled their plot. But I shrewdly said, "What do you want me to do?"

"Foul the intakes," said the technician quickly.

Despite myself, I snorted in anger and surprise. "Betray a sacred trust? How can I?"

"It's for your own sake, Ishmael. Here's how it works—you and your crew will plug up the intakes, and the water plant will stop working. The whole island will panic. Human maintenance crews will go down to see what's what, but as soon as they clear the valves, you go back and foul them again. Emergency water supplies will have to be rushed to St. Croix. It'll focus public attention on the fact that this island is dependent on dolphin labor—underpaid, overworked dolphin labor! During the crisis we'll step forward to tell the world your story. We'll get every human being to cry out in outrage against the way you're being treated."

I did not say that I felt no outrage myself. Instead I cleverly replied, "There could be dangers in this for me."

"Nonsense!"

"They will ask me why I have not cleared the valves. It is my responsibility. There will be trouble."

For a while we debated the point. Then the technician said, "Look, Ishmael, we know there are a few risks. But we're willing to offer extra payment if you'll handle the job."

"Such as?"

"Spools. Anything you'd like to hear, we'll get for you. I know you've got literary interests. Plays, poetry, novels, all that sort of stuff. After hours, we'll feed literature to you by the bushel if you'll help us."

I had to admire their slickness. They knew how to motivate me.

"It's a deal," I said.

"Just tell us what you'd like."

"Anything about love."

"*Love?*"

"Love. Man and woman. Bring me love poems. Bring me stories of famous lovers. Bring me descriptions of the sexual embrace. I must understand these things."

"He wants the *Kama Sutra*," said the one on the left.

"Then we bring him the *Kama Sutra*," said the one on the right.

Category 4: My Response to the Criminals

They did not actually bring me the *Kama Sutra*. But they brought me a good many other things, including one spool that quoted at length from the *Kama Sutra*. For several weeks I devoted myself intensively to a study of human love literature. There were maddening gaps in the texts, and I still lack real comprehension of much that goes on between man and woman. The joining of body to body does not puzzle me; but I am baffled by the dialectics of the chase, in which the male must be predatory and the woman must pretend to be out of season; I am mystified by the morality of temporary mating as distinct from permanent ["marriage"]; I have no grasp of the intricate systems of taboos and prohibitions that humans have invented. This has been my one intellectual failure: at the end of my studies I knew little more of how to conduct myself with Lisabeth than I had before the conspirators had begun slipping me spools in secret.

Now they called on me to do my part.

Naturally I could not betray the station. I knew that these men were not the enlightened foes of dolphin exploitation that they claimed to be; for some private reason they wished the station shut down, that was all, and they had used their supposed sympathies with my species to win my cooperation. I do not feel exploited.

Was it improper of me to accept spools from them if I had no intention of aiding them? I doubt it. They wished to use me; instead I used them. Sometimes a superior species must exploit its inferiors to gain knowledge.

They came to me and asked me to foul the valves that evening. I said, "I am not certain what you actually wish me to do. Will you instruct me again?"

Cunningly I had switched on a recording device used by Lisabeth in her study sessions with the station dolphins. So they told me again about how fouling the valves would throw the island into panic and cast a spotlight on dolphin abuse. I questioned them repeatedly, drawing out details and also giving each man a chance to place his voiceprints on record. When proper incrimination had been achieved, I said, "Very well. On my next shift I'll do as you say."

"And the rest of your maintenance squad?"

"I'll order them to leave the valves untended for the sake of our species."

They left the station, looking quite satisfied with themselves. When they were gone, I beaked the switch that summoned Lisabeth. She came from her living quarters rapidly. I showed her the spool in the recording machine.

"Play it," I said grandly. "And then notify the island police!"

Category 5: The Reward of Heroism

The arrests were made. The three men had no concern with dolphin exploitation whatsoever. They were members of a disruptive group ["revolutionaries"] attempting to delude a naive dolphin into helping them cause chaos on the island. Through my loyalty, courage, and intelligence I had thwarted them.

Afterward Lisabeth came to me at the rest tank and said; "You were wonderful, Ishmael. To play along with them like that, to make them record their own confession—marvelous! You're a wonder among dolphins, Ishmael."

I was in a transport of joy.

The moment had come. I blurted, "Lisabeth, I love you."

My words went booming around the walls of the tank as they burst from the speakers. Echoes amplified and modulated them into grotesque barking noises more worthy of some miserable moron of a seal. *"Love you...love you...love you..."*

"Why, Ishmael!"

"I can't tell you how much you mean to me. Come live with me and be my love. Lisabeth, Lisabeth, Lisabeth!"

Torrents of poetry broke from me. Gales of passionate rhetoric escaped my beak. I begged her to come down into the tank and let me embrace her. She laughed and said she wasn't dressed for swimming. It was true: she had just come from town after the arrests. I implored. I begged. She yielded. We were alone; she removed her garments and entered the tank; for an instant I looked upon beauty bare. The sight left me shaken—those ugly swinging milk glands normally so wisely concealed, the strips of sickly white skin where the sun had been unable to reach, that unexpected patch of additional body hair—but once she was in the water I forgot my love's imperfections and rushed toward her. "Love!" I cried "Blessed Love!" I wrapped my fins about her in what I imagined was the human embrace. "Lisabeth! Lisabeth!" We slid below the surface. For the first time in my life I knew true passion, the kind of which the poets sing, that overwhelms even the coldest mind. I crushed her to me. I was aware of her forelimb-ends ["fists"] beating against my pectoral zone, and took it at first for a sign that my passion was being reciprocated; then it reached my love-hazed brain that she might be short of air. Hastily I surfaced. My darling Lisabeth, choking and gasping, sucked in breath and struggled to escape me. In shock I released her. She fled the tank and fell along its rim, exhausted, her pale body quivering. "Forgive me," I boomed. "I love you, Lisabeth! I saved the station out of love for you!" She managed to lift her lips as a sign that she did not feel anger for me [a "smile"]. In a faint voice she said, "You almost drowned me, Ishmael!"

"I was carried away by my emotions. Come back into the tank. I'll be more gentle. I promise! To have you near me—"

"Oh, Ishmael! What are you saying?"

"I love you! I love you!"

I heard footsteps. The power-plant man, Dr. Madison, came running. Hastily Lisabeth cupped her hands over her milk glands and pulled her discarded garments over the lower half of her body. That pained me, for if she chose to hide such things from him, such ugly parts of herself, was that not an indication of her love for him?

"Are you all right, Liz?" he asked. "I heard yelling—"

"It's nothing, Jeff. Only Ishmael. He started hugging me in the tank. He's in love with me, Jeff, can you imagine? In *love* with me!"

They laughed together at the folly of the love-smitten dolphin.

Before dawn came I was far out to sea. I swam where dolphins swim, far from man and his things. Lisabeth's mocking laughter rang within me. She had not meant to be cruel. She who knows me better than anyone else had not been able to keep from laughing at my absurdity.

Nursing my wounds, I stayed at sea for several days, neglecting my duties at the station. Slowly, as the pain gave way to a dull ache, I headed back toward the island. In passing I met a female of my own kind. She was newly come into her season and offered herself to me, but I told her to follow me, and she did. Several times I was forced to warn off other males who wished to make use of her. I led her to the station, into the lagoon the dolphins use in their sport. A member of my crew came out to investigate—Mordred, it was—and I told him to summon Lisabeth and tell her I had returned.

Lisabeth appeared on the shore. She waved to me, smiled, called my name.

Before her eyes I frolicked with the female dolphin. We did the dance of mating; we broke the surface and lashed it with our flukes; we leaped, we soared, we bellowed.

Lisabeth watched us. And I prayed: *Let her become jealous.*

I seized my companion and drew her to the depths and violently took her, and set her free to bear my child in some other place. I found Mordred again. "Tell Lisabeth," I instructed him, "that I have found another love, but that someday I may forgive her."

Mordred gave me a glassy look and swam to shore.

My tactic failed. Lisabeth sent word that I was welcome to come back to work, and that she was sorry if she had offended me; but there was no hint of jealousy in her message. My soul has turned to rotting seaweed within me. Once more I clear the intake valves, like the good beast I am, I, Ishmael, who has read Keats and Donne. Lisabeth! Lisabeth! Can you feel my pain?

Tonight by darkness I have spoken my story. You who hear this, whoever you may be, aid a lonely organism, mammalian and aquatic, who desires more intimate contact with a female of a different species. Speak kindly of me to Lisabeth. Praise my intelligence, my loyalty, and my devotion.

Tell her I give her one more chance. I offer a unique and exciting experience. I will wait for her, tomorrow night, by the edge of the reef. Let her swim to me. Let her embrace poor lonely Ishmael. Let her speak the words of love.

From the depths of my soul...from the depths...Lisabeth, the foolish beast bids you good night, in grunting tones of deepest love.

RINGING THE CHANGES

In the summer of 1968—the midpoint of that feverish year, catastrophic for me and for the world in general, a year full of assassinations, political turbulence, and general social weirdity—Anne McCaffrey said she was editing an anthology called Alchemy & Academe and asked me for a story. I didn't understand what the title meant, and couldn't get a clear answer from Annie, but I went ahead anyway. Alchemy, I figured, involves changing things. So that August I wrote a story about changes for her. In keeping with the casual attitudes of what was rapidly becoming the legendary era known as the Sixties, I cavalierly chose to regard the "academe" part of the title as irrelevant. Apparently that was okay, because Annie bought the story. (When the anthology appeared in 1970 it carried the subtitle, "A Collection of Original Stories Concerning Themselves with Transmutations, Mental and Elemental, Alchemical and Academic." I wish Annie had said so in the first place. But that was what I wrote anyway, so I guess it made little difference that I had never been clear about the nature of her theme.)

The book was full of good stories by people like James Blish, Samuel R. Delany, Gene Wolfe, Norman Spinrad, and Carol Emshwiller. So were a lot of other anthologies of that period; but this one happened to be edited by Anne McCaffrey, who was soon to become enormously famous as the author of the Dragons of Pern series. Thanks to Annie's immense subsequent success, Alchemy & Academe stayed in print for more than twenty years, getting reissued regularly, right along with all the other McCaffrey books— and "Ringing the Changes" brought me a nice royalty check every now *and then for quite a long time. It pays to pick the right editor for the anthologies you sell your stories to.*

There has been a transmission error in the shunt room, and several dozen bodies have been left without minds, while several dozen minds are held in the stasis net, unassigned and, for the moment, unassignable. Things like this have happened before, which is why changers take out identity insurance, but never has it happened to so many individuals at the same time. The shunt is postponed. Everyone must be returned to his original identity; then they will start over. Suppressing the news has proved to be impossible. The area around the hospital has been besieged by the news media. Hover-cameras stare rudely at the building at every altitude from twelve to twelve hundred feet. Trucks are angle-parked in the street. Journalists trade tips, haggle with hospital personnel for the names of the bereaved, and seek to learn the identities of those involved in the mishap. "If I knew, I'd tell you," says Jaime Rodriguez, twenty-seven. "Don't you think I could use the money? But we don't know. That's the whole trouble, we don't know. The data tank was the first thing to blow."

The shunt room has two antechambers, one on the west side of the building, the other facing Broadway; one is occupied by those who believe they are related to the victims, while in the other can be found the men from the insurance companies. Like everyone else, the insurance men have no real idea of the victims' names, but they do know that various clients of theirs were due for shunting today, and with so many changers snarled up at once, the identity-insurance claims may ultimately run into the millions. The insurance men confer agitatedly with one another, dictate muttered memoranda, scream telephone calls into their cufflinks, and show other signs of distress, although several of them remain cool enough to conduct ordinary business while here; they place stock market orders and negotiate assignations with nurses. It is, however, a tense and difficult situation, whose final implications are yet unknown.

Dr. Vardaman appears, perspired, paternal. "We're making every effort," he says, "to reunite each changer with the proper identity matrix. I'm fully confident. Only a matter of time. Your loved ones, safe and sound."

"We aren't the relatives," says one of the insurance men.

"Excuse me," says Dr. Vardaman, and leaves.

The insurance men wink and tap their temples knowingly. They peer beyond the antechamber door.

"Cost us a fortune," one broker says.

"Not your money," an adjuster points out.

"Raise premiums, I guess."

"Lousy thing. Lousy thing. Lousy thing. Could have been me."

"You a changer?"

"Due for a shunt next Tuesday."

"Tough luck, man. You could have used a vacation."

The antechamber door opens. A plump woman with dark-shadowed eyes enters. "Where are they?" she asks. "I want to see them! My husband was shunting today!"

She begins to sob and then to shriek. The insurance men rush to comfort her. It will be a long and somber day.

Now go on with the story

After a long time in the stasis net, the changer decides that something must have gone wrong with the shunt. It has never taken this long before. Something as simple as a shift of persona should be accomplished quickly, like the pulling of a tooth: *out, shunt, in.* Yet minutes or possibly hours have gone by, and the shunt has not come. What are they waiting for? I paid good money for a shunt. Something wrong somewhere, I bet.

Get me out of here. Change me.

The changer has no way of communicating with the hospital personnel. The changer, at present, exists only as a pattern of electrical impulses held in the stasis net. In theory it is possible for an expert to communicate in code even across the stasis gap, lighting up nodes on a talkboard; it was in this way that preliminary research into changing was carried out. But this changer has no such skills, being merely a member of the lay public seeking temporary identity transformation, a holiday sojourn in another's skull. The changer must wait in limbo.

A voice impinges. "This is Dr. Vardaman, addressing all changers in the net. There's been a little technical difficulty, here. What we need to do now is put you all back in the bodies you started from, which is just a routine reverse shunt, as you know, and when everybody is sorted out we can begin again. Clear? So the next thing that's going to happen to you is that you'll get shunted, only you won't be changed, heh-heh, at least we don't *want* you to be changed. As soon as you're able to speak to us, please tell your nurse if you're back in the right body, so we can disconnect you from the master switchboard, all right? Here we go, now, one, two, three—"

—Shunt.

This body is clearly the wrong one, for it is female. The changer trembles, taking possession of the cerebral fibers and driving pitons into the autonomic nervous system. A hand rises and touches a breast. Erectile tissue responds. The skin is soft and the flesh is firm. The changer strokes a cheek. Beardless. He searches now for vestigial personality traces. He finds a name, Vonda Lou, and the image of a street, wide and dusty, a small town in a flat region, with squat square-fronted buildings set well back from the pavement, and gaudy automobiles parked sparsely in front of them. Beyond the town the zone of dry red earth begins; far away are the bare brown mountains. This is no place for the restless. A soothing voice says, "They catch us, Vonda Lou, they gonna take a baseball bat, jam it you know where," and Vonda Lou replies, "They ain't gone catch us anyway," and the other voice says, "But if they do, but if they do?" The room is warm but not humid. There are crickets outside. Cars without mufflers roar by. Vonda Lou says, "Stop worrying and put your head here. *Here*. That's it. Oh, nice—" There is a giggle. They change positions. Vonda Lou says, "No fellow ever did that to you, right?" The soft voice says, "Oh, Vonda Lou—" And Vonda Lou says, "One of these days we gone get out of this dime-store town—" Her hands clutch yielding flesh. In her mind dances the image of a drum majorette parading down the dusty main street, twirling a baton, lifting knees high and pulling the white shorts tight over the smug little rump, yes, yes, look at those things jiggle up there, look all the nice stuff, and the band plays *Dixie* and the football team comes marching by, and Vonda Lou laughs, thinking of that big hulking moron and how he had tried to dirty her, putting his paws all over her, that dumb Billy Joe who figured he was going to score, and all the time Vonda Lou was laughing at him inside, because it wasn't the halfback but the drum majorette who had what she wanted, and—

Voice: "Can you hear me? If there has been a proper matching of body and mind, please raise your right hand."

The changer lifts left hand.

—shunt

The world here is dark green within a fifty-yard radius of the helmet lamp, black beyond. The temperature is 38 degrees F. The pressure is six atmospheres. One moves like a crab within one's jointed suit, scuttling along the bottom. Isolated clumps of gorgonians wave in the current. To the left, one can see as though through a funnel the cone of light that rises to the surface, where the water is blue. Along the face of the submerged cliff are coral outcroppings, but not here, not this deep, where sunlight is of a primal coldness.

One moves cautiously, bothered by the pressure drag. One clutches one's collecting rod tightly, stepping over nodules of manganese and silicon, swinging the lamp in several directions, searching for the places where the bottom drops away. One is uneasy and edgy here, not because of the pressure or the dark or the chill, but because one is cursed with an imagination, and one cannot help but think of the kraken in the pit. One dreams of Tennyson's dreamless beast, below the thunders of the upper deep. Faintest sunlights flee about his shadowy sides: above him swell huge sponges of millennial growth and height.

One comes now to the brink of the abyss.

There hath he lain for ages and will lie, battening upon huge seaworms in his sleep, until the latter fire shall heat the deep; then once by man and angels to be seen, in roaring he shall rise and on the surface die. Yes. One is moved, yes. One inclines one's lamp, hoping its beam will strike a cold glittering eye below. Far, far beneath in the abysmal sea. There is no sign of the thick ropy tentacles, the mighty beak.

"Going down in, now," one says to those above.

One has humor as well as imagination. One pauses at the brink, picks up a chalky stone, inscribes on a boulder crusted with the tracks of worms the single word:

NEMO

One laughs and flips aside the stone, and launches one's self into the abyss, kicking off hard against the continental shelf. Down. And down. Seeking wondrous grot and secret cell.

The changer sighs, thinking of debentures floated on the Zurich exchange, of contracts for future delivery of helium and plutonium, of puts and calls and margins. He will not enter the abyss; he will not see the kraken; feebly he signals with his left hand.

—*shunt*

A middle-aged male, at least. There's hope in that. A distinct paunch at the middle. Some shortness of breath. Faint stubble on face. The legs feel heavy, with swollen feet; a man gets tired easily at a certain age, when his responsibilities are heavy. The sound of unanswered telephones rings in his ears. Everything is familiar: the tensions, the frustrations, the fatigue, the sense of things unfinished and things uncommenced, the staleness in the mouth, the emptiness in the gut. This must be the one. Home again, all too soon?

Q: Sir, in the event of an escalation of the crisis, would you request an immediate meeting of the Security Council, or would you attempt to settle matters through quasidiplomatic means as was done in the case of the dispute between Syria and the Maldive Islands?

A: Let's not put the horse in the cart, shall we?

Q: According to last Monday's statement by the Bureau of the Budget, this year's deficit is already running twelve billion ahead of last, and we're only halfway through the second quarter. Have you given any concern to the accusation of the Fiscal Responsibility Party that this is the result of a deliberate Communist-dictated plan to demoralize the economy?

A: What do you think?

Q: Is there any thought of raising the tax on personality-shunting?

A: Well, now, there's already a pretty steep tax on that, and we don't want to do anything that'll interfere with the rights of American citizens to move around from body to body, as is their God-given and constitutional right. So I don't think we'll change that tax any.

Q: Sir, we understand that you yourself have done some shunting. We—

A: Where'd you hear that?

Q: I think it was Representative Spear, of Iowa, who said the other day that it's well known that the President visits a shunt room every time he's in New York, and—

A: You know these Republicans. They'll say anything at all about a Democrat.

Q: Mr. President, does the Administration have any plans for ending sexual discrimination in public washrooms?

A: I've asked the Secretary of the Interior to look into that, inasmuch as it might involve interstate commerce and also being on Federal property, and we expect a report at a later date.

Q: Thank you, Mr. President.

The left hand stirs and rises. Not this one, obviously. The hand requests a new phase-shift. The body is properly soggy and decayed, yes. But one must not be deceived by superficialities. This is the wrong one. Out, please. Out.

—shunt

The crowd stirred in anticipation as Bernie Kingston left the on-deck circle and moved toward the plate, and by the time he was in the batter's box they were standing.

Kingston glanced out at the imposing figure of Ham Fillmore, the lanky Hawks southpaw on the mound. *Go ahead*, Bernie thought, *I'm ready for you.*

He wiggled the bat back and forth two or three times and dug in hard, waiting for the pitch. It was a low, hard fastball, delivered by way of first base, and it shot past him before he had a chance to offer. "Strike one," he heard. He looked down toward third to see if the manager had any sign for him.

But Danner was staring at him blankly. *You're on your own*, he seemed to be saying.

The next pitch was right in the groove, and Bernie lined it effortlessly past the big hurler's nose and on into right field for a single. The crowd roared its approval as he trotted down to first.

"Good going, kid," said Jake Edwards, the first-base coach, when Bernie got there. Bernie grinned. Base hits always felt good, and he loved to hear the crowd yell.

The Hawks' catcher came out to the mound and called a conference. Bernie wandered around first, doing some gardening with his spikes. With one out and the score tied in the eighth, he couldn't blame the Hawks for wanting to play it close to the belt.

As soon as the mound conference broke up it was the Stags' turn to call time. "Come here, kid," Jake Edwards called.

"What's the big strategy this time?" Bernie asked boredly.

"No lip, kid. Just go down on the second pitch."

Bernie shrugged and edged a few feet off the base. Ham Fillmore was still staring down at his catcher, shaking off signs, and Karl Folsom, the Stag cleanup man, was waiting impatiently at the plate.

"Take a lead," the coach whispered harshly. "Go on, Kingston—get down that line."

The hurler finally was satisfied with his sign, and he swung into the windup. The pitch was a curve, breaking far outside. Folsom didn't venture at it, and the ball hit the dirt and squirted through the catcher's big mitt. It trickled about fifteen feet back of the plate.

Immediately the Hawks' shortstop moved in to cover second in case Bernie might be going. But Bernie had no such ideas. He stayed put at first.

"What's the matter, lead in ya pants?" called a derisive voice from the Hawk dugout.

Bernie snarled something and returned to the base. He glanced over at third, and saw Danner flash the steal sign.

He leaned away from first cautiously, five, six steps, keeping an eye cocked at the mound.

The pitcher swung into a half-windup—Bernie broke for second— his spikes dug furiously into the dusty basepath—

Out! Out! Out! The left hand upraised! Not this one, either! Out! Get me out!

—*shunt*

Through this mind go dreams of dollars, and the changer believes they have finally made the right match-up. He takes the soundings and finds much here that is familiar. Dow-Jones Industrials 1453.28, down 8.29. Confirmation of the bear signal by the rails. Penetration of the August 13 lows. Watch the arbitrage spread you get by going short on the common while picking up 10,000 of the $1.50 convertible preferred at—

The substance is right; so is the context. But the tone is wrong, the changer realizes. This man loves his work.

The changer tours this man's mind from the visitors' gallery.

— we can unload 800 shares in Milan at 48, which gives us two and a half points right there, and then after they announce the change in redemption ratio I think we ought to drop another thousand on the Zurich board—

—give me those Tokyo quotes! Damn you, you sleepy bastard, don't slow me up! Here, here, Kansai Electric Power, I want the price in yen, not the American Depositary crap—

—pick up twenty-two percent of the voting shares through street names before we announce the tender offer, that's the right way to do it, then hit them hard from a position of strength and watch the board of directors fold up in two days—

—I think we can work it with the participating preference stock, if we give them just a little hint that the dividend might go up in January, and of course they don't have to know that after the merger we're going to throw them all out anyway, so—

—why am I in it? Why, for the fun of it!—

Yes. The sheer joy of wielding power. The changer lingers here, sadly wondering why it is that this man, who after all functions in the same environment as the changer himself, shows such fierce gusto, such delight in finance for the sake of finance, while the changer derives only sour tastes and dull aches from all his getting. It's because he's so young, the changer decides. The thrill hasn't yet worn off for him. The changer surveys the body in which he is temporarily a resident. He makes himself aware of the flat belly's firm musculature, of the even rhythms of the heart, of the lean flanks. This man is at most forty years old, the changer concludes. Give him thirty more years and ten million more dollars and he'll know how hollow it all is. The futility of existence, the changer thinks. You feel it at seventeen, you feel it at seventy, but often you fail to feel it in between. I feel it. I feel it. And so this body can't be mine. Lift the left hand. Out.

"We are having some difficulties," Dr. Vardaman confesses, "in achieving accurate pairings of bodies and minds." He tells this to the insurance men, for there is every reason to be frank with them. "At the time of the transmission error we were left with—ah—twenty-nine minds in the stasis net. So far we've returned eleven of them to their proper bodies. The others—"

"Where are the eleven?" asks an adjuster.

"They're recuperating in the isolation ward," Dr. Vardaman replies. "You understand, they've been through three or four shunts apiece today, and that's pretty strenuous. After they've rested, we'll offer them the option to undergo the contracted-for change as scheduled, or to take a full refund."

"Meanwhile we got eighteen possible identity-insurance claims," says another of the insurance men. "That's something like fifteen million bucks. We got to know what you're doing to get the others back in the right bodies."

"Our efforts are continuing. It's merely a matter of time until everyone is properly matched."

"And if some of them die while you're shunting them?"

"What can I say?" Dr. Vardaman says. "We're making every attempt."

To the relatives he says, "There's absolutely no cause for alarm. Another two hours and we'll have it all straightened out. Please be assured that none of the clients involved are suffering any hardship or inconvenience, and in fact this may be a highly interesting and entertaining experience for them."

"My husband," the plump woman says. "Where's my husband?"

—shunt

The changer is growing weary of this. They have had him in five bodies, now. How many more times will they shove him about? Ten? Twenty? Sixteen thousand? He knows that he can free himself from this wheel of transformations at any time. Merely raise the right hand, claim a body as one's own. They'd never know. Walk right out of the hospital, threatening to sue everybody in sight; they scare easily and won't interfere. Pick your body. Be anyone who appeals to you. Pick fast, though, because if you wait too long they'll hit the right combination and twitch you back into the body you started from. Tired, defeated, old, do you want that?

Here's your chance, changer. Steal another man's body. Another woman's if that's your kick. You could have walked out of here as that dyke from Texas. Or that diver. That ballplayer. That hard young market sharpie. Or the President. Or this new one, now—take your pick, changer.

What do you want to be? Essence precedes existence. They offer you your choice of bodies. Why go back to your own? Why pick up a stale identity, full of old griefs?

The changer considers the morality of such a deed.

The chances are good of getting away with it. Others in this mess are probably doing the same thing; it's musical chairs with souls, and if eight or nine take the wrong bodies, they'll never get it untangled. Of course, if I switch, someone else switches and gets stuck with my body. Aging. Decrepit. Who wants to be a used-up stockbroker? On the other hand, the changer realizes, there are consolations. The body he wishes to abandon is wealthy, and that wealth would go to the body's claimant. Maybe someone thought of that already, and grabbed my identity. Maybe that's why I'm being shunted so often into these others. The shunt-room people can't find the right one.

The changer asks himself what his desires are.

To be young again? To play Faust? No. Not really. He wants to rest. He wants peace. There is no peace for him in returning to his proper self. Too many ghosts await him there. The changer's needs are special.

The changer examines this latest body into which he has been shunted.

Quite young. Male. Undergraduate, mind stuffed full of Kant, Hegel, Fichte, Kierkegaard. Wealthy family. Curling red hair; sleek limbs; thoughts of willing girls, holidays in Hawaii, final exams, next fall's clothing styles. Adonis on a lark, getting himself changed as a respite from the academic pace? But no: the changer probes more deeply and finds a flaw, a fatal one. There is anguish beneath the young man's self-satisfaction, and rightly so, for this body is defective, it is gravely marred. The changer is surprised and saddened, and then feels joy and relief, for this body fills his very need and more. He sees for himself the hope of peace with honor, a speedier exit, a good deed. It is a far, far better thing. He will volunteer.

His right hand rises. His eyes open.

"This is the one," he announces. "I'm home again!" His conscience is clear.

Once the young man was restored to his body, the doctors asked him if he still wished to undergo the change he had contracted for. He was entitled to this one final adventure, which they all knew would have to be his last changing, since the destruction of the young man's white corpuscles was nearly complete. No, he said, he had had enough excitement during the mixup in the shunt room, and craved no further changes. His doctors agreed he was wise, for his body might not be able to stand the strain of another shunt; and they took him back to the terminal ward. Death came two weeks later, peacefully, very peacefully.

SUNDANCE

One reason Ed Ferman waited two years to use "Ishmael in Love" in Fantasy and Science Fiction *was that I was now sending him stories at a rapid clip, and he kept moving them into print ahead of "Ishmael." This was one of them, dating from September, 1968. I was still living in rented quarters—in exile, as I thought of it then—but I had begun to adapt by now to the changed circumstances that the fire had brought, and I was working at something like the old pace. I was working at a new level of complexity, too—sure of myself and my technique, willing now to push the boundaries of the short-story form in any direction that seemed worth exploring. Stretching my technical skills was something that had concerned me as far back as 1955 and "The Songs of Summer"—but I had been a novice writer then, still a college undergraduate, and now I was in my thirties and approaching the height of my creative powers. So I did "Sundance" by way of producing a masterpiece in the original sense of the word—that is, a piece of work which is intended to demonstrate to a craftsman's peers that he has ended his apprenticeship and has fully mastered the intricacies of his trade.*

Apparently I told Ed Ferman something about the story's nature while I was working on it, and he must have reacted with some degree of apprehensiveness, because the letter I sent him on October 22, 1968 that accompanied the submitted manuscript says, "I quite understand your hesitation to commit yourself in advance to a story when you've been warned it's experimental; but it's not all that experimental....I felt that the only way I could properly convey the turmoil in the protagonist's mind, the gradual dissolution of his hold on reality, was through the constant changing of persons and tenses; but as I read it through I

241

*think everything remains clear despite the frequent derailments of the reader."
And I added, "I don't mean to say that I intend to disappear into the deep end
of experimentalism. I don't regard myself as a member of any 'school' of s-f, and
don't value obscurity for its own sake. Each story is a technical challenge
unique unto itself, and I have to go where the spirit moves me. Sometimes it
moves me to a relatively conventional strong-narrative item like 'Fangs of the
Trees,' and sometimes to a relatively avant-garde item like this present
'Sundance'; I'm just after the best way of telling my story, in each case."*

*Ferman responded on Nov 19 with: "You should do more of this sort of
thing. 'Sundance' is by far the best of the three I've seen recently. It not only
works; it works beautifully. The ending—with the trapdoor image and that
last line—is perfectly consistent, and just fine." He had only one suggestion:
that I simplify the story's structure a little, perhaps by eliminating the occasional use of second-person narrative. But I wasn't about to do that. I replied
with an explanation of why the story kept switching about between first person narrative, second person, third person present tense, and third person past
tense. Each mode had its particular narrative significance in conveying the
various reality-levels of the story, I told him: the first-person material was the
protagonist's interior monolog, progressively more incoherent and untrustwor-
thy; the second-person passages provided objective description of his actions,
showing his breakdown from the outside, but not so far outside as third person
would be—and so forth. Ferman was convinced, and ran the story as is.*

*And it became something of a classic almost immediately after Ed ran it
in his June, 1969 issue. Though it was certainly a kind of circus stunt, it was
a stunt that worked, and it attracted widespread attention, including a place
on the ballot for the Nebula award the following year. (But I had "Passengers"
on the same ballot, and had no wish to compete with myself. Shrewdly if
somewhat cynically, I calculated that the more accessible "Passengers" had a
better chance of winning the award, and had "Sundance" removed from the
ballot. And that was how I came to win a Nebula with my second-best story
of 1969.) "Sundance" has since been reprinted dozens of times, both in science-fiction anthologies and in textbooks of literature. Here it is once more.*

Today you liquidated about 50,000 Eaters in Sector A, and now you
are spending an uneasy night. You and Herndon flew east at dawn,
with the green-gold sunrise at your backs, and sprayed the neural pellets

over a thousand hectares along the Forked River. You flew on into the prairie beyond the river, where the Eaters have already been wiped out, and had lunch sprawled on that thick, soft carpet of grass where the first settlement is expected to rise. Herndon picked some juiceflowers, and you enjoyed half an hour of mild hallucinations. Then, as you headed toward the copter to begin an afternoon of further pellet spraying, he said suddenly, "Tom, how would you feel about this if it turned out that the Eaters weren't just animal pests? That they were people, say, with a language and rites and a history and all?"

You thought of how it had been for your own people.

"They aren't," you said.

"Suppose they were. Suppose the Eaters—"

"They aren't. Drop it."

Herndon has this streak of cruelty in him that leads him to ask such questions. He goes for the vulnerabilities; it amuses him. All night now his casual remark has echoed in your mind. Suppose the Eaters...suppose the Eaters...suppose...suppose...

You sleep for a while, and dream, and in your dreams you swim through rivers of blood.

Foolishness. A feverish fantasy. You know how important it is to exterminate the Eaters fast, before the settlers get here. They're just animals, and not even harmless animals at that; ecology-wreckers is what they are, devourers of oxygen-liberating plants, and they have to go. A few have been saved for zoological study. The rest must be destroyed. Ritual extirpation of undesirable beings, the old, old story. But let's not complicate our job with moral qualms, you tell yourself. Let's not dream of rivers of blood.

The Eaters don't even *have* blood, none that could flow in rivers, anyway. What they have is, well, a kind of lymph that permeates every tissue and transmits nourishment along the interfaces. Waste products go out the same way, osmotically. In terms of process, it's structurally analogous to your own kind of circulatory system, except there's no network of blood vessels hooked to a master pump. The life-stuff just oozes through their bodies as though they were amoebas or sponges or some other low-phylum form. Yet they're definitely high-phylum in nervous system, digestive setup, limb-and-organ template, etc. Odd, you think. The thing about aliens is that they're alien, you tell yourself, not for the first time.

The beauty of their biology for you and your companions is that it lets you exterminate them so neatly.

You fly over the grazing grounds and drop the neural pellets. The Eaters find and ingest them. Within an hour the poison has reached all sectors of the body. Life ceases; a rapid breakdown of cellular matter follows, the Eater literally falling apart molecule by molecule the instant that nutrition is cut off; the lymph-like stuff works like acid; a universal lysis occurs; flesh and even the bones, which are cartilaginous, dissolve. In two hours, a puddle on the ground. In four, nothing at all left. Considering how many millions of Eaters you've scheduled for extermination here, it's sweet of the bodies to be self-disposing. Otherwise what a charnel house this world would become!

Suppose the Eaters…

Damn Herndon. You almost feel like getting a memory-editing in the morning. Scrape his stupid speculations out of your head. If you dared. If you dared.

In the morning he does not dare. Memory-editing frightens him; he will try to shake free of his newfound guilt without it. The Eaters, he explains to himself, are mindless herbivores, the unfortunate victims of human expansionism, but not really deserving of passionate defense. Their extermination is not tragic; it's just too bad. If Earthmen are to have this world, the Eaters must relinquish it. There's a difference, he tells himself, between the elimination of the Plains Indians from the American prairie in the nineteenth century and the destruction of the bison on that same prairie. One feels a little wistful about the slaughter of the thundering herds; one regrets the butchering of millions of the noble brown woolly beasts, yes. But one feels outrage, not mere wistful regret, at what was done to the Sioux. There's a difference. Reserve your passions for the proper cause.

He walks from his bubble at the edge of the camp toward the center of things. The flagstone path is moist and glistening. The morning fog has not yet lifted, and every tree is bowed, the long, notched leaves heavy with droplets of water. He pauses, crouching, to observe a spider-analog spinning its asymmetrical web. As he watches, a small amphibian, delicately shaded turquoise, glides as inconspicuously as possible over the mossy ground. Not inconspicuously enough; he gently lifts the little creature and puts it on the back of his hand. The gills flutter in anguish, and the amphibian's sides quiver. Slowly, cunningly, its color changes until it matches the coppery tone of the hand. The camouflage is excellent. He lowers his hand and the amphibian scurries into a puddle. He walks on.

He is forty years old, shorter than most of the other members of the expedition, with wide shoulders, a heavy chest, dark glossy hair, a blunt, spreading nose. He is a biologist. This is his third career, for he has failed as an anthropologist and as a developer of real estate. His name is Tom Two Ribbons. He has been married twice but has had no children. His great-grandfather died of alcoholism; his grandfather was addicted to hallucinogens; his father had compulsively visited cheap memory-editing parlors. Tom Two Ribbons is conscious that he is failing a family tradition, but he has not found his own mode of self-destruction.

In the main building he discovers Herndon, Julia, Ellen, Schwartz, Chang, Michaelson, and Nichols. They are eating breakfast; the others are already at work. Ellen rises and comes to him and kisses him. Her short soft yellow hair tickles his cheeks. "I love you," she whispers. She has spent the night in Michaelson's bubble. "I love you," he tells her, and draws a quick vertical line of affection between her small pale breasts. He winks at Michaelson, who nods, touches the tops of two fingers to his lips, and blows them a kiss. We are all good friends here, Tom Two Ribbons thinks.

"Who drops pellets today?" he asks.

"Mike and Chang," says Julia. "Sector C."

Schwartz says, "Eleven more days and we ought to have the whole peninsula clear. Then we can move inland."

"If our pellet supply holds up," Chang points out.

Herndon says, "Did you sleep well, Tom?"

"No," says Tom. He sits down and taps out his breakfast requisition. In the west, the fog is beginning to burn off the mountains. Something throbs in the back of his neck. He has been on this world nine weeks now, and in that time it has undergone its only change of season, shading from dry weather to foggy. The mists will remain for many months. Before the plains parch again, the Eaters will be gone and the settlers will begin to arrive. His food slides down the chute and he seizes it. Ellen sits beside him. She is a little more than half his age; this is her first voyage; she is their keeper of records, but she is also skilled at editing. "You look troubled," Ellen tells him. "Can I help you?"

"No. Thank you."

"I hate it when you get gloomy."

"°It's a racial trait," says Tom Two Ribbons.

"I doubt that very much."

"The truth is that maybe my personality reconstruct is wearing thin. The trauma level was so close to the surface. I'm just a walking veneer, you know."

Ellen laughs prettily. She wears only a sprayon half-wrap. Her skin looks damp; she and Michaelson have had a swim at dawn. Tom Two Ribbons is thinking of asking her to marry him, when this job is over. He has not been married since the collapse of the real estate business. The therapist suggested divorce as part of the reconstruct. He sometimes wonders where Terry has gone and whom she lives with now. Ellen says, "You seem pretty stable to me, Tom."

"Thank you," he says. She is young. She does not know.

"If it's just a passing gloom I can edit it out in one quick snip."

"Thank you," he says. "No."

"I forgot. You don't like editing."

"My father—"

"Yes?"

"In fifty years he pared himself down to a thread," Tom Two Ribbons says. "He had his ancestors edited away, his whole heritage, his religion, his wife, his sons, finally his name. Then he sat and smiled all day. Thank you, no editing."

"Where are you working today?" Ellen asks.

"In the compound, running tests."

"Want company? I'm off all morning."

"Thank you, no," he says, too quickly. She looks hurt. He tries to remedy his unintended cruelty by touching her arm lightly and saying, "Maybe this afternoon, all right? I need to commune a while. Yes?"

"Yes," she says, and smiles, and shapes a kiss with her lips.

After breakfast he goes to the compound. It covers a thousand hectares east of the base; they have bordered it with neutral-field projectors at intervals of eighty meters, and this is a sufficient fence to keep the captive population of two hundred Eaters from straying. When all the others have been exterminated, this study group will remain. At the southwest corner of the compound stands a lab bubble from which the experiments are run: metabolic, psychological, physiological, ecological. A stream crosses the compound diagonally. There is a low ridge of grassy hills at its eastern edge. Five distinct copses of tightly clustered knifeblade trees are separated by patches of dense savanna. Sheltered beneath the glass are the oxygen-plants, almost completely hidden except for the photosynthetic spikes that jut to heights of three or four meters at regular intervals, and the lemon-colored respiratory bodies, chest high, that make the grassland sweet and dizzying with exhaled gases. Through the fields move the Eaters in a straggling herd, nibbling delicately at the respiratory bodies.

Tom Two Ribbons spies the herd beside the stream and goes toward it. He stumbles over an oxygen-plant hidden in the grass but deftly recovers his balance and, seizing the puckered orifice of the respiratory body, inhales deeply. His despair lifts. He approaches the Eaters. They are spherical, bulky, slow-moving creatures, covered by masses of coarse orange fur. Saucer-like eyes protrude above narrow rubbery lips. Their legs are thin and scaly, like a chicken's, and their arms are short and held close to their bodies. They regard him with bland lack of curiosity. "Good morning, brothers!" is the way he greets them this time, and he wonders why.

I noticed something strange today. Perhaps I simply sniffed too much oxygen in the fields; maybe I was succumbing to a suggestion Herndon planted; or possibly it's the family masochism cropping out. But while I was observing the Eaters in the compound, it seemed to me, for the first time, that they were behaving intelligently, that they were functioning in a ritualized way.

I followed them around for three hours. During that time they uncovered half a dozen outcroppings of oxygen-plants. In each case they went through a stylized pattern of action before starting to munch. They:

Formed a straggly circle around the plants.

Looked toward the sun.

Looked toward their neighbors on left and right around the circle.

Made fuzzy neighing sounds only after having done the foregoing.

Looked toward the sun again.

Moved in and ate.

If this wasn't a prayer of thanksgiving, a saying of grace, then what was it? And if they're advanced enough spiritually to say grace, are we not therefore committing genocide here? Do chimpanzees say grace? Christ, we wouldn't even wipe out chimps the way we're cleaning out the Eaters! Of course, chimps don't interfere with human crops, and some kind of coexistence would be possible, whereas Eaters and human agriculturalists simply can't function on the same planet. Nevertheless, there's a moral issue here. The liquidation effort is predicated on the assumption that the intelligence level of the Eaters is about on par with that of oysters, or, at best, sheep. Our consciences stay clear because our poison is quick and painless and because the Eaters thoughtfully dissolve upon dying, sparing us the mess of incinerating millions of corpses. But if they pray—

I won't say anything to the others just yet. I want more evidence, hard, objective. Films, tapes, record cubes. Then we'll see. What if I can show that we're exterminating intelligent beings? My family knows a little about genocide, after all, having been on the receiving end just a few centuries back. I doubt that I could halt what's going on here. But at the very least I could withdraw from the operation. Head back to Earth and stir up public outcries.

I hope I'm imagining this.

I'm not imagining a thing. They gather in circles; they look to the sun; they neigh and pray. They're only balls of jelly on chicken-legs, but they give thanks for their food. Those big round eyes now seem to stare accusingly at me. Our tame herd here knows what's going on: that we have descended from the stars to eradicate their kind, and that they alone will be spared. They have no way of fighting back or even of communicating their displeasure, but they *know*. And hate us. Jesus, we have killed two million of them since we got here, and in a metaphorical sense I'm stained with blood, and what will I do, what can I do?

I must move very carefully, or I'll end up drugged and edited.

I can't let myself seem like a crank, a quack, an agitator. I can't stand up and *denounce!* I have to find allies. Herndon, first. He surely is onto the truth; he's the one who nudged me to it, that day we dropped pellets. And I thought he was merely being vicious in his usual way!

I'll talk to him tonight.

He says, "I've been thinking about that suggestion you made. About the Eaters. Perhaps we haven't made sufficiently close psychological studies. I mean, if they really *are* intelligent—"

Herndon blinks. He is a tall man with glossy dark hair, a heavy beard, sharp cheekbones. "Who says they are, Tom?"

"You did. On the far side of the Forked River, you said—"

"It was just a speculative hypothesis. To make conversation."

"No, I think it was more than that. You really believed it."

Herndon looks troubled. "Tom, I don't know what you're trying to start, but don't start it. If I for a moment believed we were killing intelligent creatures, I'd run for an editor so fast I'd start an implosion wave."

"Why did you ask me that thing, then?" Tom Two Ribbons says.

"Idle chatter."

"Amusing yourself by kindling guilts in somebody else? You're a bastard, Herndon. I mean it."

"Well, look, Tom, if I had any idea that you'd get so worked up about a hypothetical suggestion—" Herndon shakes his head. "The Eaters aren't intelligent beings. Obviously. Otherwise we wouldn't be under orders to liquidate them."

"Obviously," says Tom Two Ribbons.

Ellen said, "No, I don't know what Tom's up to. But I'm pretty sure he needs a rest. It's only a year and a half since his personality reconstruct, and he had a pretty bad breakdown back then."

Michaelson consulted a chart. "He's refused three times in a row to make his pellet-dropping run. Claiming he can't take time away from his research. Hell, we can fill in for him, but it's the idea that he's ducking chores that bothers me."

"What kind of research is he doing?" Nichols wanted to know.

"Not biological," said Julia. "He's with the Eaters in the compound all the time, but I don't see him making any tests on them. He just watches them."

"And talks to them," Chang observed.

"And talks, yes," Julia said.

"About what?" Nichols asked.

"Who knows?"

Everyone looked at Ellen. "You're closest to him," Michaelson said. "Can't you bring him out of it?"

"I've got to know what he's in, first," Ellen said. "He isn't saying a thing."

You know that you must be very careful, for they outnumber you, and their concern for your welfare can be deadly. Already they realize you are disturbed, and Ellen has begun to probe for the source of the disturbance. Last night you lay in her arms and she questioned you, obliquely, skillfully, and you knew what she is trying to find out. When the moons appeared she suggested that you and she stroll in the compound, among the sleeping Eaters. You declined, but she sees that you have become involved with the creatures.

You have done probing of your own—subtly, you hope. And you are aware that you can do nothing to save the Eaters. An irrevocable commitment has been made. It is 1876 all over again; these are the bison, these are the Sioux, and they must be destroyed, for the railroad is on its way. If you speak out here, your friends will calm you and pacify you and edit you, for they do not see what you see. If you return to Earth to agitate, you will be mocked and recommended for another reconstruct. You can do nothing. You can do nothing.

You cannot save, but perhaps you can record.

Go out into the prairie. Live with the Eaters; make yourself their friend; learn their ways. Set it down, a full account of their culture, so that at least that much will not be lost. You know the techniques of field anthropology. As was done for your people in the old days, do now for the Eaters.

He finds Michaelson. "Can you spare me for a few weeks?" he asks.

"Spare you, Tom? What do you mean?"

"I've got some field studies to do. I'd like to leave the base and work with Eaters in the wild."

"What's wrong with the ones in the compound?"

"It's the last chance with wild ones, Mike. I've got to go."

"Alone, or with Ellen?"

"Alone."

Michaelson nods slowly. "All right, Tom. Whatever you want. Go. I won't hold you here."

I dance in the prairie under the green-gold sun. About me the Eaters gather. I am stripped; sweat makes my skin glisten; my heart pounds. I talk to them with my feet, and they understand.

They understand.

They have a language of soft sounds. They have a god. They know love and awe and rapture. They have rites. They have names. They have a history. Of all this I am convinced.

I dance on thick grass.

How can I reach them? With my feet, with my hands, with my grunts, with my sweat. They gather by the hundreds, by the thousands, and I dance. I must not stop. They cluster about me and make their sounds. I am a conduit for strange forces. My great-grandfather should see me now! Sitting on his porch in Wyoming, the firewater in his hand, his brain rotting—see me now, old one! See the dance of Tom Two Ribbons! I talk to these strange ones with my feet under a sun that is the wrong color. I dance. I dance.

"Listen to me," I say. "I am your friend, I alone, the only one you can trust. Trust me, talk to me, teach me. Let me preserve your ways, for soon the destruction will come."

I dance, and the sun climbs, and the Eaters murmur.

There is the chief. I dance toward him, back, toward, I bow, I point to the sun, I imagine the being that lives in that ball of flame, I imitate the sounds of these people, I kneel, I rise, I dance. Tom Two Ribbons dances for you.

I summon skills my ancestors forgot. I feel the power flowing in me. As they danced in the days of the bison, I dance now, beyond the Forked River.

I dance, and now the Eaters dance too. Slowly, uncertainly, they move toward me, they shift their weight, lift leg and leg, sway about. "Yes, like that!" I cry. "Dance!"

We dance together as the sun reaches noon height.

Now their eyes are no longer accusing. I see warmth and kinship. I am their brother, their redskinned tribesman, he who dances with them. No longer do they seem clumsy to me. There is a strange ponderous grace in their movements. They dance. They dance. They caper about me. Closer, closer, closer!

We move in holy frenzy.

They sing, now, a blurred hymn of joy. They throw forth their arms, unclench their little claws. In unison they shift weight, left foot forward, right, left, right. Dance, brothers, dance, dance, dance! They press against me. Their flesh quivers; their smell is a sweet one. They gently thrust me across the field, to a part of the meadow where the grass is deep and untrampled. Still dancing, we seek for the oxygen-plants, and find clumps of them beneath the grass, and they make their prayer and seize them with their awkward arms, separating the respiratory bodies from the photosynthetic spikes. The plants, in anguish, release floods of oxygen. My mind reels. I laugh and sing. The Eaters are nibbling the lemon-colored perforated globes, nibbling the stalks as well. They thrust their plants at me. It is a religious ceremony, I see. Take from us, eat with us, join with us, this is the body, this is the blood, take, eat, join. I bend forward and put a lemon-colored globe to my lips. I do not bite; I nibble, as they do, my teeth slicing away the skin of the globe. Juice spurts into my mouth while oxygen drenches my nostrils. The Eaters sing hosannas. I should be in full paint for this, paint of my forefathers, feathers too, meeting their religion in the regalia of what should have been mine. Take, eat, join. The juice of the oxygen-plant flows in my veins. I embrace my brothers. I sing, and as my voice leaves my lips it becomes an arch that glistens like new steel, and I pitch my song lower, and the arch turns to tarnished silver. The Eaters crowd close. The scent of their bodies is fiery red to me. Their soft cries are puffs of steam. The sun is very warm; its rays are tiny jagged pings of puckered sound, close to the top of my range of hearing, plink! plink! plink! The thick grass hums to me, deep and rich, and the wind hurls points of flame along the prairie. I devour another oxygen-plant, and then a third. My brothers laugh and shout. They tell me of their gods, the god of warmth, the god of food, the god of pleasure, the god of death, the god of holiness, the god of wrongness, and the others. They recite for me the names of their kings, and I hear their voices as splashes of green mold on the clean sheet of the sky. They instruct me in their holy rites. I must remember this, I tell myself, for when it is gone it will never come again. I continue to dance. They continue to dance. The color of the hills becomes rough and coarse, like abrasive gas. Take, eat, join. Dance. They are so gentle!

I hear the drone of the copter, suddenly.

It hovers far overhead. I am unable to see who flies in it. "No!" I scream. "Not here! Not these people! Listen to me! This is Tom Ribbons! Can't you hear me? I'm doing a field study here! You've no right—!"

My voice makes spirals of blue moss edged with red sparks. They drift upward and are scattered by the breeze.

I yell, I shout, I bellow. I dance and shake my fists. From the wings of the copter the jointed arms of the pellet-distributors unfold. The gleaming spigots extend and whirl. The neural pellets rain down into the meadow, each tracing a blazing track that lingers in the sky. The sound of the copter becomes a furry carpet stretching to the horizon, and my shrill voice is lost in it.

The Eaters drift away from me, seeking the pellets, scratching at the roots of the grass to find them. Still dancing, I leap into their midst, striking the pellets from their hands, hurling them into the stream, crushing them to powder. The Eaters growl black needles at me. They turn away and search for more pellets. The copter turns and flies off, leaving a trail of dense oily sound. My brothers are gobbling the pellets eagerly.

There is no way to prevent it.

Joy consumes them and they topple and lie still. Occasionally a limb twitches; then even this stops. They begin to dissolve. Thousands of them melt on the prairie, sinking into shapelessness, losing spherical forms, flattening, ebbing into the ground. The bonds of the molecules will no longer hold. It is the twilight of protoplasm. They perish. They vanish. For hours I walk the prairie. Now I inhale oxygen; now I eat a lemon-colored globe. Sunset begins with the ringing of leaden chimes. Black clouds make brazen trumpet calls in the east and the deepening wind is a swirl of coaly bristles. Silence comes. Night falls. I dance. I am alone.

The copter comes again, and they find you, and you do not resist as they gather you in. You are beyond bitterness. Quietly you explain what you have done and what you have learned, and why it is wrong to exterminate these people. You describe the plant you have eaten and the way it affects your senses, and as you talk of the blessed synesthesia, the texture of the wind and the sound of the clouds and the timbre of the sunlight, they nod and smile and tell you not to worry, that everything will be all right soon, and they touch something cold to your forearm, so cold that it is a whir and a buzz and the deintoxicant sinks into your vein and soon the ecstasy drains away, leaving only the exhaustion and the grief.

He says, "We never learn a thing, do we? We export all our horrors to the stars. Wipe out the Armenians, wipe out the Jews, wipe out the Tasmanians, wipe out the Indians, wipe out everyone who's in our way, and do the same damned murderous thing. You weren't with me out there. You didn't dance with them. You didn't see what a rich, complex culture the Eaters have. Let me tell you about their tribal structure. It's dense: seven levels of matrimonial relationships, to begin with, and an exogamy factor that requires—"

Softly Ellen says, "Tom, darling, nobody's going to harm the Eaters."

"And the religion," he goes on. "Nine gods, each one an aspect of *the* god. Holiness and wrongness both worshiped. They have hymns, prayers, a theology. And we, the emissaries of the god of wrongness—"

"We're not exterminating them," Michaelson says. "Won't you understand that, Tom? This is all a fantasy of yours. You've been under the influence of drugs, but now we're clearing you out. You'll be clean in a little while. You'll have perspective again."

"A fantasy?" he says bitterly. "A drug dream? I stood out in the prairie and saw you drop pellets. And I watched them die and melt away. I didn't dream that."

"How can we convince you?" Chang asks earnestly. "What will make you believe? Shall we fly over the Eater country with you and show you how many millions there are?"

"But how many millions have been destroyed?" he demands.

They insist that he is wrong. Ellen tells him again that no one has ever desired to harm the Eaters. "This is a scientific expedition, Tom. We're here to *study* them. It's a violation of all we stand for to injure intelligent lifeforms."

"You admit that they're intelligent?"

"Of course. That's never been in doubt."

"Then why drop the pellets?" he asks. "Why slaughter them?"

"None of that has happened, Tom," Ellen says. She takes his hand between her cool palms. "Believe us. Believe us."

He says bitterly, "If you want me to believe you, why don't you do the job properly? Get out the editing machine and go to work on me. You can't simply *talk* me into rejecting the evidence of my own eyes."

"You were under drugs all the time," Michaelson says.

"I've never taken drugs! Except for what I ate in the meadow, when I danced—and that came after I had watched the massacre going on for weeks and weeks. Are you saying that it's a retroactive delusion?"

"No, Tom," Schwartz says. "You've had this delusion all along. It's part of your therapy, your reconstruct. You came here programmed with it."

"Impossible," he says.

Ellen kisses his fevered forehead. "It was done to reconcile you to mankind, you see. You had this terrible resentment of the displacement of your people in the nineteenth century. You were unable to forgive the industrial society for scattering the Sioux, and you were terribly full of hate. Your therapist thought that if you could be made to participate in an imaginary modern extermination, if you could come to see it as a necessary operation, you'd be purged of your resentment and able to take your place in society as—"

He thrusts her away. "Don't talk idiocy! If you knew the first thing about reconstruct therapy, you'd realize that no reputable therapist could be so shallow. There are no one-to-one correlations in reconstructs. No, don't touch me. Keep away. Keep away."

He will not let them persuade him that this is merely a drug-born dream. It is no fantasy, he tells himself, and it is no therapy. He rises. He goes out. They do not follow him. He takes a copter and seeks his brothers.

The sun is much hotter today. The Eaters are more numerous. Today I wear paint, today I wear feathers. My body shines with my sweat. They dance with me, and they have a frenzy in them that I have never seen before. We pound the trampled meadow with our feet. We clutch for the sun with our hands. We sing, we shout, we cry. We will dance until we fall.

This is no fantasy. These people are real, and they are intelligent, and they are doomed. This I know.

We dance. Despite the doom, we dance.

My great-grandfather comes and dances with us. He too is real. His nose is like a hawk's, not blunt like mine, and he wears the big headdress, and his muscles are like cords under his brown skin. He sings, he shouts, he cries.

Others of my family join us.

We eat the oxygen-plants together. We embrace the Eaters. We know, all of us, what it is to be hunted.

The clouds make music and the wind takes on texture and the sun's warmth has color.

We dance. We dance. Our limbs know no weariness.

The sun grows and fills the whole sky, and I see no Eaters now, only my own people, my father's fathers across the centuries, thousands of gleaming skins, thousands of hawk's noses, and we eat the plants, and we find sharp sticks and thrust them into our flesh, and the sweet blood flows and dries in the blaze of the sun, and we dance, and we dance, and some of us fall from weariness, and we dance, and the prairie is a sea of bobbing headdresses, an ocean of feathers, and we dance, and my heart makes thunder, and my knees become water, and the sun's fire engulfs me, and I dance, and I fall, and I dance, and I fall, and I fall, and I fall.

Again they find you and bring you back. They give you the cool snout on your arm to take the oxygen-plant drug from your veins, and then they give you something else so you will rest. You rest and you are very calm. Ellen kisses you and you stroke her soft skin, and then the others come in and they talk to you, saying soothing things, but you do not listen, for you are searching for realities. It is not an easy search. It is like falling through many trapdoors, looking for the one room whose floor is not hinged. Everything that has happened on this planet is your therapy, you tell yourself, designed to reconcile an embittered aborigine to the white man's conquest; nothing is really being exterminated here. You reject that and fall through and realize that this must be the therapy of your friends; they carry the weight of accumulated centuries of guilts and have come here to shed that load, and you are here to ease them of their burden, to draw their sins into yourself and give them forgiveness. Again you fall through, and see that the Eaters are mere animals who threaten the ecology and must be removed; the culture you imagined for them is your hallucination, kindled out of old churnings. You try to withdraw your objections to this necessary extermination, but you fall through again and discover that there is no extermination except in your mind, which is troubled and disordered by your obsession with the crime against your ancestors, and you sit up, for you wish to apologize to these friends of yours, these innocent scientists whom you have called murderers. And you fall through.

HOW IT WAS WHEN THE PAST WENT AWAY

Early in November of 1968 I was able to move back into my fire-damaged house, though the repairs were still going on nine months after the disaster. Platoons of workmen continued to bang away daily on the ground floor of the enormous house, but the repairs to the second-floor living quarters and my three-room office on the third floor were finished, and I insisted on returning to the house as soon as it became possible for us to inhabit it even in part.

I felt a sense of immense relief at finding myself in my familiar quarters once again—far more elegant now, having been rebuilt from scratch to our specific design, than they had been before the fire. And in a kind of fierce jubilation I wrote, with great speed, a 22,000-word novella to serve as the lead piece for an anthology I was editing called Three For Tomorrow, *to be published in the summer of 1969.*

The theme of the book, propounded in an introduction by Arthur C. Clarke, was that "with increasing technology goes increasing vulnerability; the more Man 'conquers' (sic) Nature, the more prone he becomes to artificial catastrophe." So the collection was one of the first environmentalist s-f books, I guess. Roger Zelazny wrote a fast-paced suspense story, James Blish provided a dazzling nightmare vision of the Manhattan of the future, and I did a takeoff on the then-current paranoia about someone's putting LSD in some city's water supply, substituting in my story a memory-destroying drug for the hallucinogenic one.

It happened that I had just come back from an extended visit to San Francisco; and so I set my story in that beautiful city, working in all sorts of little details of local color—little dreaming that in another couple of years I would suddenly decide to sell my magnificently rebuilt New York mansion, abandon the city of my birth forever, and transplant myself to the Bay Area.

The day that an antisocial fiend dumped an amnesifacient drug into the city water supply was one of the finest that San Francisco had had in a long while. The damp cloud that had been hovering over everything for three weeks finally drifted across the bay into Berkeley that Wednesday, and the sun emerged, bright and warm, to give the old town its warmest day so far in 2003. The temperature climbed into the high twenties, and even those oldsters who hadn't managed to learn to convert to the centigrade thermometer knew it was hot. Airconditioners hummed from the Golden Gate to the Embarcadero. Pacific Gas & Electric recorded its highest one-hour load in history between two and three in the afternoon. The parks were crowded. People drank a lot of water, some a good deal more than others. Toward nightfall, the thirstiest ones were already beginning to forget things. By the next morning, everybody in the city was in trouble, with a few exceptions. It had really been an ideal day for committing a monstrous crime.

On the day before the past went away, Paul Mueller had been thinking seriously about leaving the state and claiming refuge in one of the debtor sanctuaries—Reno, maybe, or Caracas. It wasn't altogether his fault, but he was close to a million in the red, and his creditors were getting unruly. It had reached the point where they were sending their robot bill collectors around to harass him in person, just about every three hours.

"Mr. Mueller? I am requested to notify you that the sum of $8,005.97 is overdue in your account with Modern Age Recreators, Inc. We have applied to your financial representative and have discovered your state of insolvency, and therefore, unless a payment of $395.61 is made by the eleventh of this month, we may find it necessary to begin confiscation procedures against your person. Thus I advise you—"

"—the amount of $11,554.97, payable on the ninth of August, 2002, has not yet been received by Luna Tours, Ltd. Under the credit laws of 1995 we have applied for injunctive relief against you and anticipate receiving a decree of personal service due, if no payment is received by—"

"—interest on the unpaid balance is accruing, as specified in your contract, at a rate of 4 percent per month—"

"—balloon payment now coming due, requiring the immediate payment of—"

Mueller was growing accustomed to the routine. The robots couldn't call him—Pacific Tel & Tel had cut him out of their data net months ago—and so they came around, polite blank-faced machines stenciled with corporate emblems, and in soft purring voices told him precisely how deep in the mire he was at the moment, how fast the penalty charges were piling up, and what they planned to do to him unless he settled his debts instantly. If he tried to duck them, they'd simply track him down in the streets like indefatigable process servers, and announce his shame to the whole city. So he didn't duck them. But fairly soon their threats would begin to materialize.

They could do awful things to him. The decree of personal service, for example, would turn him into a slave; he'd become an employee of his creditor, at a court-stipulated salary, but every cent he earned would be applied against his debt, while the creditor provided him with minimal food, shelter, and clothing. He might find himself compelled to do menial jobs that a robot would spit at, for two or three years, just to clear one debt. Personal confiscation procedures were even worse; under that deal he might well end up as the actual servant of one of the executives of a creditor company, shining shoes and folding shirts. They might also get an open-ended garnishment plan, under which he and his descendants, if any, would pay a stated percentage of their annual income down through the ages until the debt, and the compounding interest thereon, was finally satisfied. There were other techniques for dealing with delinquents, too.

He had no recourse to bankruptcy. The states and the federal government had tossed out the bankruptcy laws in 1995, after the so-called credit epidemic of the 1980s when for a while it was actually fashionable to go irretrievably into debt and throw yourself on the mercy of the courts. The haven of easy bankruptcy was no more; if you became insolvent, your creditors had you in their grip. The only way out was to jump to a debtor sanctuary, a place where local laws barred any extradition for a credit offense. There were about a dozen such sanctuaries, and you could live well there, provided you had some special skill that you could sell at a high price. You needed to make a good living, because in a debtor sanctuary everything was on a strictly cash basis—cash in advance, at that, even for a haircut. Mueller had a skill he thought would see him through: he was an artist, a maker of sonic sculptures, and his work was always in good demand. All he needed was a few thousand dollars to purchase the basic tools of his trade—his last set of sculpting equipment had been repossessed a few weeks ago—and he could set up a studio in one of the sanctuaries, beyond the reach of the robot hounds. He imagined he could still find a friend who would lend him a few thousand dollars. In the name of art, so to speak. In a good cause.

If he stayed within the sanctuary area for ten consecutive years, he would be absolved of his debts and could come forth a free man. There was only one catch, not a small one. Once a man had taken the sanctuary route, he was forever barred from all credit channels when he returned to the outside world. He couldn't even get a post office credit card, let alone a bank loan. Mueller wasn't sure he could live that way, paying cash for everything all the rest of his life. It would be terribly cumbersome and dreary. Worse: it would be barbaric.

He made a note on his memo pad: *Call Freddy Munson in morning and borrow three bigs. Buy ticket to Caracas. Buy sculpting stuff.*

The die was cast—unless he changed his mind in the morning.

He peered moodily out at the row of glistening whitewashed just-post-Earthquake houses descending the steeply inclined street that ran down Telegraph Hill toward Fisherman's Wharf. They sparkled in the unfamiliar sunlight. A beautiful day, Mueller thought. A beautiful day to drown yourself in the bay. Damn. Damn. Damn. He was going to be forty years old soon. He had come into the world on the same bleak day that President John Kennedy had left it. Born in an evil hour, doomed to a dark fate. Mueller scowled. He went to the tap and got a glass of water. It was the only thing he could afford to drink, just now. He asked himself how he ever managed to get into such a mess. Nearly a million in debt!

He lay down dismally to take a nap.

When he woke, toward midnight, he felt better than he had felt for a long time. Some great cloud seemed to have lifted from him, even as it had lifted from the city that day. Mueller was actually in a cheerful mood. He couldn't imagine why.

In an elegant townhouse on Marina Boulevard, the Amazing Montini was rehearsing his act. The Amazing Montini was a professional mnemonist: a small dapper man of sixty, who never forgot a thing. Deeply tanned, his dark hair slicked back at a sharp angle, his small black eyes glistening with confidence, his thin lips fastidiously pursed. He drew a book from a shelf and let it drop open at random. It was an old one-volume edition of Shakespeare, a familiar prop in his nightclub act. He skimmed the page, nodded, looked briefly at another, then another and smiled his inward smile. Life was kind to the Amazing Montini. He earned a comfortable $30,000 a week on tour, having converted a freakish gift into a profitable enterprise. Tomorrow night he'd open for a week at Vegas; then to Manila, Tokyo, Bangkok, Cairo, on around the globe. In twelve weeks he'd earn his year's intake; then he'd relax once more.

It was all so easy. He knew so many good tricks. Let them scream out a twenty-digit number; he'd scream it right back. Let them bombard him with long strings of nonsense syllables; he'd repeat the gibberish flawlessly. Let them draw intricate mathematical formulas on the computer screen; he'd reproduce them down to the last exponent. His memory was perfect, both for visuals and auditories, and for the other registers as well.

The Shakespeare thing, which was one of the simplest routines he had, always awed the impressionable. It seemed so fantastic to most people that a man could memorize the complete works, page by page. He liked to use it as an opener.

He handed the book to Nadia, his assistant. Also his mistress; Montini liked to keep his circle of intimates close. She was twenty years old, taller than he was, with wide frost-gleamed eyes and a torrent of glowing, artificially radiant azure hair: up to the minute in every fashion. She wore a glass bodice, a nice container for the things contained. She was not very bright, but she did the things Montini expected her to do, and did them quite well. She would be replaced, he estimated, in about eighteen more months. He grew bored quickly with his women. His memory was too good.

"Let's start," he said.

She opened the book. "Page 537, left-hand column."

Instantly the page floated before Montini's eyes. "*Henry VI, Part Two*," he said. "*King Henry:* Say, man, were these thy words? *Horner:* An't shall please your majesty, I never said nor thought any such matter: God is my witness, I am falsely accused by the villain. *Peter:* By these ten bones, my lords, he did speak them to me in the garret one night, as we were scouring my Lord of York's armour. *York:* Base dunghill villain, and—"

"Page 778, right-hand column," Nadia said.

"*Romeo and Juliet*. Mercutio is speaking…'an eye would spy out such a quarrel? Thy head is as fill of quarrels as an egg is full of meat, and yet thy head hath been beaten as addle as an egg for quarreling. Thou hast quarreled with a man for coughing in the street, because he hath wakened thy dog that hath lain asleep in the sun. Didst thou not—'"

"Page 307, starting fourteen lines down on the right side."

Montini smiled. He liked the passage. A screen would show it to his audience at the performance.

"*Twelfth Night*," he said. "The Duke speaks: 'Too old, by heaven. Let still the woman take an elder than herself, so wears she to him, so sways she level in her husband's heart: For, boy, however we do praise ourselves, our fancies are more giddy and unfirm—'"

"Page 495, left-hand column."

"Wait a minute," Montini said. He poured himself a tall glass of water and drank it in three quick gulps. "This work always makes me thirsty."

Taylor Braskett, Lt. Comdr., Ret., US Space Service, strode with springy stride into his Oak Street home, just outside Golden Gate Park. At seventy-one, Commander Braskett still managed to move in a jaunty way, and he was ready to step back into uniform at once if his country needed him. He believed his country did need him, more than ever, now that socialism was running like wildfire through half the nations of Europe. Guard the home front, at least. Protect what's left of traditional American liberty. What we ought to have, Commander Braskett believed, is a network of C-bombs in orbit, ready to rain hellish death on the enemies of democracy. No matter what the treaty says, we must be prepared to defend ourselves.

Commander Braskett's theories were not widely accepted. People respected him for having been one of the first Americans to land on Mars, of course, but he knew that they quietly regarded him as a crank, a crackpot, an antiquated minuteman still fretting about the redcoats. He had enough of a sense of humor to realize that he did cut an absurd figure to these young people. But he was sincere in his determination to help keep America free—to protect the youngsters from the lash of totalitarianism, whether they laughed at him or not. All this glorious sunny day he had been walking through the park, trying to talk to the young ones, attempting to explain his position. He was courteous, attentive, eager to find someone who would ask him questions. The trouble was that no one listened. And the young ones—stripped to the waist in the sunshine, girls as well as boys, taking drugs out in the open, using the foulest obscenities in casual speech—at times, Commander Braskett almost came to think that the battle for America had already been lost. Yet he never gave up all hope.

He had been in the park for hours. Now, at home, he walked past the trophy room, into the kitchen, opened the refrigerator, drew out a bottle of water. Commander Braskett had three bottles of mountain spring water delivered to his home every two days; it was a habit he had begun fifty years ago, when they had first started talking about putting fluorides in the water. He was not unaware of the little smiles they gave him when he admitted that he drank only bottled spring water, but he didn't mind; he had outlived many of the smilers already, and attributed his perfect health to his refusal to touch the polluted, contaminated water that most other people drank. First chlorine, then fluorides. Probably they were putting in some other things by now, Commander Braskett thought.

He drank deeply.

You have no way of telling what sort of dangerous chemicals they might be putting in the municipal water system these days, he told himself. Am I a crank? Then I'm a crank. But a sane man drinks only water he can trust.

Fetally curled, knees pressed almost to chin, trembling, sweating, Nate Haldersen closed his eyes and tried to ease himself of the pain of existence. Another day. A sweet, sunny day. Happy people playing in the park. Fathers and children. He bit his lip, hard, just short of laceration intensity. He was an expert at punishing himself.

Sensors mounted in his bed in the Psychotrauma Ward of Fletcher Memorial Hospital scanned him continuously, sending a constant flow of reports to Dr. Bryce and his team of shrinks. Nate Haldersen knew he was a man without secrets. His hormone count, enzyme ratios, respiration, circulation, even the taste of bile in his mouth—it all became instantaneously known to hospital personnel. When the sensors discovered him slipping below the depression line, ultrasonic snouts came nosing up from the recesses of the mattress, proximity nozzles that sought him out in the bed, found the proper veins, squirted him full of dynajuice to cheer him up. Modern science was wonderful. It could do everything for Haldersen except give him back his family.

The door slid open. Dr. Bryce came in. The head shrink looked his part: tall, solemn yet charming, gray at the temples, clearly a wielder of power and an initiate of mysteries. He sat down beside Haldersen's bed. As usual, he made a big point of not looking at the row of computer outputs next to the bed that gave the latest details of Haldersen's condition.

"Nate?" he said. "How goes?"

"It goes," Haldersen muttered.

"Feel like talking a while?"

"Not specially. Get me a drink of water?"

"Sure," the shrink said. He fetched it and said, "It's a gorgeous day. How about a walk in the park?"

"I haven't left this room in two and a half years, doctor. You know that."

"Always a time to break loose. There's nothing physically wrong with you, you know."

'I just don't feel like seeing people," Haldersen said. He handed back the empty glass. "More?"

"Want something stronger to drink?"

"Water's fine." Haldersen closed his eyes. Unwanted images danced behind the lids: the rocket liner blowing open over the pole, the passengers spilling out like autumn seeds erupting from a pod, Emily tumbling down, down, falling eighty thousand feet, her golden hair swept by the thin cold wind, her short skirt flapping at her hips, her long lovely legs clawing at the sky for a place to stand. And the children falling beside her, angels dropping from heaven, down, down, toward the white soothing fleece of the polar ice. They sleep in peace, Haldersen thought, and I missed the plane, and I alone remain. And Job spake, and said, Let the day perish wherein I was born, and the night in which it was said, There is a man child conceived.

"It was eleven years ago," Dr. Bryce told him. "Won't you let go of it?"

"Stupid talk coming from a shrink. Why won't it let go of *me?*"

"You don't want it to. You're too fond of playing your role."

"Today is talking-tough day, eh? Get me some more water."

"Get up and get it yourself," said the shrink.

Haldersen smiled bitterly. He left the bed, crossing the room a little unsteadily, and filled his glass. He had had all sorts of therapy—sympathy therapy, antagonism therapy, drugs, shock, orthodox freuding, the works. They did nothing for him. He was left with the image of an opening pod; and falling figures against the iron-blue sky. The Lord gave, and the Lord hath taken away; blessed be the name of the Lord. My soul is weary of my life. He put the glass to his lips. Eleven years. I missed the plane. I sinned with Marie, and Emily died, and John, and Beth. What did it feel like to fall so far? Was it like flying? Was there ecstasy in it? Haldersen filled the glass again.

"Thirsty today, eh?"

"Yes," Haldersen said.

"Sure you don't want to take a little walk?"

"You know I don't.' Haldersen shivered. He turned and caught the psychiatrist by the forearm. "When does it end, Tim? How long do I have to carry this thing around?"

"Until you're willing to put it down."

"How can I make a conscious effort to forget something? Tim, Tim, isn't there some drug I can take, something to wash away a memory that's killing me?"

"Nothing effective."

"You're lying," Haldersen murmured. "I've read about the amnesifacients. The enzymes that eat memory-RNA. The experiments with diisopropyl fluorophosphate. Puromycin. The—"

Dr. Bryce said, "We have no control over their operations. We can't simply go after a single block of traumatic memories while leaving the rest of your mind unharmed. We'd have to bash about at random, hoping we got the trouble spot, but never knowing what else we were blotting out. You'd wake up without your trauma, but maybe without remembering anything else that happened to you between, say, the age of fourteen and forty. Maybe in fifty years we'll know enough to be able to direct the dosage at a specific—"

"I can't wait fifty years."

"I'm sorry, Nate."

"Give me the drug anyway. I'll take my chances on what I lose."

"We'll talk about that some other time, all right? The drugs are experimental. There'd be months of red tape before I could get authorization to try them on a human subject. You have to realize—"

Haldersen turned him off. He saw only with his inner eye, saw the tumbling bodies, reliving his bereavement for the billionth time, slipping easily back into his self-assumed role of Job. *I am a brother to dragons, and a companion to owls. My skin is black upon me, and my bones are burned with heat. He hath destroyed me on every side, and I am gone: and mine hope hath he removed like a tree.*

The shrink continued to speak. Haldersen continued not to listen. He poured himself one more glass of water with a shaky hand.

It was close to midnight on Wednesday before Pierre Gerard, his wife, their two sons and their daughter had a chance to have dinner. They were the proprietors, chefs, and total staff of the Petit Pois restaurant on Sansome Street, and business had been extraordinary, exhaustingly good all evening. Usually they were able to eat about half past five, before the dinner rush began, but today people had begun coming in early—made more expansive by the good weather, no doubt—and there hadn't been a free moment for anybody since the cocktail hour. The Gerards were accustomed to brisk trade, for theirs was perhaps the most popular family-run bistro in the city, with a passionately devoted clientele. Still, a night like this was too much!

They dined modestly on the evening's miscalculations: an overdone rack of lamb, some faintly corky Château Beychevelle '97, a fallen soufflé, and such. They were thrifty people. Their one extravagance was the Evian water that they imported from France. Pierre Gerard had not set foot in his native Lyons for thirty years, but he preserved many of the customs of the motherland, including the traditional attitude toward water. A Frenchman does not drink much water, but what he does drink comes always from the bottle, never from the tap. To do otherwise is to risk a diseased liver. One must guard one's liver.

That night Freddy Munson picked up Helene at her flat on Geary and drove across the bridge to Sausalito for dinner, as usual, at Ondine's. Ondine's was one of only four restaurants, all of them famous old ones, at which Munson ate in fixed rotation. He was a man of firm habits. He awakened religiously at six each morning, and was at his desk in the brokerage house by seven, plugging himself into the data channels to learn what had happened in the European finance markets while he slept. At half past seven local time the New York exchanges opened and the real day's work began. By half past eleven, New York was through for the day, and Munson went around the corner for lunch, always at the Petit Pois, whose proprietor he had helped to make a millionaire by putting him into Consolidated Nucleonics' several components two and a half years before the big merger. At half past one, Munson was back in the office to transact business for his own account on the Pacific Coast exchange; three days a week he left at three, but on Tuesdays and Thursdays he stayed as late as five in order to catch some deals on the Honolulu and Tokyo exchanges. Afterwards, dinner, a play or concert, always a handsome female companion. He tried to get to sleep, or at least to bed, by midnight.

A man in Freddy Munson's position *had* to be orderly. At any given time, his thefts from his clients ranged from six to nine million dollars, and he kept all the details of his jugglings in his head. He couldn't trust putting them on paper because there were scanner eyes everywhere; and he certainly didn't dare employ the data net, since it was well known that anything you confided to one computer was bound to be accessible to some other computer somewhere, no matter how tight a privacy seal you slapped on it. So Munson had to remember the intricacies of fifty or more illicit transactions, a constantly changing chain of embezzlements, and a man who practices such necessary disciplines of memory soon gets into the habit of extending discipline to every phase of his life.

Helene snuggled close. Her faintly psychedelic perfume drifted toward his nostrils. He locked the car into the Sausalito circuit and leaned back comfortably as the traffic-control computer took over the steering. Helene said, "At the Bryce place last night I saw two sculptures by your bankrupt friend."

"Paul Mueller?"

"That's the one. They were very good sculptures. One of them buzzed at me."

"What were you doing at the Bryce's?"

"I went to college with Lisa Bryce. She invited me over with Marty."

"I didn't realize you were that old," Munson said.

Helene giggled. "Lisa's a lot younger than her husband, dear. How much does a Paul Mueller sculpture cost?"

"Fifteen, twenty thousand, generally. More for specials."

"And he's broke, even so?"

"Paul has a rare talent for self-destruction," Munson said. "He simply doesn't comprehend money. But it's his artistic salvation, in a way. The more desperately in debt he is, the finer his work becomes. He creates out of his despair, so to speak. Though he seems to have overdone the latest crisis. He's stopped working altogether. It's a sin against humanity when an artist doesn't work."

"You can be so eloquent, Freddy," Helene said softly.

When the Amazing Montini woke Thursday morning, he did not at once realize that anything had changed. His memory, like a good servant, was always there when he needed to call on it, but the array of perfectly fixed facts he carried in his mind remained submerged until required. A librarian might scan shelves and see books missing; Montini could not detect similar vacancies of his synapses. He had been up for half an hour, had stepped under the molecular bath and had punched for his breakfast and had awakened Nadia to tell her to confirm the pod reservations to Vegas, and finally, like a concert pianist running off a few arpeggios to limber his fingers for the day's chores, Montini reached into his memory bank for a little Shakespeare and no Shakespeare came.

He stood quite still, gripping the astrolabe that ornamented his picture window, and peered out at the bridge in sudden bewilderment. It had never been necessary for him to make a conscious effort to recover data. He merely looked and it was there; but where was Shakespeare? Where was the left hand column of page 136, and the right hand column of page 654, and the right hand column of page 806, sixteen lines down? Gone? He drew blanks. The screen of his mind showed him only empty pages.

Easy. This is unusual, but it isn't catastrophic. You must be tense, for some reason, and you're forcing it, that's all. Relax, pull something else out of storage—

The *New York Times*, Wednesday, October 3, 1973. Yes, there it was, the front page, beautifully clear, the story on the baseball game down in the lower right-hand corner, the headline about the jet accident big and black, even the photo credit visible. Fine. Now let's try—

The *St. Louis Post-Dispatch*, Sunday, April 19, 1987. Montini shivered. He saw the top four inches of the page, nothing else. Wiped clean.

He ran through the files of other newspapers he had memorized for his act. Some were there. Some were not. Some, like the *Post-Dispatch*, were obliterated in part. Color rose to his cheeks. Who had tampered with his memory?

He tried Shakespeare again. Nothing.

He tried the 1997 Chicago data-net directory. It was there.

He tried his third-grade geography textbook. It was there, the big red book with smeary print.

He tried last Friday's five-o'clock xerofax bulletin. Gone.

He stumbled and sank down on the divan he had purchased in Istanbul, he recalled, on the nineteenth of May, 1985, for 4,200 Turkish pounds. "Nadia!" he cried. "Nadia!" His voice was little more than a croak. She came running, her eyes only half frosted, her morning face askew.

"How do I look?" he demanded. "My mouth—is my mouth right? My eyes?"

"Your face is all flushed."

"Aside from that!"

"I don't know," she gasped. "You seem all upset, but—"

"Half my mind is gone," Montini said. "I must have had a stroke. Is there any facial paralysis? That's a symptom. Call my doctor, Nadia! A stroke, a stroke! It's the end for Montini!"

Paul Mueller, awakening at midnight on Wednesday and feeling strangely refreshed, attempted to get his bearings. Why was he fully dressed, and why had he been asleep? A nap, perhaps, that had stretched on too long? He tried to remember what he had been doing earlier in the day, but he was unable to find a clue. He was baffled but not disturbed; mainly he felt a tremendous urge to get to work. The images of five sculptures, fully planned and begging to be constructed, jostled in his mind. Might as well start right now, he thought. Work through till morning. That small twittering silvery one—that's a good one to start with. I'll block out the schematics, maybe even do some of the armature—

"Carole?" he called. "Carole, are you around?"

His voice echoed through the oddly empty apartment.

For the first time Mueller noticed how little furniture there was. A bed—a cot, really, not their double bed—and a table, and a tiny insulator unit for food, and a few dishes. No carpeting. Where were his sculptures, his private collection of his own best work? He walked into his studio and found it bare from wall to wall, all of his tools mysteriously swept away, just a few discarded sketches on the floor. And his wife? "Carole? *Carole?*"

He could not understand any of this. While he dozed, it seemed, someone had cleaned the place out, stolen his furniture, his sculptures, even the carpet. Mueller had heard of such thefts. They came with a van, brazenly, posing as moving men. Perhaps they had given him some sort of drug while they worked. He could not bear the thought that they had taken his sculptures; the rest didn't matter, but he had cherished those dozen pieces dearly. I'd better call the police, he decided, and rushed toward the handset of the data unit, but it wasn't there either. Would burglars take *that* too?

Searching for some answers, he scurried from wall to wall, and saw a note in his own handwriting. *Call Freddy Munson in the morning and borrow three bigs. Buy ticket to Caracas. Buy sculpting stuff.*

Caracas? A vacation, maybe? And why buy sculpting stuff? Obviously the tools had been gone before he fell asleep, then. Why? And where was his wife? What was going on? He wondered if he ought to call Freddy right now, instead of waiting until morning. Freddy might know. Freddy was always home by midnight, too. He'd have one of his damn girls with him and wouldn't want to be interrupted, but to hell with that; what good was having friends if you couldn't bother them in a time of crisis?

Heading for the nearest public communicator booth, he rushed out of his apartment and nearly collided with a sleek dunning robot in the hallway. The things show no mercy, Mueller thought. They plague you at all hours. No doubt this one was on its way to bother the deadbeat Nicholson family down the hall.

The robot said, "Mr. Paul Mueller? I am a properly qualified representative of International Fabrication Cartel, Amalgamated. I am here to serve notice that there is an unpaid balance in your account to the extent of $9,150.55, which as of 0900 hours tomorrow morning will accrue compounded penalty interest at a rate of 5 percent per month. since Since you have not responded to our three previous requests for payment. I must further inform you—"

"You're off your neutrinos," Mueller snapped. "I don't owe a dime to IFC. For once in my life I'm in the black, and don't try to make me believe otherwise."

The robot replied patiently, "Shall I give you a printout of the transactions? On the fifth of January, 2003, you ordered the following metal products from us: three 4-meter tubes of antiqued iridium, six 10-centimeter spheres of—"

"The fifth of January, 2003, happens to be three months from now," Mueller said "and I don't have time to listen to crazy robots. I've got an important call to make. Can I trust you to patch me into the datanet without garbling things?"

"I'm not authorized to permit you to make use of my facilities."

"Emergency override," said Mueller. "Human being in trouble. Go argue with that one!"

The robot's conditioning was sound. It yielded at once to his assertion of an emergency and set up a relay to the main communications net. Mueller supplied Freddy Munson's number. "I can provide audio only," the robot said, putting the call through. Nearly a minute passed. Then Freddy Munson's familiar deep voice snarled from the speaker grille in the robot's chest, "Who is it and what do you want?"

"It's Paul. I'm sorry to bust in on you, Freddy, but I'm in big trouble. I think I'm losing my mind, or else everybody else is."

"Maybe everybody else is. What's the problem?"

"All my furniture's gone. A dunning robot is trying to shake me down for nine bigs. I don't know where Carole is. I can't remember what I was doing earlier today. I've got a note here about getting tickets to Caracas that I wrote myself, and I don't know why. And—"

"Skip the rest," Munson said. "I can't do anything for you. I've got problems of my own."

"Can I come over, at least, and talk?"

"Absolutely not!" In a softer voice Munson said, "Listen, Paul, I didn't mean to yell, but something's come up here, something very distressing—"

"You don't need to pretend. You've got Helene with you and you wish I'd leave you alone. Okay."

"No. Honestly," Munson said. "I've got problems, suddenly. I'm in a totally ungood position to give you any help at all. I need help myself."

"What sort? Anything I can do for you?"

"I'm afraid not. And if you'll excuse me, Paul—"

"Just tell me one thing, at least. Where am I likely to find Carole? Do you have any idea?"

"At her husband's place, I'd say."

"*I'm* her husband."

There was a long pause. Munson said finally, "Paul, she divorced you last January and married Pete Castine in April."

"No," Mueller said.

"What, no?"

"No, it isn't possible."

"Have you been popping pills, Paul? Sniffing something? Smoking weed? Look, I'm sorry, but I can't take time now to—"

"At least tell me what day today is."

"Wednesday."

"Which Wednesday?"

"Wednesday the eighth of May. Thursday the ninth, actually, by this time of night."

"And the year?"

"For Christ's sake, Paul—"

"The *year?*"

"2003."

Mueller sagged. "Freddy, I've lost half a year somewhere! For me it's last October. 2002. I've some weird kind of amnesia. It's the only explanation."

"Amnesia," Munson said. The edge of tension left his voice. "Is that what you've got? Amnesia? Can there be such a thing as an epidemic of amnesia? Is it contagious? Maybe you better come over here after all. Because amnesia's my problem too."

Thursday, May 9, promised to be as beautiful as the previous day had been. The sun once again beamed on San Francisco; the sky was clear, the air warm and tender. Commander Braskett awoke early as always, punched for his usual Spartan breakfast, studied the morning xerofax news, spent an hour dictating his memoirs, and, about nine, went out for a walk. The streets were strangely crowded, he found, when he got down to the shopping district along Haight Street. People were wandering aimlessly, dazedly, as though they were sleepwalkers. Were they drunk? Drugged? Three times in five minutes Commander Braskett was stopped by young men who wanted to know the date. Not the time, the *date*. He told them, crisply, disdainfully; he tried to be tolerant, but it was difficult for him not to despise people who were so weak that they were unable to refrain from poisoning their minds with stimulants and narcotics and psychedelics and similar trash. At the corner of Haight and Masonic a forlorn-looking pretty girl of about seventeen, with wide blank blue eyes, halted him and said, "Sir, this city is San Francisco, isn't it? I mean, I was supposed to move here from Pittsburgh in May, and if this is May, this is San Francisco, right?" Commander Braskett nodded brusquely and turned away, pained.

He was relieved to see an old friend, Lou Sandler, the manager of the Bank of America office across the way. Sandler was standing outside the bank door. Commander Braskett crossed to him and said, "Isn't it a disgrace, Lou, the way this whole street is filled with addicts this morning? What is it, some historical pageant of the 1960s?" And Sandler gave him an empty smile and said, "Is that my name? Lou? You wouldn't happen to know the last name too, would you? Somehow it's slipped my mind." In that moment Commander Braskett realized that something terrible had happened to his city and perhaps to his country, and that the leftist takeover he had long dreaded must now be at hand, and that it was time for him to don his old uniform again and do what he could to strike back at the enemy.

In joy and in confusion, Nate Haldersen awoke that morning realizing that he had been transformed in some strange and wonderful way. His head was throbbing, but not painfully. It seemed to him that a terrible weight had been lifted from his shoulders, that the fierce dead hand about his throat had at last relinquished its grip.

He sprang from bed, full of questions.

Where am I? What kind of place is this? Why am I not at home? Where are my books? Why do I feel so happy?

This seemed to be a hospital room.

There was a veil across his mind. He pierced its filmy folds and realized that he had committed himself to—to Fletcher Memorial—last August—no, the August before last—suffering with a severe emotional disturbance brought on by—brought on by—

He had never felt happier than this moment.

He saw a mirror. In it was the reflected upper half of Nathaniel Haldersen, Ph.D. Nate Haldersen smiled at himself. Tall, stringy, long-nosed man, absurdly straw-colored hair, absurd blue eyes, thin lips, smiling. Bony body. He undid his pajama top. Pale, hairless chest; bump of bone like an epaulet on each shoulder. I have been sick a long time, Haldersen thought. Now I must get out of here, back to my classroom. End of leave of absence. Where are my clothes?

"Nurse? Doctor?"' He pressed his call button three times. "Hello? Anyone here?"

No one came. Odd; they always came. Shrugging, Haldersen moved out into the hall. He saw three orderlies, heads together, buzzing at the far end. They ignored him. A robot servitor carrying breakfast trays glided past. A moment later one of the younger doctors came running through the hall, and would not stop when Haldersen called to him. Annoyed, he went back into his room and looked about for clothing. He found none, only a little stack of magazines on the closet floor. He thumbed the call button three more times. Finally one of the robots entered the room.

"I am sorry," it said, "but the human hospital personnel are busy at present. May I serve you, Dr. Haldersen?"

"I want a suit of clothing. I'm leaving the hospital."

"I am sorry, but there is no record of your discharge. Without authorization from Dr. Bryce, Dr. Reynolds, or Dr. Kamakura, I am not permitted to allow your departure."

Haldersen sighed. He knew better than to argue with a robot. "Where are those three gentlemen right now?"

"They are occupied, sir. As you may know, there is a medical emergency in the city this morning, and Dr. Bryce and Dr. Kamakura are helping to organize the committee of public safety. Dr. Reynolds did not report for duty today and we are unable to trace him. It is believed that he is a victim of the current difficulty."

"What current difficulty?"

"Mass loss of memory on the part of the human population," the robot said.

"An epidemic of amnesia?"

"That is one interpretation of the problem."

"How can such a thing—" Haldersen stopped. He understood now the source of his own joy this morning. Only yesterday afternoon he had discussed with Tim Bryce the application of memory-destroying drugs to his own trauma and Bryce had said—

Haldersen no longer knew the nature of his own trauma.

"Wait," he said, as the robot began to leave the room. "I need information. Why have I been under treatment here?"

"You have been suffering from social displacements and dysfunctions whose origin, Dr. Bryce feels, lies in a situation of traumatic personal loss."

"Loss of what?"

"Your family, Dr. Haldersen."

"Yes. That's right. I recall, now—I had a wife and two children. Emily. And a little girl—Margaret, Elizabeth, something like that. And a boy named John. What happened to them?"

"They were passengers aboard Intercontinental Airways Flight 103, Copenhagen to San Francisco, September 5, 1991. The plane underwent explosive decompression over the Arctic Ocean and there were no survivors."

Haldersen absorbed the information as calmly as though he were hearing of the assassination of Julius Caesar.

"Where was I when the accident occurred?"

"In Copenhagen," the robot replied. "You had intended to return to San Francisco with your family on Flight 103; however, according to your data file here, you became involved in an emotional relationship with a woman named Marie Rasmussen, whom you had met in Copenhagen, and failed to return to your hotel in time to go to the airport. Your wife, evidently aware of the situation, chose not to wait for you. Her subsequent death, and that of your children, produced a traumatic guilt reaction in which you came to regard yourself as responsible for their terminations."

"I *would* take that attitude, wouldn't I?" Haldersen said. "Sin and retribution. Mea culpa, mea maxima culpa. I always had a harsh view of sin, even when I was sinning. I should have been an Old Testament prophet."

"Shall I provide more information, sir?"

"Is there more?"

"We have in the files Dr. Bryce's report headed, *The Job Complex: A Study in the Paralysis of Guilt.*"

"Spare me that," Haldersen said. "All right, go."

He was alone. The Job Complex, he thought. Not really appropriate, was it? Job was a man without sin, and yet he was punished grievously to satisfy a whim of the Almighty. A little presumptuous, I'd say, to identify myself with him. Cain would have been a better choice. Cain said unto the Lord, My punishment is greater than I can bear. But Cain was a sinner. I was a sinner. I sinned and Emily died for it. When, eleven, eleven-and-a-half years ago? And now I know nothing at all about it except what the machine just told me. Redemption through oblivion, I'd call it. I have expiated my sin and now I'm free. I have no business staying in this hospital any longer. Strait is the gate, and narrow is the way, which leadeth unto life, and few there be that find it. I've got to get out of here. Maybe I can be of some help to others.

He belted his bathrobe, took a drink of water, and went out of the room. No one stopped him. The elevator did not seem to be running, but he found the stairs, and walked down, a little creakily. He had not been this far from his room in more than a year. The lowest floors of the hospital were in chaos—doctors, orderlies, robots, patients, all milling around excitedly. The robots were trying to calm people and get them back to their proper places. "Excuse me," Haldersen said serenely. "Excuse me. Excuse me." He left the hospital, unmolested, by the front door. The air outside was as fresh as young wine; he felt like weeping when it hit his nostrils. He was free. Redemption through oblivion. The disaster high above the Arctic no longer dominated his thoughts. He looked upon it precisely as if it had happened to the family of some other man, long ago. Haldersen began to walk briskly down Van Ness, feeling vigor returning to his legs with every stride. A young woman, sobbing wildly, erupted from a building and collided with him. He caught her, steadied her, was surprised at his own strength as he kept her from toppling. She trembled and pressed her head against his chest. "Can I do anything for you?" he asked. "Can I be of any help?"

❋

Panic had begun to enfold Freddy Munson during dinner at Ondine's Wednesday night. He had begun to be annoyed with Helene in the midst of the truffled chicken breasts, and so he started to think about the details of business; and to his amazement he did not seem to have the details quite right in his mind; and so he felt the early twinges of terror.

The trouble was that Helene was going on and on about the art of sonic sculpture in general and Paul Mueller in particular. Her interest was enough to arouse faint jealousies in Munson. Was she getting ready to leap from his bed to Paul's? Was she thinking of abandoning the wealthy, glamorous, but essentially prosaic stockbroker for the irresponsible, impecunious, fascinatingly gifted sculptor? Of course, Helene kept company with a number of other men, but Munson knew them and discounted them as rivals; they were nonentities, escorts to fill her idle nights when he was too busy for her. Paul Mueller, however, was another case. Munson could not bear the thought that Helene might leave him for Paul. So he shifted his concentration to the day's maneuvers. He had extracted a thousand shares of the $5.87 convertible preferred of Lunar Transit from the Schaeffer account, pledging it as collateral to cover his shortage in the matter of the Comsat debentures, and then, tapping the Howard account for five thousand Southeast Energy Corporation warrants, he had—or had those warrants come out of the Brewster account? Brewster was big on utilities. So was Howard, but that account was heavy on Mid-Atlantic Power, so would it also be loaded with Southeast Energy? In any case, had he put those warrants up against the Zurich uranium futures, or were they riding as his markers in that Antarctic oil-lease thing? He could not remember.

He could not remember.

He could not remember.

Each transaction had been in its own compartment. The partitions were down, suddenly. Numbers were spilling about in his mind as though his brain were in free fall. All of today's deals were tumbling. It frightened him. He began to gobble his food, wanting now to get out of here, to get rid of Helene, to get home and try to reconstruct his activities of the afternoon. Oddly, he could remember quite clearly all that he had done yesterday—the Xerox switch, the straddle on Steel—but today was washing away minute by minute.

"Are you all right?" Helene asked.

"No, I'm not," he said. "I'm coming down with something."

"The Venus virus. Everybody's getting it."

"Yes, that must be it. The Venus virus. You'd better keep clear of me tonight."

They skipped dessert and cleared out fast. He dropped Helene off at her flat; she hardly seemed disappointed, which bothered him, but not nearly so much as what was happening to his mind. Alone, finally, he tried to jot down an outline of his day, but even more had left him now. In the restaurant he had known which stocks he had handled, though he wasn't sure what he had done with them. Now he couldn't even recall the specific securities. He was out on the limb for millions of dollars of other people's money, and every detail was in his mind, and his mind was falling apart. By the time Paul Mueller called, a little after midnight, Munson was growing desperate. He was relieved, but not exactly cheered, to learn that whatever strange thing had affected his mind had hit Mueller a lot harder. Mueller had forgotten everything since last October.

"You went bankrupt,' Munson had to explain to him. "You had this wild scheme for setting up a central clearinghouse for works of art, a kind of stock exchange—the sort of thing only an artist would try to start. You wouldn't let me discourage you. Then you began signing notes, and taking on contingent liabilities, and before the project was six weeks old you were hit with half a dozen lawsuits and it all began to go sour."

"When did this happen, precisely?"

"You conceived the idea at the beginning of November. By Christmas yon you were in severe trouble. You already had a bunch of personal debts that had gone unpaid from before, and your assets melted away and you hit a terrible bind in your work and couldn't produce a thing. You really don't remember a thing of this, Paul?"

"Nothing."

"After the first of the year the fastest moving creditors started getting decrees against you. They impounded everything you owned except the furniture, and then they took the furniture. You borrowed from all of your friends, but they couldn't give you enough, because you were borrowing thousands and you owed hundreds of thousands."

"How much did I hit you for?"

"Eleven bigs," Munson said. "But don't worry about that now."

"I'm not. I'm not worrying about a thing. I was in a bind in my work, you say?" Mueller chuckled. "That's all gone. I'm itching to start making things. All I need are the tools—I mean, money to buy the tools."

" What would they cost?"

"Two-and-a-half bigs," Mueller said.

Munson coughed. "All right. I can't transfer the money to your account, because your creditors would lien it right away. I'll get some cash at the bank. You'll have three bigs tomorrow, and welcome to it."

"Bless you, Freddy," Mueller said. "This kind of amnesia is a good thing, eh? I was so worried about money that I couldn't work. Now I'm not worried at all. I guess I'm still in debt, but I'm not fretting. Tell me what happened to my marriage, now."

"Carole got fed up and turned off," said Munson. "She opposed your business venture from the start. When it began to devour you, she did what she could to untangle you from it, but you insisted on trying to patch things together with more loans and she filed for a decree. When she was free, Pete Castine moved in and grabbed her."

"That's the hardest part to believe. That she'd marry an art dealer, a totally noncreative person, a—a parasite, really—"

"They were always good friends," Munson said. "I won't say they were lovers, because I don't know, but they were close. And Pete's not that horrible. He's got taste, intelligence, everything an artist needs except the gift. I think Carole may have been weary of gifted men, anyway."

"How did I take it?" Mueller asked.

"You hardly seemed to notice, Paul. You were so busy with your financial shenanigans."

Mueller nodded. He sauntered to one of his own works, a three-meter-high arrangement of oscillating rods that ran the whole sound spectrum into high kilohertzes, and passed two fingers over the activator eye. The sculpture began to murmur. After a few moments Mueller said, "You sounded awfully upset when I called, Freddy. You say you have some kind of amnesia too?"

Trying to be casual about it, Munson said, "I find I can't remember some important financial transactions I carried out today. Unfortunately, my only record of them is in my head. But maybe the information will come back to me when I've slept on it."

"There's no way I can help you with that."

"No. There isn't."

"Freddy, where is this amnesia coming from?"

Munson shrugged. "Maybe somebody put a drug in the water supply, or spiked the food, or something. These days, you never can tell. Look, I've got to do some work, Paul. If you'd like to sleep here tonight—"

"I'm wide awake; thanks. I'll drop by again in the morning."

When the sculptor was gone, Munson struggled for a feverish hour to reconstruct his data, and failed. Shortly before two he took a four-hour sleep pill. When he awakened, he realized in dismay that he had no memories whatever for the period from April 1 to noon yesterday. During those five weeks he had engaged in countless securities transactions, using other people's property as his collateral, and counting on his ability to get each marker in his game back into its proper place before anyone was likely to go looking for it. He had always been able to remember everything. Now he could remember nothing. He reached his office at seven in the morning, as always, and out of habit plugged himself into the data channels to study the Zurich and London quotes, but the prices on the screen were strange to him, and he knew that he was undone.

At that same moment of Thursday morning Dr. Timothy Bryce's house computer triggered an impulse and the alarm voice in his pillow said quietly but firmly, "It's time to wake up, Dr. Bryce." He stirred but lay still. After the prescribed ten-second interval the voice said, a little more sharply, "It's time to wake up, Dr. Bryce." Bryce sat up, just in time; the lifting of his head from the pillow cut off the third, much sterner, repetition which would have been followed by the opening chords of the *Jupiter* Symphony. The psychiatrist opened his eyes.

He was surprised to find himself sharing his bed with a strikingly attractive girl.

She was a honey blonde, deeply tanned, with light-brown eyes, full pale lips, and a sleek, elegant body. She looked to be fairly young, a good twenty years younger than he was—perhaps twenty-five, twenty-eight. She wore nothing, and she was in a deep sleep, her lower lip sagging in a sort of involuntary pout. Neither her youth nor her beauty nor her nudity surprised him; he was puzzled simply because he had no notion who she was or how she had come to be in bed with him. He felt as though he had never seen her before. Certainly he didn't know her name. Had he picked her up at some party last night? He couldn't seem to remember where he had been last night. Gently he nudged her elbow.

She woke quickly, fluttering her eyelids, shaking her head.

"Oh," she said, as she saw him, and clutched the sheet up to her throat. Then, smiling, she dropped it again. "That's foolish. No need to be modest *now*, I guess."

"I guess. Hello."

"Hello," she said. She looked as confused as he was.

"This is going to sound stupid," he said, "but someone must have slipped me a weird weed last night, because I'm afraid I'm not sure how I happened to bring you home. Or what your name is."

"Lisa," she said. "Lisa—Falk." She stumbled over the second name. "And you're—"

"Tim Bryce."

"You don't remember where we met?"

"No," he said.

"Neither do I."

He got out of bed, feeling a little hesitant about his own nakedness, and fighting the inhibition off. "They must have given us both the same thing to smoke, then. You know"—he grinned shyly—"I can't even remember if we had a good time together last night. I hope we did."

"I think we did," she said. "I can't remember it either. But I feel good inside—the way I usually do after I've—" She paused. We couldn't have met only just last night, Tim."

"How can you tell?"

"I've got the feeling that I've known you longer than that."

Bryce shrugged. "I don't see how. I mean, without being too coarse about it, obviously we were both high last night, really floating, and we met and came here and—"

"No. I feel at home here. As if I moved in with you weeks and weeks ago."

"A lovely idea. But I'm sure you didn't."

"Why do I feel so much at home here, then?"

"In what way?"

"In every way." She walked to the bedroom closet and let her hand rest on the touchplate. The door slid open; evidently he had keyed the house computer to her fingerprints. Had he done that last night too? She reached in. "My clothing," she said. "Look. All these dresses, coats, shoes. A whole wardrobe. There can't be any doubt. We've been living together and don't remember it!"

A chill swept through him. "What have they done to us? Listen, Lisa, let's get dressed and eat and go down to the hospital together for a checkup. We—"

"Hospital?"

"Fletcher Memorial. I'm in the neurological department. Whatever they slipped us last night has hit us both with a lacunary retrograde amnesia—a gap in our memories—and it could be serious. If it's caused brain damage, perhaps it's not irreversible yet, but we can't fool around."

She put her hands to her lips in fear. Bryce felt a sudden warm urge to protect this lovely stranger, to guard and comfort her, and he realized he must be in love with her, even though he couldn't remember who she was. He crossed the room to her and seized her in a brief, tight embrace; she responded eagerly, shivering a little. By a quarter to eight they were out of the house and heading for the hospital through unusually light traffic. Bryce led the girl quickly to the staff lounge. Ted Kamakura was there already, in uniform. The little Japanese psychiatrist nodded curtly and said, "Morning, Tim."

Then he blinked. "Good morning, Lisa. How come *you're* here?"

"You know her?" Bryce asked.

"What kind of a question is that?"

"A deadly serious one."

"Of course I know her," Kamakura said, and his smile of greeting abruptly faded. "Why? Is something wrong about that?"

"You may know her, but I don't," said Bryce.

"Oh, God. Not you too!"

"Tell me who she is, Ted."

"She's your wife, Tim. You married her five years ago."

By half past eleven Thursday morning the Gerards had everything set up and going smoothly for the lunch rush at the Petit Pois. The soup caldron was bubbling, the escargot trays were ready to be popped in the oven, the sauces were taking form. Pierre Gerard was a bit surprised when most of the lunchtime regulars failed to show up. Even Mr. Munson, always punctual at half past eleven, did not arrive. Some of these men had not missed weekday lunch at the Petit Pois in fifteen years. Something terrible must have happened on the stock market, Pierre thought, to have kept all these financial men at their desks, and they were too busy to call him and cancel their usual tables. That must be the answer. It was impossible that any of the regulars would forget to call him. The stock market must be exploding. Pierre made a mental note to call his broker after lunch and find out what was going on.

※

About two Thursday afternoon, Paul Mueller stopped into Metchnikoff's Art Supplies in North Beach to try to get a welding pen, some raw metal, loudspeaker paint, and the rest of the things he needed for the rebirth of his sculpting career. Metchnikoff greeted him sourly with, "No credit at all, Mr. Mueller, not even a nickel!"

"It's all right. I'm a cash customer this time."

The dealer brightened. "In that case it's all right, maybe. You finished with your troubles?"

" I hope so," Mueller said.

He gave the order. It came to about $2,300; when the time came to pay, he explained that he simply had to run down to Montgomery Street to pick up the cash from his friend Freddy Munson, who was holding three bigs for him. Metchnikoff began to glower again. "Five minutes!" Mueller called. "I'll be back in five minutes!" But when he got to Munson's office, he found the place in confusion, and Munson wasn't there. "Did he leave an envelope for a Mr. Mueller?" he asked a distraught secretary. "I was supposed to pick something important up here this afternoon. Would you please check?" The girl simply ran away from him. So did the next girl. A burly broker told him to get out of the office. "We're closed, fellow," he shouted. Baffled, Mueller left.

Not daring to return to Metchnikoff's with the news that he hadn't been able to raise the cash after all, Mueller simply went home. Three dunning robots were camped outside his door, and each one began to croak its cry of doom as he approached. "Sorry," Mueller said, "I can't remember a thing about any of this stuff," and he went inside and sat down on the bare floor, angry, thinking of the brilliant pieces he could be turning out if he could only get his hands on the tools of his trade. He made sketches instead. At least the ghouls had left him with pencil and paper. Not as efficient as a computer screen and a light-pen, maybe, but Michelangelo and Benvenuto Cellini had managed to make out all right without computer screens and light-pens.

At four o'clock the door bell rang.

"Go *away*," Mueller said through the speaker. "See my accountant! I don't want to hear any more dunnings, and the next time I catch one of you idiot robots by my door I'm going to—"

"It's me, Paul," a nonmechanical voice said.

Carole.

He rushed to the door. There were seven robots out there, surrounding her, and they tried to get in; but he pushed them back so she could enter. A robot didn't dare lay a paw on a human being. He slammed the door in their metal faces and locked it.

Carole looked fine. Her hair was longer than he remembered it, and she had gained about eight pounds in all the right places, and she wore an iridescent peekaboo wrap that he had never seen before, and which was really inappropriate for afternoon wear, but which looked splendid on her. She seemed at least five years younger than she really was; evidently a month and a half of marriage to Pete Castine had done more for her than nine years of marriage to Paul Mueller. She glowed. She also looked strained and tense, but that seemed superficial, the product of some distress of the last few hours.

"I seem to have lost my key," she said.

"What are you doing here?"

"I don't understand you, Paul."

"I mean why'd you come here?"

"I *live* here."

"Do you?' He laughed harshly. "Very funny."

"You always did have a weird sense of humor, Paul." She stepped past him. "Only this isn't any joke. Where is everything? The furniture, Paul. My things." Suddenly she was crying. "I must be breaking up. I wake up this morning in a completely strange apartment, all alone, and I spend the whole day wandering in a sort of daze that I don't understand at all, and now I finally come home and find that you've pawned every damn thing we own, or something and—" She bit her knuckles. "Paul?"

She's got it too, he thought. The amnesia epidemic.

He said quietly, "This is a funny thing to ask, Carole, but will you tell me what today's date is?"

"Why—the fourteenth of September—or is it the fifteenth—"

"2002?"

"What do you think? 1776?"

She's got it worse than I have, Mueller told himself. She's lost a whole extra month. She doesn't remember my business venture. She doesn't remember my losing all the money. *She doesn't remember divorcing me.* She thinks she's still my wife.

"Come in here," he said, and led her to the bedroom. He pointed to the cot that stood where their bed had been. "Sit down, Carole. I'll try to explain. It won't make much sense but I'll try to explain."

Under the circumstances, the concert by the visiting New York Philharmonic for Thursday evening was cancelled. Nevertheless the orchestra assembled for its rehearsal at half past two in the afternoon. The union required so many rehearsals—with pay—a week; therefore the orchestra rehearsed, regardless of external cataclysms. But there were problems. Maestro Alvarez, who used an electronic baton and proudly conducted without a score, thumbed the button for a downbeat and realized abruptly, with a sensation as of dropping through a trapdoor, that the Brahms Fourth was wholly gone from his mind. The orchestra responded raggedly to his faltering leadership. Some of the musicians had no difficulties, but the concertmaster stared in horror at his left hand, wondering how to finger the strings for the notes his violin was supposed to be yielding, and second oboe could not find the proper keys, and the first bassoon had not yet even managed to remember how to put his instrument together.

By nightfall, Tim Bryce had managed to assemble enough of the story so that he understood what had happened, not only to himself and to Lisa, but to the entire city. A drug, or drugs, almost certainly distributed through the municipal water supply, had leached away nearly everyone's memory. The trouble with modern life, Bryce thought, is that technology gives us the potential for newer and more intricate disasters every year, but it doesn't seem to give us the ability to ward them off. Memory drugs were old stuff, going back thirty, forty years. He had studied several types of them himself. Memory is partly a chemical and partly an electrical process; some drugs went after the electrical end, jamming the synapses over which brain transmissions travel, and some went after the molecular substrata in which long-term memories are locked up. Bryce knew ways of destroying short-term memories by inhibiting synapse transmission, and he knew ways of destroying the deep long-term memories by washing out the complex chains of ribonucleic acid, brain-RNA, by which they are inscribed in the brain. But such drugs were experimental, tricky, unpredictable; he had hesitated to use them on human subjects; he certainly had never imagined that anyone would simply dump them into an aqueduct and give an entire city a simultaneous lobotomy.

His office at Fletcher Memorial had become an improvised center of operations for San Francisco. The mayor was there, pale and shrunken; the chief of police, exhausted and confused, periodically turned his back and popped a pill; a dazed-looking representative of the communications net hovered in a corner, nervously monitoring the hastily rigged system through which the committee of public safety that Bryce had summoned could make its orders known throughout the city.

The mayor was no use at all. He couldn't even remember having run for office. The chief of police was in even worse shape: he had been up all night because he had forgotten, among other things, his home address, and he had been afraid to query a computer about it for fear he'd lose his job for drunkenness. By now the chief of police was aware that he wasn't the only one in the city having memory problems today, and he had looked up his address in the files and even telephoned his wife, but he was close to collapse. Bryce had insisted that both men stay here as symbols of order; he wanted only their faces and their voices, not their fumble-headed official services.

A dozen or so miscellaneous citizens had accumulated in Bryce's office too. At five in the afternoon he had broadcast an all-media appeal, asking anyone whose memory of recent events was unimpaired to come to Fletcher Memorial. "If you haven't had any city water in the past twenty-four hours, you're probably all right. Come down here. We need you." He had drawn a curious assortment. There was a ramrod-straight old space hero, Taylor Braskett, a pure-foods nut who drank only mountain water. There was a family of French restaurateurs, mother, father, three grown children, who preferred mineral water flown in from their native land. There was a computer salesman named McBurney who had been in Los Angeles on business and hadn't had any of the drugged water. There was a retired cop named Adler who lived in Oakland, where there were no memory problems; he had hurried across the bay as soon as he heard that San Francisco was in trouble. That was before all access to the city had been shut off at Bryce's orders. And there were some others, of doubtful value but of definitely intact memory.

The three screens that the communications man had mounted provided a relay of key points in the city. Right now one was monitoring the Fisherman's Wharf district from a camera atop Ghirardelli Square, one was viewing the financial district from a helicopter over the old Ferry Building Museum, and one was relaying a pickup from a mobile truck in Golden Gate Park. The scenes were similar everywhere: people milling about, asking questions, getting no answers. There wasn't any sign of looting yet. There were no fires. The police, those of them able to function, were out in force, and antiriot robots were cruising the bigger streets, just in case they might be needed to squirt their stifling blankets of foam at suddenly panicked mobs.

Bryce said to the mayor, "At half past six I want you to go on all media with an appeal for calm. We'll supply you with everything you have to say."

The mayor moaned.

Bryce said, "Don't worry. I'll feed you the whole speech by bone relay. Just concentrate on speaking clearly and looking straight into the camera. If you come across as a terrified man, it can be the end for all of us. If you look cool, we may be able to pull through."

The mayor put his face in his hands.

Ted Kamakura whispered, "You can't put him on the channels, Tim! He's a wreck, and everyone will see it!"

"The city's mayor has to show himself," Bryce insisted. "Give him a double jolt of bracers. Let him make this one speech and then we can put him to pasture."

"Who'll be the spokesman, then?" Kamakura asked. "You? Me? Police Chief Dennison?"

"I don't know," Bryce muttered. "We need an authority-image to make announcements every half hour or so, and I'm damned if I'll have time. Or you. And Dennison—"

"Gentlemen, may I make a suggestion?" it was the old spaceman Braskett. "I wish to volunteer as spokesman. You must admit I have a certain look of authority. And I'm accustomed to speaking to the public."

Bryce rejected the idea instantly. That right-wing crackpot, author of passionate nut letters to every news medium in the state, that latterday Paul Revere? Him, spokesman for the committee? But in the moment of rejection came acceptance. Nobody really paid attention to far-out political activities like that; probably nine people out of ten in San Francisco thought of Braskett, if at all, simply as the hero of the first Mars expedition.

He was a handsome old horse, too, elegantly upright and lean. Deep voice; unwavering eyes. A man of strength and presence.

Bryce said, "Commander Braskett, if we were to make you chairman of the committee of public safety—"

Ted Kamakura gasped.

"—would I have your assurance that such public announcements as you would make would be confined entirely to statements of the policies arrived at by the entire committee?"

Commander Braskett smiled glacially. "You want me to be a figurehead, is that it?"

"To be our spokesman, with the official title of chairman."

"As I said: to be a figurehead. Very well, I accept. I'll mouth my lies like an obedient puppet, and I won't attempt to inject any of my radical, extremist ideas into my statements. Is that what you wish?"

"I think we understand each other perfectly," Bryce said, and smiled, and got a surprisingly warm smile in return.

He jabbed now at his data board. Someone in the path lab eight stories below his office answered, and Bryce said, "Is there an up-to-date analysis yet?"

Madison appeared on the screen. He ran the hospital's radioisotope department, normally: a beefy, red-faced man who looked as though he ought to be a beer salesman. He knew his subject. "It's definitely the water supply, Tim," he said at once. "We tentatively established that an hour and a half ago, of course, but now there's no doubt. I've isolated traces of two different memory-suppressant drugs, and there's the possibility of a third. Whoever it was was taking no chances."

"What are they?" Bryce asked.

"Well, we've got a good jolt of acetylcholine terminase," Madison said, "which will louse up the synapses and interfere with short-term memory fixation. Then there's something else, perhaps a puromycin-derivative protein dissolver, which is going to work on the brain-RNA and smashing up older memories. I suspect also that we've been getting one of the newer experimental amnesifacients, something that I haven't isolated yet, capable of working its way deep and cutting out really basic motor patterns. So they've hit us high, low, and middle."

"That explains a lot. The guys who can't remember what they did yesterday, the guys who've lost a chunk out of their adult memories, and the ones who don't even remember their names—this thing is working on people at all different levels."

"Depending on individual metabolism, age, brain structure, and how much water they had to drink yesterday, yes."

"Is the water supply still tainted?" Bryce asked.

"Tentatively, I'd say no. I've had water samples brought me from the upflow districts, and everything's okay there. The water department has been running its own check; they say the same. Evidently the stuff got into the system early yesterday, came down into the city, and is generally gone by now. Might be some residuals in the pipes; I'd be careful about drinking water even today."

"And what does the pharmacopoeia say about the effectiveness of these drugs?"

Madison shrugged. "Anybody's guess. You'd know that better than I. Do they wear off?"

"Not in the normal sense," said Bryce. "What happens is the brain cuts in a redundancy circuit and gets access to a duplicate set of the affected memories, eventually—shifts to another track, so to speak—provided a duplicate of the sector in question was there in the first place, and provided that the duplicate wasn't blotted out also. Some people are going to get chunks of their memories back, in a few days or a few weeks. Others won't."

"Wonderful," Madison said. "I'll keep you posted, Tim."

Bryce cut off the call and said to the communications man, "You have that bone relay? Get it behind His Honor's ear."

The mayor quivered. The little instrument was fastened in place.

Bryce said, "Mr. Mayor, I'm going to dictate a speech, and you're going to broadcast it on all media, and it's the last thing I'm going to ask of you until you've had a chance to pull yourself together. Okay? Listen carefully to what I'm saying, speak slowly, and pretend that tomorrow is election day and your job depends on how well you come across now. You won't be going on live. There'll be a fifteen-second delay, and we have a wipe circuit so we can correct any stumbles, and there's absolutely no reason to be tense. Are you with me? Will you give it all you've got?"

"My mind is all foggy."

"Simply listen to me and repeat what I say into the camera's eye. Let your political reflexes take over. Here's your chance to make a hero of yourself. We're living history right now, Mr. Mayor. What we do here today will be studied the way the events of the 1906 fire were studied. Let's go, now. Follow me. *People of the wonderful city of San Francisco—*"

The words rolled easily from Bryce's lips, and, wonder of wonders, the mayor caught them and spoke them in a clear, beautifully resonant voice. As he spun out his speech, Bryce felt a surging flow of power going through himself, and he imagined for the moment that he was the elected leader of the city, not merely a self-appointed emergency dictator. It was an interesting, almost ecstatic feeling. Lisa, watching him in action, gave him a loving smile.

He smiled at her. In this moment of glory he was almost able to ignore the ache of knowing that he had lost his entire memory archive of his life with her. Nothing else gone, apparently. But, neatly, with idiot selectivity, the drug in the water supply had sliced away everything pertaining to his five years of marriage. Kamakura had told him, a few hours ago, that it was the happiest marriage of any he knew. Gone. At least Lisa had suffered an identical loss, against all probabilities. Somehow that made it easier to bear; it would have been awful to have one of them remember the good times and the other know nothing. He was almost able to ignore the torment of loss while he kept busy. Almost.

"The mayor's going to be on in a minute," Nadia said. "Will you listen to him? He'll explain what's been going on."

"I don't care," said the Amazing Montini dully.

"It's some kind of epidemic of amnesia. When I was out before, I heard all about it. *Everyone's* got it. It isn't just you! And you thought it was a stroke, but it wasn't. You're all right."

"My mind is a ruin."

"It's only temporary." Her voice was shrill and unconvincing. "It's something in the air, maybe. Some drug they were testing that drifted in. We're all in this together. I can't remember last week at all."

"What do I care?" Montini said. "Most of these people, they have no memories even when they are healthy. But me? Me? I am destroyed. Nadia, I should lie down in my grave now. There is no sense in continuing to walk around."

The voice from the loudspeaker said, "Ladies and gentlemen, His Honor Elliot Chase, the Mayor of San Francisco."

"Let's listen," Nadia said.

The mayor appeared on the wallscreen, wearing his solemn face, his we-face-a-grave-challenge-citizens face. Montini glanced at him, shrugged, looked away.

The mayor said, "People of the wonderful city of San Francisco, we have just come through the most difficult day in nearly a century, since the terrible catastrophe of April, 1906. The earth has not quaked today, nor have we been smitten by fire, yet we have been severely tested by sudden calamity.

"As all of you surely know, the people of San Francisco have been afflicted since last night by what can best be termed an epidemic of amnesia. There has been mass loss of memory, ranging from mild cases of forgetfulness to near-total obliteration of identity. Scientists working at Fletcher Memorial Hospital have succeeded in determining the cause of this unique and sudden disaster.

"It appears that criminal saboteurs contaminated the municipal water supply with certain restricted drugs that have the ability to dissolve memory structures. *The effect of these drugs is temporary.* There should be no cause for alarm. Even those who are most severely affected will find their memories gradually beginning to return, and there is every reason to expect full recovery in a matter of hours or days."

"He's lying," said Montini.

"The criminals responsible have not yet been apprehended, but we expect arrests momentarily. The San Francisco area is the only affected region, which means the drugs were introduced into the water system just beyond city limits. Everything is normal in Berkeley, in Oakland, in Marin County, and other outlying areas.

"In the name of public safety I have ordered the bridges to San Francisco closed, as well as the Bay Area Rapid Transit and other means of access to the city. We expect to maintain these restrictions at least until tomorrow morning. The purpose of this is to prevent disorder and to avoid a possible influx of undesirable elements into the city while the trouble persists. We San Franciscans are self-sufficient and can look after our own needs without outside interference. However, I have been in contact with the president and with the governor, and they both have assured me of all possible assistance.

"The water supply is at present free of the drug, and every precaution is being taken to prevent a recurrence of this crime against one million innocent people. However, I am told that some lingering contamination may remain in the pipes for a few hours. I recommend that you keep your consumption of water low until further notice, and that you boil any water you wish to use.

"Lastly, Police Chief Dennison, myself, and your other city officials will be devoting full time to the needs of the city so long as the crisis lasts. Probably we will not have the opportunity to go before the media for further reports. Therefore, I have taken the step of appointing a committee of public safety, consisting of distinguished laymen and scientists of San Francisco, as a coordinating body that will aid in governing the city and reporting to its citizens. The chairman of this committee is the well-known veteran of so many exploits in space, Commander Taylor Braskett. Announcements concerning the developments in the crisis will come from Commander Braskett for the remainder of the evening, and you may consider his words to be those of your city officials. Thank you."

Braskett came on the screen. Montini grunted. "Look at the man they find! A maniac patriot!"

"But the drug will wear off," Nadia said. "Your mind will be all right again."

"I know these drugs. There is no hope. I am destroyed." The Amazing Montini moved toward the door. "I need fresh air. I will go out. Goodbye, Nadia."

She tried to stop him. He pushed her aside. Entering Marina Park, he made his way to the yacht club; the doorman admitted him, and took no further notice. Montini walked out on the pier. The drug, they say, is temporary. It will wear off. My mind will clear. I doubt this very much. Montini peered at the dark, oily water, glistening with light reflected from the bridge. He explored his damaged mind, scanning for gaps. Whole sections of memory were gone. The walls had crumbled, slabs of plaster falling away to expose bare lath. He could not live this way. Carefully, grunting from the exertion, he lowered himself via a metal ladder into the water, and kicked himself away from the pier. The water was terribly cold. His shoes seemed immensely heavy. He floated toward the island of the old prison, but he doubted that he would remain afloat much longer. As he drifted, he ran through an inventory of his memory, seeing what remained to him and finding less than enough. To test whether even his gift had survived, he attempted to play back a recall of the mayor's speech, and found the words shifting and melting. It is just as well, then, he told himself, and drifted on, and went under.

❋

Carole insisted on spending Thursday night with him.

"We aren't man and wife any more," he had to tell her. "You divorced me."

"Since when are you so conventional? We lived together before we were married, and now we can live together after we were married. Maybe we're inventing a new sin, Paul. Postmarital sex."

"That isn't the point. The point is that you came to hate me because of my financial mess, and you left me. If you try to come back to me now, you'll be going against your own rational and deliberate decision of last January."

"For me last January is still four months away," she said. "I don't hate you. I love you. I always have and always will. I can't imagine how I would ever have come to divorce you, but in any case I don't remember divorcing you, and you don't remember being divorced by me, and so why can't we just keep going from the point where our memories leave off?"

"Among other things, because you happen to be Pete Castine's wife now."

"That sounds completely unreal to me. Something you dreamed."

"Freddy Munson told me, though. It's true."

"If I went back to Pete now," Carole said, "I'd feel sinful. Simply because I supposedly married him, you want me to jump into bed with him? I don't want him. I want you. Can't I stay here?"

"If Pete—"

"If Pete, if Pete, if Pete! In my mind I'm Mrs. Paul Mueller, and in your mind I am too, and to hell with whatever Freddy Munson told you, and everything else. This is a silly argument, Paul. Let's quit it. If you want me to get out, tell me so right now in that many words. Otherwise let me stay."

He couldn't tell her to get out.

He had only the one small cot, but they managed to share it. It was uncomfortable, but in an amusing way. He felt twenty years old again for a while. In the morning they took a long shower together, and then Carole went out to buy some things for breakfast, since his service had been cut off and he couldn't punch for food. A dunning robot outside the door told him, as Carole was leaving, "The decree of personal service due has been requested, Mr. Mueller, and is now pending a court hearing."

"I know you not," Mueller said. "Begone!"

Today, he told himself, he would hunt up Freddy Munson somehow and get that cash from him, and buy the tools he needed, and start working again. Let the world outside go crazy; so long as he was working, all was well. If he couldn't find Freddy, maybe he could swing the purchase on Carole's credit. She was legally divorced from him and none of his credit taint would stain her; as Mrs. Peter Castine she should surely be able to get hold of a couple of bigs to pay Metchnikoff. Possibly the banks were closed on account of the memory crisis today, Mueller considered; but Metchnikoff surely wouldn't demand cash from Carole. He closed his eyes and imagined how good it would feel to be making things once more.

Carole was gone an hour. When she came back, carrying groceries, Peter Castine was with her.

"He followed me," Carole explained. "He wouldn't let me alone."

He was a slim, poised, controlled man, quite athletic, several years older than Mueller—perhaps into his fifties already—but seemingly very young. Calmly he said, "I was sure that Carole had come here. It's perfectly understandable, Paul. She was here all night, I hope?"

"Does it matter?" Mueller asked.

"To some extent. I'd rather have had her spending the night with her former husband than with some third party entirely."

"She was here all night, yes," Mueller said wearily.

"I'd like her to come home with me now. She *is* my wife, after all."

"She has no recollection of that. Neither do I."

"I'm aware of that." Castine nodded amiably. "In my own case, I've forgotten everything that happened to me before the age of twenty-two. I couldn't tell you my father's first name. However, as a matter of objective reality, Carole's my wife, and her parting from you was rather bitter, and I feel she shouldn't stay here any longer."

"Why are you telling all this to me?" Mueller asked. "If you want your wife to go home with you, ask her to go home with you."

"So I did. She says she won't leave unless you direct her to go."

"That's right," Carole said. "I know whose wife I *think* I am. If Paul throws me out I'll go with you. Not otherwise."

Mueller shrugged. "I'd be a fool to throw her out, Pete. I need her and I want her, and whatever breakup she and I had isn't real to us. I know it's tough on you, but I can't help that. I imagine you'll have no trouble getting an annulment once the courts work out some law to cover cases like this."

Castine was silent for a long moment.

At length he said, "How has your work been going, Paul?"

"I gather that I haven't turned out a thing all year."

"That's correct."

"I'm planning to start again. You might say that Carole has inspired me."

"Splendid," said Castine without intonation of any kind. "I trust this little mixup over our—ah—shared wife won't interfere with the harmonious artist-dealer relationship we used to enjoy?"

"Not at all," Mueller said. "You'll still get my whole output. Why the hell should I resent anything you did? Carole was a free agent when you married her. There's only one little trouble."

"Yes?"

"I'm broke. I have no tools, and I can't work without tools, and I have no way of buying tools."

"How much do you need?"

"Two and a half bigs."

Castine said, "Where's your data pickup? I'll make a credit transfer."

"The phone company disconnected it a long time ago."

"Let me give you a check, then. Say, three thousand even? An advance against future sales." Castine fumbled for a while before locating a blank check. "First one of these I've written in five years, maybe. Odd how you get accustomed to spending by telephone. Here you are, and good luck. To both of you." He made a courtly, bitter bow. "I hope you'll be happy together. And call me up when you've finished a few pieces, Paul. I'll send the van. I suppose you'll have a phone again by then." He went out.

"There's a blessing in being able to forget," Nate Haldersen said. "The redemption of oblivion, I call it. What's happened to San Francisco this week isn't necessarily a disaster. For some of us, it's the finest thing in the world."

They were listening to him—at least fifty people, clustering near his feet. He stood on the stage of the bandstand in the park, just across from the De Young Museum. Shadows were gathering. Friday, the second full day of the memory crisis, was ending. Haldersen had slept in the park last night, and he planned to sleep there again tonight; he realized after his escape from the hospital that his apartment had been shut down long ago and his possessions were in storage. It did not matter. He would live off the land and forage for food. The flame of prophecy was aglow in him.

"Let me tell you how it was with me," he cried. "Three days ago I was in a hospital for mental illness. Some of you are smiling, perhaps, telling me I ought to be back there now, but no! You don't understand. I was incapable of facing the world. Wherever I went, I saw happy families, parents and children, and it made me sick with envy and hatred, so that I couldn't function in society. Why? Why? Because my own wife and children were killed in an air disaster in 1991, that's why, and I missed the plane because I was committing sin that day, and for my sin they died, and I lived thereafter in unending torment! But now all that is flushed from my mind. I have sinned, and I have suffered, and now I am redeemed through merciful oblivion!"

A voice in the crowd called, "If you've forgotten all about it, how come you're telling the story to us?"

"A good question! An excellent question!" Haldersen felt sweat bursting from his pores, adrenaline pumping in his veins. "I know the story only because a machine in the hospital told it to me, yesterday morning. But it came to me from the outside, a secondhand tale. The experience of it within me, the scars, all that has been washed away. The pain of it is gone. Oh, yes, I'm sad that my innocent family perished, but a healthy man learns to control his grief after eleven years, he accepts his loss and goes on. I was sick, sick right *here*, and I couldn't live with my grief, but now I can, I look on it objectively, do you see! And that's why I say there's a blessing in being able to forget. What about you, out there? There must be some of you who suffered painful losses too, and now can no longer remember them, now have been redeemed and released from anguish. Are there any? Are there? Raise your hands. Who's been bathed in holy oblivion? Who out there knows that he's been cleansed, even if he can't remember what it is he's been cleansed from?"

Hands were starting to go up.

Freddy Munson had spent Thursday afternoon, Thursday night, and all of Friday holed up in his apartment with every communications link to the outside turned off. He neither took nor made calls, ignored the telescreens, and had switched on the xerofax only three times in the thirty-six hours.

He knew that he was finished, and he was trying to decide how to react to it.

His memory situation seemed to have stabilized. He was still missing only five weeks of market maneuvers. There wasn't any further decay—not that that mattered; he was in trouble enough—and, despite an optimistic statement last night by Mayor Chase, Munson hadn't seen any evidence that memory loss was reversing itself. He was unable to reconstruct any of the vanished details.

There was no immediate peril, he knew. Most of the clients whose accounts he'd been juggling were wealthy old bats who wouldn't worry about their stocks until they got next month's account statements. They had given him discretionary powers, which was how he had been able to tap their resources for his own benefit in the first place. Up to now, Munson had always been able to complete each transaction within a single month, so the account balanced for every statement. He had dealt with the problem of the securities withdrawals that the statements ought to show by gimmicking the house computer to delete all such withdrawals provided there was no net effect from month to month; that way he could borrow 10,000 shares of United Spaceways or Comsat or IBM for two weeks, use the stock as collateral for a deal of his own, and get it back into the proper account in time with no one the wiser. Three weeks from now, though, the end-of-the-month statements were going to go out showing all of his accounts peppered by inexplicable withdrawals, and he was going to catch hell.

The trouble might even start earlier, and come from a different direction. Since the San Francisco trouble had begun, the market had gone down sharply, and he would probably be getting margin calls on Monday. The San Francisco exchange was closed, of course; it hadn't been able to open Thursday morning because so many of the brokers had been hit hard by amnesia. But New York's exchanges were open, and they had reacted badly to the news from San Francisco, probably out of fear that a conspiracy was afoot and the whole country might soon be pushed into chaos. When the local exchange opened again on Monday, if it opened, it would most likely open at the last New York prices, or near them, and keep on going down. Munson would be asked to put up cash or additional securities to cover his loans. He certainly didn't have the cash, and the only way he could get additional securities would be to dip into still more of his accounts, compounding his offense; on the other hand, if he didn't meet the margin calls they'd sell him out and he'd never be able to restore the stock to the proper accounts, even if he succeeded in remembering which shares went where.

He was trapped. He could stick around for a few weeks, waiting for the ax to fall, or he could get out right now. He preferred to get out right now.

And go where?

Caracas? Reno? Sao Paulo? No, debtor sanctuaries wouldn't do him any good, because he wasn't an ordinary debtor. He was a thief, and the sanctuaries didn't protect criminals, only bankrupts. He had to go farther, all the way to Luna Dome. There wasn't any extradition from the moon. There'd be no hope of coming back, either.

Munson got on the phone, hoping to reach his travel agent. Two tickets to Luna, please. One for him, one for Helene; if she didn't feel like coming, he'd go alone. No, not round trip. But the agent didn't answer. Munson tried the number several times. Shrugging, to decided to order direct, and called United Spaceways next. He got a busy signal. "Shall we wait-list your call?" the data net asked. "It will be three days, at the present state of the backlog of calls, before we can put it through."

"Forget it," Munson said.

He had just realized that San Francisco was closed off, anyway. Unless he tried to swim for it, he couldn't get out of the city to go to the spaceport, even if he did manage to buy tickets to Luna. He was caught here until they opened the transit routes again. How long would that be? Monday, Tuesday, next Friday? They couldn't keep the city shut forever—could they?

What it came down to, Munson saw, was a contest of probabilities. Would someone discover the discrepancies in his accounts before he found a way of escaping to Luna, or would his escape access become available too late? Put on those terms, it became an in interesting gamble instead of a panic situation. He would spend the weekend trying to find a way out of San Francisco, and if he failed, he would try to be a stoic about facing what was to come.

Calm, now, he remembered that he had promised to lend Paul Mueller a few thousand dollars, to help him equip his studio again. Munson was unhappy over having let that slip his mind. He liked to be helpful. And, even now, what were two or three bigs to him? He had plenty of recoverable assets. Might as well let Paul have a little of the money before the lawyers start grabbing it.

One problem. He had less than a hundred in cash on him—who bothered carrying cash?—and he couldn't telephone a transfer of funds to Mueller's account, because Paul didn't have an account with a data net any more, or even a phone. There wasn't any place to get that much cash, either, at this hour of evening, especially with the city paralyzed. And the weekend was coming. Munson had an idea, though. What if he went shopping with Mueller tomorrow, and simply charged whatever the sculptor needed to his own account? Fine. He reached for the phone to arrange the date, remembered that Mueller could not be called, and decided to tell Paul about it in person. Now. He could use some fresh air, anyway.

He half expected to find robot bailiffs outside, waiting to arrest him. But of course no one was after him yet. He walked to the garage. It was a fine night, cool, starry, with perhaps just a hint of fog in the west. Berkeley's lights glittered through the haze. The streets were quiet. In time of crisis people stay home. He drove quickly to Mueller's place. Four robots were in front of it. Munson eyed them edgily, with the wary look of the man who knows that the sheriff will be after him too in a little while. But Mueller, when he came to the door, took no notice of the dunners.

Munson said, "I'm sorry I missed connections with you. The money I promised to lend you—"

"It's all right, Freddy. Pete Castine was here this morning and I borrowed the three bigs from him. I've got my studio set up again. Come in and look?"

Munson entered. "Pete Castine?"

"A good investment for him. He makes money if he has work of mine to sell, right? It's in his best interest to help me get started again. Carole and I have been hooking things up all day."

"Carole?" Munson said. Mueller showed him into the studio. The paraphernalia of a sonic sculptor sat on the floor—a welding pen, a vacuum bell, a big texturing vat, some ingots and strands of wire, and such things. Carole was feeding discarded packing cases into the wall disposal unit. Looking up, she smiled uncertainly and ran her hand through her long dark hair.

"Hello, Freddy."

"Everybody good friends again?" he asked, baffled.

"Nobody remembers being enemies," she said. She laughed. "Isn't it wonderful to have your memory blotted out like this?"

"Wonderful," Munson said bleakly.

✹

Commander Braskett said, "Can I offer you people any water?"

Tim Bryce smiled. Lisa Bryce smiled. Ted Kamakura smiled. Even Mayor Chase, that poor empty husk, smiled. Commander Braskett understood those smiles. Even now, after three days of close contact under pressure, they thought he was nuts.

He had had a week's supply of bottled water brought from his home to the command post here at the hospital. Everybody kept telling him that the municipal water was safe to drink now, that the memory drugs were gone from it; but why couldn't they comprehend that his aversion to public water dated back to an era when memory drugs were unknown? There were plenty of other chemicals in the reservoir, after all.

He hoisted his glass in a jaunty toast and winked at them.

Tim Bryce said, "Commander, we'd like you to address the city again at half past ten this morning."

Braskett scanned the sheet. It dealt mostly with the relaxation of the order to boil water before drinking it. "You want me to go on all media," he said, "and tell the people of San Francisco that it's safe for them to drink from the taps, eh? That's a bit awkward for me. Even a figurehead spokesman is entitled to some degree of personal integrity."

Bryce looked briefly puzzled. Then he laughed and took the text back. "You're absolutely right, commander. I can't ask you to make this announcement, in view of—ah—your particular beliefs. Let's change the plan. You open the spot by introducing me, and I'll discuss the no-boiling thing. Will that be all right?"

Commander Braskett appreciated the tactful way they deferred to his special obsession. "I'm at your service, doctor," he said gravely.

✹

Bryce finished speaking and the camera lights left him. He said to Lisa, "What about lunch? Or breakfast, or whatever meal it is we're up to now."

"Everything's ready Tim. Whenever you are."

They ate together in the holograph room, which had become the kitchen of the command post. Massive cameras and tanks of etching fluid surrounded them. The others thoughtfully left them alone. These brief shared meals were the only fragments of privacy he and Lisa had had, in the fifty-two hours since he had awakened to find her sleeping beside him.

He stared across the table in wonder at this delectable blonde girl who they said was his wife. How beautiful her soft brown eyes were against that backdrop of golden hair! How perfect the line of her lips, the curve of her earlobes! Bryce knew that no one would object if he and Lisa went off and locked themselves into one of the private rooms for a few hours. He wasn't that indispensable; and there was so much he had to begin relearning about his wife. But he was unable to leave his post. He hadn't been out of the hospital or even off this floor for the duration of the crisis; he kept himself going by grabbing the sleep wire for half an hour every six hours. Perhaps it was an illusion born of too little sleep and too much data, but he had come to believe that the survival of the city depended on him. He had spent his career trying to heal individual sick minds; now he had a whole city to tend to.

"Tired?" Lisa asked.

"I'm in the tiredness beyond feeling tired. My mind is so clear it that my skull wouldn't cast a shadow. I'm nearing nirvana."

"The worst is over, I think. The city's settling down."

"It's still bad, though. Have you seen the suicide figures?"

"Bad?"

"Hideous. The norm in San Francisco is 220 a year. We've had close to five hundred in the last two and a half days. And that's just the reported cases, the bodies discovered and so on. Probably we can double the figure. Thirty suicides reported Wednesday night, about two hundred on Thursday, the same on Friday, and about fifty so far this morning. At least it seems as if the wave is past its peak."

"But *why*, Tim?"

"Some people react poorly to loss. Especially the loss of a segment of their memories. They're indignant—they're crushed—they're scared—and they reach for the exit pill. Suicide's too easy now, anyway. In the old days you reacted to frustration by smashing the crockery; now you go a deadlier route. Of course, there are special cases. A man named Montini they fished out of the bay—a professional mnemonist, who did a trick act at nightclubs, total recall. I can hardly blame him for caving in. And I suppose there were a lot of others who kept their business in their heads—gamblers, stock-market operators, oral poets, musicians—who might decide to end it all rather than try to pick up the pieces."

"But if the effects of the drug wear off—"

"Do they?" Bryce asked.

"You said so yourself."

"I was making optimistic noises for the benefit of the citizens. We don't have any experimental history for these drugs and human subjects. Hell, Lisa, we don't even know the dosage that was administered; by the time we were able to get water samples most of the system had been flushed clean, and the automatic monitoring devices at the city pumping station were rigged as part of the conspiracy so they didn't show a thing out of the ordinary. I've got no idea at all if there's going to be any measurable memory recovery."

"But there is, Tim. I've already started to get some things back."

"*What?*"

"Don't scream at me like that! You scared me."

He clung to the edge of the table. "Are you really recovering?"

"Around the edges. I remember a few things already. About us."

"Like what?"

"Applying for the marriage license. I'm standing stark naked inside a diagnostat machine and a voice on the loudspeaker is telling me to look straight into the scanners. And I remember the ceremony, a little. Just a small group of friends, a civil ceremony. Then we took the pod to Acapulco."

He stared grimly. "When did this start to come back?"

"About seven this morning, I guess."

"Is there more?"

"A bit. Our honeymoon. The robot bellhop who came blundering in on our wedding night. You don't—"

"Remember it? No. No. Nothing. Blank."

"That's all I remember, this early stuff."

"Yes, of course," he said. "The older memories are always the first to return in any form of amnesia. The last stuff in is the first to go." His hands were shaking, not entirely from fatigue. A strange desolation crept over him. Lisa remembered. He did not. Was it a function of her youth, or of the chemistry of her brain, or—?

He could not bear the thought that they no longer shared an oblivion. He didn't want the amnesia to become one-sided for them; it was humiliating not to remember his own marriage when she did. You're being irrational, he told himself. Physician, heal thyself!

"Let's go back inside," he said.

"You haven't finished your—"

"Later."

He went into the command room. Kamakura had phones in both hands and was barking data into a recorder. The screens were alive with morning scenes, Saturday in the city, crowds in Union Square. Kamakura hung up both calls and said, "I've got an interesting report from Dr. Klein at Letterman General. He says they're getting the first traces of memory recovery this morning. Women under thirty, only."

"Lisa says she's beginning to remember too," Bryce said.

"Women under thirty," said Kamakura. "Yes. Also the suicide rate is definitely tapering. We may be starting to come out of it."

"Terrific," Bryce said hollowly.

Haldersen was living in a ten-foot-high bubble that one of his disciples had blown for him in the middle of Golden Gate Park, just west of the Arboretum. Fifteen similar bubbles had gone up around his, giving the region the look of an up-to-date Eskimo village in the plastic igloos. The occupants of the camp, aside from Haldersen, were men and women who had so little memory left that they did not know who they were or where they lived. He had acquired a dozen of these lost ones on Friday, and by late afternoon on Saturday he had been joined by some forty more. The news somehow was moving through the city that those without moorings were welcome to take up with the group in the park. It had happened that way during the 1906 disaster, too.

The police had been around a few times to check on them. The first time, a portly lieutenant had tried to persuade the whole group to move to Fletcher Memorial. "That's where most of the victims are getting treatment, you see. The doctors give them something, and then we try to identify them and find their next of kin—"

"Perhaps it's best for these people to remain away from their next of kin for a while," Haldersen suggested. "Some meditation in the park—and exploration of the pleasures of having forgotten—that's all we're doing here." He would not go to Fletcher Memorial himself except under duress. As for the others, he felt he could do more for them in the park than anyone in the hospital could.

The second time the police came, Saturday afternoon when his group was much larger, they brought a mobile communications system. "Dr. Bryce of Fletcher Memorial wants to talk to you," a different lieutenant said.

Haldersen watched the screen come alive. "Hello, doctor. Worried about me?"

"I'm worried about everyone, Nate. What the hell are you doing in the park?"

"Founding a new religion, I think."

"You're a sick man. You ought to come back here."

"No, doctor. I'm not sick any more. I've had my therapy and I'm fine. It was a beautiful treatment: selective obliteration, just as I prayed for. The entire trauma is gone."

Bryce appeared fascinated by that; his frowning expression of official responsibility vanished a moment, giving place to a look of professional concern. "Interesting," he said. "We've got people who've forgotten only nouns, and people who've forgotten who they married, and people who've forgotten how to play the violin. But you're the first one who's forgotten a trauma. You still ought to come back here, though. You aren't the best judge of your fitness to face the outside environment."

"Oh, but I am," Haldersen said. "I'm doing fine. And my people need me."

"Your people?"

"Waifs. Strays. The total wipeouts."

"We want those people in the hospital, Nate. We want to get them back to their families."

"Is that necessarily a good deed? Maybe some of them can use a spell of isolation from their families. These people look happy, Dr. Bryce. I've heard there are a lot of suicides, but not here. We're practicing mutual supportive therapy. Looking for the joys to be found in oblivion. It seems to work."

Bryce stared silently out of the screen for a long moment. Then he said impatiently, "All right, have it your own way for now. But I wish you'd stop coming on like Jesus and Freud combined, and leave the park. You're still a sick man, Nate, and the people with you are in serious trouble. I'll talk to you later."

The contact broke. The police, stymied, left.

Haldersen spoke briefly to his people at five o'clock. Then he sent them out as missionaries to collect other victims. "Save as many as you can," he said. "Find those who are in complete despair and get them into the park before they can take their own lives. Explain that the loss of one's past is not the loss of all things."

The disciples went forth. And came back leading those less fortunate than themselves. The group grew to more than one hundred by nightfall. Someone found the extruder again and blew twenty more bubbles as shelters for the night. Haldersen preached his sermon of joy, looking out at the blank eyes, the slack faces, of those whose identities had washed away on Wednesday. "Why give up?" he asked them. "Now is your chance to create new lives for yourself. The slate is clean! Choose the direction you will take, define your new selves through the exercise of free will—you are reborn in holy oblivion, all of you. Rest, now, those who have just come to us. And you others, go forth again, seek out the wanderers, the drifters, the lost ones hiding in the corners of the city—"

As he finished, he saw a knot of people bustling toward him from the direction of the South Drive. Fearing trouble, Haldersen went out to meet them; but as he drew close he saw half a dozen disciples, clutching a scruffy, unshaven, terrified little man. They hurled him at Haldersen's feet. The man quivered. His eyes glistened; his wedge of a face, sharp-chinned, sharp of cheekbones, was pale.

"It's the one who poisoned the water supply!" someone called. "We found him in a rooming house on Judah Street. With a stack of drugs in his room, and the plans of the water system, and a bunch of computer programs. He admits it. He admits it!"

Haldersen looked down. "Is this true?" he asked. "Are you the one?"

The man nodded.

"What's your name?"

"Won't say. Want a lawyer."

"Kill him now!" a woman shrieked. "Pull his arms and legs off!"

"Kill him!" came an answering cry from the other side of the group. "Kill him!"

The congregation, Haldersen realized, might easily turn into a mob.

He said, "Tell me your name, and I'll protect you. Otherwise I can't be responsible."

"Skinner," the man muttered miserably.

"Skinner. And you contaminated the water supply."

Another nod.

"Why?"

"To get even."

"With whom?"

"Everyone. Everybody."

Classic paranoid. Haldersen felt pity. Not the others; they were calling out for blood.

A tall man bellowed, "Make the bastard drink his own drug!"

"No, kill him! Squash him!"

The voices became more menacing. The angry faces came closer.

"Listen to me," Haldersen called, and his voice cut through the murmurings. "There'll be no killing here tonight."

"What are you going to do, give him to the police?"

"No," said Haldersen. "We'll hold communion together. We'll teach this pitiful man the blessings of oblivion, and then we'll share new joys ourselves. We are human beings. We have the capacity to forgive even the worst of sinners. Where are the memory drugs? Did someone say you had found the memory drugs? Here. Here. Pass it up here. Yes. Brothers, sisters, let us show this dark and twisted soul the nature of redemption. Yes. Yes. Fetch some water, please. Thank you. Here, Skinner. Stand him up, will you? Hold his arms. Keep him from falling down. Wait a second, until I find the proper dose. Yes. Yes. Here, Skinner. Forgiveness. Sweet oblivion."

It was so good to be working again that Mueller didn't want to stop. By early afternoon on Saturday his studio was ready; he had long since worked out the sketches of the first piece; now it was just a matter of time and effort, and he'd have something to show Pete Castine. He worked on far into the evening, setting up his armature and running a few tests of the sound sequences that he proposed to build into the piece. He had some interesting new ideas about the sonic triggers, the devices that would set off the sound effects when the appreciator came within range. Carole had to tell him, finally, that dinner was ready. "I didn't want to interrupt you," she said, "but it looks like I have to, or you won't ever stop."

"Sorry. The creative ecstasy."

"Save some of that energy. There are other ecstasies. The ecstasy of dinner, first."

She had cooked everything herself. Beautiful. He went back to work again afterward, but at half past one in the morning Carole interrupted him. He was willing to stop, now. He had done an honest day's work, and he was sweaty with the noble sweat of a job well done. Two minutes under the molecular cleanser and the sweat was gone, but the good ache of virtuous fatigue remained. He hadn't felt this way in years.

He woke to Sunday thoughts of unpaid debts.

"The robots are still there," he said. "They won't go away, will they? Even though the whole city's at a standstill, nobody's told the robots to quit."

"Ignore them," Carole said.

"That's what I've been doing. But I can't ignore the debts. Ultimately there'll be a reckoning."

"You're working again, though! You'll have an income coming in."

"Do you know what I owe?" he asked. "Almost a million. If I produced one piece a week for a year, and sold each piece for twenty bigs, I might pay everything off. But I can't work that fast, and the market can't possibly absorb that many Muellers, and Pete certainly can't buy them all for future sale."

He noticed the way Carole's face darkened at the mention of Pete Castine.

He said, "You know what I'll have to do? Go to Caracas, like I was planning before this memory thing started. I can work there, and ship my stuff to Pete. And maybe in two or three years I'll have paid off my debt, a hundred cents on the dollar, and I can start fresh back here. Do you know if that's possible? I mean, if you jump to a debtor sanctuary, are you blackballed for credit forever, even if you pay off what you owe?"

"I don't know," Carole said distantly.

"I'll find that out later. The important thing is that I'm working again, and I've got to go someplace where I can work without being hounded. And then I'll pay everybody off. You'll come with me to Caracas, won't you?"

"Maybe we won't have to go," Carole said.

"But how—"

"You should be working now, shouldn't you?"

He worked, and while he worked he made lists of creditors in his mind, dreaming of the day when every name on every list was crossed off. When he got hungry he emerged from the studio and found Carole sitting gloomily in the living room. Her eyes were red and puffy-lidded.

"What's wrong?" he asked. "You don't want to go to Caracas?"

"Please, Paul—let's not talk about it—"

"I've really got no alternative. I mean, unless we pick one of the other sanctuaries. Sao Paulo? Spalato?"

"It isn't that, Paul."

"What, then?"

"I'm starting to remember again."

The air went out of him. "Oh," he said.

"I remember November, December, January. The crazy things you were doing, the loans, the financial juggling. And the quarrels we had. They were terrible quarrels."

"Oh."

"The divorce. I remember, Paul. It started coming back last night, but you were so happy I didn't want to say anything. And this morning it's much clearer. You still don't remember any of it?"

"Not a thing past last October."

"I do," she said, shakily. "You hit me, do you know that? You cut my lip. You slammed me against the wall, right over there, and then you threw the Chinese vase at me and it broke."

"Oh. Oh."

She went on, "I remember how good Pete was to me, too. I think I can almost remember marrying him, being his wife. Paul, I'm scared. I feel everything fitting into place in my mind, and it's as scary as if my mind was breaking into pieces. It was so good, Paul, these last few days. It was like being a newlywed with you again. But now all the sour parts are coming back, the hate, the ugliness, it's all alive for me again. And I feel so bad about Pete. The two of us, Friday, shutting him out. He was a real gentleman about it. But the fact is that he saved me when I was going under, and I owe him something for that."

"What do you plan to do?" he asked quietly.

"I think I ought to go back to him. I'm his wife. I've got no right to stay here."

"But I'm not the same man you came to hate," Mueller protested. "I'm the old Paul; the one from last year and before. The man you loved. All the hateful stuff is gone from me."

"Not from me, though. Not now."

They were both silent.

"I think I should go back, Paul."

"Whatever you say."

"I think I should. I wish you all kinds of luck, but I can't stay here. Will it hurt your work if I leave again?"

"I won't know until you do."

She told him three or four times that she felt she ought to go back to Castine, and then, politely, he suggested that she should go back right now, if that was how she felt, and she did. He spent half an hour wandering around the apartment, which seemed so awfully empty again. He nearly invited one of the dunning robots in for company. Instead, he went back to work. To his surprise, he worked quite well, and in an hour he had ceased thinking about Carole entirely.

Sunday afternoon, Freddy Munson set up a credit transfer and managed to get most of his liquid assets fed into an old account he kept at the Bank of Luna. Toward evening, he went down to the wharf and boarded a three-man hovercraft owned by a fisherman willing to take his chances with the law. They slipped out into the bay without running lights and crossed the bay on a big diagonal, landing some time later a few miles north of Berkeley. Munson found a cab to take him to the Oakland airport, and caught the midnight shuttle to LA, where, after a lot of fancy talking, he was able to buy his way aboard the next Luna-bound rocket, lifting off at ten o'clock Monday morning. He spent the night in the spaceport terminal. He had taken with him nothing except the clothes he wore; his fine possessions, his paintings, his suits, his Mueller sculptures, and all the rest remained in his apartment, and ultimately would be sold to satisfy the judgments against him. Too bad. He knew that he wouldn't be coming back to Earth again, either, not with a larceny warrant or worse awaiting him. Also too bad. It had been so nice for so long, here, and who needed a memory drug in the water supply? Munson had only one consolation. It was an article of his philosophy that sooner or later, no matter how neatly you organized your life, fate opened a trapdoor underneath your feet and catapulted you into something unknown and unpleasant. Now he knew that it was true even for him.

Too, too bad. He wondered what his chances were of starting over up there. Did they need stockbrokers on the moon?

Addressing the citizenry on Monday night, Commander Braskett said, "The committee of public safety is pleased to report that we have come through the worst part of the crisis. As many of you have already discovered, memories are beginning to return. The process of recovery will be more swift for some than others, but great progress has been made. Effective at six A.M. tomorrow, access routes to and from San Francisco will reopen. There will be normal mail services and many businesses will return to normal. Fellow citizens, we have demonstrated once again the real fiber of the American spirit. The founding fathers must be smiling down upon us today! How superbly we avoided chaos, and how beautifully we pulled together to help one another in what could have been an hour of turmoil and despair!

"Dr. Bryce requests me to remind you that anyone still suffering severe impairment of memory—especially those experiencing loss of identity, confusion of vital functions, or other disability—should report to the emergency ward at Fletcher Memorial Hospital. Treatment is available there, and computer analysis is at the service of those unable to find their homes and loved ones. I repeat—"

Tim Bryce wished that the good commander hadn't slipped in that plug for the real fiber of the American spirit, especially in view of the necessity to invite the remaining victims to the hospital with his next words. But it would be uncharitable to object. The old spaceman had done a beautiful job all weekend as the Voice of the Crisis, and some patriotic embellishments now were harmless.

The crisis, of course, was nowhere near as close to being over as Commander Braskett's speech had suggested, but public confidence had to be buoyed.

Bryce had the latest figures. Suicides now totaled nine hundred since the start of trouble on Wednesday; Sunday had been an unexpectedly bad day. At least forty thousand people were still unaccounted for, although they were tracing one thousand an hour and getting them back to their families or else into an intensive-care section. Probably seven hundred and fifty thousand more continued to have memory difficulties. Most children had fully recovered, and many of the women were mending; but older people, and men in general, had experienced scarcely any memory recapture. Even those who were nearly healed had no recall of events of Tuesday and Wednesday, and probably never would; for large numbers of people, though, big blocks of the past would have to be learned from outside, like history lessons.

Lisa was teaching him their marriage that way.

The trips they had taken—the good times, the bad—the parties, the friends, the shared dreams—she described everything as vividly as she could, and he fastened on each anecdote, trying to make it a part of himself again. He knew it was hopeless, really. He'd know the outlines, never the substance. Yet it was probably the best he could hope for.

He was so horribly tired, suddenly.

He said to Kamakura, "Is there anything new from the park yet? That rumor that Haldersen's actually got a supply of the drug?"

"Seems to be true, Tim. The word is that he and his friends caught the character who spiked the water supply, and relieved him of a roomful of various amnesifacients."

"We've got to seize them," Bryce said.

Kamakura shook his head. "Not just yet. Police are afraid of any actions in the park. They say it's a volatile situation."

"But if those drugs are loose—"

"Let me worry about it, Tim. Look, why don't you and Lisa go home for a while? You've been here without a break since Thursday."

"So have—"

"No. Everybody else has had a breather. Go on, now. We're over the worst. Relax, get some real sleep, make some love. Get to know that gorgeous wife of yours again a little."

Bryce reddened. "I'd rather stay here until I feel I can afford to leave."

Scowling, Kamakura walked away from him to confer with Commander Braskett. Bryce scanned the screens, trying to figure out what was going on in the park. A moment later, Braskett walked over to him.

"Dr. Bryce?"

"What?"

"You're relieved of duty until sundown Tuesday."

"Wait a second—"

"That's an order, doctor. I'm chairman of the committee of public safety, and I'm telling you to get yourself out of this hospital. You aren't going to disobey an order, are you?"

"Listen, commander—"

"Out. No mutiny, Bryce. Out! Orders."

Bryce tried to protest, but he was too weary to put up much of a fight. By noon, he was on his way home, soupy-headed with fatigue. Lisa drove. He sat quite still, struggling to remember details of their marriage. Nothing came.

She put him to bed. He wasn't sure how long he slept; but then he felt her against him; warm, satin-smooth.

"Hello," she said. "Remember me?"

"Yes," he lied gratefully. "Oh, yes, yes, yes!"

Working right through the night, Mueller finished his armature by dawn on Monday. He slept awhile, and in early afternoon began to paint the inner strips of loudspeakers on: a thousand speakers to the inch, no more than a few molecules thick, from which the sounds of his sculpture would issue in resonant fullness. When that was done, he paused to contemplate the needs of his sculpture's super-structure, and by seven that night was ready to move to the next phase. The demons of creativity possessed him; he saw no reason to eat and scarcely any to sleep.

At eight, just as he was getting up momentum for the long night's work, he heard a knock at the door. Carole's signal. He had disconnected the doorbell, and robots didn't have the sense to knock. Uneasily, he went to the door. She was there.

"So?" he said.

"So I came back. So it starts all over."

"What's going on?"

"Can I come in?" she asked.

"I suppose. I'm working, but come in."

She said, "I talked it over with Pete. We both decided I ought to go back to you."

"You aren't much for consistency, are you?"

"I have to take things as they happen. When I lost my memory, I came to you. When I remembered things again, I felt I ought leave. I didn't *want* to leave. I felt I *ought* to leave. There's a difference."

"Really," he said.

"Really. I went to Pete, but I didn't want to be with him. I want to be here."

"I hit you and made your lip bleed. I threw the Ming vase at you."

"It wasn't Ming, it was K'ang-hsi."

"Pardon me. My memory still isn't so good. Anyway, I did terrible things to you, and you hated me enough to want a divorce. So why come back?"

"You were right, yesterday. You aren't the man I came to hate. You're the old Paul."

"And if my memory of the past nine months returns?"

"Even so," she said. "People change. You've been through hell and come out the other side. You're working again. You aren't sullen and nasty and confused. We'll go to Caracas, or wherever you want, and you'll do your work and pay your debts, just as you said yesterday."

"And Pete?"

"He'll arrange an annulment. He's being swell about it."

"Good old Pete," Mueller said. He shook his head. "How long will this neat happy ending last, Carole? If you think there's a chance you'll be bouncing back in the other direction by Wednesday, say so now. I'd rather not get involved again, in that case."

"No chance. None."

"Unless I throw the Chi'ien-lung vase at you."

"K'ang-hsi," she said.

"Yes. K'ang-hsi." He managed to grin. Suddenly he felt the accumulated fatigue of these days register all at once. "I've been working too hard," he said. "An orgy of creativity to make up for lost time. Let's go for a walk."

"Fine," she said.

They went out, just as a dunning robot was arriving. "Top of the evening to you, sir," Mueller said.

"Mr. Mueller, I represent the accounts receivable department of Acme Brass and—"

"See my attorney," he said.

Fog was rolling in off the sea now. There were no stars. The downtown lights were invisible. He and Carole walked west, toward the park. He felt strangely light-headed, not entirely from lack of sleep. Reality and dream had merged; these were unusual days. They entered the park from the Panhandle and strolled toward the museum area, arm in arm, saying nothing much to one another. As they passed the conservatory Mueller became aware of a crowd up ahead, thousands of people staring in the direction of the music shell. "What do you think is going on?" Carole asked. Mueller shrugged. They edged through the crowd.

Ten minutes later they were close enough to see the stage. A tall, thin, wild-looking man with unruly yellow hair was on the stage. Beside him was a small, scrawny man in ragged clothing, and there were a dozen others flanking them, carrying ceramic bowls.

"What's happening?" Mueller asked someone in the crowd.

"Religious ceremony."

"Eh?"

"New religion. Church of Oblivion. That's the head prophet up there. You haven't heard about it yet?"

"Not a thing."

"Started around Friday. You see that ratty-looking character next to the prophet?"

"Yes."

"He's the one that put the stuff in the water supply. He confessed and they made him drink his own drug. Now he doesn't remember a thing, and he's the assistant prophet. Craziest damn stuff!"

"And what are they doing up there?"

"They've got the drug in those bowls. They drink and forget some more. They drink and forget some more."

The gathering fog absorbed the sounds of those on the stage. Mueller strained to listen. He saw the bright eyes of fanaticism, the alleged contaminator of the water looked positively radiant. Words drifted out into the night.

"Brothers and sisters...the joy, the sweetness of forgetting...come up here with us, take communion with us...oblivion...redemption...even for the most wicked...forget...forget..."

They were passing the bowls around on stage, drinking, smiling. People were going up to receive the communion, taking a bowl, sipping, nodding happily. Toward the rear of the stage the bowls were being refilled by three sober-looking functionaries.

Mueller felt a chill. He suspected that what had been born in this park during this week would endure, somehow, long after the crisis of San Francisco had become part of history; and it seemed to him that something new and frightening had been loosed upon the land.

"Take...drink...forget..." the prophet cried.

And the worshippers cried, *"Take...drink...forget..."*

The bowls were passed.

"What's it all *about?*" Carole whispered.

"Take...drink...forget..."

"Take...drink...forget..."

"Blessed is the sweet oblivion."

"Blessed is the sweet oblivion."

"Sweet if it is to lay down the burden of one's soul."

"Sweet it is to lay down the burden of one's soul."

"Joyous it is to begin anew."

"Joyous it is to begin anew."

The fog was deepening. Mueller could barely see the aquarium building just across the way. He clasped his hand tightly around Carole's and began to think about getting out of the park.

He had to admit, though, that these people might have hit on something true. Was he not better off for having taken a chemical into his bloodstream, and thereby shedding a portion of his past? Yes, of course. And yet—to mutilate one's mind this way, deliberately, happily, to drink deep of oblivion—

"Blessed are those who are able to forget," the prophet said.

"*Blessed are those who are able to forget,*" the crowd roared in response.

"Blessed are those who are able to forget," Mueller heard his own voice cry. And he began to tremble. And he felt sudden fear: He sensed the power of this strange new movement, the gathering strength of the prophet's appeal to unreason. It was time for a new religion, maybe, a cult that offered emancipation from all inner burdens. They would synthesize this drug and turn it out by the ton, Mueller thought, and repeatedly dose cities with it, so that everyone could be converted, so that everyone might taste the joys of oblivion. No one will be able to stop them. After a while no one will *want* to stop them. And so we'll go on, drinking deep, until we're washed clean of all pain and all sorrow, of all sad recollection, we'll sip a cup of kindness and part with auld lang syne, we'll give up the griefs we carry around, and we'll give up everything else, identity, soul, self, mind. We will drink sweet oblivion. Mueller shivered. Turning suddenly, tugging roughly at Carole's arm, he pushed through the joyful worshipping crowd, and hunted somberly in the fogwrapped night, trying to find some way out of the park.

A HAPPY DAY IN 2381

This was the era when the anthology of original stories came to replace the science-fiction magazine as the central zone of short science fiction. Some appeared in hard covers, like Damon Knight's Orbit *and Roger Elwood's* Continuum. *Some came out as paperbacks, like Terry Carr's* Universe, *Bob Hoskins'* Infinity, *Samuel R. Delany's* Quark, *and my own* New Dimensions. *All of those were periodical publications, appearing anywhere from annually to quarterly, but also there were plenty of one-shots, like Harlan Ellison's* Dangerous Visions, *Joe Elder's* The Farthest Reaches, *Anne McCaffrey's* Alchemy and Academe, *and the innumerable titles that the indefatigable anthologist Roger Elwood was soon to loose on the publishing world.*

Harry Harrison, an old friend of mine who had been a key figure in science fiction for many years both as editor and writer, joined the original-anthology bandwagon in 1969 with Nova, *a hard-cover series destined to see four volumes over the next five years. He asked me to write a story for his first issue, and I responded in March, 1969 with "A Happy Day in 2381," a story that grew out of my interest in the work of the visionary architect Paolo Soleri. Soleri, just then, was getting a lot of attention with his concept of "arcologies": supersized apartment buildings, each packing many thousands of inhabitants into a single gigantic tower so that open space could be conserved to meet agricultural needs in our overpopulated future. I was fascinated by the elaborate architectural blueprints had drawn for these fantastic buildings, and saw both an upside and a downside to the scheme, an ambivalence which is reflected in the portrayal of the Urban Monad culture that I invented for my story.*

317

"A Happy Day in 2381" was published in Harry's Nova in 1970. By then it had occurred to me that the Urban Monad idea was too good to drop after a single short story, and I was at work at a whole series of them—"In the Beginning," which I did for another original-story anthology called Science Against Man, and four others—"The Throwbacks," "The World Outside," "We Are Well Organized," and "All the Way Up, All the Way Down," that I wrote for Galaxy Science Fiction, where Ejler Jakobsson had replaced Fred Pohl as editor. A year or so later I pulled the six of them together into the novel The World Inside. Reprinting all six here would be pretty much the same as inserting that novel into this collection, which I don't want to do; but, inasmuch as I had no idea that I was beginning a novel when I wrote "A Happy Day in 2381" for Harry Harrison, I include it here as a sample of the whole group.

Here is a happy day in 2381. The morning sun is high enough to reach the uppermost fifty stories of Urban Monad 116. Soon the building's entire eastern face will glitter like the sea at dawn.. Charles Mattern's window, activated by the dawn's early photons, deopaques. He stirs. God bless, he thinks. His wife stirs. His four children, who have been up for hours, now can officially begin the day. They rise and parade around the bedroom, singing:

"God bless, god bless, god bless!
God bless us every one!
God bless Daddo, god bless Mommo, god bless you and me!
God bless us all, the short and tall,
Give us f er-til-I-tee!"

They rush toward their parents' sleeping platform. Mattern rises and embraces them. Indra is eight, Sandor is seven, Marx is five, Cleo is three. It is Charles Mattern's secret shame that his family is so small. Can a man with only four children truly be said to have reverence for life? But Principessa's womb no longer flowers. The medics have said she will not bear again. At twenty-seven she is sterile. Mattern is thinking of taking in a second woman. He longs to hear the yowls of an infant again; in any case, a man must do his duty to god.

Sandor says, "Daddo, Siegmund is still here. He came in the middle of the night to be with Mommo."

The child points. Mattern sees. On Principessa's side of the sleeping platform, curled against the inflation pedal, lies fourteen-year-old Siegmund Kluver, who had entered the Mattern home several hours after midnight to exercise his rights of propinquity. Siegmund is fond of older women. Now he snores; he has had a good workout. Mattern nudges him. "Siegmund? Siegmund, it's morning!" The young man's eyes open. He smiles at Mattern, sits up, reaches for his wrap. He is quite handsome. He lives on the 787th floor and already has one child and another on the way.

"Sorry," says Siegmund. "I overslept. Principessa really drains me. A savage, she is!"

"Yes, she's quite passionate," Mattern agrees. So is Siegmund's wife, Mattern has heard. When she is a little older, Mattern plans to try her. Next spring, perhaps.

Siegmund sticks his head under the molecular cleanser. Principessa now has risen from bed. She kicks the pedal and the platform deflates swiftly. She begins to program breakfast. Indra switches on the screen. The wall blossoms with light and color. "Good morning," says the screen. "The external temperature, if anybody's interested, is 28°. Today's population figures at Urbmon 116 are 881,115, which is +102 since yesterday and +14,187 since the first of the year. God bless, but we're slowing down! Across the way at Urbmon 117 they added 131 since yesterday, including quads for Mrs. Hula Jabotinsky. She's eighteen and has had seven previous. A servant of god, isn't she? The time is now 0620. In exactly forty minutes Urbmon 116 will be honored by the presence of Nicanor Gortman, the visiting sociocomputator from Hell, who can be recognized by his outbuilding costume in crimson and ultraviolet. Dr. Gortman will be the guest of the Charles Matterns of the 799th floor. Of course we'll treat him with the same friendly blessmanship we show one another. God bless Nicanor Gortman! Turning now to news from the lower levels of Urbmon 116—"

Principessa says, "Hear that, children? We'll have a guest, and we must be blessworthy toward him. Come and eat."

When he has cleansed himself, dressed, and eaten, Charles Mattern goes to the thousandth-floor landing stage to greet Nicanor Gortman. Mattern passes the floors on which his brothers and sisters and their families live. Three brothers, three sisters. Four of them younger than he, two older. One brother died, unpleasantly, young. Jeffrey. Mattern rarely thinks of Jeffrey. He rises through the building to the summit. Gortman has been touring the tropics and now is going to visit a typical urban monad in the temperate zone. Mattern is honored to have been named the official host. He steps out on the landing stage, which is at the very tip of Urbmon 116. A forcefield shields him from the fierce winds that sweep the lofty spire. He looks to his left and sees the western face of Urban Monad 115 still in darkness. To his right, Urbmon 117's eastern windows sparkle. Bless Mrs. Hula Jabotinsky and her eleven littles, Mattern thinks. Mattern can see other urbmons in the row, stretching on and on toward the horizon, towers of super-stressed concrete three kilometers high, tapering ever so gracefully. It is as always a thrilling sight. God bless, he thinks. God bless, god bless, god bless!

He hears a cheerful hum of rotors. A quickboat is landing. Out steps a tall, sturdy man dressed in high-spectrum garb. He must be the visiting sociocomputator from Hell.

"Nicanor Gortman?" Mattern asks.

"Bless god. Charles Mattern?"

"God bless, yes. Come."

Hell is one of the eleven cities of Venus, which man has reshaped to suit himself. Gortman has never been on Earth before. He speaks in a slow, stolid way, no lilt in his voice at all; the inflection reminds Mattern of the way they talk in Urbmon 84, which Mattern once visited on a field trip. He has read Gortman's papers: solid stuff, closely reasoned. "I particularly liked *Dynamics of the Hunting Ethic*," Mattern tells him while they are in the dropshaft. "Remarkable. A revelation."

"You really mean that?" Gortman asks, flattered.

"Of course. I try to keep up with a lot of the Venusian journals. It's so fascinatingly alien to read about hunting wild animals."

"There are none on Earth?"

"God bless, no," Mattern says. "We couldn't allow that! But I love reading about such a different way of life as you have."

"It is escape literature for you?" asks Gortman.

Mattern looks at him strangely. "I don't understand the reference."

"What you read to make life on Earth more bearable for yourself."

"Oh, no. No. Life on Earth is quite bearable, let me assure you. It's what I read for *amusement*. And to obtain a necessary parallax, you know, for my own work," says Mattern. They have reached the 799th level. "Let me show you my home first." He steps from the dropshaft and beckons to Gortman. "This is Shanghai. I mean, that's what we call this block of forty floors, from 761 to 800. I'm in the next-to-top level of Shanghai; which is a mark of my professional status. We've got twenty-five cities altogether in Urbmon 116. Reykjavik's on the bottom and Louisville's on the top."

"What determines the names?"

"Citizen vote. Shanghai used to be Calcutta, which I personally prefer, but a little bunch of malcontents on the 775th floor rammed a referendum through in '75."

"I thought you had no malcontents in the urban monads," Gortman says.

Mattern smiles. "Not in the usual sense. But we allow certain conflicts to exist. Man wouldn't be man without conflicts, even here!"

They are walking down the eastbound corridor toward Mattern's home. It is now 0710, and children are streaming from their homes in groups of three and four, rushing to get to school. Mattern waves to them. They sing as they run along. Mattern says, "We average 6.2 children per family on this floor. It's one of the lowest figures in the building, I have to admit. High status people don't seem to breed well. "They've got a floor in Prague—I think it's 117—that averages 9.9 per family! Isn't that glorious?"

"You are speaking with irony?" Gortman asks.

"Not at all." Mattern feels an uptake of tension. "We *like* children. We *approve* of breeding. Surely you realized that before you set out on this tour of— "

"Yes, yes," says Gortman hastily. "I was aware of the general cultural dynamic. But I thought perhaps your own attitude—"

"Ran counter to norm? Just because I have a scholar's detachment, you shouldn't assume that I disapprove in any way of my cultural matrix."

"I regret the implication. And please don't think I show disapproval of your matrix either, although your world is quite strange to me. Bless god, let us not have strife, Charles."

"God bless, Nicanor. I didn't mean to seem touchy."

They smile. Mattern is dismayed by his show of irritation.

Gortman says, "What is the population of the 799th floor?"

"805, last I heard."

"And of Shanghai?"

"About 33,000."

"And of Urbmon 116?"

"881,000."

"And there are fifty urban monads in this constellation of houses."

"Yes."

"Making some forty million people," Gortman says. "Or somewhat more then than the entire human population of Venus. Remarkable!"

"And this isn't the biggest constellation, not by any means!" Mattern's voice rings with pride. "Sansan is bigger, and so is Boswash. And there are several bigger ones in Europe—Berpar, Wienbud, I think two others. With more being planned!"

"A global population of—"

"—Seventy-five billion," Mattern cries. "God bless! There's never been anything like it! No one goes hungry! Everybody happy! Plenty of open space! God's been good to us, Nicanor!" He pauses before a door labeled 79915. "Here's my home. What I have is yours, dear guest." They go in.

Mattern's home is quite adequate. He has nearly ninety square meters of floor space. The sleeping platform deflates; the children's cots retract; the furniture can easily be moved to provide play area. Most of the room, in fact, is empty. The screen and the data terminal occupy two-dimensional areas of wall that once had to be taken up by television sets, bookcases, desks, file drawers, and other encumbrances. It is an airy, spacious environment, particularly for a family of just six.

The children have not yet left for school; Principessa has held them back, to meet the guest, and so they are restless. As Mattern enters, Sandor and Indra are struggling over a cherished toy, the dream stirrer. Mattern is astounded. Conflict in the home? Silently, so their mother will not notice, they fight. Sandor hammers his shoes into his sister's shins. Indra, wincing, claws her brother's cheek. "God *bless*," Mattern says sharply. "Somebody wants to go down the chute, eh?" The children gasp. The toy drops. Everyone stands at attention. Principessa looks up, brushing a lock of dark hair from her eyes; she has been busy with the youngest child and has not even heard them come in.

Mattern says, "Conflict sterilizes. Apologize to each other."

Indra and Sandor kiss and smile. Meekly Indra picks up the toy and hands it to Mattern, who gives it to his younger son Marx. They are all staring now at the guest. Mattern says to him, "What I have is yours, friend:" He makes introductions. Wife, children. The scene of conflict has unnerved him a little, but he is relieved when Gortman produces four small boxes and distributes them to the children. Toys. A blessful gesture. Mattern points to the deflated sleeping platform. "This is where we sleep. There's ample room for three. We wash at the cleanser, here. Do you like privacy when voiding waste matter?"

"Please, yes."

"You press this button for the privacy shield. We excrete in this. Urine here, feces here. Everything is reprocessed, you understand. We're a thrifty folk in the urbmons."

"Of course," Gortman says.

Principessa says, "Do you prefer that we use the shield when we excrete? I understand some outbuilding people do."

"I would not want to impose my customs on you," says Gortman.

Smiling, Mattern says, "We're a post-privacy culture, of course. But it wouldn't be any trouble for us to press the button if—" He falters. "There's no general nudity taboo on Venus, is there? I mean, we have only this one room, and—"

"I am adaptable," Gortman insists. "A trained sociocomputator must be a cultural relativist, of course!"

"Of course," Mattern agrees, and he laughs nervously.

Principessa excuses herself from the conversation and sends the children, still clutching their new toys, off to school.

Mattern says, "Forgive me for being over-obvious, but I must bring up the matter of your sexual prerogatives. We three will share a single platform. My wife is available to you, as am I. Avoidance of frustration, you see, is the primary rule of a society such as ours. And do you know our custom of nightwalking?"

"I'm afraid I—"

"Doors are not locked in Urbmon 116. We have no personal property worth mentioning, and we all are socially adjusted. At night it is quite proper to enter other homes. We exchange partners in this way all the time; usually wives stay home and husbands migrate, though not necessarily. Each of us has access at any time to any other adult member of our community."

"Strange," says Gortman. "I'd think that in a society where there are so many people, an exaggerated respect for privacy would develop, not a communal freedom."

"In the beginning we had many notions of privacy. They were allowed to erode, god bless! Avoidance of frustration must be our goal, otherwise impossible tensions develop. And privacy is frustration."

"So you can go into any room in this whole gigantic building and sleep with—"

"Not the whole building," Mattern interrupts. "Only Shanghai. We frown on nightwalking beyond one's own city." He chuckles. "We do impose a few little restrictions on ourselves, so that our freedoms don't pall."

Gortman looks at Principessa. She wears a loinband and a metallic cup over her left breast. She is slender but voluptuously constructed, and even though her childbearing days are over she has not lost the sensual glow of young womanhood. Mattern is proud of her, despite everything.

Mattern says, "Shall we begin our tour of the building?"

They go out. Gortman bows gracefully to Principessa as they leave. In the corridor, the visitor says, "Your family is smaller than the norm, I see."

It is an excruciatingly impolite statement, but Mattern is tolerant of his guest's faux pas. Mildly he replies, "We would have had more children, but my wife's fertility had to be terminated surgically. It was a great tragedy for us."

"You value large families here?"

"We value life. To create new life is the highest virtue. To prevent life from coming into being is the darkest sin. We all love our big bustling world. Does it seem unendurable to you? Do we seem unhappy?"

"You seem surprisingly well adjusted," Gorman says. "Considering that—" He stops.

"Go on."

"Considering that there are so many of you. And that you spend your whole lives inside a single colossal building. You never do go out, do you?"

"Most of us never do," Mattern admits. "I have traveled, of course— a sociocomputator needs perspective, obviously. But Principessa has never been below the 350th floor. Why should she go anywhere? The secret of our happiness is to create self-contained villages of five or six floors within the cities of forty floors within the urbmons of 1000 floors. We have no sensation of being overcrowded or cramped. We know our neighbors; we have hundreds of dear friends; we are kind and loyal and blessworthy to one another."

"And everybody remains happy forever?"

"Nearly everybody."

"Who are the exceptions?" Gortman asks.

"The flippos," says Mattern. "We endeavor to minimize the frictions of living in such an environment; as you see, we never refuse a reasonable request, we never deny one another anything. But sometimes there are those who abruptly can no longer abide by our principles. They flip; they thwart others; they rebel. It is quite sad."

"What do you do with flippos?"

"We remove them of course," Mattern says. He smiles, and they enter the dropshaft once again.

Mattern has been authorized to show Gortman the entire urbmon, a tour that will take several days. He is a little apprehensive; he is not as familiar with some parts of the structure as a guide should be. But he will do his best.

"The building," he says, "is made of superstressed concrete. It is constructed about a central service core 200 meters square, . Originally, the plan was to have fifty families per floor, but we average about 120 today, and the old apartments have all been subdivided into single-room occupancies. We are wholly self-sufficient, with our own schools, hospitals, sports arenas, houses of worship, and theaters."

"Food?"

"We produce none, of course. But we have contractual access to the agricultural communes. I'm sure you've seen that nearly seven eighths of the land area of this continent is used for food-production; and then there are the marine farms. There's plenty of food, now that we no longer waste space by spreading out horizontally over good land."

"But aren't you at the mercy of the food-producing communes?"

"When were city-dwellers not at the mercy of farmers?" Mattern asks. "But you seem to regard life on Earth as a thing of fang and claw. We are vital to them—their only market. They are vital to us—our only source of food. Also we provide necessary services to them, such as repair of their machines. The ecology of this planet is neatly in mesh. We can support many billions of additional people. Some day, god blessing, we will."

The dropshaft, coasting downward through the building, glides into its anvil at the bottom. Mattern feels the oppressive bulk of the whole urbmon over him, and tries not to show his uneasiness. He says, "The foundation of the building is 400 meters deep. We are now at the lowest level. Here we generate our power." They cross a catwalk and peer into an immense generating room, forty meters from floor to ceiling, in which sleek turbines whirl. "Most of our power is obtained," he explains, "through combustion of compacted solid refuse. We burn everything we don't need, and sell the residue as fertilizer. We have auxiliary generators that work on accumulated body heat, also."

"I was wondering about that," Gortman murmurs.

Cheerily Mattern says, "Obviously 800,000 people within one sealed enclosure will produce an immense quantity of heat. Some of this is directly radiated from the building through cooling fins along the outer surface. Some is piped down here and used to run the generators. In winter, of course, we pump it evenly through the building to maintain temperature. The rest of the excess heat is used in water purification and similar things."

They peer at the electrical system for a while. Then Mattern leads the way to the reprocessing plant. Several hundred schoolchildren are touring it; silently they join the tour.

The teacher says, "'Here's where the urine comes down, see?" She points to gigantic plastic pipes. "It passes through the flash chamber to be distilled, and the pure water is drawn off here—follow me, now—you remember from the flow chart, about how we recover the chemicals and sell them to the farming communes—"

Mattern and his guest inspect the fertilizer plant, too, where fecal reconversion is taking place. Gortman asks a number of questions. He seems deeply interested. Mattern is pleased; there is nothing more significant to him than the details of the urbmon way of life, and he had feared that this stranger from Venus, where men live in private houses and walk around in the open, would regard the urbmon way as repugnant or hideous.

They go onward. Mattern speaks of air-conditioning, the system of dropshafts and liftshafts, and other such topics.

"It's all wonderful," Gore says. "I couldn't imagine how one little planet with seventy-five billion people could even survive, but you've turned it into—into—"

"Utopia?" Mattern suggests.

"I meant to say that, yes," says Gorman.

*

Power production and waste disposal are not really Mattern's specialties. He knows how such things are handled, here, but only because the workings of the urbmon are so enthralling to him. His real field of study is sociocomputation, naturally, and he has been asked to show the visitor how the social structure of the giant building is organized. Now they go up, into the residential levels.

"This is Reykjavik," Mattern announces. "'Populated chiefly by maintenance workers. We try not to have too much status stratification, but each city does have its predominant populations—engineers, academics, entertainers, you know. My Shanghai is mostly academic. Each profession is clannish." They walk down the hall. Mattern feels edgy here, and he keeps talking to cover his nervousness. He tells how each city within the urbmon develops its characteristic slang, its way of dressing, its folklore and heroes.

"Is there much contact between cities?" Gortman asks.

"We try to encourage it. Sports, exchange students, regular mixer evenings."

"Wouldn't it be even better if you encouraged intercity nightwalking?"

Mattern frowns. "We prefer to stick to our propinquity groups for that. Casual sex with people from other cities is a mark of a sloppy soul."

"I see."

They enter a large room. Mattern says, "This is a newlywed dorm. We have them every five or six levels. When adolescents mate, they leave their family homes and move in here. After they have their first child they are assigned to homes of their own."

Puzzled, Gortman asks, "But where do you find room for them all? I assume that every room in the building is full, and you can't possibly have as many deaths as births, so—how—?"

"Deaths do create vacancies, of course. If your mate dies and your children are grown, you go to a senior citizen dorm, creating room for establishment of a new family unit. But you're correct that most of our young people don't get accommodations in the building, since we form new families at about two percent a year and deaths are far below that. As new urbmons are built, the overflow from the newlywed dorms is sent to them. By lot. It's hard to adjust to being expelled, they say, but there are compensations in being among the first group into a new building, you acquire automatic status. And so we're constantly over-flowing, casting out our young, creating new combinations of social units—utterly fascinating, eh? Have you read my paper, *Structural Metamorphosis in the Urbmon Population?*"

"I know it well," Gortman replies. He looks about tine the dorm. A dozen couples are having intercourse on a nearby platform. "They seem so young," he says.

"Puberty comes early among us. Girls generally marry at twelve, boys at thirteen. First child about a year later, god blessing."

"And nobody tries to control fertility at all."

"*Control fertility?*" Mattern clutches his genitals in shock at the unexpected obscenity. Several copulating couples look up, amazed. Someone giggles. Mattern says, "Please don't use that phrase again. Particularly if you're near children. We don't—ah—think in terms of control."

"But—"

"We hold that life is sacred. Making new life is blessed. One does one's duty to god by reproducing." Mattern smiles. "To be human is to meet challenges through the exercise of intelligence, right? And one challenge is the multiplication of inhabitants in a world that has seen the conquest of disease and the elimination of war. We could limit births, I suppose, but that would be sick, a cheap way out. Instead we've met the challenge of overpopulation triumphantly, wouldn't you say? And so we go on and on, multiplying joyously, our numbers increasing by three billion a year, and we find room for everyone, and food for everyone. Few die, and many are born, and the world fills up, and god is blessed, and life is rich and pleasant, and as you see we are all quite happy. We have matured beyond the infantile need to place insulation between man and man. Why go outdoors? Why yearn for forests and deserts? Urbmon 116 holds universes enough for us. The warnings of the prophets of doom have proved hollow. Can you deny that we are happy here? Come with me. We will see a school now."

The school Mattern has chosen is in a working-class district of Prague, on the 108th floor. He thinks Gortman will find it particularly interesting, since the Prague people have the highest reproductive rate in Urban Monad 116, and families of twelve or fifteen are not at all unusual. Approaching the school door, they hear the clear treble voices singing of the blessedness of god. Mattern joins the singing; it is a hymn he sang too, when he was their age dreaming of the big family he would have:

"And now he plants the holy seed,
That grows in Mommo's womb,
And now a little sibling comes—"

There is an unpleasant and unscheduled interruption. A woman rushes toward Mattern and Gortman in the corridor. She is young, untidy, wearing only a flimsy gray wrap; her hair is loose; she is well along in pregnancy. "Help!" she shrieks. "My husband's gone flippo!" She hurls herself, trembling, into Gortman's arms. The visitor looks bewildered.

Behind her there runs a man in his early twenties, haggard, blood-shot. He carries a fabricator torch whose tip glows with heat. "Goddam bitch," he mumbles. "Allatime babies! Seven babies already and now number eight and I gonna go off my *head!*" Mattern is appalled. He pulls the woman away from Gortman and shoves the visitor through the door of the school.

"Tell them there's a flippo out here," Mattern says. "Get help, fast!" He is furious that Gortman should witness so atypical a scene, and wishes to get him away from it.

The trembling girl cowers behind Mattern. Quietly Mattern says, "Let's be reasonable, young man. You've spent your whole life in urb-mons, haven't you? You understand that it's blessed to create. Why do you suddenly repudiate the principles on which—"

"Get the hell away from her or I gonna burn you too!"

The young man feints with the torch, straight at Mattern's face. Mattern feels the heat and flinches. The young man swipes past him at the woman. She leaps away, but she is clumsy with girth, and the torch slices her garment. Pale white flesh is exposed with a brilliant burn-streak down it. She cups her jutting belly and falls, screaming. The young man jostles Mattern aside and prepares to thrust the torch into her side. Mattern tries to seize his arm. He deflects the torch; it chars the floor. The young man, cursing, drops it and throws himself on Mattern, pounding in frenzy with his fists. "Help me!" Mattern calls. "Help!"

Into the corridor erupt dozens of schoolchildren. They are between eight and eleven years old, and they continue to sing their hymn as they pour forth. They pull Mattern's assailant away. Swiftly, smoothly, they cover him with their bodies. He can dimly be seen beneath the flailing, thrashing mass. Dozens more pour from the schoolroom and join the heap. A siren wails. A whistle blows. The teacher's amplified voice booms, "The police are here! Everyone off!"

Four men in uniform have arrived. They survey the situation. The injured woman lies groaning, rubbing her burn. The insane man is unconscious; his face is bloody and one eye appears to be destroyed. "What happened?" a policeman asks. "Who are you?"

"Charles Mattern, sociocomputator, 799th level, Shanghai. The man's a flippo. Attacked his pregnant wife with the torch. Attempted to attack me."

The policemen haul the flippo to his feet. He sags in their midst. The police leader says, rattling the words into one another, "Guilty of atrocious assault on woman of childbearing years currently carrying unborn life, dangerous antisocial tendencies, by virtue of authority vested in me I pronounce sentence of erasure, carry out immediately. Down the chute with the bastard, boys!" They haul the flippo away. Medics arrive to care for the woman. The children, once again singing, return to the classroom.

Nicanor Gortman looks dazed and shaken. Mattern seizes his arm and whispers fiercely, "All right, those things happen sometimes. But it was a billion to one against having it happen right here where you were! It isn't typical! It isn't typical!"

They enter the classroom.

The sun is setting. The western face of the neighboring urban monad is streaked with red. Nicanor Gortman sits quietly at dinner with the members of the Mattern family. The children, voices tumbling one over another, talk of their day at school. The evening news comes on the screen; the announcer mentions the unfortunate event on the 108th floor. "The mother was not seriously injured," he says, "and no harm came to her unborn child." Principessa murmurs, "Bless god." After dinner Mattern requests copies of his most recent technical papers from the data terminal, and gives them to Gortman to read at his leisure. Gortman thanks him.

"You look tired," Mattern says.

"It was a busy day. And a rewarding one."

"Yes. We really traveled, didn't we?"

Mattern is tired too. They have visited nearly three dozen levels already; he has shown Gortman town meetings, fertility clinics, religious services, business offices. Tomorrow there will be much more to see. Urban Monad 116 is a varied, complex community. And a happy one, Mattern tells himself firmly. We have a few little incidents from time to time, but we're *happy*.

The children, one by one, go to sleep, charmingly kissing Daddo and Mommo and the visitor goodnight and running across the room, sweet nude little pixies, to their cots. The lights automatically dim. Mattern feels faintly depressed; the unpleasantness on 108 has spoiled what was otherwise an excellent day. Yet he still thinks that he has succeeded in helping Gortman see past the superficialities to the innate harmony and serenity of the urbmon way. And now he will allow the guest to experience for himself one of their techniques for minimizing the interpersonal conflicts that could be so destructive to their kind of society. Mattern rises.

"It's nightwalking time," he says. "I'll go. You stay here…with Principessa." He suspects that the visitor would appreciate some privacy.

Gortman looks uneasy.

"Go on," Mattern says. "Enjoy yourself. People don't deny happiness to people, here. We weed the selfish ones out early. Please. What I have is yours. Isn't that so, Principessa?"

"Certainly," she says.

Mattern steps out of the room, walks quickly down the corridor, enters the dropshaft and descends to the 770th floor. As he steps out he hears sudden angry shouts, and he stiffens, fearing that he will become involved in another nasty episode, but no one appears. He walks on. He passes the black door of a chute access door, and shivers a little, and suddenly he thinks of the young man with the fabricator torch, and where that young man probably is now. And then, without warning, there swims up from memory the face of the brother he had once had who had gone down that same chute, the brother one year his senior, Jeffrey, the whiner, the stealer, Jeffrey the selfish, Jeffrey the unadaptable, Jeffrey who had had to be given to the chute. For an instant Mattern is stunned and sickened, and he seizes a doorknob in his dizziness.

The door opens. He goes in. He has never been a nightwalker on this floor before. Five children lie asleep in their cots, and on the sleeping platform are a man and a woman, both younger than he is, both asleep. Mattern removes his clothing and lies down on the woman's left side. He touches her thigh, then her breast. She opens her eyes and he says, "Hello. Charles Mattern, 799."

"Gina Burke," she says. "My husband Lenny."

Lenny awakens. He sees Mattern, nods, turns over, and returns to sleep. Mattern kisses Gina Burke lightly on the lips. She opens her arms to him. He shivers a little in his need, and sighs as she receives him. God bless, he thinks. It has been a happy day in 2381, and now it is over.

$(NOW + n, NOW - n)$

I am a dour and unsmiling sort of man who actually has a lively if dry sense of humor: no one survives decade after decade of professional writing, as I have, without a sense of humor. A lot of the things I find amusing, though, evidently don't seem funny to other people, as I found out when I compiled an anthology of humorous science fiction and a number of startled reviewers commented on the dark tone of many of the stories.

So be it. Perhaps what I mistake for humor is actually irony, wit, or some other species of controlled and understated playfulness. I serve notice here that I think "(Now + n, Now − n)" is a comic story. Perhaps its comedy is one of tone rather than of situation; perhaps it's really no funnier than Macbeth, and my perceptions of what humor is are all cockeyed. At least grant me that it's a cleverly done time-paradox story, even if you don't get any laughs out of it. I may not know what funny is, but I defy anyone to tell me that I don't know my way around the twists and turns of time-travel.

I wrote this one in June of 1969, but it foreshadows the tone and sardonic approach I would be taking in the many stories I did in 1971, 1972, and 1973. Like the previous story in this book it was written at the request of Harry Harrison for his anthology Nova, and appeared in the second volume of that series.

All had been so simple, so elegant, so profitable for ourselves. And then we met the lovely Selene and nearly were undone. She came into our lives during our regular transmission hour on Wednesday, October 7, 1987, between six and seven p.m. Central European Time. The moneymaking hour. I was in satisfactory contact with myself and also with myself. (Now − n) was due on the line first, and then I would hear from (now + n).

I was primed for some kind of trouble. I knew trouble was coming, because on Monday, while I was receiving messages from the me of Wednesday, there came an inexplicable and unexplained break in communications. As a result I did not get data from (now + n) concerning the prices of the stocks in our carryover portfolio from last week, and I was unable to take action. Two days have passed, and I am the me of Wednesday who failed to send the news to me of Monday, and I have no idea what will happen to interrupt contact. Least of all did I anticipate Selene.

In such dealings as ours no distractions are needed, sexual or otherwise. We must concentrate wholly. At any time there is steady low-level contact among ourselves; we feel one another's reassuring presence. But transmission of data from self to self requires close attention.

I tell you my method. Then maybe you understand my trouble.

My business is investments. I do all my work at this same hour. At this hour it is midday in New York; the Big Board is still open. I can put through quick calls to my brokers when my time comes to buy or sell.

My office at the moment is the cocktail lounge known as the Celestial Room in the Henry VIII Hotel, south of the Thames. My office may be anywhere. All I need is a telephone. The Celestial Room is aptly named. The room orbits endlessly on a silent oiled track. Twittering sculptures in the so-called galactic mode drift through the air, scattering cascades of polychromed light upon those who sip drinks. Beyond the great picture windows of this supreme room lies the foggy darkness of the London evening, which I ignore. It is all the same to me, wherever I am: London, Nairobi, Karachi, Istanbul, Pittsburgh. I look only for an adequately comfortable environment, air that is safe to admit to one's lungs, service in the style I demand, and a telephone line. The individual characteristics of an individual place do not move me. I am like the ten planets of our solar family: a perpetual traveler, but not a sightseer.

Myself who is (now − n) is ready to receive transmission from myself who is (now). "Go ahead, (now + n)." he tells me. ((To him I am (now + *n*). To myself I am (now). Everything is relative; *n* is exactly forty-eight hours these days.))

"Here we go, (now − *n*)." I say to him.

I summon my strength by sipping at my drink. Chateau d'Yquem '79 in a sleek Czech goblet. Sickly sweet stuff; the waiter was aghast when I ordered it *before dinner.* Horreurs! Quel aperitif! But the wine makes transmission easier. It greases the conduit, somehow. I am ready.

My table is a single elegant block of glittering irradiated crystal, iridescent, cunningly emitting shifting moire patterns. On the table, unfolded, lies today's European edition of the *Herald Tribune.* I lean forward. I take from my breast pocket a sheet of paper, the printout listing the securities I bought on Monday afternoon. Now I allow my eyes to roam the close-packed type of the market quotations in my newspaper. I linger for a long moment on the heading, so there will be no mistake: *Closing New York Prices, Tuesday, October 6.* To me they are yesterday's prices. To (now − *n*) they are tomorrow's prices. (Now − *n*) acknowledges that he is receiving a sharp image.

I am about to transmit these prices to the me of Monday. You follow the machination, now?

I scan and I select.

I search only for the stocks that move five percent or more in a single day. Whether they move up or move down is immaterial; motion is the only criterion, and we go short or long as the case demands. We need fast action because our maximum survey span is only ninety-six hours at present, counting the relay from (now + *n*) back to (now − *n*) by way of (now). We cannot afford to wait for leisurely capital gains to mature; we must cut our risks by going for the quick, violent swings, seizing our profits as they emerge. The swings have to be violent. Otherwise brokerage costs will eat up our gross.

I have no difficulty choosing the stocks whose prices I will transmit to Monday's me. They are the stocks on the broker's printout, the ones we have already bought; obviously (now − *n*) would not have bought them unless Wednesday's me had told him about them, and now that I am Wednesday's me, I must follow through. So I send:

Arizona Agrochemical, 79?, + 6?
Canadian Transmutation, 116, + 4?

Commonwealth Dispersals, 12, − 1?
Eastern Electric Energy, 41, + 2
Great Lakes Bionics, 66, + 3 ?

And so on through *Western Offshore Corp.,* 99, − 8. Now I have transmitted to (now − *n*) a list of Tuesday's top twenty high-percentage swingers. From his vantage-point in Monday, (now − *n*) will begin to place orders, taking positions in all twenty stocks on Monday afternoon. I know that he has been successful, because the printout from my broker gives confirmations of all twenty purchases at what now are highly favorable prices.

(Now − *n*) then signs off for a while and (now + *n*) comes on. He is transmitting from Friday, October 9. He gives me Thursday's closing prices on the same twenty stocks, from Arizona Agrochemical to Western Offshore. He already knows which of the twenty I will have chosen to sell today, but he pays me the compliment of not telling me; he merely gives me the prices. He signs off, and, in my role as (now), I make my decisions. I sell Canadian Transmutation, Great Lakes Bionics, and five others; I cover our short sale on Commonwealth Dispersals. The rest of the positions I leave undisturbed for the time being, since they will sell at better prices tomorrow, according to the word from (now + *n*). I can handle those when I am Friday's me.

Today's sequence is over.

In any given sequence—and we have been running about three a week—we commit no more than five or six million dollars. We wish to stay inconspicuous. Our pre-tax profit runs at about nine percent a week. Despite our network of tax havens in Ghana, Fiji, Grand Cayman, Liechtenstein, and Bolivia, through which our profits are funneled, we can bring down to net only about five percent a week on our entire capital. This keeps all three of us in a decent style and compounds prettily. Starting with $5,000 six years ago at the age of twenty-five, I have become one of the world's wealthiest men, with no other advantages than intelligence, persistence, and extrasensory access to tomorrow's stock prices.

It is time to deal with the next sequence. I must transmit to (now − *n*) the Tuesday prices of the stocks in the portfolio carried over from last week, so that he can make his decisions on what to sell. I know what he has sold, but it would spoil his sport to tip my hand. We treat ourselves fairly. After I have finished sending (now − *n*) those prices, (now + *n*) will come online again and will transmit to me an entirely new list of stocks in which I must take positions before Thursday morning's New York opening. He will be able to realize profits in those on Friday. Thus we go from day to day, playing our shifting roles.

But this was the day on which Selene intersected our lives.

I had emptied my glass. I looked up to signal the waiter, and at that moment a slender, dark-haired girl, alone, entered the Celestial Room. She was tall, graceful, glorious. She was expensively clad in a clinging monomolecular wrap that shuttled through a complex program of wavelength shifts, including a microsecond sweep of total transparency that dazzled the eye while still maintaining a degree of modesty. Her features were a match for her garment: wide-set glossy eyes, delicate nose, firm lips lightly outlined in green. Her skin was extraordinarily pale. I could see no jewelry on her (why gild refined gold, why paint the lily?) but on her lovely left cheekbone I observed a small decorative band of ultraviolet paint, obviously chosen for visibility in the high-spectrum lighting of this unique room.

She conquered me. There was a mingling of traits in her that I found instantly irresistible: she seemed both shy and steel-strong, passionate and vulnerable, confident and ill at ease. She scanned the room, evidently looking for someone, not finding him. Her eyes met mine and lingered.

Somewhere in my cerebrum (now − n) said shrilly, as I had said on Monday, "I don't read you, (now + n). I don't read you!"

I paid no heed. I rose. I smiled to the girl, and beckoned her toward the empty chair at my table. I swept my *Herald Tribune* to the floor. At certain times there are more important things than compounding one's capital at five percent per week. She glowed gratefully at me, nodding, accepting my invitation.

When she was about twenty feet from me, I lost all contact with (now − n) and (now + n).

I don't mean simply that there was an interruption in the transmission of words and data among us. I mean that I lost all sense of the presence of my earlier and later selves. That warm, wordless companionship, that ourselvesness, that harmony that I had known constantly since we had established our linkage five years ago, vanished as if switched off. On Monday, when contact with (now + n) broke, I still had had (now − n). Now I had no one.

I was terrifyingly alone, even as ordinary men are alone, but more alone than that, for I had known a fellowship beyond the reach of other mortals. The shock of separation was intense.

Then Selene was sitting beside me, and the nearness of her made me forget my new solitude entirely.

She said, "I don't know where he is and I don't care. He's been late once too often. Finito for him. Hello, you. I'm Selene Hughes."

"Aram Kevorkian. What do you drink?"

"Chartreuse on the rocks. Green. I knew you were Armenian from halfway across the room."

I am Bulgarian, thirteen generations. It suits me to wear an Armenian name. I did not correct her. The waiter hurried over; I ordered chartreuse for her, a sake martini for self. I trembled like an adolescent. Her beauty was disturbing, overwhelming, astonishing. As we raised glasses I reached out experimentally for (now − n) or (now + n). Silence. Silence. But there was Selene.

I said, "You're not from London."

"I travel a lot. I stay here a while, there a while. Originally Dallas. You must be able to hear the Texas in my voice. Most recent port of call, Lima. For the July skiing. Now London."

"And the next stop?"

"Who knows? What do you do, Aram?"

"I invest."

"For a living?"

"So to speak. I struggle along. Free for dinner?"

"Of course. Shall we eat in the hotel?"

"There's the beastly fog outside," I said.

"Exactly."

Simpatico. Perfectly. I guessed her for twenty-four, twenty-five at most. Perhaps a brief marriage three or four years in the past. A private income, not colossal but nice. An experienced woman of the world, and yet also somehow still retaining a core of innocence, a magical softness of the soul. I loved her instantly. She did not care for a second cocktail. "I'll make dinner reservations," I said, as she went off to the powder room. I watched her walk away. A supple walk, flawless posture, supreme shoulderblades. When she was about twenty feet from me I felt my other selves suddenly return. "What's happening?" (now − n) demanded furiously. "Where did you go? Why aren't you sending?"

"I don't know yet."

"Where the hell are the Tuesday prices on last week's carryover stocks?"

"Later," I told him.

"Now. Before you blank out again."

"The prices can wait," I said, and shut him off. To (now + n) I said, "All right. What do you know that I ought to know?"

Myself of forty-eight hours hence said, "We have fallen in love."

"I'm aware of that. But what blanked us out?"

"She's psi-suppressant. She absorbs all the transmission energy we put out."

"Impossible! I've never heard of any such thing."

"No?" said (now + n). "Brother, this past hour has been the first chance I've had to get through to you since Wednesday, when we got into this mess. It's no coincidence that I've been with her just about one hundred percent of the time since Wednesday evening, except for a few two-minute breaks, and then I couldn't reach you because you must have been with her in your time sequence. And so—"

"How can this be?" I cried. "What'll happen to us if? No. No, you bastard, you're rolling me over. I don't believe you. There's no way that she could be causing it."

"I think I know how she does it," said (now + n). "There's a—"

At that moment Selene returned, looking even more radiantly beautiful, and silence descended once more.

We dined well. Chilled Mombasa oysters, salade niçoise, filet of Kobe beef rare, washed down by Richebourg '77. Occasionally I tried to reach myselves. Nothing. I worried a little about how I was going to get the Tuesday prices to (now − n) on the carryover stuff, and decided to forget about it. Obviously I hadn't managed to get them to him, since I hadn't received any printout on sales out of that portfolio this evening, and if I hadn't reached him, there was no sense in fretting about reaching him. The wonderful thing about this telepathy across time is the sense of stability it gives you: whatever has been, must be, and so forth.

After dinner we went down one level to the casino for our brandies and a bit of gamblerage. "Two thousand pounds' worth," I said to the robot cashier, and put my thumb to his charge plate, and the chips came skittering out of the slot in his chest. I gave half the stake to Selene. She played high-grav-low-grav, and I played roulette; we shifted from one table to the other according to whim and the run of our luck. In two hours she tripled her stake and I lost all of mine. I never was good at games of chance. I even used to get hurt in the market before the market ceased being a game of chance for me. Naturally, I let her thumb her winnings into her own account, and when she offered to return the original stake I just laughed.

Where next? Too early for bed.

"The swimming pool?" she suggested.

"Fine idea," I said. But the hotel had two, as usual. "Nude pool or suit pool?"

"Who owns a suit?" she asked, and we laughed and took the dropshaft to the pool.

There were separate dressing rooms, M and W. No one frets about showing flesh, but shedding clothes still has lingering taboos. I peeled fast and waited for her by the pool. During this interval I felt the familiar presence of another self impinge on me: (now – n). He wasn't transmitting, but I knew he was there. I couldn't feel (now + n) at all. Grudgingly I began to admit that Selene must be responsible for my communications problem. Whenever she went more than twenty feet away, I could get through to myselves. How did she do it, though? And could it be stopped? Mao help me, would I have to choose between my livelihood and my new beloved?

The pool was a vast octagon with a trampoline diving web and a set of underwater psych-lights making rippling patterns of color. Maybe fifty people were swimming and a few dozen more were lounging beside the pool, improving their tans. No one person can possibly stand out in such a mass of flesh, and yet when Selene emerged from the women's dressing room and began the long saunter across the tiles toward me, the heads began to turn by the dozens. Her figure was not notably lush, yet she had the automatic magnetism that only true beauty exercises. She was definitely slender, but everything was in perfect proportion, as though she had been shaped by the hand of Phidias himself. Long legs, long arms, narrow wrists, narrow waist, small high breasts, miraculously outcurving hips. The *Primavera* of Botticelli. The *Leda* of Leonardo. She carried herself with ultimate grace. My heart thundered.

Between her breasts she wore some sort of amulet: a disk of red metal in which geometrical symbols were engraved. I hadn't noticed it when she was clothed.

"My good-luck piece," she explained. "I'm never without it." And she sprinted laughing to the trampoline, and bounded, and hovered, and soared, and cut magnificently through the surface of the water. I followed her in. We raced from angle to angle of the pool, testing each other, searching for limits and not finding them. We dived and met far below, and locked hands, and bobbed happily upward. Then we lay under the warm quartz lamps. Then we tried the sauna. Then we dressed.

We went to her room.

She kept the amulet on even when we made love. I felt it cold against my chest as I embraced her.

But what of the making of money? What of the compounding of capital? What of my sweaty little secret, the joker in the Wall Street pack, the messages from beyond by which I milked the market of millions? On Thursday no contact with my other selves was scheduled, but I could not have made it even if it had been. It was amply clear: Selene blanked my psi field. The critical range was twenty feet. When we were farther apart than that, I could get through; otherwise, not. How did it happen? How? How? How? An accidental incompatibility of psionic vibrations? A tragic canceling out of my powers through proximity to her splendid self? No. No. No. No.

On Thursday we roared through London like a conflagration, doing the galleries, the boutiques, the museums, the sniffer palaces, the pubs, the sparkle houses. I had never been so much in love. For hours at a time I forgot my dilemma. The absence of myself from myself, the separation that had seemed so shattering in its first instant, seemed trivial. What did I need *them* for, when I had *her*?

I needed them for the moneymaking. The moneymaking was a disease that love might alleviate but could not cure. And if I did not resume contact soon, there would be calamities in store.

Late Thursday afternoon, as we came reeling giddily out of a sniffer palace on High Holborn, our nostrils quivering, I felt contact again. (Now + n) broke through briefly, during a moment when I waited for a traffic light and Selene plunged wildly across to the far side of the street.

"The amulet's what does it," he said. "That's the word I get from—"

Selene rushed back to my side of the street. "Come *on*, silly! Why'd you wait?"

Two hours later, as she lay in my arms, I swept my hand up from her satiny haunch to her silken breast and caught the plaque of red metal between two fingers. "Love, won't you take this off?" I said innocently. "I hate the feel of a piece of cold slithery metal coming between us when—"

There was terror in her dark eyes. "I couldn't, Aram! I *couldn't!*"

"For me, love?"

"Please. Let me have my little superstition." Her lips found mine. Cleverly she changed the subject. I wondered at her tremor of shock, her frightened refusal.

Later we strolled along the Thames, and watched Friday coming to life in fogbound dawn. Today I would have to escape from her for at least an hour, I knew. The laws of time dictated it. For on Wednesday, between six and seven p.m. Central European Time, I had accepted a transmission from myself of (now + *n*), speaking out of Friday, and Friday had come and I was that very same (now + *n*), who must reach out at the proper time toward his counterpart at (now − *n*) on Wednesday. What would happen if I failed to make my rendezvous with time in time, I did not know. Nor wanted to discover. The universe, I suspected, would continue regardless. But my own sanity—my grasp on that universe—might not.

It was narrowness. All glorious Friday I had to plot how to separate myself from radiant Selene during the cocktail hour, when she would certainly want to be with me. But in the end it was simplicity. I told the concierge, "At seven minutes after six send a message to me in the Celestial Room. I am wanted on urgent business must come instantly to computer room for intercontinental data patch, person to person. So?" Concierge replied, "We can give you the patch right at your table in the Celestial Room." I shook my head firmly. "Do it as I say. Please." I put thumb to gratuity account of concierge and signaled an account transfer of five pounds. Concierge smiled.

Seven minutes after six, message-robot scuttles into Celestial Room, comes homing in on table where I sit with Selene. "Intercontinental data patch, Mr. Kevorkian," says robot. "Wanted immediately. Computer room." I turn to Selene. "Forgive me, love. Desolated, but must go. Urgent business. Just a few minutes."

She grasps my arm fondly. "Darling, no! Let the call wait. It's our anniversary now. Forty-eight hours since we met!"

Gently I pull arm free. I extend arm, show jewelled timepiece. "Not yet, not yet! We didn't meet until half past six Wednesday. I'll be back in time to celebrate." I kiss tip of supreme nose. "Don't smile at strangers while I'm gone," I say, and rush off with robot.

I do not go to computer room. I hurriedly buy a Friday *Herald Tribune* in the lobby and lock myself in men's washroom cubicle. Contact now is made on schedule with (now − *n*), living in Wednesday, all innocent of what will befall him that miraculous evening. I read stock prices, twenty securities, from Arizona Agrochemical to Western Offshore Corp. I sign off and study my watch. (Now − *n*) is currently closing out seven long positions and the short sale on Commonwealth Dispersals. During the interval I seek to make contact with (now + *n*) ahead of me on Sunday evening. No response. Nothing.

Presently I lose contact also with (now − *n*). As expected; for this is the moment when the me of Wednesday has for the first time come within Selene's psi-suppressant field. I wait patiently. In a while (Selene − *n*) goes to powder room. Contact returns.

(Now − *n*) says to me, "All right. What do you know that I ought to know?"

"We have fallen in love," I say.

Rest of conversation follows as per. What has been, must be. I debate slipping in the tidbit I have received from (now + *n*) concerning the alleged powers of Selene's amulet. Should I say it quickly, before contact breaks? Impossible. It was not said to me. The conversation proceeds until at the proper moment I am able to say, "I think I know how she does it. There's a—"

Wall of silence descends. (Selene − *n*) has returned to the table of (now − *n*). Therefore I (now) will return to the table of Selene (now). I rush back to the Celestial Room. Selene, looking glum, sits alone, sipping drink. She brightens as I approach.

"See?" I cry. "Back just in time. Happy anniversary, darling. Happy, happy, happy, happy!"

When we woke Saturday morning we decided to share the same room thereafter. Selene showered while I went downstairs to arrange the transfer. I could have arranged everything by telephone without getting out of bed, but I chose to go in person to the desk, leaving Selene behind. You understand why.

In the lobby I received a transmission from (now + n), speaking out of Monday, October 12. "It's definitely the amulet," he said. "I can't tell you how it works, but it's some kind of mechanical psi-suppressant device. God knows why she wears it, but if I could only manage to have her lose it we'd be all right. It's the amulet. Pass it on."

I was reminded, by this, of the flash of contact I had received on Thursday outside the sniffer palace in High Holborn. I realized that I had another message to send, a rendezvous to keep with him who has become (now − n).

Late Saturday afternoon, I made contact with (now − n) once more, only momentarily. Again I resorted to a ruse in order to fulfill the necessary unfolding of destiny. Selene and I stood in the hallway, waiting for a dropshaft. There were other people. The dropshaft gate raised open and Selene went in, followed by others. With an excess of chivalry I let all the others enter before me, and "accidentally" missed the closing of the gate. The dropshaft descended with Selene. I remained alone in the hall. My timing was good; after a moment I felt the inner warmth that told me of proximity to the mind of (now − n). "The amulet's what does it," I said. "That's the word I get from—" Aloneness intervened.

During the week beginning Monday, October 12, I received no advance information on the fluctuations of the stock market at all. Not in five years had I been so deprived of data. My linkings with (now − n) and (now + n) were fleeting and unsatisfactory. We exchanged a sentence here, a blurt of hasty words there, no more. Of course, there were moments every day when I was apart from the fair Selene long enough to get a message out. Though we were utterly consumed by our passion for one another, nevertheless I did get opportunities to elude the twenty-foot radius of her psi-suppressant field. The trouble was that my opportunities to send did not always coincide with the opportunities of (now − n) or (now + n) to receive. We remained linked in a 48-hour spacing, and to alter that spacing would require extensive discipline and infinitely careful coordination, which none of ourselves were able to provide in such a time. So any contact with myselves had to depend on a coincidence of apartnesses from Selene.

I regretted this keenly. Yet there was Selene to comfort me. We reveled all day and reveled all night. When fatigue overcame us we grabbed a two-hour deepsleep wire and caught up with ourselves, and then we started over. I plumbed the limits of ecstasy. I believe it was like that for her.

Though lacking my unique advantage, I also played the market that week. Partly it was compulsion: my plungings had become obsessive. Partly, too, it was at Selene's urgings. "Don't you neglect your work for me," she purred. "I don't want to stand in the way of making *money*."

Money, I was discovering, fascinated her nearly as intensely as it did me. Another evidence of compatibility. She knew a good deal about the market herself and looked on, an excited spectator, as I each day shuffled my portfolio.

The market was closed Monday: Columbus Day. Tuesday, queasily operating in the dark, I sold Arizona Agrochemical, Consolidated Luna, Eastern Electric Energy, and Western Offshore, reinvesting the proceeds in large blocks of Meccano Leasing and Holoscan Dynamics. Wednesday's *Tribune*, to my chagrin, brought me the news that Consolidated Luna had received the Copernicus franchise and had risen 9 points in the final hour of Tuesday's trading. Meccano Leasing, though, had been rebuffed in the Robomation takeover bid and was off 4 since I had bought it. I got through to my broker in a hurry and sold Meccano, which was down even further that morning. My loss was $125 000—plus $250,000 more that I had dropped by selling Consolidated Luna too soon. After the market closed on Wednesday, the directors of Meccano Leasing unexpectedly declared a five-for-two split and a special dividend in the form of a one-for-ten distribution of cumulative participating high-depreciation warrants. Meccano regained its entire Tuesday-Wednesday loss and tacked on 5 points beyond.

I concealed the details of this from Selene. She saw only the glamor of my speculations: the telephone calls, the quick computations, the movements of hundreds of thousands of dollars. I hid the hideous botch from her, knowing it might damage my prestige.

On Thursday, feeling battered and looking for the safety of a utility, I picked up 10,000 Southwest Power and Fusion at 38, only hours before the explosion of SPF's magnetohydrodynamic generating station in Las Cruces which destroyed half a county and neatly peeled $90,000 off the value of my investment when the stock finally traded after a delayed opening, on Friday. I sold. Later came news that SPF's insurance would cover everything. SPF recovered, whereas Holoscan

Dynamics plummeted 11, costing me $140,000 more. I had not known that Holoscan's insurance subsidiary was the chief underwriter for SPF's disaster coverage.

All told, that week I shed more than $500,000. My brokers were stunned. I had a reputation for infallibility among them. Most of them had become wealthy simply by duplicating my own transactions for their own accounts.

"Sweetheart, what *happened?*" they asked me.

My losses the following week came to $1,250,000. Still no news from (now + n). My brokers felt I needed a vacation. Even Selene knew I was losing heavily, by now. Curiously, my run of bad luck seemed to intensify her passion for me. Perhaps it made me look tragic and Byronic to be getting hit so hard.

We spent wild days and wilder nights. I lived in a throbbing haze of sensuality. Wherever we went we were the center of all attention. We had that burnished sheen that only great lovers have. We radiated a glow of delight all up and down the spectrum.

I was losing millions.

The more I lost, the more reckless my plunges became, and the deeper my losses became.

I was in real danger of being wiped out, if this went on.

I had to get away from her.

Monday, October 26. Selene has taken the deepsleep wire and in the next two hours will flush away the fatigue of three riotous days and nights without rest. I have only pretended to take the wire. When she goes under, I rise. I dress. I pack. I scrawl a note for her. *"Business trip. Back soon. Love, love, love, love."* I catch noon rocket for Istanbul.

Minarets, mosques, Byzantine temples. Shunning the sleep wire, I spend next day and a half in bed in ordinary repose. I wake and it is forty-eight hours since parting from Selene. Desolation! Bitter solitude! But I feel (now + n) invading my mind.

"Take this down," he says brusquely. "Buy 5,000 FSP, 800 CCG, 150 LC, 200 T, 1,000 TXN, 100 BVI. Go short 200 BA, 500 UCM, 200 LOC. Clear? Read back to me."

I read back. Then I phone in my orders. I hardly care what the ticker symbols stand for. If (now + n) says to do, I do.

An hour and a half later the switchboard tells me, "A Miss Hughes to see you, sir."

She has traced me! Calamitas calamitatum! "Tell her I'm not here," I say. I flee to the roofport. By copter I get away. Commercial jet shortly brings me to Tel Aviv. I take a room at the Hilton and give absolute instructions am not to be disturbed. Meals only to room, also *Herald Trib* every day, otherwise no interruptions.

I study the market action. On Friday I am able to reach (now – *n*). "Take this down," I say brusquely. "Buy 5,000 FSP, 800 CCG, 140 LC, 200 T—"

Then I call brokers. I close out Wednesday's longs and cover Wednesday's shorts. My profit is over a million. I am recouping. But I miss her terribly.

I spend agonizing weekend of loneliness in hotel room.

Monday. Comes voice of (now + *n*) out of Wednesday, with new instructions. I obey. At lunchtime, under lid of my barley soup, floats note from her. "Darling, why are you running away from me? I love you to the ninth power. S."

I get out of hotel disguised as bellhop and take El Al jet to Cairo. Tense, jittery, I join tourist group sightseeing pyramids, much out of character. Tour is conducted in Hebrew; serves me right. I lock self in hotel. *Herald Tribune* available. On Wednesday I send instructions to me of Monday, (now – *n*). I await instructions from me of Friday, (now + *n*). Instead I get muddled transmissions, noise, confusions. What is wrong? Where to flee now? Brasilia, McMurdo Sound, Anchorage, Irkutsk, Maograd? She will find me. She has her resources. There are few secrets to one who has the will to surmount them. How does she find me?

She finds me.

Note comes: "I am at Abu Simbel to wait for you. Meet me there on Friday afternoon or I throw myself from Rameses' leftmost head at sundown. Love. Desperate. S."

I am defeated. She will bankrupt me, but I must have her.

On Friday I go to Abu Simbel.

She stood atop the monument, luscious in windswept white cotton.

"I knew you'd come," she said.

"What else could I do?"

We kissed. Her suppleness inflamed me. The sun blazed toward a descent into the western desert.

"Why have you been running away from me?" she asked. "What did I do wrong? Why did you stop loving me?"

"I never stopped loving you," I said.

"Then—*why?*"

"I will tell you," I said, "a secret I have shared with no human being other than myselves."

Words tumbled out. I told all. The discovery of my gift, the early chaos of sensory bombardment from other times, the bafflement of living one hour ahead of time and one hour behind time as well as in the present. The months of discipline needed to develop my gift. The fierce struggle to extend the range of extrasensory perception to five hours, ten, twenty-four, forty-eight. The joy of playing the market and never losing. The intricate systems of speculation; the self-imposed limits to keep me from ending up with all the assets in the world; the pleasures of immense wealth. The loneliness, too. And the supremacy of the night when I met her.

Then I said, "When I'm with you it doesn't work. I can't communicate with myselves. I lost millions in the last couple of weeks, playing the market the regular way. You were breaking me."

"The amulet," she said. "It does it. It absorbs psionic energy. It suppresses the psi field."

"I thought it was that. But who ever heard of such a thing? Where did you get it, Selene? Why do you wear it?"

"I got it far, far from here," said Selene. "I wear it to protect myself."

"Against *what?*"

"Against my own gift. My terrible gift, my nightmare gift, my curse of a gift. But if I must choose between my amulet and my love it is no choice. I love you, Aram, I love you, I love you!"

She seized the metal disk, ripped it from the chain around her neck, hurled it over the brink of the monument. It fluttered through the twilight sky and was gone.

I felt $(now - n)$ and $(now + n)$ return.

Selene vanished.

For an hour I stood alone atop Abu Simbel, motionless, baffled, stunned. Suddenly Selene was back. She clutched my arm and whispered,

"Quick! Let's go to the hotel!"

"Where have you been?"

"Next Tuesday," she said. "I oscillate in time."

"What?"

"The amulet damped my oscillations. It anchored me to the time-line in the present. I got it in 2459 A.D. Someone I knew there, someone who cared very deeply for me. It was his parting gift, and he gave it knowing we could never meet again. But now—"

She vanished. Gone eighteen minutes.

"I was back in last Tuesday," she said, returning. "I phoned myself and said I should follow you to Istanbul, and then to Tel Aviv, and then to Egypt. You see how I found you?"

We hurried to her hotel overlooking the Nile. We made love, and an instant before the climax I found myself alone in bed. (Now + n) spoke to me and said, "She's been here with me. She should be on her way back to you." Selene returned. "I went to—"

"—this coming Sunday," I said. "I know. Can't you control the oscillations at all?"

"No. I'm swinging free. When the momentum really builds up, I cover centuries. It's torture, Aram. Life has no sequence, no structure. Hold me tight!"

In a frenzy we finished what we could not finish before. We lay clasped close, exhausted. "What will we do?" I cried. "I can't let you oscillate like this!"

"You must. I can't let you sacrifice your livelihood!"

"But—"

She was gone.

I rose and dressed and hurried back to Abu Simbel. In the hours before dawn I searched the sands beside the Nile, crawling, sifting, probing. As the sun's rays crested the mountain I found the amulet. I rushed to the hotel. Selene had reappeared.

"Put it on," I commanded.

"I won't. I can't deprive you of—"

"Put it on."

She disappeared. (Now + n) said, "Never fear. All will work out wondrous well."

Selene came back. "I was in the Friday after next," she said. "I had an idea that will save everything."

"No ideas. Put the amulet on."

349

She shook her head. "I brought you a present," she said, and handed me a copy of the *Herald Tribune,* dated the Friday after next. Oscillation seized her. She went and came and handed me November 19's newspaper. Her eyes were bright with excitement. She vanished. She brought me the *Herald Tribune* of November 8. Of December 4. Of November 11. Of January 18, 1988. Of December 11. Of March 5, 1988. Of December 22. Of June 16, 1997. Of December 14. Of September 8, 1990. "Enough!" I said. "Enough!" She continued to swing through time. The stack of papers grew. "I love you," she gasped, and handed me a transparent cube one inch high. "*The Wall Street Journal,* May 19, 2206," she explained. "I couldn't get the machine that reads it. Sorry." She was gone. She brought me more *Herald Tribunes,* many dates, 1988-2002. Then a whole microreel. At last she sank down, dazed, exhausted, and said, "Give me the amulet. It must be within twelve inches of my body to neutralize my field." I slipped the disk into her palm. "Kiss me," Selene murmured.

And so. She wears her amulet; we are inseparable; I have no contact with my other selves. In handling my investments I merely consult my file of newspapers, which I have reduced to minicap size and carry in the bezel of a ring I wear. For safety's sake Selene carries a duplicate.

We are very happy. We are very wealthy.

Is only one dilemma. Neither of us use the special gift with which we were born. Evolution would not have produced such things in us if they were not to be used. What risks do we run by thwarting evolution's design?

I bitterly miss the use of my power, which her amulet negates. Even the company of supreme Selene does not wholly compensate for the loss of the harmoniousness that was

(now – *n*)

(now)

(now + *n*)

I could, of course, simply arrange to be away from Selene for an hour here, an hour there, and reopen that contact. I could even have continued playing the market that way, setting aside a transmission hour every forty-eight hours outside of amulet range. But it is the continuous contact that I miss. The always presence of my other selves. If I have that contact, Selene is condemned to oscillate, or else we must part.

I wish also to find some way that her gift will be not terror but joy for her.

Is maybe a solution. Can extrasensory gifts be induced by proximity? Can Selene's oscillation pass to me? I struggle to acquire it. We work together to give me her gift. Just today I felt myself move, perhaps a microsecond into the future, then a microsecond into the past. Selene said I definitely seemed to blur.

Who knows? Will success be ours?

I think yes. I think love will triumph. I think I will learn the secret, and we will coordinate our vanishings, Selene and I, and we will oscillate as one, we will swing together through time, we will soar, we will speed hand in hand across the millennia. She can discard her amulet once I am able to go with her on her journeys.

Pray for us, (now + n), my brother, my other self, and one day soon perhaps I will come to you and shake you by the hand.

AFTER THE MYTHS WENT HOME

Ed Ferman's Fantasy and Science Fiction was to celebrate its twentieth anniversary of publication with its October, 1969 issue, and in June of that year Ferman asked me to contribute a story to the special anniversary issue. I was flattered and honored by the request—F & SF had been a favorite of mine since the age of fourteen, when I had discovered its first issue on the newsstands—and I quickly sent him "After the Myths Went Home."

To my disappointment, though, it got squeezed out of the October number. "I kept hoping to get it in," Ed told me on July 28, "but then Sturgeon came through with a story, and then I discovered that yours was a bit close in story line to a Niven piece that had to go in, and so on: no one reason, just a bunch coming together. Yours was one of several excellent stories that I didn't have room for, so I'm planning the November issue as a sort of Twentieth Anniversary Again Issue. If Harlan can do it, we can." (The reference is to Harlan Ellison's just-announced Again, Dangerous Visions, the sequel to his controversial first anthology, containing stories by authors who hadn't contributed to the earlier volume.)

Time assuages all disappointments, sooner or later. I missed out on F & S F's much-heralded Twentieth Anniversary Issue, but Ferman reprinted "Sundance"—which a vote of readers and my fellow writers had chosen as one of the best stories in the magazine's history—in the Thirtieth in October of 1979. Just by way of demonstrating my longevity and persistence I did a story for the Fortieth too, ten years later, and for the Fiftieth when 1999 rolled around, and I'm already thinking about one for the Sixtieth, which is still a couple of years in the future as I write this.

For a while in those years we were calling great ones out of the past, to find out what they were like. This was in the middle twelves—12400 to 12450, say. We called up Caesar and Antony, and also Cleopatra. We got Freud and Marx and Lenin into the same room and let them talk. We summoned Winston Churchill, who was a disappointment (he lisped and drank too much), and Napoleon, who was magnificent. We raided ten millennia of history for our sport.

But after half a century of this we grew bored with our game. We were easily bored, in the middle twelves. So we started to call up the myth people, the gods and the heroes. That seemed more romantic; this was one of Earth's romanticist eras we lived in.

It was my turn then to serve as curator of the Hall of Man, and that was where they built the machine, so I watched it going up from the start. Leor the Builder was in charge. He had made the machines that called the real people up, so this was only slightly different, no real challenge to his talents. He had to feed in another kind of data, full of archetypes and psychic currents, but the essential process of reconstruction would be the same. He never had any doubt of success.

Leor's new machine had crystal rods and silver sides. A giant emerald was embedded in its twelve-angled lid. Tinsel streamers of radiant platinum dangled from the ebony struts on which it rose.

"Mere decoration," Leor confided to me. "I could have made a simple black box. But brutalism is out of fashion."

The machine sprawled all over the Pavilion of Hope on the north face of the Hall of Man. It hid the lovely flicker-mosaic flooring, but at least it cast lovely reflections into the mirrored surfaces of the exhibit cases. Somewhere about 12570, Leor said he was ready to put his machine into operation.

We arranged the best possible weather. We tuned the winds, deflecting the westerlies a bit and pushing all clouds far to the south. We sent up new moons to dance at night in wondrous patterns, now and again coming together to spell out Leor's name. People came from all over Earth, thousands of them, camping in whisper-tents on the great plain that begins at the Hall of Man's doorstep. There was real excitement then, a tension that crackled beautifully through the clear blue air.

Leor made his last adjustments. The committee of literary advisers conferred with him over the order of events, and there was some friendly bickering. We chose daytime for the first demonstration, and tinted the sky light purple for better effect. Most of us put on our youngest bodies, though there were some who said they wanted to look mature in the presence of these fabled figures out of time's dawn.

"Whenever you wish me to begin—" Leor said.

There were speeches first. Chairman Peng gave his usual lighthearted address. The Procurator of Pluto, who was visiting us, congratulated Leor on the fertility of his inventions. Nistim, then in his third or fourth successive term as Metabolizer General, encouraged everyone present to climb to a higher level. Then the master of ceremonies pointed to me. No, I said, shaking my head, I am a very poor speaker. They replied that it was my duty, as curator of the Hall of Man, to explain what was about to unfold.

Reluctantly I came forward.

"You will see the dreams of old mankind made real today," I said, groping for words. "The hopes of the past will walk among you, and so, I think, will the nightmares. We are offering you a view of the imaginary figures by means of whom the ancients attempted to give structure to the universe. These gods, these heroes, summed up patterns of cause and effect, and served as organizing forces around which cultures could crystallize. It is all very strange to us and it will be wonderfully interesting. Thank you."

Leor was given the signal to begin.

"I must explain one thing," he said. "Some of the beings you are about to see were purely imaginary, concocted by tribal poets, even as my friend has just told you. Others, though, were based on actual human beings who once walked the Earth as ordinary mortals, and who were transfigured, given more-than-human qualities, raised to the pantheon. Until they actually appear, we will not know which figures belong to which category, but I can tell you how to detect their origin once you see them. Those who were human beings before they became myths will have a slight aura, a shadow, a darkness in the air about them. This is the lingering trace of their essential humanity, which no mythmaker can erase. So I learned in my preliminary experiments. I am now ready."

Leor disappeared into the bowels of his machine. A single pure note, high and clean, rang in the air. Suddenly, on the stage looking out to the plain, there emerged a naked man, blinking, peering around.

Leor's voice, from within the machine, said, "This is Adam, the first of all men."

And so the gods and the heroes came back to us on that brilliant afternoon in the middle twelves, while all the world watched in joy and fascination.

Adam walked across the stage and spoke to Chairman Peng, who solemnly saluted him and explained what was taking place. Adam's hand was outspread over his loins. "Why am I naked?" Adam asked. "It is wrong to be naked."

I pointed out to him that he had been naked when he first came into the world, and that we were merely showing respect for authenticity by summoning him back that way.

"But I have eaten the apple," Adam said. "Why do you bring me back conscious of shame, and give me nothing to conceal my shame? Is this proper? Is this consistent? If you want a naked Adam, bring forth an Adam who has not yet eaten the apple. But—"

Leor's voice broke in: "This is Eve, the mother of us all."

Eve stepped forth, naked also, though her long silken hair hid the curve of her breasts. Unashamed, she smiled and held out a hand to Adam, who rushed to her, crying, "Cover yourself! Cover yourself!"

Surveying the thousands of onlookers, Eve said coolly, "Why should I, Adam? These people are naked too, and this must be Eden again."

"This is not Eden," said Adam. "This is the world of our children's children's children's children."

"I like this world," Eve said. "Relax."

Leor announced the arrival of Pan the Goat-Footed.

Now Adam and Eve both were surrounded by the dark aura of essential humanity. I was surprised at this, since I doubted that there had ever been a First Man and a First Woman on whom legends could be based; yet I assumed that this must be some symbolic representation of the concept of man's evolution. But Pan the half-human monster also wore the aura. Had there been such a being in the real world?

I did not understand it then. But later I came to see that if there had never been a goat-footed man, there nevertheless had been men who behaved as Pan behaved, and out of them that lusty god had been created. As for the Pan who came out of Leor's machine, he did not remain long on the stage. He plunged forward into the audience, laughing and waving his arms and kicking his cloven hooves in the air. "Great Pan lives!" He seized in his arms the slender form of Milian, the year-wife of Divud the Archivist, and carried her away toward a grove of feather-trees on the horizon.

"He does me honor," said Milian's year-husband Divud.

Leor continued to toil in his machine.

He brought forth Hector and Achilles, Orpheus, Perseus, Loki, and Absalom. He brought forth Medea, Cassandra, Odysseus, Oedipus. He brought forth Thoth, the Minotaur, Aeneas, Salome. He brought forth Shiva and Gilgamesh, Viracocha and Pandora, Priapus and Astarte, Diana, Diomedes, Dionysus, Deucalion. The afternoon waned and the sparkling moons sailed into the sky, and still Leor labored. He gave us Clytemnestra and Agamemnon, Helen and Menelaus, Isis and Osiris. He gave us Damballa and Guede-nibo and Papa Legba. He gave us Baal. He gave us Samson. He gave us Krishna. He woke Quetzalcoatl, Adonis, Holger Dansk, Kali, Ptah, Thor, Jason, Nimrod, Set.

The darkness deepened and the creatures of myth jostled and tumbled on the stage, and overflowed on to the plain. They mingled with one another, old enemies exchanging gossip, old friends clasping hands, members of the same pantheon embracing or looking warily upon their rivals. They mixed with us, too, the heroes selecting women, the monsters trying to seem less monstrous, the gods shopping for worshippers.

Perhaps we had enough. But Leor would not stop. This was his time of glory.

Out of the machine came Roland and Oliver, Rustum and Sohrab, Cain and Abel, Damon and Pythias, Orestes and Pylades, Jonathan and David. Out of the machine came St. George, St. Vitus, St. Nicholas, St. Christopher, St. Valentine, St. Jude. Out of the machine came the Furies, the Harpies, the Pleiades, the Fates, the Norns. Leor was a romantic, and he knew no moderation.

All who came forth wore the aura of humanity.

But wonders pall. The Earthfolk of the middle twelves were easily distracted and easily bored. The cornucopia of miracles was far from exhausted, but on the fringes of the audience I saw people taking to the sky and heading for home. We who were close to Leor had to remain, of course, though we were surfeited by these fantasies and baffled by their abundance.

An old white-bearded man wrapped in a heavy aura left the machine. He carried a slender metal tube. "This is Galileo," said Leor.

"Who is he?" the Procurator of Pluto asked me, for Leor, growing weary, had ceased to describe his conjured ghosts.

I had to request the information from an output in the Hall of Man. "A latter-day god of science," I told the Procurator, "who is credited with discovering the stars. Believed to have been a historical personage before his deification, which occurred after his martyrdom by religious conservatives."

Now that the mood was on him, Leor summoned more of these gods of science, Newton and Einstein and Hippocrates and Copernicus and Oppenheimer and Freud. We had met some of them before, in the days when we were bringing real people out of lost time, but now they had new guises, for they had passed through the mythmakers' hands. They bore emblems of their special functions, symbols of knowledge and power, and they went among us offering to heal, to teach, to explain. They were nothing like the real Newton and Einstein and Freud we had seen. They stood three times the height of men, and lightnings played around their brows.

Then came a tall, bearded man with a bloodied head. "Abraham Lincoln," said Leor.

"The ancient god of emancipation," I told the Procurator, after some research.

Then came a handsome young man with a dazzling smile and also a bloodied head. "John Kennedy," said Leor.

"The ancient god of youth and springtime," I told the Procurator. "A symbol of the change of seasons, of the defeat of summer by winter."

"That was Osiris," said the Procurator. "Why are there two?"

"There are many more," I said. "Baldur, Tammuz, Mithra, Attis."

"Why did they need so many?" he asked.

Leor said, "Now I will stop."

The gods and heroes were among us. A season of revelry began.

Medea went off with Jason, and Agamemnon was reconciled with Clytemnestra, and Theseus and the Minotaur took up lodgings together. Others preferred the company of men. I spoke a while with John Kennedy, the last of the myths to come from the machine. Like Adam, the first, he was troubled at being here.

"I was no myth," he insisted. "I lived. I was real. I entered primaries and made speeches."

"You became a myth," I said. "You lived and died and in your dying you were transfigured."

He chuckled. "Into Osiris? Into Baldur?"

"It seems appropriate."

"To you, maybe. They stopped believing in Baldur a thousand years before I was born."

"To me," I said, "you and Osiris and Baldur are contemporaries. To me and all the people here. You are of the ancient world. You are thousands of years removed from us."

"And I'm the last myth you let out of the machine?"

"You are."

"Why? Did men stop making myths after the twentieth century?"

"You would have to ask Leor. But I think you are right: your time was the end of the age of myth-making. After your time we could no longer believe such things as myths. We did not *need* myths. When we passed out of the era of troubles we entered a kind of paradise where every one of us lived a myth of his own, and then why should we have to raise some men to great heights among us?"

He looked at me strangely. "Do you really believe that? That you live in paradise? That men have become gods?"

"Spend some time in our world," I said, "and see for yourself."

He went out into the world, but what his conclusions were I never knew, for I did not speak to him again. Often I encountered roving gods and heroes, though. They were everywhere. They quarreled and looted and ran amok, some of them, but we were not very upset by that, since it was how we expected archetypes out of the dawn to act. And some were gentle. I had a brief love affair with Persephone. I listened, enchanted, to the singing of Orpheus. Krishna danced for me.

Dionysus revived the lost art of making liquors, and taught us to drink and be drunk.

Loki made magics of flame for us.

Taliesin crooned incomprehensible, wondrous ballads to us.

Achilles hurled his javelin for us.

It was a season of wonder, but the wonder ebbed. The mythfolk began to bore us. There were too many of them, and they were too loud, too active, too demanding. They wanted us to love them, listen to them. Bow to them, write poems about them. They asked questions—some of them anyway—that pried into the inner workings of our world, and embarrassed us, for we scarcely knew the answers. They grew vicious and schemed against each other, sometimes causing perils for us.

Leor had provided us with a splendid diversion. But we all agreed it was time for the myths to go home. We had had them with us for fifty years, and that was quite enough.

We rounded them up, and started to put them back into the machine.

The heroes were the easiest to catch, for all their strength. We hired Loki to trick them into returning to the Hall of Man. "Mighty tasks await you there," he told them, and they hurried thence to show their valor. Loki led them into the machine and scurried out, and Leor sent them away, Herakles, Achilles, Hector, Perseus, Cuchulainn, and the rest of that energetic breed.

After that many of the demonic ones came. They said they were as bored with us as we were with them and went back into the machine of their free will. Thus departed Kali, Legba, Set, and many more.

Some we had to trap and take by force. Odysseus disguised himself as Breel, the secretary to Chairman Peng, and would have fooled us forever if the real Breel, returning from holiday in Jupiter, had not exposed the hoax. And then Odysseus struggled. Loki gave us problems. Oedipus launched blazing curses when we came for him. Daedalus clung touchingly to Leor and begged, "Let me stay, brother! Let me stay!" and had to be thrust within.

Year after year the task of finding and capturing them continued, and one day we knew we had them all. The last to go was Cassandra, who had been living alone in a distant island, clad in rags.

"Why did you send for us?" she asked. "And, having sent, why do you ship us away?"

"The game is over," I said to her. "We will turn now to other sports."

"You should have kept us," Cassandra said. "People who have no myths of their own would do well to borrow those of others, and not just as sport. Who will comfort your souls in the dark times ahead? Who will guide your spirits when the suffering begins? Who will explain the woe that will befall you? Woe! Woe!"

"The woes of Earth," I said gently, "lie in Earth's past. We need no myths."

Cassandra smiled and stepped into the machine. And was gone.

And then the age of fire and turmoil opened, for when the myths went home the invaders came, bursting from the sky. And our towers toppled and our moons fell. And the cold-eyed strangers went among us, doing as they wished with us.

And those of us who survived cried out to the old gods, the vanished heroes.

"Loki, come!"

"Achilles, defend us!"

"Shiva, release us!"

"Herakles! Thor! Gawain!"

But the gods are silent, and the heroes do not come. The machine that glittered in the Hall of Man is broken. Leor, its maker, is gone from this world. Jackals run through our gardens, and our masters stride in our streets, and we are made slaves. And we are alone beneath the frightful sky. And we are alone.

THE PLEASURE
OF THEIR COMPANY

We have reached the autumn of 1969, a time when it was starting to seem certain that the day of the science-fiction magazine was ending. Just a handful of the magazines for which I had written in the early days of my career a decade and a half earlier still survived after the distribution cataclysm of 1958 and the general attrition of the years immediately afterward, and those that were still with us were looking very unhealthy. As I mentioned in the introduction to "A Happy Day in 2381," the center of gravity of the science-fiction-short-story field was now the steadily expanding group of original-fiction anthologies. Damon Knight had started his Orbit *series in 1966, and my* New Dimensions *would follow a couple of years later, along with Terry Carr's* Universe, *Harry Harrison's* Nova, *Samuel R. Delany's* Quark, *and a whole host of one-shot collections such as Harrison's* In the Year 2000 *and Anthony Cheetham's* Science Against Man. *I did stories for just about all of them,* Quark *being the only exception that comes to mind.*

One of the best of the new series was Infinity, *published in paperback form by the same company that fifteen years earlier had brought out Larry Shaw's fine magazine* Infinity Science Fiction. *The editor this time was the long-time s-f reader and writer Bob Hoskins, who now was employed at the paperback company that had risen out of the ashes of the old* Infinity *and its companion magazines. He asked me to be a regular contributor, and as things turned out I could not have been more regular than I was:*

there were five issues of the new Infinity *and I had stories in all five of them. This was the first, written in August of 1969 and published in* Infinity One *late in 1970.*

———————

He was the only man aboard the ship, one man inside a sleek shining cylinder heading away from Bradley's World at ten thousand miles a second, and yet he was far from alone. He had wife, father, daughter, son for company, and plenty of others, Ovid and Hemingway and Plato, and Shakespeare and Goethe, Attila the Hun and Alexander the Great, a stack of fancy cubes to go with the family ones. And his old friend Juan was along, too, the man who had shared his dream, his utopian fantasy, Juan who had been with him at the beginning and almost until the end. He had a dozen fellow voyagers in all. He wouldn't be lonely, though he had three years of solitary travel ahead of him before he reached his landfall, his place of exile.

It was the third hour of his voyage. He was growing calm, now, after the frenzy of his escape. Aboard ship he had showered, changed, rested. The sweat and grime of that wild dash through the safety tunnel were gone, now, though he wouldn't quickly shake from his mind the smell of that passageway, like rotting teeth, nor the memory of his terrifying fumbling with the security gate's copper arms as the junta's storm-troopers trotted toward him. But the gate had opened, and the ship had been there, and he had escaped, and he was safe. And he was safe.

I'll try some cubes, he thought.

The receptor slots in the control room held six cubes at once. He picked six at random, slipped them into place, actuated the evoker. Then he went into the ship's garden. There were screens and speakers all over the ship.

The air was moist and sweet in the garden. A plump, toga-clad man, clean-shaven, big-nosed, blossomed on one screen and said, "What a lovely garden! How I adore plants! You must have a gift for making things grow."

"Everything grows by itself. You're—"

"Publius Ovidius Naso."

"Thomas Voigtland. Former President of the Citizens' Council on Bradley's World. Now president-in-exile, I guess. A coup d'etat by the military."

"My sympathies. Tragic, tragic!"

"I was lucky to escape alive. I may never be able to return. They've probably got a price on my head."

"I know how terrible it is to be sundered from your homeland. Were you able to bring your wife?"

"I'm over here," Lydia said. "Tom? Tom, introduce me to Mr. Naso."

"I didn't have time to bring her," Voigtland said. "But at least I took a cube of her with me."

Lydia was three screens down from Ovid, just above a clump of glistening ferns. She looked glorious, her auburn hair a little too deep in tone but otherwise quite a convincing replica. He had cubed her two years before; her face showed none of the lines that the recent troubles had engraved on it. Voigtland said to her, "Not Mr. Naso, dear. Ovid. The poet Ovid."

"Of course. I'm sorry. How did you happen to choose him?"

"Because he's charming and civilized. And he understands what exile is like."

Ovid said softly, "Ten years by the Black Sea. Smelly barbarians my only companions. Yet one learns to adapt. My wife remained in Rome to manage my property and to intercede for me—"

"And mine remains on Bradley's World," said Voigtland. "Along with—along with—"

Lydia said, "What's this about exile, Tom? What happened?"

He began to explain about McAllister and the junta. He hadn't told her, back when he was having her cubed, why he wanted a cube of her. He had seen the coup coming. She hadn't.

As he spoke, a screen brightened between Ovid and Lydia and the seamed, leathery face of old Juan appeared. They had redrafted the constitution of Bradley's World together, twenty years earlier.

"It happened, then," Juan said instantly. "Well, we both knew it would. Did they kill very many?"

"I don't know. I got out fast once they started to—" He faltered. "It was a perfectly executed coup. You're still there. I suppose you're organizing the underground resistance by now. And I—And I—"

Needles of fire sprouted in his brain.

And I ran away, he said silently.

The other screens were alive now. On the fourth, someone with white robes, gentle eyes, dark curling hair. Voigtland guessed him to be Plato. On the fifth, Shakespeare, instantly recognizable, for the cube-makers had modeled him after the First Folio portrait: high forehead, long hair, pursed quizzical lips. On the sixth, a fierce, demonic-looking little man. Attila the Hun? They were all talking, activating themselves at random, introducing themselves to one another and to him. Their voices danced along the top of his skull. He could not follow their words. Restless, he moved among the plants, touching their leaves, inhaling the perfume of their flowers.

Out of the chaos came Lydia's voice.

"Where are you heading now, Tom?"

"Rigel XIX. I'll wait out the revolution there. It was my only option once hell broke loose. Get in the ship and—"

"It's so far," she said. "You're traveling alone?"

"I have you, don't I? And Mark and Lynx, and Juan, and Dad, and all these others."

"Cubes, that's all."

"Cubes will have to do," Voigtland said. Suddenly the fragrance of the garden seemed to be choking him. He went out, into the viewing salon next door, where the black splendor of space glistened through a wide port. Screens were mounted opposite the window. Juan and Attila seemed to be getting along marvelously well; Plato and Ovid were bickering; Shakespeare brooded silently; Lydia, looking worried, stared out of her screen at him. He studied the sweep of the stars.

"Which is our world?" Lydia asked.

"This," he said.

"So small. So far away."

"I've only been traveling a few hours. It'll get smaller."

He hadn't had time to take anyone with him. The members of his family had been scattered all over the planet when the alarm came, not one of them within five hours of home—Lydia and Lynx holidaying in the South Polar Sea, Mark archaeologizing on the Westerland Plateau. The integrator net told him it was a Contingency C situation: get off-planet within ninety minutes, or get ready to die. The forces of the junta had reached the capital and were on their way to pick him up. The escape ship had been ready, gathering dust in its buried vault. He hadn't been able to reach Juan. He hadn't been able to reach anybody. He used up sixty of his ninety minutes trying to get in touch with people, and then, with stunner shells already hissing overhead, he had gone into the ship and taken off. Alone.

But he had the cubes.

Cunning things. A whole personality encapsulated in a shimmering plastic box a couple of centimeters high. Over the past few years, as the likelihood of Contingency C had grown steadily greater, Voigtland had cubed everyone who was really close to him and stored the cubes aboard the escape ship, just in case.

It took an hour to get yourself cubed; and at the end of it, they had your soul in the box, your motion habits, your speech patterns, your way of thinking, your entire package of standard reactions. Plug your cube into a receptor slot and you came to life on the screen, smiling as you would smile, moving as you would move, sounding as you would sound, saying things you would say. Of course, the thing on the screen was unreal, a computer-actuated mockup, but it was programmed to respond to conversation, to absorb new data and change its outlook in the light of what it learned, to generate questions without the need of previous inputs; in short, to behave as a real person would.

The cube-makers also could supply a cube of anyone who had ever lived, or, for that matter, any character of fiction. Why not? It wasn't necessary to draw a cube's program from a living subject. How hard was it to tabulate and synthesize a collection of responses, typical phrases, and attitudes, feed them into a cube, and call what came out Plato or Shakespeare or Attila? Naturally a custom-made synthesized cube of some historical figure ran high, because of the man-hours of research and programming involved, and a cube of someone's own departed great-aunt was even more costly, since there wasn't much chance that it could be used as a manufacturer's prototype for further sales. But there was a wide array of standard-model historicals in the catalog when he was stocking his getaway ship; Voigtland had chosen eight of them.

Fellow voyagers. Companions on the long solitary journey into exile that he knew that he might someday have to take. Great thinkers. Heroes and villains. He flattered himself that he was worthy of their company. He had picked a mix of personality types, to keep him from losing his mind on his trip. There wasn't another habitable planet within a light-year of Bradley's World. If he ever had to flee, he would have to flee *far*.

He walked from the viewing salon to the sleeping cabin, and from there to the galley, and on into the control room. The voices of his companions followed him from room to room. He paid little attention to what they were saying, but they didn't seem to mind. They were talking to each other. Lydia and Shakespeare, Ovid and Plato, Juan and Attila, like old friends at a cosmic cocktail party.

"—not for its own sake, no but I'd say it's necessary to encourage mass killing and looting in order to keep your people from losing momentum, I guess, when—"

"—such a sad moment, when Prince Hal says he doesn't know Falstaff. I cry every time—"

"— when I said what I did about poets and musicians in an ideal Republic, it was not, I assure you, with the intent that *I* should have to live in such a Republic myself—"

"— the short sword, such as the Romans use, that's best, but—"

"—a throng of men and women in the brain, and one must let them find their freedom on the page —"

"—a slender young lad is fine, but yet I always had a leaning toward the ladies, you understand—"

"—massacre as a technique of political manipulation—"

"— Tom and I read your plays aloud to one another—"

"— good thick red wine, hardly watered—"

"— I loved Hamlet the dearest, my true son he was—"

"— the axe, ah, the axe!—"

Voigtland closed his throbbing eyes. He realized that it was soon in his voyage for company, too soon, too soon. Only the first day of his escape, it was. He had lost his world in an instant, in the twinkling of an eye. He needed time to come to terms with that, time and solitude, while he examined his soul. Later he could talk to his fellow voyagers. Later he could play with his cubed playmates.

He began pulling the cubes from the slots, Attila first, then Plato, Ovid, Shakespeare. One by one the screens went dark. Juan winked at him as he vanished, Lydia dabbed at her eyes. Voigtland pulled her cube too.

When they were all gone, he felt as if he had killed them.

For three days he roamed the ship in silence. There was nothing for him to do except read, think, watch, eat, sleep, and try to relax. The ship was self-programmed and entirely homeostatic; it ran without need of him, and indeed he had no notion of how to operate it. He knew how to program a takeoff, a landing, and a change of course, and the ship did all the rest. Sometimes he spent hours in front of his viewing port, watching Bradley's World disappear into the maze of the heavens. Sometimes he took his cubes out and arranged them in little stacks, four stacks of three, then three stacks of four, then six of two. But he did not play any of them. Goethe and Plato and Lydia and Lynx and Mark remained silent. They were his opiates against loneliness; very well, he would wait until the loneliness became intolerable.

He considered starting to write his memoirs. He decided to let them wait a while, too, until time had given him a clearer perspective on his downfall.

He thought a great deal about what might be taking place on Bradley's World just now. The jailings, the kangaroo trials, the purges. Lydia in prison? His son and daughter? Juan? Were those whom he had left behind cursing him for a coward, running off to Rigel this way in his plush little escape vessel? Did you desert your planet, Voigtland. Did you run out?

No. No. No. No.

Better to live in exile than to join the glorious company of martyrs. This way you can send inspiring messages to the underground, you can serve as a symbol of resistance, you can go back someday and guide the oppressed fatherland toward freedom, you can lead the counterrevolution and return to the capital with everybody cheering...Can a martyr do any of that?

So he had saved himself. So he had stayed alive to fight another day.

It sounded good. He was almost convinced.

He wanted desperately to know what was going on back there on Bradley's World, though.

The trouble with fleeing to another star system was that it wasn't the same thing as fleeing to a mountain-top hideout or some remote island on your own world. It would take so long to get to the other system, so long to make the triumphant return. His ship was a pleasure cruiser, not really meant for big interstellar hops. It wasn't capable of heavy acceleration, and its top velocity, which it reached only after a buildup of many weeks, was less than .50 lights. If he went all the way to the Rigel system and headed right back home, six years would have elapsed on Bradley's World between his departure and his return. What would happen in those six years?

What was happening there now?

His ship had a tachyon-beam ultrawave communicator. He could reach with it any world within a sphere ten light-years in radius, in a matter of minutes. If he chose, he could call clear across the galaxy, right to the limits of man's expansion, and get an answer in less than an hour.

He could call Bradley's World and find out how all those he loved had fared in the first hours of the dictatorship.

If he did, though, he'd paint a tachyon trail like a blazing line across the cosmos. And they could track him and come after him in their ramjet fighters at .75 lights, and there was about one chance in three that they could locate him with only a single point-source coordinate, and overtake him, and pick him up. He didn't want to risk it, not yet, not while he was still this close to home.

But what if the junta had been crushed at the outset? What if the coup had failed? What if he spent the next three years foolishly fleeing toward Rigel, when all was well at home, and a single call could tell him that?

He stared at the ultrawave set. He nearly turned it on.

A thousand times during those three days he reached toward it, hesitated, halted.

Don't. Don't. They'll detect you and come after you.

But what if I don't need to keep running?

It was Contingency C. The cause was lost.

That's what our integrator net said. But machines can be wrong. Suppose our side managed to stay on top? I want to talk to Juan. I want to talk to Mark. I want to talk to Lydia.

That's why you brought the cubes along. Keep away from the ultrawave.

On the fourth day, he picked out six cubes and put them in the receptor slots.

Screens glowed. He saw his father, his son, his oldest friend. He also saw Hemingway, Goethe, Alexander the Great.

"I have to know what's happening at home," Voigtland said. "I want to call them."

"I'll tell you." It was Juan who spoke, the man who was closer to him than any brother. The old revolutionary, the student of conspiracies. "The junta is rounding up everyone who might have dangerous ideas and locking them away. It's telling everybody else not to worry, stability is here at last. McAllister is in full control; calling himself provisional president or something similar."

"Maybe not. Maybe it's safe for me to turn and go back."

"What happened?" Voigtland's son asked. His cube hadn't been activated before. He knew nothing of events since he had been cubed, ten months earlier. "Were you overthrown?"

Juan started to explain about the coup to Mark. Voigtland turned to his father. At least the old man was safe from the rebellious colonels; he had died two years ago, in his eighties, just after making the cube. The cube was all that was left of him. "I'm glad this didn't happen in your time," Voigtland said. "Do you remember, when I was a boy, and you were President of the Council, how you told me about the uprisings on other colonies? And I said, No, Bradley's World is different, we all work together here."

The old man smiled. He looked pale and waxy, an echo of the man he had been. "No world is different, Tom. Political entities go through similar cycles everywhere, and part of the cycle involves an impatience with democracy. I'm sorry that the impatience had to strike while you were in charge, son."

"Homer tells us that men would rather have their fill of sleep, love, singing, and dancing than of war," Goethe offered, smooth-voiced, courtly, civilized. "But there will always be some who love war above all else. Who can say why the gods gave us Achilles?"

" I can," Hemingway growled. "You define man by looking at the opposites inside him. Love and hate. War and peace. Kissing and killing. That's where his borders are. What's wrong with that? Every man's a bundle of opposites. So is every society. And sometimes the killers get the upper hand on the kissers. Besides, how do you know the fellows who overthrew you were so wrong?"

"Let me speak of Achilles," said Alexander, tossing his ringlets, holding his hands high. "I know him better than any of you, for I carry his spirit within me. And I tell you that warriors are best fit to rule, so long as they have wisdom as well as strength, for they have given their lives as pledges in return for the power they hold. Achilles—"

Voigtland was not interested in Achilles. To Juan he said, "I have to call. It's four days, now. I can't just sit in this ship and remain cut off."

"If you call, they're likely to catch you."

"I know that. But what if the coup failed?" Voigtland was trembling. He moved closer to the ultrawave set.

Mark said, "Dad, if the coup failed, Juan will be sending a ship to intercept you. They won't let you just ride all the way to Rigel for nothing."

Yes, Voigtland thought, dazed with relief. Yes, yes, of course. How simple. Why hadn't I thought of that?

"You hear that?" Juan asked. "You won't call?"

"I won't call," Voigtland promised.

The days passed. He played all twelve cubes, chatted with Mark and Lynx, Lydia, Juan. Idle chatter, talk of old holidays, friends, growing up. He loved the sight of his cool elegant daughter and his rugged long-limbed son, and wondered how he could have sired them, he who was short and thick-bodied, with blunt features and massive bones. He talked with his father about government, with Juan about revolution. He talked with Ovid about exile, and with Plato about the nature of injustice, and with Hemingway about the definition of courage. They helped him through some of the difficult moments. Each day had its difficult moments.

The nights were much worse.

He ran screaming and ablaze down the tunnels of his own soul. He saw faces looming like huge white lamps above him. Men in black uniforms and mirror-bright boots paraded in somber phalanxes over his fallen body. Citizens lined up to jeer him. ENEMY OF THE STATE. ENEMY OF THE STATE. ENEMY OF THE STATE. They brought Juan to him in his dreams. COWARD. COWARD. COWARD. Juan's lean bony body was ridged and gouged; he had been. put through the tortures, the wires in the skull, the lights in the eyes, the truncheons in the ribs. I STAYED. YOU FLED. I STAYED. YOU FLED. I STAYED. YOU FLED. They showed him his own face in a mirror, a jackal's face, with long yellow teeth and little twitching eyes. ARE YOU PROUD OF YOURSELF? ARE YOU PLEASED? ARE YOU HAPPY TO BE ALIVE?

He asked the ship for help. The ship wrapped him in a cradle of silvery fibers and slid snouts against his skin that filled his veins with cold droplets of unknown drugs. He slipped into a deeper sleep, and underneath the sleep, burrowing up, came dragons and gorgons and serpents and basilisks, whispering mockery as he slept. TRAITOR. TRAITOR. TRAITOR. HOW CAN YOU HOPE TO SLEEP SOUNDLY, HAVING DONE WHAT YOU HAVE DONE?

"Look," he said to Lydia, "they would have killed me within the hour. There wasn't any possible way of finding you, Mark, Juan, anybody. What sense was there in waiting longer?"

"No sense at all, Tom. You did the smartest thing."

"But was it the *right* thing, Lydia?"

Lynx said, "Father, you had no choice. It was run or die."

He wandered through the ship, making an unending circuit. How soft the walls were, how beautifully upholstered! The lighting was gentle. Restful images flowed and coalesced and transformed themselves on the sloping ceilings. The little garden was a vale of beauty. He had music, fine food, books, cubes. What was it like in the sewers of the underground now?

"We didn't need more martyrs," he told Plato. "The junta was making enough martyrs as it was. We needed leaders. What good is a dead leader?"

"Very wise, my friend. You have made yourself a symbol of heroism, distant, idealized, untouchable, while your colleagues carry on the struggle in your name," Plato said silkily. "And yet you are able to return and serve your people in the future. The service a martyr gives is limited, finite, locked to a single point in time. Eh?"

" I have to disagree," said Ovid. "If a man wants to be a hero, he ought to hold his ground and take what comes. Of course, what sane man wants to be a hero? You did well, friend Voigtland! Give yourself over to feasting and love, and live longer and more happily."

"You're mocking me," he said to Ovid.

"I do not mock. I console. I amuse. I do not mock."

In the night came tinkling sounds, faint bells, crystalline laughter. Figures capered through his brain, demons, jesters, witches, ghouls. He tumbled down into mustiness and decay, into a realm of spiders, where empty husks hung on vast arching webs. THIS IS WHERE THE HEROES GO. Hags embraced him. WELCOME TO VALHALLA. Gnarled midgets offered him horns of mead, and the mead was bitter, leaving a coating of ash on his lips. ALL HAIL. ALL HAIL. ALL HAIL.

"Help me," he said hoarsely to the cubes. "What did I bring you along for, if not to help me?"

"We're trying to help," Hemingway said. "We agree that you did the sensible thing."

"You're saying it to make me happy, You aren't sincere."

"You bastard, call me a liar again and I'll step out of this screen and—"

"Maybe I can put it another way," Juan said craftily. "Tom, you had an *obligation* to save yourself. Saving yourself was the most valuable thing you could have done for the cause. Listen, for all you knew the rest of us had already been wiped out, right?"

"Yes. Yes."

"Then what would you accomplish by staying and being wiped out too? Outside of some phony heroics, what?" Juan shook his head. "A leader in exile is better than a leader in the grave. You can direct the resistance from Rigel, if the rest of us are gone. Do you see the dynamics of it, Tom?"

"I see. I see. You make it sound so reasonable, Juan."

Juan winked. "We always understood each other."

He activated the cube of his father. "What do you say? Should I have stayed or gone?"

"Maybe stay, maybe go. How can I speak for you? Certainly taking the ship was more practical. Staying would have been more dramatic. Tom, Tom, how can I speak for you?"

"Mark?"

"I would have stayed and fought right to the end. Teeth, nails, everything. But that's me. I think maybe you did the right thing, Dad. The way Juan explains it. The right thing for *you*, that is."

Voigtland frowned. "Stop talking in circles. Just tell me this: do you despise me for going?"

"You know I don't," Mark said.

The cubes consoled him. He began to sleep more soundly, after a while. He stopped fretting about the morality of his flight. He remembered how to relax.

He talked military tactics with Attila, and was surprised to find a complex human being behind the one-dimensional ferocity. He tried to discuss the nature of tragedy with Shakespeare, but Shakespeare seemed more interested in talking about taverns, politics, and the problems of a playwright's finances. He spoke to Goethe about the second part of Faust, asking if Goethe really felt that the highest kind of redemption came through governing well, and Goethe said, yes, yes, of course. And when Voigtland wearied of matching wits with his cubed great ones, he set them going against one another, Attila and Alexander, Shakespeare and Goethe, Hemingway and Plato, and sat back, listening to such talk as mortal man had never heard. And there were humbler sessions with Juan and his family. He blessed the cubes; he blessed their makers.

"You seem much happier these days," Lydia said.

"All that nasty guilt washed away," said Lynx.

"It was just a matter of looking at the logic of the situation," Juan observed.

Mark said, "And cutting out all the masochism, the self-flagellation."

"Wait a second," said Voigtland. "Let's not hit below the belt, young man."

"But it *was* masochism, Dad. Weren't you wallowing in your guilt? Admit it."

"I suppose I—"

"And looking to us to pull you out," Lynx said. "Which we did."

" Yes. You did."

"And it's all clear to you now, eh?' Juan asked. "Maybe you *thought* you were afraid, thought you were running out, but you were actually performing a service to the republic. Eh?"

Voigtland grinned. "Doing the right thing for the wrong reason."

"Exactly. Exactly."

"The important thing is the contribution you still can make to Bradley's World," his father's voice said. "You're still young. There's time to rebuild what we used to have there."

"Yes. Certainly."

"Instead of dying a futile but heroic death," said Juan.

"On the other hand," Lynx said, "what did Eliot write? '*The last temptation is the greatest treason: To do the right deed for the wrong reason.*'"

Voigtland frowned. "Are you trying to say—"

"And it *is* true," Mark cut in, "that you were planning your escape far in advance. I mean, making the cubes and all, picking out the famous men you wanted to take—"

"As though you had decided that at the first sign of trouble you were going to skip out," said Lynx.

"They've got a point," his father said. "Rational self-protection is one thing, but an excessive concern for your mode of safety in case of emergency is another."

"I don't say you should have stayed and died," Lydia said. "I never would say that. But all the same—"

"Hold on!" Voigtland said. The cubes were turning against him suddenly. "What kind of talk is this?"

Juan said, "And strictly as a pragmatic point, if the people were to find out how far in advance you engineered your way out, and how comfortable you are as you head for exile—"

"You're supposed to help me," Voigtland shouted. "Why are you starting this? What are you trying to do?"

"You know we all love you," said Lydia.

"We hate to see you not thinking clearly, Father," Lynx said.

"Weren't you planning to run out all along?" said Mark.

"Wait! Stop! Wait!"

"Strictly as a matter of—"

Voigtland rushed into the control room and pulled the Juan-cube from the slot.

"We're trying to explain to you, dear—"

He pulled the Lydia-cube, the Mark-cube, the Lynx-cube, the father-cube.

The ship was silent.

He crouched, gasping, sweat-soaked, face rigid, eyes clenched tight shut, waiting for the shouting in his skull to die away.

An hour later, when he was calm again, he began setting up his ultrawave call, tapping out the frequency that the underground would probably be using, if any underground existed. The tachyon beam sprang across the void, an all but instantaneous carrier wave, and he heard cracklings, and then a guarded voice saying, "Four Nine Eight Three, we read your signal, do you read me? This is Four Nine Eight Three, come in, come in, who are you?"

"Voigtland," he said. "President Voigtland, calling Juan. Can you get Juan on the line?"

"Give me your numbers, and—"

"What numbers? This is *Voigtland*. I'm I don't know how many billion miles out in space, and I want to talk to Juan. Get me Juan. *Get me Juan.*"

"You wait," the voice said.

Voigtland waited, while the ultrawave spewed energy wantonly into the void. He heard clickings, scrapings, clatterings. "You still there?" the voice said, after a while. "We're patching him in. But be quick. He's busy."

"Well? Who is it?" Juan's voice, beyond doubt.

"Tom here. Tom Voigtland, Juan!"

"It's really you?" Coldly. From a billion parsecs away, from some other universe. "Enjoying your trip, Tom?"

"I had to call. To find out—to find out—how it was going, how everybody is. How Mark—Lydia—you—"

" Mark's dead. Killed the second week, trying to blow up McAllister in a parade."

"Oh. Oh."

"Lydia and Lynx are in prison somewhere. Most of the others are dead. Maybe ten of us left, and they'll get us soon, too. Of course, there's you."

"Yes."

"You bastard," Juan said quietly. "You rotten bastard. All of us getting rounded up and shot, and you get into your ship and fly away!"

"They would have killed me too, Juan. They were coming after me. I only just made it."

"You should have stayed," Juan said.

"No. No. That isn't what you just said to me! You told me I did the right thing, that I'd serve as a symbol of resistance, inspiring everybody from my place of exile, a living symbol of the overthrown government—"

"I said this?"

"You, yes," Voigtland told him. "Your cube, anyway."

"Go to hell," said Juan. "You lunatic bastard."

"Your cube— we discussed it, you explained—"

"Are you crazy, Tom? Listen, those cubes are programmed to tell you whatever you want to hear. Don't you know that? You want to feel like a hero for running away, they tell you you're a hero. It's that simple. How can you sit there and quote what my cube said to you, and make me believe that *I* said it?"

"But I— you—"

"Have a nice flight, Tom. Give my love to everybody, wherever you're going."

"I couldn't just stay there to be killed. What good would it have been? Help me, Juan! What shall I do now? Help me!"

"I don't give a damn what you do," Juan said. "Ask your cubes for help. So long, Tom."

"Juan—"

"So long, you bastard."

Contact broke.

Voigtland sat quietly for a while, pressing his knuckles together. *Listen, those cubes are programmed to tell you whatever you want to hear. Don't you know that? You want to feel like a hero for running away, they tell you you're a hero. And if you want to feel like a villain? They tell you that too. They meet all needs. They aren't people. They're cubes.*

He put Goethe in the slot. "Tell me about martyrdom," he said.

Goethe said, "It has its tempting side. One may be covered with sins, scaly and rough-skinned with them, and in a single fiery moment of self-immolation one wins redemption and absolution, and one's name is forever cherished."

He put Juan in the slot. "Tell me about the symbolic impact of getting killed in the line of duty."

"It can transform a mediocre public official into a magnificent historical figure," Juan said.

He put Mark in the slot. "Which is a better father to have: a live coward or a dead hero?"

"Go down fighting, Dad."

He put Hemingway in the slot. "What would you do if someone called you a rotten bastard?"

"I'd stop to think if he was right or wrong. If he was wrong, I'd give him to the sharks. If he was right, well, maybe the sharks would get fed anyway."

He put Lydia in the slot. Lynx. His father. Alexander. Attila. Shakespeare. Plato. Ovid.

lit In their various ways they were all quite eloquent. They spoke of bravery, self-sacrifice, nobility, redemption.

He picked up the Mark-cube. "You're dead," he said. "Just like your grandfather. There isn't any Mark anymore. What comes out of this cube isn't Mark. It's me, speaking with Mark's voice, talking through Mark's mind. You're just a dummy."

He put the Mark-cube in the ship's converter input, and it tumbled down the slideway to become reaction mass. He put the Lydia-cube in next. Lynx. His father. Alexander. Attila. Shakespeare. Plato. Ovid. Goethe.

He picked up the Juan-cube. He put it in a slot again. "Tell me the truth," he yelled. "What'll happen to me if I go back to Bradley's World?"

"You'll make your way safely to the underground and take charge, Tom. You'll help us throw McAllister out: We can win with you, Tom."

"Crap," Voigtland said. "I'll tell you what'll really happen. I'll be intercepted before I go into my landing orbit. I'll be taken down and put on trial. And then I'll be shot. Right? Right? Tell me the truth, for once. Tell me I'll be shot!"

"You misunderstand the dynamics of the situation, Tom. The impact of your return will be so great that—"

He took the Juan-cube from the slot and put it into the chute that went to the converter.

"Hello?" Voigtland said. "Anyone here?"

The ship was silent.

"I'll miss all that scintillating conversation," he said. "I miss you already. Yes. Yes. But I'm glad you're gone."

He countermanded the ship's navigational instructions and tapped out the program headed RETURN TO POINT OF DEPARTURE. His hands were shaking, just a little, but the message went through. The instruments showed him the change of course as the ship began to turn around. As it began to take him home.

Alone.

WE KNOW WHO WE ARE

The old-line science-fiction magazines were not completely dead, though. Among the survivors was the venerable Amazing Stories, *the oldest s-f magazine of all, which had gone through some hard times but was now enjoying something of a renaissance under the editorial guidance of Ted White, a well-known science-fiction fan who had lately made the move to the professional level. I had been instrumental in getting White chosen for the job; and now he turned around and asked me to do some stories for him. My work schedule was getting increasingly frantic in this phase of my career as editors crowded around asking for material—I didn't mind being in demand, but I was having trouble meeting all the requests—and in the end I wrote only this one story for White, though I did arrange for him to serialize two of my current novels,* Up the Line *and* The Second Trip. *I did "We Know Who We Are" in September of 1969 and it was published in* Amazing's *July, 1970 issue.*

I had thought, back in 1958, that my career as a science-fiction writer was just about over, since the market for such fiction had dwindled to the point where it was impossible to earn a reasonable living writing it; and indeed, as I noted in the introduction to this book, four years passed between "Delivery Guaranteed" in 1958, which concludes the first volume of this series, and "To See the Invisible Man" of 1962, which opens this second volume. But by the time we reach 1969 and "We Know Who We Are," I am back in the science-fiction business with a vengeance, coming into my most fertile era and unleashing a whole swarm of stories and novels that still stand as my most memorable work, and it will take two volumes more just to present the best of the short stories and novellas I did between 1970 and 1973—after which, as I will show in due course, there came yet another crash in science-fiction publishing and yet another retreat by me from writing the stuff. But better to tell that part of the story, I think, in the volumes ahead.

"**W**e know who we are and what we want to be," say the people of Shining City whenever they feel particularly uncertain about things. Shining City is at least a thousand years old. It may be even older, but who can be sure? It stands in the middle of a plain of purple sand that stretches from the Lake of No Return to the River Without Fish. It has room for perhaps six hundred thousand people. The recent population of Shining City has been perhaps six hundred people. They know who they are. They know what they want to be.

Things got trickier for them after the girl who was wearing clothes came walking in out of the desert.

Skagg was the first one to see her. He knew immediately that there was something unusual about her, and not just that she was wearing clothes. Anybody who ever goes out walking in the desert puts clothes on, because the heat is fierce—there being no Cool Machine out there—and the sun would roast you fast if you didn't have some kind of covering, and the sand would blow against you and pick the meat from your bones. But the unusual thing about the girl was her face. It wasn't a familiar one. Everybody in Shining City knew everybody else, and Skagg didn't know this girl at all, so she had to be a stranger, and strangers just didn't exist.

She was more than a child but less than a woman, and her body was slender and her hair was dark, and she walked the way a man would walk, with her arms swinging and her knees coming high and her legs kicking outward. When Skagg saw her he felt afraid, and he had never been afraid of a woman before.

"Hello," she said. "I speak Language. Do you?"

Her voice was deep and husky, like the wind on a winter day pushing itself between two of the city's towers. Her accent was odd, and the words came out as if she were holding her tongue in the wrong part of her mouth. But he understood her.

He said, "I speak Language, and I understand what you say. But who are you?"

"Fa Sol La," she sang.

"Is that your name?"

"That is my name. And yours?"

"Skagg.."

"Do all the people in this city have names like Skagg?"

"I am the only Skagg," said Skagg. "Where do you come from?"

She pointed eastward. "From a place beside the River Without Fish. Is this Shining City?"

"Yes," Skagg said.

"Then I am where I want to be." She unslung the pack that she was carrying over one shoulder and set it down, and then she removed her robe, so that she was as naked as he was. Her skin was very pale, and there was practically no flesh on her. Her breasts were tiny and her buttocks were flat. From where he stood, Skagg could easily have mistaken her for a boy. She picked up the pack again. "Will you take me into your city?" she asked.

They were on the outskirts, in the region of the Empty Buildings. Skagg sometimes went there when he felt that his mind was too full. Tall tapering towers sprouted here. Some were sagging and others had lost their outer trim. Repair Machines no longer functioned in this part of the city.

"Where do you want to go?" he asked.

"To the place where the Knowing Machine is," said Fa Sol La.

Frowning, he said, "How do you know about the Machine?"

"Everyone in the world knows about the Knowing Machine. I want to see it. I walked all the way from the River Without Fish to see the Knowing Machine. You'll take me there, won't you, Skagg?"

He shrugged. "If you want. But you won't be able to get close to it. You'll see. You've wasted your time."

They began to walk toward the center of the city.

She moved with such a swinging stride that he had to work hard to keep up with her. Several times she came close to him, so that her hip or thigh brushed his skin, and Skagg felt himself trembling at the strangeness of her. They were silent a long while. The morning sun began to go down and the afternoon sun started to rise, and the double light, blending, cast deceptive shadows and made her body look fuller than it was. Near the Mirror Walls a Drink Machine came up to them and refreshed them. She put her head inside it and gulped as if she had been dry for months, and then she let the fluid run out over her slim body. Not far on a Riding Machine found them and offered to transport them to the center. Skagg gestured to her to get in, but she waved a no at him.

"It's still a great distance," he said.

"I'd rather walk. I've walked this far, and I'll walk to the end. I can see things better."

Skagg sent the machine away. They went on walking. The morning sun disappeared and now only the green light of afternoon illuminated Shining City.

She said, "Do you have a woman, Skagg?"

"I don't understand."

"Do you have a woman, I said."

"I heard the words. But how does one *have* a woman? What does it mean?"

"To live with. To sleep with. To share pleasure with. To have children with."

"We live by ourselves," he said. "There's so much room here, why crowd together? We sleep sometimes with others, yes. We share pleasure with everyone. Children rarely come."

"You have no regular mates here, then?"

"I have trouble understanding. Tell me how it is in your city."

"In my city," she said, "a man and a woman live together and do all things together. They need no one else. Sometimes, they realize they do not belong together and then they split up and seek others, but often they have each other for a lifetime."

"This sounds quite strange," said Skagg.

"We call it love," said Fa Sol La.

"We have love here. All of us love all of us. We do things differently, I suppose. Does any man in your city have you, then?"

"No. Not any more. I had a man, but he was too simple for me. And I left and walked to Shining City."

She frightened him even more, now.

They had started to enter the inhabited part of the city. Behind them were the long stately avenues and massive residential structures of the dead part; ahead lay the core, with its throbbing machines and eating centers and bright lights.

"Are you happy here?" Fa Sol La asked as they stepped between a Cleansing Machine's pillars and were bathed in blue mist.

"We know who we are," Skagg said, "and what we want to be. Yes, I think we're happy."

"I think you may be wrong," she said, and laughed, and pressed her body tight up against him a moment, and sprinted ahead of him like something wild.

A Police Machine rose from the pavement and blocked her way. It shot out silvery filaments that hovered around her, ready to clamp close if she made a hostile move. She stood still. Skagg ran up and said, "It's all right. She's new to the city. Scan her and accept her."

The machine bathed both of them in an amber glow and went away.

"What are you afraid of here?" Fa Sol La asked.

"Animals sometimes come in from the desert. We have to be careful. Did it scare you?"

"It puzzled me," she said.

Others were nearing them now. Skagg saw Glorr, Derk, Prewger, and Simit; and more were coming. They crowded around the girl, none daring to touch her but everyone staring hard.

"This is Fa Sol La," said Skagg. "I discovered her. She comes from a city at the River Without Fish and walked across the desert to visit us."

"What is your city called?" Derk demanded.

"River City," she said.

"How many people live there?" asked Prewger.

"I don't know. Many but not *very* many."

"How old are you?" Simit blurted.

"Five no-suns," she said.

"Did you come alone?" Glorr said.

"Alone."

"Why did you come here?" Prewger asked.

She said, "To see the Knowing Machine," and they moved as if she had proclaimed herself to be the goddess of death.

"The Knowing Machine is dangerous," said Prewger.

"No one may get close to it," said Simit.

"We fear it," said Glorr.

"It will kill you," said Derk.

Fa Sol La said, "Where is the Knowing Machine?"

They backed away from her. Derk summoned a Soothing Machine and had a drink from it. Prewger stepped into a Shelter Machine. Simit went among the others who had gathered, whispering her answers to them. Glorr turned his face away and bowed his head.

"Why are you so afraid?" she asked.

Skagg said, "When the city was built, the builders used the Knowing Machine to make themselves like gods. And the gods killed them. They came out of the machine full of hate, and took weapons against one another, until only a few were left. And those who remained said that no one ever again would enter the Machine."

"How long ago was that?"

"How should I know?" said Skagg.

"Show me the machine."

He hesitated. He spoke a few faltering syllables of refusal.

She pressed herself close against him and rubbed her body against his. She put her teeth lightly on the lobe of his ear. She ran her fingers along the strong muscles of his back.

"Show me the machine," she said. "I love you, Skagg. Can you refuse me the machine?"

He quivered. Her strangeness attracted him powerfully. He was eight no-suns old, and he knew every woman in Shining City all too well, and though he feared this girl he also was irresistibly drawn to her.

"Come," he whispered.

They walked down sleek boulevards and glowing skyways, crossed brooks and ponds and pools, passed spiky statues and dancing beacons. It was a handsome city, the finest in the world, and Fa Sol La trilled and sighed at every beautiful thing in it.

"They say that those who live here never go anywhere else," she said. "Now I begin to understand why. Have you ever been to another city, Skagg?"

"Never."

"But you go outside sometimes?"

"To walk in the desert, yes. Most of the others never even do that."

"But outside—there are so many cities, Skagg, so many different kinds of people! A dozen cities, a whole world! Don't you ever want to see them?"

"We like it here. We know what we want."

"It's lovely here. But it isn't right for you to stay in one place forever. It isn't *human*. How would people ever have come to this world in the first place, if our ancestors had done as you folk do?"

"I don't concern myself with that. Shining City cares for us, and we prefer not to go out. Obviously most others stay close to their cities too, since you are the first visitor I can remember."

"Shining City is too remote from other cities," Fa Sol La said. "Many dream of coming here, but few dare, and fewer succeed. But we travel everywhere else. I have been in seven cities besides my own, Skagg."

The idea of that disturbed him intensely.

She went on, "Traveling opens the mind. It teaches you things about yourself that you never realized."

"We know who we are," he said.

"You only think you do."

He glared at her, turned, pointed. "This is the Knowing Machine," he said, glad to shift subjects.

They stood in the center of the great cobbled plaza before the machine. Two hundred strides to the east rose the glossy black column, flanked by the protective columns of shimmering white metal. The door-opening was faintly visible. Around the brow of the column the colors flickered and leaped, making the range of the spectrum as they had done for at least a thousand years.

"Where do I go in?" she asked.

"No one goes in."

"I'm going in. I want you to come in with me, Skagg."

He laughed. "Those who enter die."

"No. No. The machine teaches love. It opens you to the universe. It awakens your mind. We have books about it. We *know.*"

"The machine kills."

"It's a lie, Skagg, made up by people whose souls were full of hate. They didn't want anyone to experience the goodness that the machine brings. It isn't the first time that men have prohibited goodness out of the fear of love."

Skagg smiled. "I have a fear of death, girl, not of love. Go into the machine, if you like. I'll wait here."

Fury and contempt sparkled in her eyes. Without another word she strode across the plaza. He watched, admiring the trimness of her body, the ripple of her muscles. He did not believe she would enter the machine. She passed the Zone of Respect and the Zone of Obeisance and the Zone of Contemplation, and went into the Zone of Approach, and did not halt there, but entered the Zone of Peril, and as she walked on into the Zone of Impiety he cursed and started to run after her, shouting for her to halt.

Now she was on the gleaming steps. Now she was ascending. Now she had her hand on the sliding door.

"Wait!" he screamed. "No! I love you!"

"Come in with me, then."

"It will kill us!"

"Then farewell," she said, and went into the Knowing Machine.

Skagg collapsed on the rough red cobblestones of the Zone of Approach and lay there sobbing, face down, clutching at the stones with his fingers, remembering how vulnerable and fragile she had looked, and yet how strong and sturdy she was, remembering her small breasts and lean thighs, and remembering too the strangeness about her that he loved. Why had she chosen to kill herself this way?

After a long while he stood up and started to leave. Night had come and the first moons were out. The taste of loss was bitter in mouth.

"Skagg?" she called.

She was on the steps of the Knowing Machine. She ran toward him, seemingly floating, and her face was flushed and her eyes were radiant.

"You lived?" he muttered. "You came out?"

"They've been lying, Skagg. The machine doesn't kill. It's there to help. It was marvelous, Skagg."

"What happened?"

"Voices speak to you, and tell you what to do. And you put a metal thing on your head, and fire shoots through your brain, and you *see*, Skagg, you see everything for the first time."

"Everything? What everything?"

"Life. Love. Stars. The connections that hold people together. It's all there. Ecstasy. It feels like having a whole planet making love to you. You see the patterns of life, and when you come out you want everybody else to see them too, so they don't have to walk around crippled and cut off all the time. I just tried a little bit. You can take it mild, strong, any level you like. And when you take it, you begin to understand. You're in tune at last. You receive signals from the universe. It opens you, Skagg. Oh, come inside with me, won't you? I want to go in and take it stronger. And I want you to share it with me."

He eluded her grasping hand. "I'm afraid."

'Don't be. I went in. I came out."

"It's forbidden."

"Because it's good, Skagg. People have always been forbidding other people to have anything this good. And once you've had it, you'll know why. You'll see the kind of power that hate and bitterness have—and you'll know how to soar to the sky and escape that power."

She tugged at him. He moved back.

"I can't go in," he said.

"Are you that afraid of dying?"

"They tell us that the machine makes people monstrous."

"Am I a monster?"

"They tell us that there are certain things we must never know."

"Anybody who says that is the true monster, Skagg."

"Perhaps. Perhaps. But I can't. Look—they're all watching us. You see them, here in the shadows? Everybody in Shining City is here! How could I go in? How could I do something so filthy when all of them—"

"I feel so sorry for you," she said softly. "To be afraid of love—to pull back from knowledge—"

"I can't help myself."

Gently she said, "Skagg, I'm going back in, and this time I'm going to ask for the most they can give. If there's any love in your soul, come in after me. I'll wait in there for you. And afterward we'll go off together—we'll visit every city in the world together—"

He shook his head.

She came close to him. He jumped away, as if afraid she would seize him and haul him into the machine, but she went to him and kissed him, a light brushing of lips on lips, and then she turned and went back into the machine.

He did not follow, but he did not leave.

The moons crossed in the sky, and the rain-sphere passed over the city, and the birds of night followed it, and a Riding Machine came to him and offered to take him to his home, and the red light of the morning sun began to streak the sky, and still the door of the Knowing Machine did not open, and still Fa Sol La stayed within. Skagg was alone in the plaza now.

"I'll wait in there for you," she had said.

The others, his friends, his neighbors, had gone home to sleep. He was alone. At sunrise he went forward into the Zone of Peril and stayed there awhile, and after an hour he entered the Zone of Impiety, and as the full morning heat descended he found himself going up the steps quite calmly and opening the door of the Knowing Machine.

"Welcome to Therapeutic Center Seven," a deep voice said from above, speaking in Language but using an accent even less familiar than the girl's. "Please move to your left for elementary sensory expansion treatment. You will find helmets on the wall. Place a helmet snugly on your head and—"

"Where's the girl?" he asked.

The voice continued to instruct him. Skagg ignored it, and went to his right, along a corridor that curved to circle the column. He found her just around the bend. She wore a helmet and her eyes were open, but she leaned frozen against the wall, strangely pale, strangely still. He put his ear between her breasts and heard nothing. He touched her skin and it seemed already to be growing cold. She did not close her eyes when his fingertip neared them.

There was on her face an expression of such joy that he could hardly bear to look at it.

The voice said, "In the early stages of therapy, a low level of stimulation is recommended. Therefore we request that you do not attempt to draw a greater degree of intensification than you are able at this stage to—"

Skagg took the helmet from her head. He lifted her in his arms and found that she weighed almost nothing. Carefully he set her down. Then, taking another helmet from the rack, he held it with both hands for a long time, listening to the instructions and hearing once more the girl's talk of ecstasy and soaring, and comparing all that he saw here to the things that everyone always had said about the Knowing Machine. After a while he put the helmet back in the rack without using it, and picked up the girl again, and carried her body out of the machine.

As he went down the steps, he saw that the others had gathered again and were gaping at him.

"You were in the machine?" Simit asked.

"I was in the machine," said Skagg.

"It killed her but not you?" Derk wanted to know.

"She used it. I didn't. First she used it a little, and then she used it too much, and the second time it killed her." Skagg kept walking as he spoke. They followed him.

"It is death simply to go inside the machine," Prewger said.

"This is wrong," said Skagg. "You can enter safely. Death comes only from using the machine. From using it wrongly."

"She was a fool," said Glorr. "She was punished."

"Maybe so," Skagg said. "But the machine gives us love. The machine gives us goodness."

He put the girl on the ground and summoned a Service Machine. Skagg gave it the girl's pack, asking that it be outfitted with a Water Machine and a Food Machine and a Shelter Machine. The Service Machine went away and came back a short while later. After inspecting the pack, Skagg strapped it over his shoulder. Then he picked up the girl again and began to walk.

"Where are you going with her?" Glorr asked.

"Out of the city. I will find a place for her body to rest in the desert."

"When you return, will you go into the Knowing Machine again?" Simit asked.

"I won't return for a long time," said Skagg. "I have some traveling to do. First to River City, and then to other places, maybe. And then, when I've found my courage, when I know who I really am and what I really want to be, I'll come back here and go into the machine and use it as it was meant to be used. And nothing will ever be the same in Shining City again."

He walked more quickly away from them, out toward the Empty Buildings, toward the plain of purple sand. He wondered how long it would take him to reach that other city beside the River Without Fish, and whether he would meet anyone like Fa Sol La when he got there.

His friends stood watching him until he was out of sight.

"He has become a madman," said Prewger.

"A dangerous madman," Glorr said.

"Would you do such a thing?" Simit asked.

"Do you mean, go into the machine, or go to another city?" said Derk.

"Either one."

"Of course not," said Derk.

"Of course not," said Glorr as well. "I know who I am. I know what I want to be."

"Yes," Simit said, shuddering. "Why should we do such things? We know who we are."

"We know what we want to be," said Prewger.

CPSIA information can be obtained at www.ICGtesting.com
Printed in the USA
LVOW07s1801221014

410014LV00003B/910/P